DROWNING

IN DARKNESS AND LIGHT

DROWNING
IN DARKNESS AND LIGHT

GREG BOGAERTS

BEST SHORT STORIES

SHANTI ARTS PUBLISHING

BRUNSWICK, MAINE

DROWNING IN DARKNESS AND LIGHT

Published by Shanti Arts Publishing

Cover and interior design
by Shanti Arts Designs

Cover image by Artem Kovalev / unsplash.com

Shanti Arts LLC
Brunswick, Maine
www.shantiarts.com

Printed in the United States of America

ISBN: 978-1-951651-01-5 (print, softcover)
ISBN: 978-1-951651-02-2 (e-book)

LCCN: 2019952589

for my mother,

Marjorie Musson

CONTENTS

ACKNOWLEDGMENTS

Grateful acknowledgment is made to the editors of the following publications where these stories first appeared:

United States — Journals
Antipodes: "The Dome," 2002 and "Breakdown," 2016
Embodied Effigies: "The Boy's Boots," 2015
Gone Lawn: "Landscape with Three Trees and a House," 2014
The Portland Literary Journal: Portland State University, Oregon,
    "The Restaurant de la Serène at Asnières," 2003
Still Point Arts Quarterly: "Quarry Girl," 2013

Australia — Journals
Coppertales, Central Queensland University: "Hunter River Story:
    The Flood," 2006
fourW: "The Dead Landlord," 2004; "The Gamblers," 1997; "Gary,"
    2010; and "Leaving Home," 1997
Gathering Force: "The Lovers," 1997
Going Down Swinging: "Montmartre Path with Sunflowers," 2004
Inklings: "Gladys Montgomery," 1996
Kalimat: "The Narrows Beach," 2003
Overland: "Skelp Mill," 2004
Page 17: "Street Scene in Montmartre," 2007
Scarp: "Frozen," 1996
Social Alternatives Magazine, Queensland University: "The Loan," 1996
Spinechiller Magazine: "An After Death Experience," 1998
The Storytellers: "Blood," 1998

Tarralla, Swinburne University of TAFE, Melbourne: "The Alyscamps, Avenue in Arles," 2003

Time to Write, Northern Melbourne Institute of TAFE: "My Uncle," 2014

Windmills, Deakin University: "Two Schooners of Beer, Please," 2011

Australia — Collections and Anthologies

Australian Short Stories, No. 54, Pascoe Publishing: "The Release," 1996

Fellowship of Australian Writers Queensland: "Darkness in the Fire," 2000

Surf Coast Scribblers, Anglesea: "The Christmas Cake," 2003

The following stories appeared in ***Walking Paris Streets With Eugène Atget: Inspired Stories About the Ragpicker, Lampshade Vendor, and Other Characters and Places of Old France***, Shanti Arts Publishing, 2013: "Maria," and "Market Porter."

The following stories appeared in ***Beyond Sunflowers and Starry Nights: Stories Inspired by Vincent Van Gogh***, Shanti Arts Publishing, 2018: "Montmartre Path with Sunflowers," "The Alyscamps, Avenue in Arles," "The Restaurant de la Sirène at Asnières," "Landscape with Three Trees and a House," and "The Little Arlésienne."

BREAKDOWN

HE COULD SEE THE KID FROM THE CORNER OF HIS EYE. And that's what he was, a kid, barely fourteen, still a boy, a little boy, but a boy who jumped up and down as though he was chained to a pogo stick, bounced from side to side like a circus clown performing, twitched his body all over the place like a soft slug dowsed with the acid of lemon juice, could not keep still for even a second. He turned and looked at the kid to discover what the movement was that had caught his eye, and it was the kid sitting on the cement chair beside the pool, his left leg bouncing up and down, getting quicker and quicker until the leg became a blur as though the muscle, bone, blood, and arteries and veins had melted, the limb about to run, fall away from the body to puddle on the pool deck.

He wanted to walk up to the kid, sit down beside him, place a hand on the boy's jumping knee, still him, take his head with his other hand and turn the kid's face to him and tell him to stop it. It wasn't worth it, all the training, all the laps up and down the pool so many times you did them all again when you went to sleep, and rose the next morning exhausted, barely able to stand, barely able to give your parents the time of day. It wasn't worth what it did to your body and your head, the repetition of the laps made a blotched and bleeding mess of your life. It made your life a child's top spinning so quickly the edges of the painted pictures blurred until they became a mess of abstract color impossible to work out where each picture began and ended.

But he wouldn't, couldn't do that. Touch another male on the swim squad. You just didn't do that not unless you wanted to be branded a poofter, not so much because of the contact but for showing the softness of caring, not in a squad of muscle-bound, loud and raucous, testosterone-driven, challenging males, obsessed with the size of their cocks, boys, almost men, who not only challenged each other to swim races but challenged each other in everything: arm wrestling between laps, occasional fist fights just to see who was the best fighter, competition for the affection of the females on the squad — young women made into men, breasts lost by rising swells of chest muscle, legs transformed into heavy, shivering trunks of sinew because of the thousands of laps and the weight training.

He'd seen it before, the one and only time a male swimmer had touched another male swimmer. Jim Mackie's father had just died, and Jim came back to training an old man bent over, hobbled by grief, but no one not even the swim coach showed anything like care, no one offered their condolences, no one was going to make themselves seem soft by even a brief touch of a hand on Jim's shoulder. Until Mark Brown, a new member of the squad, not only took Jim by the shoulders, drew him to him and gave him a hug, but also expressed his emotions in words.

"Really sorry to hear about your Dad, Jim," said Mark, the words of comfort a death knell for the new swimmer.

The attacks started with some pushing and shoving of Mark on the pool deck, something the new swimmer took as a bit of a joke, some horsing around at first, but then changed his mind when the pushing and shoving became hard, bone-sharp elbows jabbed into his ribs, leaving long purple and black bruises rising in his flesh like plague buboes. And that's what he was to the other males in the squad and most of the females — a diseased thing, a queer, off limits to everyone — and even Jim Mackie shunned him.

On the day of the Northern District Swim Championships, as he was walking the pool deck to the starting blocks to contest a butterfly final, a cluster of male competitors closed around Mark Brown. No one could see, and one punch lashed out breaking Mark Brown's jaw, the cluster of young men broke apart to reveal the boy on his knees, holding his bleeding face, spitting teeth, then blacking out with the pain. He spent time in the hospital and didn't come back to the squad.

He looked at the kid sitting on the cement chair and the kid looked miserable, driven mad by parents who expected too much of him, drove him to the pool at four in the morning every day, drove him to swim the laps faster, drove him on during races. It was only a matter of time so, sighing, he walked to the kid, stood in front of him and waited. The kid looked up at him, spat needle words at him.

"What the fuck do you want? Leave me alone I've got to swim soon."

But the kid wasn't fooling him with the bravado. He knew there'd been a huge to-do only last week when the kid left the pool after swimming two laps, left the pool grounds and hid in the car park shivering with cold and wet, wearing only his swimmers. His parents and the coach found him and dragged him bodily back into the pool, commanding him to swim, the father telling the son not to be such a girl. And the kid resumed training, but every time he turned between laps you could see him crying, hear the sobs that wrenched like blows through him.

He took some steps backward. The kid turned his head away, his bottom lip trembling. Then, out of the morning's blue hue they came like black clots of Indian ink staining the landscape, the kid's mother and father and his coach, laughing and chatting among themselves as though they belonged to some exclusive club, until they reached the young boy. Then their faces became taught and stern as they began to berate the young boy telling him he had to try harder, swim further, contest more races. The state champs were a month away and the mother and father and coach expected, insisted, commanded that the kid should win his age championship in at least three events. After all, they said, look at all they'd done for him: running him back and forth to training at ungodly hours, feeding him the best and most expensive health foods, clothing him and educating him, the coach told the kid he neglected other swimmers because he thought the kid had something special, was a potential champion if he could stop being such a cry baby and put in some sort of an effort.

The coach stood there gabbing away as if he was the only person on earth, his hands on his hips, bent forward, peering down at the kid, cowering now on the cement chair. The coach had poor eyesight so he wore thick coke bottle bottom glasses, but even these didn't do much to help his sense of sight. He jammed his head closer to the kid, constantly berating him, trying to see the kid's face but he couldn't, and it didn't matter as long as the kid took notice and trained harder and won three age titles at the state champs.

The three of them, the parents and the coach crowded in, tied a tight knot around the kid. He couldn't see the boy anymore so he took a step closer, and then the three adults turned as one and looked at him as though he was the foulest piece of garbage that had ever crawled out of a gutter.

"What do you want, Bradly?" demanded the coach

"Why don't you piss off, Bradly," said the boy's father. "You've no business here."

"Yes, piss off Bradly, you're nothing but a dog. You can't swim, you never win races, you don't really train — not like our Michael," declared the boy's mother.

The words didn't surprise Bradly, he'd heard them directed at him many times before, he and others who were second string swimmers, plodders who would never win a school age competition let alone win a state championship. The plodders were almost untouchables in the class system that ruled the squad. He was surprised the three adults had named him, but he realized it was a form of acknowledgment that allowed them to make it clear to him that he was inferior when it came to swimming. There was no ambiguity about what they thought of him.

Behind the parents and coach, Michael was grinning, his leg going up and down faster than ever. Bradly could see his lips were dry from swimming so long in the chlorine water and when the kid spread those lips in a grotesque imitation of a smile, splits opened and blood was running down his chin, staining the white sloppy joe he wore with bright, steaming, scarlet spots of his life's blood. The kid was grinning because Bradly had become the target and that meant Michael got a respite, albeit it only of a minute or so, however long the insulting abuse lasted.

The three turned away from Bradly, took hold of Michael as though he was a prisoner they'd handcuffed and were escorting back to gaol. They took him to the end of the pool and made him swim and, as he watched them, Bradly remembered Martha Smith.

Martha, a squad member, won a state title and went to the Australian Championships, a contest to decide who would represent Australia at the next Olympics. In the final of the 100-meters freestyle, Martha was so far in front, the pool side commentators were already calling her the new Dawn Fraser, but when Martha came in to make the tumble turn to propel her back over the last lap, she stopped, dead. Instead of tumbling Martha stood up and the other girls hammered themselves into their tumble turns, their feet thumping like canon shots into the tiles of the wall, the splash of their turns obliterating Martha as though she'd sunk to the bottom of the pool, forever.

Bradly had watched her and he saw her face white, cold, withered like a carcass of meat hanging on a hook and left too long in a cold storage room. It was the end of her swimming career; no one would come near her, least of all the coach. She stayed indoors during the day, nothing her parents did could make her set one step outside the family home. Bradly heard about her, the rumors, the smug smirking whispers because he lived just around the corner. Only in the dead of night did she venture outside as though she had regained some of her old self but wanted, needed to keep it hidden lest someone try to take it away again. She wandered through the streets and, occasionally, someone peering through a curtain saw her. These were called Mad Martha sightings and became the currency of ridicule and mockery in the town and at the pool.

•

The kid won one state title and his parents and the coach drove him harder telling him he should have won the three. One morning, Michael's father came into his bedroom to get his son up to go to training and found the boy as stiff as a slab of concrete, eyes wide and staring at the ceiling. The father couldn't get the kid out of bed, no one could. Michael lay in bed for four days staring into oblivion.

The breakdown was as certain as death, as final as death, as complete as death.

AN AFTER DEATH EXPERIENCE

Lucy recoiled from the eyes, cold eyes that looked into her from sixty years ago. A cleaved crease between the stenciled eyebrows, cutting the face into two halves. She watched the mouth, the thin straight smile. She felt herself, wet. The felt hat with the fat black band tilted rakishly up.

Her nipples stirred. The ears were pointed, a demon's ears. A curved beak nose that might thrust from the old oval frame, hook and tear her flesh, pull her into a world of men wearing leather gloves with shadows the shape of towers on pearl-colored walls behind them.

Lucy shivered. She didn't want the photograph of Geoffrey's grandfather hanging in the dining room. But her husband had been insistent. After all, she had her aunts and uncles, grandfathers and grandmothers, great-grandfathers and great-grandmothers draped throughout the house. A whole gallery of black and white sternness staring at them, wherever they went.

Admonishing with clerical and critical looks, the freshly microwaved food Lucy and Geoffrey ate, the quality bottles of red wine they drank, the ease of the television eye.

But Geoffrey's grandfather, Wilton Brown, was different. The sardonic smile seemed to threaten to open. Lucy imagined a very pink wet tongue coming from the black and white lips. Slithering toward her. The stories Geoffrey told her about Wilton Brown didn't help her unease. His philandering, the kept women in flats in Mayfield, and Geoffrey's long-suffering grandmother. And finally, for her, the suicide. Driven by her husband's infidelity to take her own life. A slow self-imposed death of starvation, making Wilton Brown confront day-by-day, her emaciated form, the claws of flesh, and her dimming eyes reaching out to him. And at the end, the coffin a leaf of weight, lowered into the earth of Sandgate Cemetery.

Lucy turned. Walked away, leaving the black-coated figure staring after her, still holding the long rolled cigarette between leather-sheathed index and middle fingers. Lucy wondered whether Wilton was laughing. Laughing like Geoffrey told her he did when Geoffrey's grandmother gauntly confronted him. Laughing at the bones coming from the flesh, the eyes eclipsed moons above a black deep ocean. Inhaling, then blowing a long blue streak of smoke into her death-mask face.

Six p.m. Geoffrey and Lucy sat at the dining room table, an heirloom of cedar passed on by Geoffrey's grandparents. Stained blood red, French polished with too much stain until the wood was a black clot. No light came from the dim luster of wood. Lucy could barely see her dim form in the French polish when she lay the white lace over the wood.

Between them stood a bottle of Shiraz, a full tower of red. Thick, congealing in the final winter light. And roast pork, Geoffrey's favorite. Lucy sipped the acid red. It burned all the way down.

She could not see her husband clearly. But she could hear his teeth smashing into the crackling of the pork. He ground the hard skin of fat with his strong teeth. She could see his teeth now. Great squares that ground like a mortar and pestle, the sound of seeds fractured, grain ground to powder.

She saw his lips. Then knew, as they clasped shut over the teeth. The same thin sardonic line, the slightest curling at the end of the lips like pubic hair. She watched it. Mesmerized, the mouth opening, the teeth working, and the pink tongue that slid out at her. She expected it to disengage itself from his throat. Sliver across the table. Slide in between her legs.

Then there was light. Geoffrey had lit a candle. More romantic, he said. She watched the pearl color spread out from his mouth. Abalone shell luster across his face. Lucy's forkful of peas, paused. Plopped onto the white lace tablecloth. Rolled like cogs and wheels from a broken machine.

Lucy's eyes goggled. Geoffrey's face was the same. The same face as the face hanging on the wall just behind her husband's left shoulder.

The same deep crease in the forehead as if some jealous husband had attempted to cleave the skull in two with an ax. The same pop fly eyes, everywhere, nowhere, searching for syrup to sink its proboscis into. The same fish hook nose baited with sculptured Roman bone. The same ears, bat ears listening to the movement of her thighs as she changed position on her chair. Ready to jump. Ready to run from the house.

•

Lucy wondered where Geoffrey was. The evening absences were more frequent. She eyed his collection of antique firearms nailed to the wall. All oiled and in perfect working order. With bullets.

A real enthusiast was Geoffrey. He'd taught her how to load and fire.

"Just in case," he said.

"Just in case what?" she thought.

Lucy went into the laundry. Checked all of his shirts. Again. Searching for hair, smelling for faded perfume, looking for lipstick. Held his underpants up to the laundry window. Searched for stains, fluid fingerprints of guilt.

She wouldn't let him out by himself any more. Even insisted on driving him to work. Picked him up too. Went every morning into his office. Supervised him sitting at his desk to begin work. Scanned the carpet-quiet corridors for secretaries dressed in the uniform of black skirt, black stockings, and black high heels. Looked daggers when she found one. Would often bail her up, warning her off Geoffrey. And finally leave. Leave Geoffrey, his fingers barring her from his sight. Sniggers of fright as the office girls dived for cover.

Lucy was losing weight. Suspicion. Wearing. Stripped away her flesh. She was all polished bone. Pearl knobs and spear points of elbows, knees, shins, and fingers, almost tearing through the taught sallow skin. Her eyes were the lights of sinking ships, great ovals of wasted luminosity stuttering out distress signals across a flat black sea.

She'd taken down the photograph. Burned it. Watched as flame ate into the body of the grandfather. Watched the lips curled back in a black sneer. Watched the cigarette finally lit. Held in the gloved hands melting. The smell made her gag.

A wind sprang from among the eucalypt scrub at the back of the block. Picked up the glowing flakes of black paper. Flung them into her face. Burned small but deep pits into her scarecrow-stretched skin, a black pox from a past age.

•

Geoffrey sat beside Lucy's bed. Held the emaciated hands, claws of bone scrabbling for the lip of life. He watched her eyelids jerk, spasm in the half-light of the ward.

He'd been there for days. Had no one to see, nothing to do but to be with Lucy. Geoffrey looked at her form, barely a ripple of foothills eroded by fear under the covers.

Lucy's eyes opened for the final time. Saw Geoffrey receding, leaving. Her hand slipped like melting ice from his. Her eyes shut.

She saw the mouth. Curling a mocking welcome to her along the darkening passage of pearl. Saw the demon spark in the abalone shell eyes. No overwhelming sea of love washed to meet her. Just the mouth, the lips opening, the cigarette burning. The gloved hand leading her into the screaming silence of black and white.

WITH DEATH, A LIFE

THE TEST BORE SCREAMED, BRUTALIZED THE MORNING quiet. Hammered through cement, conglomerate, shale, dirt. Friction steam rising. Unforgiving sound of burning metal. Then silence. Pause of the construction gang, puzzled by the quiet when the metal bore was meant to barrage down through twenty meters of solid earth crust.

Jim Saul, the geotechnical engineer on site, strode to the bore, bending forward to investigate the strange peace that had come out of nowhere.

A geyser of water shocked out of the earth; a pinnacle of green, burning up into the air; a column that caught Jim, lifting him a good six feet with the force of the eruption. Jim hung up in the working wobble of water. Flat planes of sunlight, shearing into the green. Jim, his hair a burning bush of red and yellow seaweed. His open mouth, disgorging a long yell of pain and surprise into the fluid. His eyes and ears bomboras of white fire, blazing in the water.

A collapsing tower of water from around the limbs of Jim Saul. Suddenly lost in the light of the air. Falling down, slowly, it seemed. He saw the upturned, open-mouthed faces of the construction crew as he fell, saw every feature in that two-second descent. The three men suddenly not strangers who worked for him and nothing more: Fatty Smith with his ridiculous gut, hanging over his shorts, that didn't seem funny any more, but assumed a type of portly dignity; Jack Brown holding up his capable crane rigger hands that didn't look clumsy the way they usually did to Jim; Fred Jones, who Jim could never credit with being able to nut out a problem in minutes, but with a look on his face that suggested he might whip up a scaffolding and carry Jim down from the air before he fell completely.

Then the thud that made Jim see angels of light. As he lay like a broken-backed fish on the wet metal of the construction platform, he looked up at the faces of Fatty, Fred, and Jack. But he could only see hair roots of fine fire, flickering at the circumferences of dark discs, their features eclipsed from his sight, his experience.

And then the words of concern, and a new humor they usually didn't bother with when they talked to Jim Saul, a humor he felt already even in the pain of his blindness.

"Jesus Christ, Jimmy are yer alright?" from Fatty.

"Fucked if I know where th' water came from Jimmy. But have yer finished flyin' f' th' day?" from Jacky.

But then the memory, the sound of the words became blurred for Jim Saul, wire rope drawls rusted in water. There were no faces anymore.

Just the sky and the recurring imprint of the water snake stamped green into the blue as if the geyser had been tattooed into the skin of Jim's eyes. There forever, waiting to swim into focus, a tower from which he might watch the destruction of his old life.

The construction of water was still there even when the ocean of black took him from the pain in his body and the last sounds he heard: the concerned clunk of work boots, scrambling for a phone and an ambulance.

•

Jim Saul licked his lips as he lay in the lurching blood box. Tasted the salt of the water, thinking it strange. The sudden silence of the bore had been strange, the water geyser had been stranger, but the salt water was the strangest thing of all. Where the water came from Jim had no idea. Salt water bursting up in the middle of the city's CBD took some explaining.

A calmness centered in him as he remembered the peal of pain that had passed from his mouth when he'd been in the water. He felt light upon the ambulance stretcher, as though he'd passed, in the water, a heavy stone of disbelief, a stone that had been sewn up in his gut for years, holding him back from what he should know.

Jim looked out of the ambulance window, tinted deep water glass with cars like big fish swimming past. Skyscrapers grew out of the earth like deep and steep underwater canyons. Passersby, in pinks and purples and reds, darting like reef fish.

People and things he'd not noticed before, never bothered to give a second thought, but clear to him now. Different from when he drove his car to and from work with the windows up, the CD blaring full blast.

Possible concussion, cuts and bruises, the ambulance man said. Jim felt the lump at the back of his head, looked at his skin taught where the salt water had dried on it. It felt itchy and he began to rub, to scratch, anxious to rid himself of the membrane. It felt like a body bag, he thought. Too tight this old skin, constricting him, the small stars, the small fish scales of skin coming away, falling to the floor of the ambulance.

Jim was ruddy and pink like a baby born from uterine fluid, the skin like the crazed pattern of a past and purposeless life, littering the floor of the ambulance.

•

Jim Saul spent two hours in the casualty ward under observation until his wife, Megan, turned up beside his bed. She looked at him. Paused. Clamped shut her teeth on the shock before it escaped and gave her away.

She frowned, twisted the gold and diamond rings on her fingers, picked up Jim's things, bundled him out of the hospital.

She drove Jim home with sidelong glances at her husband, whose attention was caught up in the branches of bush that rushed by just below the car wheels.

Jim wound down the window, hanging halfway out like a child, tempted to reach out to touch the forest so close to the expressway built just above its canopy.

"Jimmy! Get back inside! Now! And put your seat belt back on!" chastised Megan.

Jim, with a petulant push of his mouth, obeyed Megan, clicked himself back in.

"Wasn't goin' t' do nothin'," he said childishly.

Megan burst out laughing, a river of sound that made her and Jim grin.

Megan drove into the garage and the automatic door closed behind the car. Her hand went for the door handle, but Jim leaned across, kissed her, and had her surprised and breathless before she could think. Jim Saul wasn't like this, she thought, as he edged up her skirt. Jim Saul didn't make spontaneous love outside of the bedroom, she thought, as his mouth found her vagina. Jim Saul didn't seduce his wife in a car in a garage, she thought, as she orgasmed.

They stumbled together from the car, Megan still floating, Jim with more salt water in his mouth. He pursued Megan up the internal stairs, past their two computer-game-committed children in the loungeroom, into the bedroom. Onto the bed where they made love again.

The second time, in a short time, after a long time.

•

Jim took the next day off, sat on his patio overlooking river, rock, and ravine. He sat quietly with no food or drink passing his lips. No rush of cars and mobile phones and other engineers and architects after him for a pound of his flesh.

Only the phone call from the nursing home to say his father was worse, falling in and out of unconsciousness. Jim thought about his father, his father's life, and the prospect of his father's death.

Roy Saul had been a high roller in the city with his business complex right in the eye of the city, a theater with a pub right next to it. Not a theater where Shakespeare and Chekov were staged, but a theater, more than a little sleazy, for punters who turned up with pockets full of money for Roy Saul. A theater for strip tease acts and sly backyard grog, from the pub next door, during the depressed 1930s. The place was full of amateur acts that came and went in a night because Roy didn't keep them on too long otherwise the paying public would come to realize they were forking out good money for third raters.

Jim saw the tower of water still in his line of vision as he thought about the door-to-door preachers who came offering the *Watchtower* and how his father gave them short shrift.

"Bugger off yer Bible bashin' bastards! Get out before I chuck yers out?"

Jim remembered the words of his father to him from childhood to adulthood.

"Yer here t' make money Jimmy. Yer not 't give heed to a God that doesn't exist. Remember, they're stupid bastards that believe in a life hereafter. It's this life and this life only so use th' bastard."

Jim Saul had taken the words as his text. He'd studied his arse off at university, clawed his way up to the top in the construction firm, and became half owner, and he'd accumulated rental properties. All achieved under the approving eye of his father.

Not that Roy eased up on him. He was always at him, always

obsessed with the here and now. Obsessed with turning a dollar. Jim remembered how Roy purchased the theater where he made most of his money.

The first thing his father did was to take a mattock and chop out the brass candlestick holders from the walls. Flogged the brass to a scrap metal dealer, threw the candles in the garbage, and said to his son: "This's a theater not a fuckin' church. Th' punters come 'ere for a laugh and a perve and a drink. They don't come 'ere 'f holy communion!"

As the years passed, the obsession of Roy Saul grew in intensity, especially his disgust and shame concerning Jonathon Saul, Jim's grandfather. Jonathon Saul had been a hard-working, God-fearing man, who'd worked the city seams of coal almost a hundred years ago.

Jonathon Saul was a deep earth miner who should have spent his time lying on his side in the half-dark pick-axing out coal. But the narrow tunnels were lit by Jonathon's seven-branched candelabrum, bearing seven candles that shed the light of creation deep in the dark guts of the earth. Jonathon Saul, with his God, was fearless in the earth, chopping out more coal than anyone else. Oblivious, the stories told, to the dangers of collapse and coal creep, fearless in the face of death with his seven candles set in their grimy, brass tree.

Stories of Jonathan and his seven-branched candlestick were still heard and fueled by the mystery of his disappearance. Stories that chaffed and rubbed Roy Saul right up the wrong way. Old timers, old miners still remembered Jonathon Saul and the flood of candle light that came from his bord in the yard seam.

There were old blokes who still remembered the active role Jonathon played in the church and the Sunday prayer meetings the old man held in the town or in the small mining settlements out in the bush, always drawing a big crowd to hear the word of God from the man.

"Forget yer grandfather," Roy told Jim. "He was as mad as a meat ax. An embarrassment t' th' family what with all of his God botherin'. His disappearance was th' best thing that ever happened. Good riddance!"

And now Roy Saul was about to disappear. To where Roy didn't know and had spent a lifetime denying he cared. And Jim had no idea.

Jim thought it strange he should be the one who came to demolish the theater and pub of his father to make way for the new church and manse. But that wasn't to say that Roy lost on the deal. He didn't.

He cleaned up when the church brought the buildings and the land. But Roy didn't get a chance to spend his money, chopped down by a stroke, taken to a home for care the day Jim and the engineers began demolishing the theater and the pub.

Jim was drawn to the site by something other than the contract with the church to wreck and rebuild. Something he couldn't put his finger on, something that niggled at him for months during the demolition. Like a silver bream worrying a fresh bait of strip mullet — elusive, unable to be caught. Out of sight down in the black of many fathoms.

Jim thought about his grandfather and his disappearance so many years ago. No rumor or innuendo had come down through family members; no gossip of Jonathon Saul boarding a sailing ship in the dead of night and leaving his family; no talk of Jonathon shooting through with a fancy woman. Nothing like that.

Jim had spoken to one or two old men who remembered Jonathon when they were children. They told him no one could believe Jonathon Saul could desert his family. Not a man who took in derelicts off the street and gave them a meal, not a man who would spare a sixpence to help a family with rent if he could, not a man who collected for the poor.

So the mystery remained. With another mystery: the mystery that had prodded and poked Jim these past months and intensified the weaker his father became in the home. Roy wasted to parchment skin and brittle bones and eyes that panicked in the pissy shadows of the old peoples' home. Eyes that drove Jim away, back to the building site.

The phone rang. Jim Saul rose through the baptismal wash of evening light to answer it.

•

Jim Saul buried his father with a thin scattering of business associates at the grave. At the wake, Jim and his wife and kids. No one else.

Jim went back to work, light of step as though he floated a few inches above the car park asphalt as he walked to the site.

He felt even lighter after burying his father than he had after the scream of pain in the pinnacle of water. But he was still puzzled and didn't know why. Still itchy with the mystery of his new lightness of being but not knowing where it would lead, still scratching his head about the mystery of the eruption of salt water, still beguiled by his own absence of guilt in feeling relief when his father died.

He said good day to Fatty Smith, Jack Brown, and Fred Jones and thanked them for calling the ambulance. He had a cup of tea that morning, spent fifteen minutes chewing the fat, ironing out problems with the three men who usually shied away from him. Now they seemed drawn to him, a tight shoal of men having a yak and a cup of tea. Clearer about what was going on on-site.

"We've got ourselves an underwater camera, Jimmy," said Fatty.

"Yeah, Jimmy," said Jack. "It should clear up th' mystery of the water. But I'll be buggered if we'll find out how it came to be salty."

"We've been waitin' for yer t' come back," said Fred. "Let you be th' one t' have first squizze seein' you're th' one who got dropped on his arse."

"Christ, Fred," said Jim, "you're th' one who looks as though he was dropped from a great height."

"I was on the turps last night, Jimmy," explained Fred.

"You look like it too. Afraid yer going t' die and prayin' yer will," said Jim.

Fred and Fatty and Jack raised eyebrows to each other as they followed Jim up the ramp to the bore hole and the underwater camera. Jim set the device in motion and put his eye to the lens.

What he saw astonished him: a coal mine filled with water — a labyrinth of clear water that twisted onward under the site of the proposed church. Jim witnessed, as the camera searched deeper into the tunnels, the construction of pit props, the wooden crosses holding up the roof of the warren. And he could see the furrows in the walls from the picks of the miners and some leaves of bark on some of the pit props.

Jim pushed further into the yard seam, feeling his breath shorten, his pulse quicken the deeper he went. His mouth wet and salty as he watched the tunnels, burrowing deep down under where the theater and pub of his father had been.

He found the sudden cleft of the main tunnel: a narrow opening in the strata that led a short way to the harbor. The salt water mystery explained with the sea current of water, bearing fish and seaweed into the main shaft.

Jim paused. Heart thumping like the bore. Itchy and on edge.

"Are yer okay Jimmy?" from Fatty.

"Yes, mate. Go on you three. Go and have your crib. It's two hours since we started. I'll go the rest of the way myself," said Jim.

They left him, reluctantly.

Jim focused his eyes in the crystal water as though he was in the vein of salt green, swimming down to the end of the seam. He moved as if in a dream, turned the final loop in the coal wall, could not bight back the scream that escaped from his mouth.

Hung up in the water, the man, cross-shaped in the pulse of water movement, beating in the mine beneath Jim's feet. Hair and beard long and silver in the sea currents like an instrument of God, storming through the dark to take the scales from Jim's eyes.

Pellucid blue, pouring from eye sockets of the man, holding the seven-branched candelabrum in front of him – a tree of creation with seven candles still burning in the torch light glare. Seven flames of light passing into Jim Saul's eyes.

THE CHRISTMAS CAKE

DOWN A STREET IN RICHMOND, AT THE END OF A LANE
of black cobblestones, there's a small garage made of tin and wood that
was new during the Great Depression. In the shed, under the orange
glow of a single light bulb, a man toils pulling apart and putting back
together second-hand washing machines and fridges. It's all he knows;
it's all he's done since he was old enough to leave school behind.

Under the weak wash of orange light he sweats even though it is icy
in the shed made of metal. Dressed only in shorts, t-shirt and thongs
his body seems oblivious to the cold, his head is bent and intent upon
the washing machine he's bolting back together now he's fixed the
engine. It's for the Greek lady who lives three streets away, and when
he's finished bolting the machine back together, the man will pick it up,
by himself, and load it onto a trolley that stands waiting just outside
the shed door.

A few Richmond residents might be worried or puzzled that the
man could leave the trolley out of sight. They might think someone
could come along and steal it. But the man, sweating over the machine,
knows no one will take the trolley because just about everyone around
the neighborhood knows him, respects him. It goes without saying
after almost fifteen years.

The old Greek woman, who lives three streets away, knows her
washing machine will be returned repaired. She knows the man will
wheel it around to her place on the trolley, and he won't charge her for
bringing it back, nor will he charge her for fitting the hoses back on so
she can do her loads of washing that have backed up over the last two
days while her machine was being repaired.

The woman knows the repairman will accept next to nothing for the work he's done on her washing machine. Not that he's a soft touch. He charges enough to cover the cost of parts, his labor, enough to conjure up the thinnest of profit margins, just enough to feed himself, pay the rent on the shed he uses for working his trade and in which he lives.

The neighbors always know when he's awake; they can set their watches by the noise of hammering coming from the shed. Once the sound of hammer on metal starts they know the man has risen from the bunk he sleeps in at one end of the shed. And although the repairman starts his hammering early, none of the neighbors complain; they all know how much they need him, how little he charges them to keep their washing machines and fridges in good repair.

A used white goods saint they see him as, someone who will keep their food cold and fresh, their clothes clean for next to nothing. A man who keeps to himself, speaks little, yet makes his whole existence revolve around the welfare of the people who make a map of streets and lanes in the heart and mind of the repairman.

Behind him, hanging from the tin roof above the bunk, is a Christmas cake wrapped in white muslin stained brown and golden by the sweetness of the fruit and alcohol maturing in the heart of the cake. It is the one gift the neighbors make to the man. The women in Richmond take turns to make the cake and give it to the man halfway through the year. But it is no solo effort because the men and women, and sometimes children, come through the months leading up to Christmas carrying bottles of port, rum, and sherry.

When a bearer of booze turns up at the shed door, the repairman grins, stops work, doesn't say a word, goes to the cake swinging above his bed, and undoes the string holding the cloth together. Then he will beckon toward the visitor with his work-calloused hands. The visitor walks to the bunk, stands upon the thin, foam rubber mattress, pulls out the cork in the bottle, tips, carefully, the fortified wine into the thirsty cake.

The cake is dry, it seems, all of the time, no matter how many people turn up with their bottles of wine and tip the contents into the Christmas cake. The booze soaks into the batter like a bucket of water tipped onto desert sand. The repairman stands there, smiling, watching the cake swinging from the roof, growing, ever so slightly, fatter, day by day. It swells with a belly full of sherry, port, muscat and whatever else the residents of Richmond can find, almost forgotten, hidden away in drinks cabinets, under beds, at the back of cupboards.

At night, as the repairman lies on his foam mattress with the sharp springs sticking into the tender spaces between the vertebrae of his backbone, he looks up at the cake swinging silently above him. He smells the rich fruit and fortified wine in the heart of the cake and it is enough to take away some of his memories. But it is the thought of the visitors that makes him sleep, drops him into a dreamless world of slumber.

Toward Christmas the number of visitors bringing fortified wine for the cake increases, a mild frenzy comes upon the men and women of Richmond, born from a fear that the cake will never be satisfied, that it will keep on soaking up the wine. But they all know, as does the repairman, from years past, that this will not happen. Eventually the cake is saturated with wine and the first drops fall from the muslin cloth onto the foam mattress.

Then the repairman calls a halt to the tipping of any more wine into the Christmas cake and the word goes out along the streets and lanes of Richmond. There is to be no more bringing of wine, until next year.

It is at this moment of saturation, just before Christmas, when the neighbors stop bringing wine, that the repairman ponders his past life when he was living at home with his parents in another suburb of the city. He closes the shop, sits on the bunk, ignores the drops of wine seeping through the Christmas cake cloth, falling upon his back and shoulders, staining his white t-shirt with the color of blood.

The man remembers how his parents made him the one who was always good for nothing, created a second son they could lay the blame on whenever anything went wrong. It was a queer thing, thinks the repairman, sitting on his bunk, to be allocated a scapegoat role from infancy.

Whenever the man's father was out of work on the docks because of a strike or slow orders, it was always the younger of the two sons who was responsible for the poverty of the family because the boy always ate too much. No mention was made of the elder son and two daughters, what they ate, what they got away with.

Whenever a neighbor came around to complain about a broken window or some lemons or oranges pinched from a backyard tree, it was the repairman who got the blame even though his parents knew full well it was often his brother or one of his sisters who was the culprit.

The last straw came in the repairman's last year at school. He'd barely turned fifteen and was itching to leave the foreign country of books, pens, and teachers with rules as onerous as his parents' rules. His mother, as usual, had made the Christmas cake and hung it from the kitchen ceiling. She'd forbidden lacing the cake with alcohol; she didn't hold with drinking in any shape or form. The cake was to remain tied tightly until Christmas day when it would be eaten dry.

But over the months of maturation, the cake disappeared piece by piece thanks to the hungry attention of the repairman's brother and sisters. On Christmas day, when the mother undid the string, opened the cloth, all hell broke loose because there was virtually nothing left but crumbs and the small blocks of wood the brother and sisters had placed in the parcel to fool their parents.

The repairman was blamed, but he'd had enough and walked out of the house leaving behind his accusers who he never laid eyes on again. It took him some time to find the shed in Richmond, and it took some years to establish his reputation as a tradesman of quality and reasonable prices. But the repairman became a part of the area, as recognizable and immutable as the smooth black and gray cobblestones lining the lanes of Richmond.

On Christmas day, the repairman cuts the cake down, opens the cloth, cuts the enormous sweet into wedges, places the plate containing the cake near the door. The smell of the booze is sweet on the wind, and it soon finds the noses of the men and women and some children of Richmond. They arrive in dribs and drabs, drawn to the shed by the smell of the cake.

They stand around in the shed, at the doorway, and share a slice of cake with the repairman. They all wish him a merry Christmas. Then they leave to go back to their families and the Christmas dinners cooking in ovens. But the day is full of visitors for the repairman; it is in the final hours of evening before the last of the visitors eat their wedges of cake, wish him merry Christmas, and leave him.

He goes to the bunk, lies down, looks up at the empty rag of cloth hanging limp above his head, but his stomach is full of cake, and his heart is full of the affection left for him by the men and women and children of Richmond.

DIANNE LAMBKIN

HE COULD SEE HER, DIANNE LAMBKIN, STANDING ON the edge of the tide of shadow. He could see her toe nails, painted bright red, winking in the gloom like the eyes of feral cats. He saw her turn and look straight at him across the Olympic swimming pool, across twelve cement starting blocks, across the heads of dozens of people, across the green waxy-leaved hedges that ran rattling in the sulfur-tainted wind in a thick border between her and him, across the manic thrash and splash of swimmers.

The shadow had crept closer to her in that brief moment of a hand clutch of seconds of looking at each other. He saw the dark begin to climb up her back she presented to him now. The blackness was like a stranger coming from nowhere, grabbing hold of Dianne, forcing her down on her fat knees, tearing up the back of her blue dress, reefing down the back of her white cotton panties, and ramming a big blue-veined cock into her.

He almost cried out, thought about diving into the pool, swimming across the paths of the competitors in the swimming race, pulling himself out of the stinging, chlorine-laced water, shouldering through the dozens of people on the pool deck, hurdling the hedges, grabbing hold of her, pulling her back into the light slapped all over the swimming complex like spilt paint by the giant search lights bolted atop three tall gleaming steel poles. Poles cast, made by the steel-making company when it built the pool and its buildings and made a big deal of giving it all to the city. A token gesture, really, a bribe, really, to men broken by dirt and dust and cancer and dog watch, and deafness made by giant pounding wheels and rollers and howling, hot blast furnaces.

She was wavering between the light and the dark. She turned back around and looked at him again and smiled her wide white grin — teeth square, strong, even, disconcerting in their perfection. She blinked her big blue eyes at him, slowly, opening and closing them like rusty doors, her soul barely a glimpse, a speck of light. Took a step away from the dark sea, presenting herself to him for him he realized despite his fifteen-year-old naiveté. Her large breasts seemed to swim like dolphins out of the dark into the light and look at him as though she'd opened the front of her dress, pulled down her bra, and her breasts had eyes not nipples — eyes that looked straight at him, into him.

Looking behind her, he could see the stark, dark shapes of the trees of the parkland, bordered by the edge of the pool deck and a high wire fence topped by rolls of barbed wire, gleaming like dull snake coils in the dead last light of day. The tree shapes looked like the aunts and uncles, the brothers and sisters of Dianne who'd somehow clambered over the barbed wire, leaving them bloodied and torn, to take her back home to warmth and cake and cups of tea and being tucked into bed and kissed on her forehead. Or maybe the shapes were something else, he thought.

Dianne stepped back one step and her face was lost in the stain of night coming. Shadows like long strong fingers laced together across her generous stomach, and he thought she was going to be pulled back into annihilation; he thought he'd never see her again. But then, stopping his panic rising like acidy reflux in his throat, he heard the calm and stern voice. Dianne's sister, Susan, talking to Dianne across the pool. He saw Dianne step back into the light as though her sister's words had fish hooks attached to every one, strong fine lines and sharp steel hooks pulling back Dianne away from the dark park of slippery grass and gnarled grotesque trees.

"Come back, Dianne, right now. They don't care about you, they only want one thing, you know that, really," said Susan.

The words were like clear ringing bells cutting through the noise of swimmers and people on the pool deck and the strident clamor of works knock off traffic crunching by, mill workers honking anger and tiredness and frustration just outside the pool. He saw the anger flush through Dianne's face, then the confusion of her not understanding, finally that incomprehension that made her face a dull mask tipping close to the edge of stupidity. And he wondered why he wanted to look at her, wondered why he lusted after her.

Susan's words took on a ragged edge of desperation.

"What would Mum say if she knew?"

It was Susan's last card, and he watched Dianne's face crease with anger, a long deep crevice seeming to cleave right through the center. Then the male smell came, the smell of sweat and underarm and testosterone settling over the pool like a suffocating invisible dome.

The odor smoothed Dianne's face, took away the wrinkles of doubt and anger as though someone had slammed a red hot steel iron into her face and ironed it all away. She smiled and turned away from her sister. He saw the movement from the corner of his eye, a movement like the hissing, vicious untangling of a knot of entwined rats.

They stormed across his line of sight, black crazy crotchets of hyperactivity, jumping, skipping with endless adolescent strength, pushing one another under the pretense of play, of camaraderie when underneath it was serious. It would only take one shove too hard and fists would start flying the way fists flew at the pub just down the road the steel workers patronized seven days and seven nights a week. Four of them were there and he watched them move toward Dianne who turned away and faced them.

He felt the cold like a giant splinter slivering into his flesh. He felt as though someone had taken long steel sharp-ended spikes and driven them with a heavy hammer into the soft cartilage between his vertebrae, as though the spikes of steel kept him upright, kept him prisoner, unable to move, forcing him to watch, to witness.

And he knew all of them from school. The Untouchables they were called not so much because they could throw and duck a punch but because of their reputation, mostly made by their big, nasty mouths that spilled insults and abuse like rivers of raw sewerage raging into the ocean. Verbal bullies, he thought of them. Not your traditional bullies who'd punch the shit out of you if you didn't hand over your lunch money. But the sticks and stones of their words broke the bones of many students who shied away from the group, left them alone, let them do whatever they wanted rather than suffer the acid sting of their words.

And he knew all of their fathers because his father worked in the industries with them, so there was no escaping the Untouchables. They were there outside of school at the pool, at the works annual picnic, at informal family get-togethers, slouching outside the milk bar on the corner, flinging smart arse comments at anyone who passed. He was always made to attend works get-togethers by his father. The last event had been an open day at the works when families got to visit the mills, walk through them and see what their husbands, brothers, uncles, and friends did, see where their lives were slowly slaughtered, second by second, day by day, week by week, year by year.

As he watched the four approach Dianne, he remembered walking into the lunch room with his mother and father and his two sisters in tow and the reaction of shock from his mother and sisters when they saw the girlie posters on the walls. Naked women covering all of the walls, but not just naked — women on all fours with huge dildos jammed half way into their vaginas or anuses, women on all fours with cocks in their mouths, some women with their mouths opened to display the thick cum shooting in, others on all fours being fucked from behind and sucking off another bloke kneeling in front of them, others being fucked anally and vaginally at the same time.

He still remembered the puzzled look on his father's face, something far more confronting than the women plastered to the walls of the crib room, a look that changed from confusion to anger when his father's wife and two daughters went at him, telling him that it was disgraceful, offensive to display women like that. His father didn't understand, he didn't get it, and more than that, he wasn't going to put up with three females getting stuck into him for no good reason, not with his mates and their families close by.

"What's wrong with yers yer stupid bitches? All of the blokes look at them all the time. There's nothing wrong with it," declared his father.

His voice was as final as the crash of a cobble of steel when a hot bar was aligned incorrectly and smashed into the rollers, the half-hot slab rising like a giant glowering backbone, falling onto the mill floor, workers rushing away to safety, sometimes. His mother apologized to her husband all the way home, the woman anxious not to upset him because the man would sulk for weeks because of the perceived insult. Sometimes the man, if angry enough, insulted enough, would let go with a punch that ironed out his wife unconscious on the kitchen floor.

They were gathering around Dianne now, clustering closer to her so he could only see fragments of her dress as though the four of them had torn it to rags that clung limply to her form. He should go there, walk around the pool to them and try to stop them, but he'd tried that before, put up with the derision from the four adolescents, but it was Dianne who'd decided then as she would now if he tried it again. It was her that laughed at him, told him he was a little poncy poofter, sent him away, the laughter of the Untouchables snapping like hungry tundra wolves at his heels.

He watched her now, persuaded by weasel words to step into the park darkness. It was as though one of the sink holes leading to the old coal shafts had opened and swallowed her, Dianne lost in an underworld, a maze of shafts and tunnels that cancered through the town, beneath it, a labyrinth where she might wander raving until the release of death.

He saw the roll of Glad Wrap held by one of the four, the boy tapping it against his leg, his mouth stretched wide with glee. All of them, all four of them would wrap their erections around with the Glad Wrap. They wouldn't buy condoms. Not for Dianne.

YOU'LL NEVER LEAVE HERE

THE HEAD SWAM AROUND THE CORNER OF THE TILES, A silent and careful placing of the face at the edge of the two rows of yellow tiles. The cheek nestled next to the black line of grime where the two rows of tiles met in a long hard joint. None of the men in the shower aware of the presence of the face watching them, the slitted eyes with the thick lid flesh stretched above so the olive-black pits of eyes smoldered and shifted far back in the skull. The eyes watching them, watching the thirty men from B crew in the shower trying to wash away the grit and shit from the shift on the floor of the mill.

The grin in the face as it continued to watch the pasty flesh and the futile efforts of the men to scrub out the dirt of steelmaking. Dirt that leeched under their skin and made strange gray marks, fan sprays of gray-like tattoos, fan sprays of gray like the prickle of a fish's backbone spikes. Markings of ownership the men battled to remove so they could go home to their wives and children and sit at the table for tea or breakfast. And not need to go to the bathroom to scrub themselves under the shower again.

Not need to go to the bathroom because the marks of dirt were still there and they wanted to sit at the table with their wives and children, wives and children with skin and flesh the luminous luster of fine pearls fished up from the depths of the ocean. The men aliens in their own homes when they sat next to the bright beams of their spouses and offspring, when they looked at the veins of dirt and grease creasing through the lines of their own hands. The men leaving grimy fingerprints on cutlery and porcelain and on the furniture.

And they came back to the works and the showers and the face that came and watched them at the end of every shift because they needed the money, because they had come to feel they belonged in the mill among the dirt and not in their homes.

The face continued to watch them and none of the men had noticed it even though they knew it would be there at the end of every shift to grin at them and to mock them. So tired were they, they did not bother or think to look up from the hot water and soap suds they lathered into their bodies.

The face with rags of hot water steam drifting across it so it seemed as though it was swimming up from a deep hole of black water toward the white light of the neon strips above the showers.

"You'll never leave here," the face suddenly said, and most of the thirty men looked up.

Some of them grinned and turned away from the face and continued to scrub themselves. Others laughed. Nervously. Others told the face to go and fuck itself.

"Go on, Jim. Piss off. Go on fuck off and leave us in peace," said one, then turned his back so he wouldn't have to see the grin in the face.

"Yeah, fuck off, Stingray," said another, but with a laugh in the words to lessen their force because Jim Ray was his foreman, their foreman.

The face coming out from behind the corner of the shower recess. Coming out, fleshing out, hardening under the merciless neon light. So all the men could see it. Could see the grin that spread like the opening of a cave with a shelf of darkness cutting back into the bone. With only a few teeth left, small wedges of yellowed porcelain but pointed and roughened and sharp on the edges.

Some of the men looking up nervously now, looking away from their bodies lathered soapy and glistening like seals under the white light. The men looking at the man and the body that ballooned from the neck into a ball of flesh. As though the head was of the same part as the torso. One round circle of head and eyes and shoulders and stomach. Like the body of a stingray swimming quietly through the thick mist of steam that came from the showers.

"You'll never leave here," the face and the body said again.

Jim Ray, the foreman, known without real affection as Stingray to the men because of his name, because his tongue was as sharp and as poisonous as the barbed tail of a stingray, because of the shape of his head and body. The body that seemed to grow bigger every day. That seemed to move with even more stealth the more the works hired more men to come and work at the mill.

The foreman stood at the lip of the shower and grinned. No more words for them. Just the glee that sprang from him like the bodies of fish chopping salt water in a feeding frenzy. The foreman with his shark smile and only his eyes moving. His body blocking the exit for the men to go to their lockers to towel themselves dry and get out the front gate.

"Come on Stingray, get outta th' way," said one and pushed past the foreman. The grease and grime on the overalls of the foreman rubbing off onto the clean body of the man. Who did not see the fin-shaped barb of grease on his side.

Others pushing past the man who would not move. Who stood and grinned and let the men push past. Who left his mark on them all.

Jim Ray stepping one step closer so his stomach hung into the shower recess. Where Tim Brown was the only one left now. Tim Brown who was not a tradesman, who was not employed as a subcontractor with his own business. Tim Brown who was a laborer without any skills, who'd left school as soon as possible and went straight to the steel works because there was good money to be made there. Because his girlfriend was four months pregnant with Tim's child.

Tim who'd been there for ten years and him only in his twenties and not having known any other life. His father and brothers all in the mills.

Tim Brown with three kids and two cars to pay off and a mortgage as well. Tim Brown the resident "lifer" in the mill because he could never leave because of his debts to banks and finance companies, because of his debts to his wife and children.

Something the Stingray never let him forget. Something he reminded Tim of now as the foreman's big stomach blocked the way out of the showers for Tim Brown. Tim Brown naked and wet and looking at the man with something approaching fear. Because it looked as though the Stingray had eaten all of the men from B crew. Had swallowed every one of them whole. And would vomit them back into being when they were needed in twelve hours time to roll and tie and twist the hot metal that came from the belly of the furnace.

Tim Brown gulped down his fear and went to leave but the foreman would not move.

"You'll never leave here," he repeated and stepped into the shower recess. Blocked the entrance and left thick ripples of grease on the tiles from the soles of his work boots. Tim Brown struggling to get past the bulk of the man but caught in the soft flesh of the stomach.

Pushed against the wall of yellow tiles slimy from the sweat and grease of thirty bodies. The flesh of the foreman jamming the small man fast. The flab like the fat Tim Brown came across occasionally in the fish he caught out of the Hunter River and cleaned.

Fish that had fed on the refuse of men, fast food scraps dumped in the river upstream and the bream and whiting and taylor feeding on the doughy waste. The trim, clean white meat of the fish thickening into white strips of fat marbled among the guts and bones of the fish.

Tim Brown having to fillet his catch carefully these days. Careful to cut away the lines of fat, careful to clean the guts of the fish. And present what remained to his wife who would cook and dish up the catch for the family.

Tim Brown starting to lose his breath as the grin in the face widened and the man leaned hard against Tim. Leaned hard against the tiles.

"Leave him alone, Stingray," said Brian Jones, one of the fitters coming up behind the foreman.

The foreman grinning and stepping back. Moving his bulk out of the shower and Tim Brown on his hands and knees catching his breath. Looking up to hear the words come again from the foreman before he swam out of Tim's sight.

"You'll never leave here."

Tim Brown grabbing the soap from the tile holder and lathering himself all over. Again. Scrubbing at the grease and dirt marks the Stingray had left on his body. Scrubbing in vain and knowing the only way to get rid of the grease and dirt was to use the pumice stone and salt water.

The pumice stone his wife gave him when he went fishing. Tim with his line set in the water, leaning over the side of his aluminum dinghy and scrubbing himself with the pumice stone and salt water. As the boat drifted from the mangroves of Hexham down river into the widening fan of the estuary that flared into wide water under the arch of the Stockton Bridge.

The river and estuary Tim Brown would be fishing tomorrow because he'd finished ten straight shifts tying watch springs of hot, recently-rolled metal. The worst job in the mill and a permanent position for Tim because he had no choice, because the Stingray made sure he stayed there even after ten years of Tim bent over the coils of hot metal. Ten years of looping the wire around the metal and tying it fast so it wouldn't unwind and spring apart like intestines shooting out from the belly of a fish full of row and caught and cut from arsehole to gills by the knife of a fisherman.

Tim Brown tumbled from the mill and legged it for the front gate. Sinking down into the sand drifts that had been a feature of the works from when it opened almost a century ago. The works sited on low-lying ground next to the Hunter River, the site built up by the dredging of the river channel and pumping the sand and shell and fish onto the place where the mills would go.

The small man struggling through the grit heading for the gate where he could see his wife waiting for him in the car. Vicki Brown with her matronly arms crossed over the top of the steering wheel of the car. Waiting with some impatience for her husband.

"I thought you weren't going to ever leave that place," she said as Tim hauled himself into the seat beside her.

He looked at her sideways and sighed. Turned his face away and looked out of the window at the pyramids of black coal heaped along the side of the road leading out of the works. Heaps of black coal that shed sheets of black dust that coated Tim and his wife and children as they slept. Dust from the coal the company used to fire steel into existence.

He looked back at Vicki jockeying the rust bucket ute through the exodus of mill workers in their cars. Looked at the lines of gray dirt grained into her brow from the works and the effort of feeding and cleaning and scolding her children. And he wondered whether he would ever escape the works and the mill and the Stingray and take his wife and kids away to somewhere cleaner and quieter. Away from the hot metal bang and roll they could hear in their sleep.

Tim's house a small miner's cottage only two blocks of houses away from the main gate of the works.

He turned his head away and saw the small red Datsun scoot up the inside of the ute, the Datsun with the face of the Stingray floating above the wheel. And the loud honk honking of the horn and the grin turned toward Tim. Mocking him, telling him there was no escape even when he left the works.

•

Tim Brown watched the canopy of mangroves open into clean wide water. The brown and black stench of sticky mangrove mud slipping under the bottom of the aluminum dinghy. The small craft nosing into the estuary that widened into veins and arteries of streams and the channels of the main river.

Tim with his cane basket half filled with whiting and a few bream. Tim using the slick and slippery blood worms he threaded onto the white steel of his hook. The small man, by himself, and drifting with the many flows of the estuary. The smooth drift that sometimes became an eddy of currents meeting and knotting and twirling the dinghy in circles. Until the boat found a break in the twist of stream and river and open ocean currents and freed itself. Released Tim back into one of the smooth cables of current that divined a course toward the sea. Toward the works that loomed on the horizon.

The steel stacks jammed hard against the wharf built along the bank of the Hunter River. The familiar stench finding the nose of Tim Brown as he pulled in a big bream that bristled wet and silver spikes. Tim carefully folding flat the scrub of needles. Allowing his hand to close unharmed around the body of the bream. The bream with the dark body of an estuary fish caught close to the works. Not the bright metallic silver with a tinge of green or bronze found on the back of open ocean fish.

Tim Brown placed the bream in the basket and baited his hook. Let the line over the side of the boat. Watched the blood worm sink into the green metal sheen of the water. Watched the steel works opposite his boat now. Saw the mill where he worked, the soot-smutted iron of the walls and the roof and the sound of the hot steel being rolled. A sound that did not stop, day and night, twelve hour shifts about, except when the furnace went down for repairs.

Tim watched as the entrance of the mill came into view and he could see the worms of hot orange steel billets being rolled. He could see the tendrils of steam hissing and curling as the jets of water played onto the molten metal. He could see the men he knew, he worked with, dashing about on the mill floor.

And he felt the heavy downward pull on his line, not the usual sharp jag of a whiting running away like a freight train with the line, not the usual shy and cunning pick of a bream at the bait. But a heavy lazy weight on the line.

"Feels like a big fat flathead," said Tim to himself.

Tim pulling the line in slowly because he didn't have a steel trace on his line and a flathead would see-saw through the line if he pulled too hard. Tim slow and careful and not panicking until he saw the color come in the water. Until he saw the flap and shudder of the stingray in the water next to the boat. The flap and shudder of the body, a good two feet in diameter, running up the line into the hands of Tim Brown. Who shook with something like dread and fear.

Who felt the nausea rise in his throat when he saw the spiracles, or breathing holes, placed behind the eyes. The breathing holes like another pair of eyes so the ray seemed to be looking at him with four eyes. Seemed to hold his eyes and not let him go. As if Tim was the fish caught by the stingray, caught in the upper world of air and likely to be pulled, by the ray, into the water and taken down into some deep and narrow hole in the bed of the river.

Tim Brown watched with a certain fascination as the stingray creased itself into running rolls of movement. Earthquake ripples of movement that revealed the white underbelly of the fish. The ray flapping hard against the metal of the dinghy. As if it were trying to slide up the side of the boat. Tim Brown lost, frozen from any sort of action.

But seeing the eyes looking at him, the disgust in Tim antagonizing him into action. Tim leaning over to cut the line. Let the ray go free. Let himself go free. His hand clutching the knife close to the water to cut the line as close as possible to the stingray. So as not to lose too much line.

The blunt edge of the knife at the line when the stingray wrenched its bulk backward. Creased itself almost in half and whipped its long wire rope tail in an arc. Drops of water lashing like bright fire sparks. The barb in an orbit that ended embedded in the index finger of Tim Brown.

Who cried blue murder. Tried to free himself but the barb jammed through the top joint of the finger and the barb tip protruding out the other side. The pain of the wound rippling like muscle through the tissue of his hand. Tim seeing the hand beginning to bloat already, to swell from the stingray barb.

Tim calming himself. Leaning down, his body over the side of the boat. His legs hooked under the seat to stop him going over the side. Tim taking the knife in his good hand and slashing at the tail. Severing the stingray tail from the flesh of the big body. Leaving the spool of line go with the ray. Pulling himself back into the boat with the long tail twitching at the end of his index finger.

Tim Brown arched but a moment in pain before he seated himself and turned over the outboard motor. The spluttering into life of the engine and Tim steering the dinghy with one hand, the other hand swelling and the tail of the ray still lashing about the boat. Tim keeping the pain at bay. Pushing it to the back of his mind the way he did whenever he burned himself on one of the coils of hot steel.

Tim who had slipped with fatigue, had fallen asleep bent over the hot steel and burned his hands. Had administered his own medicine of dripping and Vicki's cold cream when he got home, rather than deal with the Stingray, rather than report the accidents and have the foreman after him even more for causing him trouble.

Tim cut the engine and turned the boat sideways into the wharf. With one hand tied the small vessel to the bottom rung of the ladder running up the side of the gray wooden pylons. Using one good hand pulled himself up the rungs with his other hand turning septic quickly from the ray tail trailing from his finger.

Tim stumbling through the sand drifts toward the entrance of the mill and finding Brian Jones puffing on a rollie and sipping a cup of tea.

"Jesus Christ, Timmy!!" declared Brian and dropped his tea and fag when he saw the hand of Tim with the stingray tail attached.

"Brian, get those bolt cutters," Tim said.

"Christ, Tim, yer can't do that!" said Brian.

"Don't argue, Brian. There's not time to take me to hospital. I might lose me hand for all I know if I leave it too long. Get the cutters, Brian," demanded Tim Brown.

Brian Jones disappearing into the murk of the mill and returning with the cutters. Returning with the Stingray lurching hot on his heels.

"Okay, do it, Brian," said Tim and placed his swollen hand on one of the steps leading into the mill.

Brian Jones with the cutters closed around the finger and Brian looking at Tim once more. Who nodded. The cutters closed and the blood engorged finger swimming through the air with the tail of the ray trailing and switching the blood that bloomed from the severed finger.

The Stingray turning his head away with the sickness rising in his throat. The emblems of black bad blood flowering from the finger stump of Tim's hand. Dropping on the cement and the dirt, dropping on the boots of the Stingray. The old cracked and thirsty leather drinking in the blood of Tim Brown. The Stingray panicking and turning away with fear and swimming back into the soupy light of the mill.

While Brian tied the torn hose of Tim's index finger with twine from his tool box.

•

Tim Brown swung the rusty ute out onto the highway. With Vicki jammed in the front with the three kids. A ute and some sandwiches and a few dollars their only possessions after the house was sold and the works paid out Tim and the mortgage and other bills were paid.

Tim and Vicki and the three kids heading south away from the works.

HER MOUTH

I SAW HER THROUGH THE GLASS, NOT A DIRECT, NERVE slicing view but a shattered flash like a startled white bird trying to take flight but brought back down to earth by a double-barreled barrage of gunshot. I didn't take any notice of her because of the glass wall between us in the café. But then something commanded me to glance through the glass and I saw her with her three friends — all grown women, all confident, all at ease in their own skins — or so it seemed.

I looked back to my wife sitting opposite and said something to her, still not registering who it was on the other side of the glass, the young woman with her friends sitting outside in the laneway that ran down the side of the café. From the corner of my eye I was aware of a bustle and tussle of toddlers that belonged to the other three women. Then I glanced through the partition again, and it was her mouth that made me remember; she had the same mouth as her grandmother, my aunt.

The young woman's mouth was a belligerent straight line that turned down at the corners and ran in deep ravines in the flesh as though a scowl had slid from her brow, took flight from her ski jump nose, and landed in place in the gaping hole waiting for the mouth. Her grandmother's mouth made an old woman of the young woman sitting in the café as though she'd been punished severely for most of her short life.

That mouth brought back all the memories, the tidal wave of black poison none of us had been able to escape. I looked directly at her mouth, and it was an enforced tattoo, the ink squeezed, smeared by brutal fingers and thumbs into cuts made by a dirty razor blade. The mouth was more than a blemish, it was a mark of ownership, a stamp of belligerence and arrogance that would claim the young woman, making her part of the kith and kin of her grandmother.

The picture of her grandmother formed in my head for the first time in years. I'd spent a long time making myself not remember her, but now there was no choice for me, just as there'd been no choice for the woman sitting on the other side of the glass in another world, but it was my world, too, whether I liked it or not.

My aunt stormed out of the past a dark, squat troll of bluff and bluster, a monster of deceit. She stood directly in the center of my mind's eye and I wondered about my soul, if it was possible for other people to tear the anima into rags until there was only a hobbling goblin left, a reflection of the abuser, the controller.

And I heard the deep masculine voice coming from my aunt's mouth in my mind, the voice always suggesting the owner would rather have a fight than a feed so you better back off if you knew what was good for you; you better let her have her own way whether it was right or wrong. As I shakily attempted to replace the cup of café latte in the saucer, spilling most of it down the front of me, burning the flesh of my chest so I had to stifle a cry of pain, I realized the deep, masculine voice I was hearing also came from the young woman on the other side of the glass.

It made the glass quiver, quenching the voices of the three other women. I looked at them and their faces were all the same as though someone had taken hold of the bone and flesh of the inside of their heads and pulled hard caving in mouths, collapsing eye sockets, slitting shut lids, quaking mouths into pinched chain smokers' mouths, the women unable to respond to the young woman with her mouth yanked down at the corners.

In my skull my aunt danced with glee, stomping her hobnailed boots up and down, and I remembered what my mother had said about her, her sister, that she'd been the rough and tumble tomboy of the family, the one who'd take on anyone anywhere, the self-declared strong one. And I looked at her granddaughter through the glass and wondered whether she was the same.

I saw that the two toddlers and the baby had stopped squirming their energy against the laps and breasts of their mothers. Like their mothers they were silent, looking straight at the young childless woman as though there was something about her that commanded complete attention. The baby opened its mouth and the dummy fell like a glistening brown flower, tumbling through the soupy café air, bits of spit flying; it landed on the stone cobbled floor, the pacifier covered with dirt. Absently the mother bent down, reached under the table, picked up the dummy, and without cleaning it, placed it back in the baby's mouth. The child sucked and swallowed. The mother had not taken her eyes from the face of my aunt's granddaughter.

I searched my mind for the granddaughter's name and I thought it was Beth, but I couldn't be sure and that was because her grandparents had robbed her of her name and her identity, destroyed who she was or might have been. Beth, sitting on the other side of the glass might well be an impostor, a mannequin made and molded by her grandmother, Selina, and her grandfather, Stan.

I thought of the royal commission into sexual abuse underway, how all the victims, those that hadn't suicided, spoke about making themselves survive, forcing themselves to establish an identity, forcing themselves to get and hold down a job, forcing themselves into marriage and struggling to make it work. But most of all I thought about how they wondered what they might have been like as people if as children hadn't been raped or forced to perform fellatio.

I looked back through the glass and Beth was still speaking, and the women and their children were still listening, silent, unmoving. I wondered if the women were confidants, the only people who knew what had befallen Beth other than her immediate family. Were the three friends the ones she turned to when the flashbacks came like nightmares of the Great War with shadowy soldiers, in the darkness storming over ramparts with cold steel cocked upward? Did she ring them and plead with them to meet her at the café again so they could debrief her once more with chit chat and coffee and cake and careful and compassionate listening?

What if they didn't know? Would that explain the way they were mesmerized by Beth, stilled to statues by the strangeness of the young woman who did and said things that stunned and amused the three women? Did the three come to be entertained, go home together without Beth, gossip about Beth's latest performance, shriek with laughter at her latest antics?

What if Beth hadn't told them anything? How could she continue to chat and drink coffee as though nothing had happened? Had she turned out the same as her grandmother, keeping up appearances, refusing to talk about the family disgrace and pain, or was she simply strong, keeping her own counsel, able to overcome the abuse, not needing others to prop her up?

She'd stopped speaking. I risked a look and they were still staring at her, and then one woman began to speak, tentatively, almost apologetically, and the other two women took up her lead, but their voices weren't the high sparrow chatter of before. Their voices were quiet like visitors to a mausoleum and their bodies were still unmoving.

I looked at Beth's plate and there was one round of plain white bread on it, and she was spreading margarine on the bread. No fancy, tasty pasta or pizza or a toasted open melt, but plain bread, Beth like a nineteenth-century prisoner in a London gaol. Next to her elbow was a glass half full of water, no hot, frothy café latte or cup of strong long black coffee.

It was starting to happen again, those coils of the snake unwrapping carefully, almost mechanically, disengaging one by one, pre-ordained, rising upward in spirals, dancing closer to where I was. I was seeing Beth as a prisoner forever condemned to austerity and confinement of all sorts. The abuse took on new shapes, new shadows, mutated into so many forms it always took you by surprise.

I'd come to the city for the first time in three years. I'd felt that it would be okay to venture back, that time and tide, etc. would have washed over the clambering, clodhopper imprints of my aunt and uncle, that there couldn't be anything or anyone left to remind me, but there she was, one of the victims, as though she'd been sitting in the café for three years behind the glass, waiting for me to turn up just so she could remind me that she

and her sister
and her cousin
and my mother
and me
and the others I didn't know about
would never be let off the hook.

I looked at Beth, saw her mouth chasm open, saw her throat fall apart like a nineteenth-century rubble-brick and limestone chimney during an earthquake, and from the yawning openings spewed thick black spider web, bolts and reams and meters of it swirling out, curling around me, stretching through the café door, sucking black tendrils, seeking the others to hold them close in a sticky mess of obscenity and suffering.

I thought I was going to pass out. And then I saw her in the thin opaque glass window that gave privacy to the café patrons from the passersby. My mother unfolded, a flame burning white, unmoving, my dead mother a bright beacon of possible deliverance. I felt myself calm, my nerves, masses of red, raw wires, settling back into bone, flesh, skin, muscle.

My aunt, still stamping up and down, still belligerent, was now blown into ragged puffs of black smoke by my mother's presence, which was like a southerly buster bustling up the NSW coast, bulldozing heavy heat from the land, allowing people to breathe, again, finally.

And I remembered it all, again, everything that began a minute after I finished eating Christmas dinner at my parents' place years ago. I'd stepped onto the veranda to get some fresh air when my father collared me.

"Your Uncle Stan's a pedophile, he's been abusing his granddaughters for years. It's just come out. Your mother's going to tell you herself in the next couple of weeks so don't let on I've told you."

And then he was gone, the veranda door slamming behind him, me standing there, stunned. He'd set the tone, the pattern for the coming ordeal, the secrecy and playacting of my Aunt Selina and Uncle Stan; their pretense and lies were somehow established by my father telling me of the family scandal, unable to hold back and let my mother tell me, my father insistent that I should cover up the fact he'd told me.

A week later I got a breathless phone call from my father.

"Your mother's going to ring you and ask you to come over. She's going to tell you about Stan so pretend you don't know anything."

Two minutes later she rang, and I went over and I had to stand there listening to my tearful mother telling me the story, and I had to pretend I didn't know, had to pretend to be shocked. And all the while I was tempted to tell her that Dad had already told me. I didn't, but it was the last time I didn't tell the truth because soon I was enveloped in a barrage of lies and pretense coming from my aunt and uncle, aided and abetted by an extended family of ancient aunts and uncles who found the issue too difficult to tackle, and a multitude of cousins who didn't seem to give a fuck.

My mother suffered terribly and never recovered from the news of the sexual abuse of the three young girls. I got sick and tired of finding my mother in tears when I visited so I consulted a clinical psychologist I knew who said that I needed to gather together all the victims and people affected and have my Uncle Stan acknowledge he'd done it and have him apologize to all of them.

That ended that so-called solution because those involved in their seventies and eighties would not put into action something suggested by a psychologist. To do so would be tantamount to admitting insanity on their part, a weakness of the mind that had no part in the working class city.

Not that my uncle would have ever admitted guilt, let alone apologized to the victims and those affected. I thought, as did my mother, that Selina and Stan would at least show some contrition and guilt, but we couldn't have been more wrong.

My mother thought her sister would leave Stan. Instead, my aunt commissioned a portrait session of her family using a well known photographer. Stan featured prominently in all of the photos, all of which were blown up to a huge size and hung on every wall in my aunt's house. Was it an ultimate act of denial on her part of the sexual abuse or an ultimate act of defiance of what people thought, or both?

And so the insidious grinding process began. My parents made the decision not to go to any social functions if Selina and Stan attended. My parents were the only ones in the large extended family to take a stand. My aunt Selina rang my mother every now and then and abused the living daylights out of her for refusing to turn up to family get-togethers. Selina was simply furious that someone would stand up to her and not turn a blind eye to what had happened. But the other old aunts and uncles continued to turn up and rub shoulders with Stan, and one reason was that he was the only one of them left with a car and a driver's license. He ran all of the "oldies" around and for that they were all prepared to ignore the fact that he'd digitally penetrated his three granddaughters for years.

The irony of it all was that my parents became the outcasts in the family. By staying away they became invisible and none of the other family members were prepared to make the effort to go and see them. Mum and Dad were simply too difficult because what they were doing was simply too difficult to deal with.

I looked at my mother burning in the strip of opaque glass in the café, but she did not waver. I could not see her face clearly but there seemed a calmness about her she hadn't possessed during life, especially during her final years when the Alzheimer's locked shut its padlock upon her mind and body. I wondered now whether there was a greater understanding in her about what had happened to her in her life on earth; was the place where she'd gone somewhere that enabled her to perceive what she'd been through with a divine clarity? Would I ever manage the same as I struggled in the here and now to come to terms with the damaged young woman sitting on the other side of the glass?

I glanced at Beth and saw the smudged dirty fingerprints upon the glass, fingerprints that suddenly seemed to attach to her face and body as though the marks on the glass had leaped like small hostile stinging insects onto her. I realized she was leprosy white as though something had attached itself to her and sucked the life blood from her body. I was reminded of some of the fish I'd caught off the tidal rock platform next to the baths over the years, a bream or drummer with a blind white parasite that had torn open the fish's side and attached itself with seething claws and rampaging nippers to an intestine, feeding off the food the host had scavenged from submerged rock shelves.

I remembered the first time I encountered my aunt and uncle after the news had broken of the sexual abuse. I went with Jan to the funeral and wake of my Uncle Brian who'd died of a brain tumor. Maybe it was because it had been so long since I'd seen Stan and Selina that made me vulnerable, but I should have been wary. But I'd underestimated their ability to control, and I hadn't understood clearly at that stage that the pair were without shame.

As Jan and I sat in my Aunt Christine's kitchen, an open hand waiting to be shaken was shoved under my nose, and I automatically took it and shook it before I looked up and saw who the hand belonged to. It was too late. I was shaking my Uncle Stan's hand and he looked smug because his plan had come off.

Before I could react, Stan broke the handshake, moved to Jan and kissed her on both sides of her face. Jan's reaction was the same as mine — automatic, unthinking — and she responded with air kisses. This, I understood later, was all for show, meant to make it clear to everyone at the wake that some of my immediate family were still on good terms with Stan and Selina. It was punishment by Stan and Selina toward my mother for refusing to socialize with her sister and brother-in-law.

I told my mother later and she was mortified.

"They set it all up. My sister and her husband would have discussed what they were going to do. They would have planned it all in advance," she said.

My aunt's and uncle's determination to keep up appearances and not to own any blame whatsoever continued unabated over the years. But what was more insidious was their strategy of blaming the victims and making out that anyone who stood up to them was somehow mentally deficient, a curiosity to be mocked and ridiculed.

Jan and I walked into the chapel for the viewing of my mother's body after she died from a heart attack due to high sugar levels and neglect by some of those closest to her. When we walked in, I saw Selina sitting with three of her daughters. She saw me and turned to her three daughters and said, "Oh, oh, here he is, I'm still in trouble with him."

This was followed by her deep masculine laughter, joined in by the deep masculine laughter of her three daughters. They were making out as if I were the one with the problem, not them, and that Stan had done nothing.

I'd continued to refuse to associate with my aunt and uncle even though Mum had caved in because the Alzheimer's had robbed her memory of the abuse ever happening. When my first book was published, I made a point of not inviting Stan and Selina to the launch.

Jan and I sat down near the front near my mother's open coffin and soon Stan came over and attempted to offer his condolences.

"Look, go and sit back down. I don't want anything to do with you," I told him and for once, clearly non-plussed, he did what he was told.

But there were plenty of people sitting behind us who were watching this closely. Selina got up next and came over to us and said to me, "I'm sorry. I'm genuinely sorry."

I could have told her that I held her and her husband at least partly responsible for Mum's death. Mum was never the same after she learned of the abuse; her diabetes rampaged out of control because of the stress. Up until she found out, she had controlled the disease with diet and exercise. There's a strong connection between untreated diabetes and dementia, and although I cannot prove it, I felt Mum's descent into Alzheimer's was linked to the stress caused by the sexual abuse, her sister's abusive phone calls, and being made an outsider by her own family.

I looked at my aunt and did not respond. Hopefully, the look I gave her was one of complete contempt, but by then I knew I was fighting a losing battle because the two people I was dealing with were ruthless and would stop at nothing to bow others to their will.

The story of how my aunt and uncle managed to worm their way back into my mother's presence is worth recounting. For years Mum refused to have Stan in the house; she allowed her sister in, and when Selina got over the threshold all hell would break loose because her husband had to sit in the car. Mum wouldn't back down.

But my aunt sensed Mum's deterioration of mind due to dementia, and one day Mum opened the front door and there were Selina and Stan standing on the doorstep, Selina holding a cat. Mum's cat had just died and everyone knew Mum just loved cats. My aunt and uncle presented her with the new moggy and Mum let them both in. They had won, once more.

My father didn't do anything to try to forestall my aunt and uncle's insidious tactics. He let them come into the house and he and Mum started going to social occasions with Stan and Selina in attendance. Mum had talked to me years before about how difficult it was to hold firm to her resolution not to associate with her sister and her husband.

"Your father has stuck by me now. I just hope he doesn't change his mind if things get even more difficult," she said.

I looked at Beth and I wondered whether all of the women in her family had mouths like that; I wondered whether her cousin in South Australia had the same turned down mouth Beth wore like a grotesque stigmata. I couldn't remember the cousin's name.

The abuse was like a virus infecting everyone, taking away their characters. The abuse was like my mother's Alzheimer's, burrowing through my brain, taking away memory and experience of life, love, and pleasure.

My coffee tasted bitter and the pizza was bland as I remembered how the girl in South Australia lost her mind, self-harming, screaming, mad with rage and pain, slamming herself against doors and walls. It went on for years and her parents, David and Meg, didn't know the cause of it. Umpteen psychologists were consulted but to no avail. The young girl's behavior became so bad that David and Meg had to undertake therapy themselves.

Finally, somehow, it all came out and David rang his father-in-law and abused the living daylights out of him and then cut all ties with Stan and Selina. But six months later, because Meg loves her mother, she decided to resume contact. She rang home and her father answered. He said, "Well, after all the trouble you and your husband have caused, I don't think we want to talk to you at all."

David, a store manager, had always been under stress and had a drinking problem that he eventually overcame, but Stan and Selina seized upon it as a way of shedding any blame for the behavior of their granddaughter.

"Your daughter's behavior has nothing to do with your father," Selina told Meg. "It's David's drinking that caused it."

I looked at Beth again and I wondered whether she'd reacted the same way as her cousin in South Australia. Did Beth self-harm, cutting her arms with razors? Did she slam herself into walls or starve herself or lay awake at night reliving her visitor looming above her? There was no way of telling; the poker-faced woman gave no hint of any emotion. Again, was it strength, or was it an insistence that all was well, a keeping up of appearances, or did she love her grandmother too?

Beth's appearance was otherworldly as though she'd withdrawn from the here and now. Her wan and fey appearance was emphasized by her white dress, white shoes and pale makeup. Only the crucifix, hanging from her neck, blazed bright gold. I knew that all of Selina and Stan's daughters and granddaughters had become born-again Christians, and I wondered whether that had enabled some sort of forgiveness of Stan. But was it forgiveness or blind stupidity to excuse a man for doing that, or, once more, was it a means of keeping up appearances in the form of a God-fearing family all pure and forgiven and delivered from sin and evil?

The women were getting ready to leave the café; bags, purses and children were retrieved. But Beth sat, not moving, as though she would never move again, never smile, never lose herself in laughter. She had a sister who had been abused and I wondered about her. Was she the same as Beth, a virtual ghost lost on this world, and what about the sisters' mother, Dianne?

The last time I'd seen Dianne was at the viewing of my mother's body. Jan and I got up and went for the door of the chapel, but before we could escape Dianne was walking toward me. As she came she shook her head and smiled in the same way her mother always had, the gestures telling me it was me who had the problem and that she, Dianne, had come to terms a long time ago with her father's abuse of her children.

"I read your stories in the paper," she said to me.

She poured out flattery like a jug of maple syrup poured on my head, thickly running, clogging my eyes and ears, and I realized Dianne thought she could smooth things over between her parents and me. Either she didn't understand the enormity of what her parents had done, or she was intent on keeping up appearances like her mother. Or she was stupid.

"Bye, Beth,"

The three women and their children waved to the young woman still sitting in the café and left. My mother burned steadily. Memory of my aunt huffed and puffed black clouds of smoke. My wife watched me from across the wooden desert of the table.

When it came out about my uncle molesting his granddaughters, I became very close to my mother because we spent months discussing the issue. You could say it was a type of debriefing for us both. Along with forming the resolution not to have anything to do with Stan and Selina, my mother came to some realizations. She said to me, "My sister, Selina, is an intelligent woman. There's no way she couldn't have known what Stan was doing to those girls over such a long period of time. I think she turned a blind eye to it and allowed it to go on. Selina always made herself out to be the strong one, the rough and tough one ready to have a go at anyone, but she's not strong, she's weak, really weak."

The flame of my mother folded in the opaque glass; my aunt mumbled in my ear like a distant storm that wouldn't go away.

I got up and looked at Beth sitting there, perfectly still, staring out through the café at the passersby who laughed and joked. A pair of lovers stopped briefly and kissed, then stumbled on. Mothers pushed strollers full of fat babies.

I knew Beth would always be there waiting for me if I came back to the café. Waiting for a life, waiting out a life sentence.

TWO SCHOONERS OF BEER, PLEASE

I WAS DRIVING A CAB IN NEWCASTLE LATE FRIDAY night and, as usual, the city had been more of a war zone than a place where civilized human beings lived and played. After the last fare where two blokes sat in the back and told me stories about how they made a habit of putting taxi drivers in the boots of their cabs, dowsing the cabbies with petrol and setting them alight, I'd had enough of downtown Newcastle, so I headed toward the Wickham rail gates which, mercifully, for a change, were up.

I needed to get away, and I reckoned that if I could get across the rickety bridge to Carrington, I could find a narrow and dark street where only the giant rats running about scavenging food would bother me. Carrington is riddled with narrow streets; they're the places where the shit collectors used to go with their horses and carts, driving down the lanes that ran at the back of the houses.

Newcastle Council in its wisdom turned the sanitary byways into streets, and many is the time I have had to drive the cab onto the footpath so a car coming the other way could get past.

In Carrington I knew that no drunks would bother me, no one would jump into the cab and threaten to bash me, no one would get in and throw up all over the dashboard, and no one would abuse me for going the long way when I hadn't.

The Wickham gates began to disappear in the dark glass of the rear view vision mirror. Then the lights on the gates began to flash red and the bells began to ring. I'd just managed to get through before they came down. I took this as a good omen because if I'd ended up waiting for a train to pass through someone would have broken into the vehicle and demanded me to take them home and not turn on the meter while waiting at the gates. Always a guaranteed source of contention, and often the cause of fist fights between cabbies and truculent and recalcitrant passengers who just won't be told.

The turn off to the bridge was in sight. Hope of release, albeit temporary, rose in my heart. But then a blinding blur of brown and white metal shot across the front of the cab missing me by inches. The Morris Major continued on out of control, smashing through the doors of the pub on the corner that had just shut for the night.

I pulled the cab over, got out and climbed through the hole in the hotel, splinters of wood and brick dust falling like a pall on my head. The Morris Major had come to rest two feet from the bar.

A barmaid, who had been washing and wiping beer glasses, stood behind the bar, her mouth ajar, her face a mask of terror, one hand holding a wet glass, the other hand holding a towel. The passenger in the runaway car had a similar expression of frozen horror on his face.

Not so the driver of the Morris, who grinned, wound down the window, stuck his head out and said to the barmaid, "Two schooners of beer, please."

HUNTER RIVER STORY

The Flood

June Sattler could hear her father even though he was a good distance away from where she stood on the veranda of the farmhouse. His voice was loud because her father had had a few beers already even though it was only mid-morning. The neighbors were over and Stan Sattler was never one to do things by halves when it came to hospitality.

He'd laid on the drinks from early morning when June was milking the cows and her mother was working her way along the rows of cauliflowers with a hoe removing any weeds. But Stan, as far as he was concerned, had more important things to attend to. And he told his wife and daughter so.

"I have to be out there with the neighbors drinkin' and spinnin' them some yarns and jokes because it's expected of me. I'm the biggest fruit and vegetable farmer along the Hunter River. It wouldn't do to be selfish when it comes to putting on a spread for those farmers around here who haven't made a good go of it like I have," he said.

And June, as she stood at the railing and listened to one of her father's well-rehearsed punch lines, had to admit he was probably right. The local farmers and their wives did look to Stan Sattler for leadership, they depended on his continued success to encourage them to keep farming the soil and slough off the adversities of flood and drought when they came.

Stan's spread of food and drink was proof of his continuing success. June remembered the sigh of relief from the guests when Stan pulled back the yellow antique lace cloth covering the food and bottles of wine and beer trembling on a trestle. It was as though some of the men and their wives had had doubts about her father's continuing ability to make a profit from growing fruit and vegetables in the red soil left by the river when it flooded.

The sight of the wooden trestle, bowed in the middle by the weight of the largesse of the soil, put their fears to rest. And Stan howled with laughter when he saw the change come over the salt-gray faces of his guests because he knew what they had been thinking. He saw them as children, insecure, with a need to be petted, prodded a bit by a caring parent. There was no doubt in Stan's mind — and June's mind — that that parent was Stan Sattler.

All six foot six of him with his ripe, corn-colored hair, the long beard, silver now with age, winnowing in the wind when it blew across the paddocks studded with green vegetables. He was a huge man with a huge voice that commanded respect, love, and affection. Stan got those things without the slightest trouble.

June knew it only too well. It hadn't been that long ago when she was a young girl of thirteen and madly devoted to her father, at jealous odds with her mother. June worshiped him, followed him everywhere he went on the farm. His daughter was a second shadow for Stan. June could not leave her father alone. She begged to stay home from school to be with him to stop her mother from being alone with him.

It was his voice she loved as much as anything, that clear melodious bellow that came from the chambers of his heart, thought June. That's how she imagined it. The words her father said were amplified, refined through the four chambers of his heart before he allowed them into his throat and out his mouth. Loud words, but heavy with the honey of the man, soft and caressing on the skin of any woman who strayed into the path of the farmer.

She'd seen him almost seduce the wife of a farmer at one of their dos recently. Not that Stan set out to do it; he just couldn't help it. He didn't know that so many women could not resist that voice that seemed born out of the creamy textured red soil Stan plowed, planted, and harvested year after year.

So it came as a complete surprise to Stan when the woman's husband started swinging wild punches at him. He backed away, dismissed the man as having had too much to drink while the other men dragged away the irate husband.

It had always been that way for as long as June could remember. Her father had always ambled through their lives without a concern in the world because Stan Sattler was mindless of the great gifts of charm and physical strength that had been granted to him. He wore them loosely like an old unwashed jumper. He paid little heed to using them for good or evil simply because he didn't realize those gifts were there at his disposal.

His charm and strength were things Stan only rolled out for show when they were needed. He only charmed the arses of blowflies when he had the neighbors over because it was in his interests to do so. He needed to be sure he was respected, looked up to, consulted on all manner of farming concerns. Charm was the way he prized open the clam shell mouths of the normally reticent men and women from the farms.

June had seen her father, over the years, perform acts of strength that ensured his place of primacy among the other men along the river. Even though he was pushing fifty, the years hadn't diminished the strength of that big body.

•

Last May, in the flood season, when the river rose and noisily chewed away at the levee banks, the men along the waterway arose one morning to find the banks breached in a dozen places where the river had risen dramatically overnight. They soon found the cause: a giant tree bole jammed into the bridge at a narrow neck of the river. The tree trunk caused a rising of water that slipped into the town and surrounding farms. Little could be done to shift the tree trunk, so many a man, standing along the river banks, frowned with the pessimistic certainty that he was about to lose everything to the river. Again.

That was until Stan, shod with his hobnailed boots, scooted out onto the trunk as though he was a kid again playing hopscotch. On his back he had an ax, the metal blade shining brightly under the slate-blue sky of rain clouds. Quickly the battle began, the blade arcing up and down, the yellow chips of wood flying in a rain of grain.

But none of the men watching would have it that even Stan Sattler could shift the huge dismembered tree; it was just too big. And Stan for once had bitten off more than he could chew or chop. But they still hoped, in their heart of hearts, that he might succeed because it would mean the saving of their farms, their families.

June, as she listened to her father entertaining his guests, could still hear the first creaking of the timber that May day as Stan opened up a long gap in the trunk, the raging water coming up through the long opening. She'd stood on the river bank with the others, not just the farmers, but the townspeople as well, the small businessmen and shopkeepers come to watch the mad man standing on the water of the river in flood.

Because that's what it looked like as Stan chopped the opening wider and the water rose around his boots, then reached above his ankles. Not that it stopped Stan Sattler. He ignored the water, chopped into it to find the grain with his ax. Explosions of the silty torrent came from the blade, the water soaked the axeman, left the fine particles of red soil on his huge form until Stan was covered with the red sediment so he appeared to bleed under the old rind of sunlight.

Groan and shriek of wood came as the man severed the two halves of the trunk and no one, not even June, used to her father performing miracles from day to day, thought Stan could survive as the two halves of wood floated away from the bridge, releasing the tidal wave of water damned for too long.

The axeman had time to clutch the steel webbing of the bridge as the bulge of water engulfed him. The watchers still talk about it till this day, the way Stan held on with the river consuming him, as though the man had been swallowed into the gut of some beast that gobbled up anything and anyone in its path. The force of the current tore at the hair and beard of the man submerged in the water. Cables of current pulling back the yellow and silver strands like seaweed at the bottom of the ocean with the tidal trade of waves coming and going, pulling at the weed, trying to tear it free from rock.

They could see Stan as clear as day because the sun broke out of the shelf of cloud and blasted a blood-red thread of light through the cliff of water so the farmer was fringed with fire beneath the river. And they could see the bits of wood, the bits of bones from drowned, dismembered animals nicking the flesh of Stan as he held on for dear life. Fine capillaries of blood leaked from his body, worked through the water.

Not that Stan would have admitted to being worried about getting out alive from the flood. When the river finally dropped away from his limbs, he yelled with laughter as though it was the biggest joke in the world that the Hunter River thought it could end his life. But none of the people on the bank, including June, were laughing. In fact you'd have thought Stan had died and they were there for his funeral, so solemn were they.

Although Stan had saved them and their farms, the men and women couldn't find it in themselves to celebrate. And it angered Stan, upset him when they walked away in silence, leaving him standing there, soaked through, his hands empty because the river had managed to carry off the ax.

It unnerved his neighbors that a man could treat the river with such indifference, almost contempt. They knew, despite Stan's enormous strength, despite his ability to win against the odds, that there would be a reckoning with the river even though none of them were up to the task of telling Stan so.

•

June looked at him coming up the path as the guests left full of food and drink. There was a slight stagger in the step of the man. Something she hadn't seen before, but she dismissed it as soon as she saw his boyish grin break his face. And that's what he was like, she realized. He was just a big boy who played his way through life without a thought or care in the world.

As he approached the veranda, as the noise of the cars leaving faded, as he boomed his hearty, half-drunken hello to his daughter, June saw the marks in his skin. The healed-over cuts and scratches made by the animal bone and wood splinter when Stan was swallowed by the river last May. Raised and red were some of the marks, some of them shone white like seed pearls, her father scratched at them.

At times he didn't know it, wasn't aware that he was rubbing the small scars from his battle with the tree and the river. He'd awoken earlier in the week, in the middle of the night, with the bed sheets littered with river debris because some wood splinters and specks of animal bone had worked their way free of his flesh in the night.

Only a few days after the get-together of the neighbors, without warning of any kind, the river rose in the night. And the strange thing was that there was no rain recorded in the highlands, no blockage of any kind to dam the river to explain the flood.

It rose quietly, not the noise of last May when the water howled like a thousand demons possessed, the shatter of wood and carcasses against banks and bridges like detonators exploding on the rail line, not too far from the river.

Quietly the river rose, flooded into the bedroom of Stan Sattler, who awoke to find the water gripping his throat. Icy cold was the water, Stan clutched his throat because it felt as though the steel ring of river water had frozen the blood in the cords of veins and arteries knotting their way through his flesh and bone.

In the morning the flood was gone leaving nothing behind it, not the usual evidence of silt and bloated carcasses. Nothing. Other than Stan Sattler who'd lost his voice. A frog's croak was all the river left Stan with, and he stood at his front gate and wept bitter tears, tried to ignore his neighbors who came to laugh at him when he tried to converse with them with his thin, raspy voice.

Stan Sattler, now that he'd lost that melodious voice, was Samson with his hair shorn. It was as though he'd been stripped naked for all of his neighbors to see, and what they saw was a figure to ridicule, not a form of strength to be feared and admired. News spread and all and sundry came to converse with the man who used to reduce women to quivering and compliant willingness. It was soon up and down the river, from the Hunter Valley heights of Dungog, where the river was born, to the harbor of Newcastle where the river spent itself. People came to hear about the diminishing of Stan.

His body wasted quickly as though the vanished voice took with it the muscle that had performed so many feats of strength. And he began to stay indoors, shunning the daylight and the eyes of the men and women who came to gawk then cackle like the hens in the yard. Stan started staying indoors to avoid seeing the river as much as anything.

It was the cold water at his throat that had taken his voice and his standing in the community. Left him sitting in the rocker in the darkness of the loungeroom, afraid to walk out into the day to see the river flowing onward, unstoppable, an element in the landscape that gave life and took life.

June and her mother could do nothing with him. His remaining strength defied their attempts to get him moving again, make him work the farm, do his bit around the place when it came to planting, tending, and harvesting the fruit and vegetables. But the river was time passing, it was age catching up with Stan Sattler, bringing him many days of reckoning to ponder his hubris.

And, eventually, he was almost forgotten by his neighbors and his family because he stayed away from them. Locked in the house, lost in a twilight world no one wanted anything to do with. June and her mother only registered his presence when they were confronted with a task on the farm almost too difficult for them to perform. It was then that Stan made his presence felt by his absence, an irritation to June and her mother.

June and her mother discovered the soil of their farm was infertile because of the countless crops it had produced for Stan. He'd never been one to put much back into the soil, he always assumed the river would flood, right on cue, replenish the soil, make it ready for yet another planting.

Vegetables and fruit withered, Stan Sattler stayed locked away, still only capable of uttering the thinnest of sounds to his wife and daughter.

June and her mother were desperate to save the farm. One day, when it began to rain, June was standing on the veranda and she smelled it. The smell of flood whenever it rained came from the walls of the house. She knew what was causing that smell of floodwater. It was the soil left in the walls of the house from all the floods over the years. The rich red loam was stored between the inside plaster and the outer wood.

Not one to think twice, June took hold of a loose board and reefed it from the wall. The grain sobbed, the board came off in June's hand, thick soil poured from the opening. Behind June, her mother stood, but not for long. She knew what her daughter had in mind. The two women tore the boards from the house, released the soil from the walls, shoveled it into two wheelbarrows, carted it to the paddocks, shoveled it onto the barren ground.

A week it took to top dress some of the farm with the soil from the walls of the house and enough of the paddocks were replenished to plant fruit and vegetables. June and her mother weren't ones to do things by halves. They not only pulled away the outer boards from the house to get at the good soil, they also dismembered the inside plaster just so as they were sure that every shovelful, every teaspoonful of rich red dirt had been recovered to top dress the farm.

And in the middle of the framework of the house, Stan Sattler sat in his rocking chair, his milky blue eyes blinking in the glare of daylight, his flesh as pale as rice. Still unable to speak, not that his daughter and wife paid him any heed. They were too busy trying to save the farm. They worked around him when they came to tear up the floorboards to get at the last of the flood soil. Using an ax, June chopped around her father, left him rocking on a small island of wood. June and her mother shoveled the soil into barrows, took it off to the paddocks to continue replenishing the farm.

•

June stood on the railway station waiting for the train to take her to Newcastle. The track followed the river to the coastal port and the town hall where June was heading for the end of the week dance. The place where the steelworkers, grown men came to meet women, to dance, to make love, to propose marriage.

THE SKELP MILL

JIMMY THE KID BUSTLES ACROSS THE FACTORY FLOOR.
He's a man on a mission of mercy so he's got no time for things as trivial
as work. Today is Christmas day and he's there with B crew at the Skelp
Mill because it's triple time on public holidays and Jimmy's got three
kids from two failed marriages to support. But then again, there're the
other children he's got to look after today, the men of B crew most of
whom would rather be at home with their wives and kids than working
in the dirt and shit of the mill.

"Triple time can go and fuck itself!" says one of the fitters to Jimmy
as he waddles by.

Bright orange steel bars roll past Jimmy the Kid as he heads for
the back of the reheating furnace. He ignores the hot metal; he
may be a fat bastard as he admits to the other blokes when they're
showering after a shift, but he's light on his feet should a cobble
come about when he's close to that hot shit that pays his wages and
feeds his kids.

A cobble is when the hot steel doesn't go through a roller cleanly.
Instead of the roller rolling the hot metal flatter and wider, the molten
metal hits an obstruction in the roller because of incorrect alignment
and then you see the men on the mill floor run like buggery. A huge
dinosaur spine of hot metal rises to the corrugated iron roof of the mill
then falls back to the floor sighing with white fire and red sparks flying
in every direction like crackers on a public holiday.

Jimmy hasn't time to think of maiming because he's got to get to the
back of the reheating furnace. It's the heart of the mill because it's the
place the cold metal ingots are placed to be reheated before coming out

the arse end of the furnace to be rolled into giant watch springs and shipped off to GMH.

Jimmy the Kid's on a mission because he knows just about everyone in the mill is as cranky as a cut snake because B crew has been working five twelve hours shifts a week, day work and dog watch, for months now. Just to keep up with demand. Jimmy's no psychologist, but he knows that today being Christmas day is just as likely to be the straw that breaks the camel's back. Not being at home with their families rubs most of the mill hands, the tradesmen, the operators, the floor sweepers right up the wrong way. It'll take the smallest of incidents and there'll be a blue make no mistake.

"It'll be on for fucking young and old," mutters Jimmy to himself as he finds the back of the furnace. Just like when George Mackeroff lost his temper last week when Jim Davis, by mistake, drank George's can of coke out of the fridge in the crib room. "Christ almighty," thinks Jimmy, "you could have knocked me down with a feather to see George throwing them big haymakers at Jim."

George Mackeroff is one of nature's gentlemen. The rest of the crew love him like a father or grandfather the way he comes in every second day with a basket full of the vegetables he's grown in his backyard in Mayfield East and tells the blokes to help themselves. All of the men on B crew are tetchy, on edge, since that incident with George because they know that if someone as placid as George Mackeroff can be set off by the unintentional filching of a can of coke then all of them must be close to the edge.

From the corner of his eye, Jimmy sees Al Brown, one of the furnace men and one bastard who shouldn't be talked to because he isn't to be trusted. Al Brown is a spy of sorts; he listens into all the conversations among the men and reports back to management. Any dissent, any likelihood of a strike is nipped in the bud if possible.

Jimmy swerves around Al as the furnace man goes to open his mouth to engage Jimmy in conversation. Al Brown has a terrible lisp and the story goes his speech impediment is a result of having his tongue stuck so far up the super's arse he can't pronounce his words correctly.

But dobbers of any kind aren't treated kindly in the mill. When Al Brown is on dog watch, one or some of the men sneak out of the side gate and walk the two blocks to the furnace man's house where Mrs. Brown may be waiting to entertain them. But there's a pecking order in the mill and the position of furnace man carries with it some status, so Al Brown's wife feels she can pick and choose when being unfaithful to her husband. She only sleeps with Italians from the mill because they've got such big cocks.

Jimmy the Kid sees the big metal box lined with steel shelves inside almost completed and Marco Stavros putting the finishing touches to the box of metal screwed into the hindquarters of the reheating furnace. A grin brighter than Nobby's Lighthouse spreads across Jimmy's fat face. But he cannot help but notice that Marco is miserable, worn down like the others by the constant long shifts, so he doesn't launch into the usual routine he and Jimmy have perfected over the years in the Skelp Mill.

Usually when they meet Marco begins with: "Fuck me fuckin' dead I've had a fuckin' gut full of this fuckin' place. That's it Jimmy the fuckin' Kid, I'm fuckin' well goin' fuckin' home. Don't fuckin' well try t' fuckin' stop me. This fuckin' place is fuckin' dreadful."

Jimmy's reply is: "Now, now, Marco, it's not that bad. There's no need to get so upset. I know how you fucking feel."

Marco's response, with mock horror on his face is: "Such language you use Jimmy the Kid. You wouldn't fuckin' well hear me fuckin' well fuckin' swearing like fuckin' that."

It's a sketch they put on for the crew, all of whom have placed bets over the years as to how many times Marco Stavros can say "fuck" in one minute. But no one knows what the record number of "fucks" is in a minute because no one has been able to count that quickly.

Marco looks at Jimmy now and says, "Jimmy the Kid, just what is this box of metal doing attached to the furnace?"

"I'm going to cook Christmas dinner in it," says Jimmy.

"You're fuckin' well goin' to do fuckin' what?!" says Marco.

Not answering again, Jimmy the Kid is off, away from his foreign order oven, heading for the crib room where he's got two big boxes of potatoes and pumpkins placed in the bottom of the fridge. In his haste, he almost runs straight into Sleepy Bob standing in front of one of the rollers.

Sleepy Bob is one of the men who attempt to keep the rollers in good order, but more importantly in alignment so there won't be cobbles of steel all over the mill floor. Jimmy knows it's a pain in the arse, a cobble, not just because it means a drop in the slim production bonus the men get, but because the crane usually has to be used to pull the renegade lump of steel out of the rollers. The partly rolled ingot has usually twisted into a knot of rapidly cooling steel. Sometimes the crane dragging out the steel means damage to a roller and extra work for Sleepy Bob because he'll have to replace the damaged roller with a new one and align the bastard to boot.

Sleepy Bob is called Sleepy Bob because he falls asleep standing up especially on dogwatch. That's what the other men on B crew reckon. You can go up to Sleepy Bob and talk to him with your face only inches away from his face and he won't hear you. He'll stare straight ahead, won't blink because to all intents and purposes he's asleep.

But Jimmy the Kid knows it's the wheels of the rollers that hypnotize Bob so it seems as though he's fallen asleep standing up. He's really awake but he's like one of the chooks Jimmy brought to feed the men this Christmas day. Jimmy watched the butcher in his backyard drag his finger in the dirt in front of the chook's beak. Over and over the butcher dragged his finger through the dirt until the poor bird was hypnotized, couldn't move until the butcher gave it a good kick up the arse. Then chopped its head off and laughed, watching the body sprinting madly around the yard, the neck pluming blood everywhere. And a dozen kids from the neighborhood lining the top of the paling fence come to watch.

Jimmy pauses to look at Bob. He doesn't need a kick up the arse to wake him up, Jimmy knows. There's nothing the matter with Bob. It's his way of coping with the dreadful boredom, the monotony of steel making.

Jimmy trundles down the cement ramp leading to the crib room. He ducks between the men drinking their tea and coffee on the ramp because it's the rule of management that crib time is to be spent on the mill floor, unlike lunch when the crew can sit down in the crib room and eat and play five hundred.

Many of the men manage a smile for Jimmy, some poke him in the roles of fat on his ribs, some give him a mouthful of cheek, but that's okay. If they didn't show their affection for the fat man by pulling his leg or insulting him, Jimmy would know there was something wrong. To be called a cunt by some men of B crew is the warmest form of affection they can bestow, thinks Jimmy.

Inside the crib room Jimmy sees the walls covered by posters of naked women, but he has to look up to see them. Whenever a man on B crew decides to place a picture of a naked woman on a wall of the crib room, he doesn't stand on the cement floor to do it. He'll get up on one of the tables, raise himself on the tips of his toes and paste the naked woman as high up as he can manage.

Jimmy knows the men exalt women, they love them, even worship them, and that's why they make sure the women are given the highest of places. It is as though the naked brunettes with big breasts, the red heads with long legs, the blonds with long legs and big breasts are looking over the men, somehow keeping them safe until they escape the grease and dirt of the mill.

But the men of B crew would tell you that this is all bullshit and the only reason they put the women high on the walls is so they can look up any time and get an eyeful of a whopping great set of tits or a plump desirable snatch.

The only other man in the crib room, Cowboy, is sleeping. He's sleeping because he's been working for three days, on and off, at the mill. He's actually living there in a sense because he's what's called a "lifer." Jimmy shivers because he's close to being a lifer himself. A lifer is a man who is in so much debt, usually due to failed marriages and children to support or just plain bad financial management, he has to work forever. Usually a lifer has no trade. He's only good for performing the most menial of jobs around the mill. So management know he will do whatever they tell him to and if they demand him to work never-ending shifts, he'll do it. And like Cowboy, sometimes it's not worth going home so he'll sleep on one of the benches until he's due to go back onto the mill floor.

Cowboy is grimy from three days of tying coils of hot metal with loops of wire. Jimmy looks at him and he can see the salt of sweat that's dried, formed a cocoon that will only come off when Cowboy gets around to having a shower. He'll have to ask one of the other men to scrub his back and shoulders for him to get the shit off.

Jimmy can see the mouth of the man clawed into deep creases because Cowboy has taken so many salt tablets because working close to hot metal all the time washes the salt from him. His mouth looks like a chook's arse, thinks Jimmy.

Another man, Crazy Horse, comes down the steps into the crib room. Jimmy and the men know Crazy Horse is called that simply because he is completely nuts and prepared to do almost anything to maintain his reputation as a loon. It keeps most of the mill bullies at bay because they don't know just what Crazy Horse might do and they're not prepared to risk finding out.

Like the time Crazy Horse got a cutthroat razor, Christ knows from where, and half shaved one of the fitters who'd been working two "doublers" back to back. The man was so fatigued, so deeply slumbering on one of the wooden benches in the crib room, he didn't feel a thing when Crazy Horse shaved off the left hand side of his mustache and beard. Only when the men on the mill floor keeled over with laugher, did the fitter realize that something was up.

Crazy Horse goes up to Cowboy now and bends his head close to the sleeping man. Cowboy is out like a light but Crazy Horse whispers in his ear: "Elvis Presley is a fuckin' prick with ears."

The effect is galvanizing. Cowboy is awake in an instant. He jumps up, eyes blazing fire. He jumps up on the table and clenches his fists and yells at the top of his lungs, "Elvis Presley is not a fuckin' prick with ears! Elvis Presley is the greatest singer the world has ever seen and heard! Elvis is the one and only!"

And so it goes with Crazy Horse, grinning, standing quietly listening to Cowboy rave. Jimmy hasn't time to listen the way he usually would, he has things to do and the first thing is to cut up a whole box of potatoes, pumpkins, and onions. And he's got some bottles of olive oil to rub the potatoes and pumpkin with before he puts them in the metal box with the dozen chooks. Providing it'll all fit. But he's not sure about the olive oil. It's taken years for Marco Stavros to educate him into using olive oil rather than the dripping Jimmy's mother used at every meal when he was a kid.

"Still don't know about this wog muck," says Jimmy to himself.

He holds up the bottle of olive oil to the soupy light filtering through the window half buried by earth and bricks. It's as if he's expecting so see something alive and swimming, wriggling in the olive oil. But there's nothing there except the beautiful green and amber color and Jimmy does have to admit the olive oil crisps the vegetables like nothing else.

Jimmy starts with the onions, peeling them, cutting them into thin rings he'll put in at the last minute when everything else is almost done. It doesn't matter how much he turns his head away while he is peeling and cutting, the fumes are so strong the tears flow down his flushed, capillary-broken cheeks.

Stan Blake comes into the crib room and of course he's drunk just like he usually is when he's at work.

"Fuck me, Jimmy! What's wrong? Who's died?" says Stan.

Stan doesn't even see the onions Jimmy's cutting because the extra three schooners he downed at the Stag and Hunter up the road, just before he started the shift, obliterate that. The Stag and Hunter, nicknamed the Staggering Hunter by the men of B crew, is the regular watering hole of the men.

From the corner of his eye, Jimmy watches Stan lurch across the floor toward a bench and flop down on the seat. Jimmy sees the chest of the man begin the rise and fall, heave with deep breaths and Jimmy the Kid knows Stan might be sleeping deeply thanks to the booze or he might be crying.

It wouldn't be the first time Stan Blake got pissed and went to the crib room and cried. Not that any of the men say anything when they come across the big, former first grade rugby league prop forward, sobbing. They don't try to talk to Stan because they know how embarrassed he'd be. There's no talking out this matter of fear. Stan Blake works at the end of the mill that houses the twist chute. It's the place where the rolled steel emerges onto big moving tables of steel.

The rolled hot steel is flat on the moving tables. It is Stan Blake's job to step onto the moving tables, step up to the giant tongue of hot rolled steel. Take the huge tongs he carries, get a grip on the end of the steel with them and turn the hot steel up on its edge to feed into the twist chute.

Once this is done the steel is rolled at enormous speed into the clock springs of metal. But Stan Blake is convinced he's going to slip one day just as he's turning the hot tongue of metal on its side to feed into the twist chute. That's why he drinks, to take away, to numb that fear he will end up melted to a maimed mess of flesh and bone.

But it's the booze that's going to make his fear a reality if he keeps on drinking the way he does, Jimmy knows as he finishes peeling the onions but the tears keep washing down his face. Jimmy remembers the old Stan Blake, the man who worked his present job without a care in the world, without a thought that he might slip and fall onto the hot metal. It just cannot be explained, Stan's fear that seemed to come almost overnight.

A bit like being in a war thinks Jimmy as he starts peeling the potatoes. Constantly under fire so one day you lose your nerve and suddenly you're a wreck because of the shell shock. That's what Jimmy sees when he looks at Stan Blake, a man suffering shell shock. Jimmy's got an uncle who served in the Pacific. Jimmy sees the tremors in the old soldier's body, the composed vacancy in the uncle's eyes hiding the fear when they meet occasionally.

But while the others on B crew can sympathize with Stan Blake, the sympathy only reaches to a point because they cannot afford to connect too closely with the man because they fear they will end up like him. When they see him crying in the crib room they know there's only a hair's breadth between Stan Blake and themselves.

Another man comes down into the crib room. It's Davo', the foreman for this shift, and like many of the men his nickname is his name. Most of the men of B crew would be pushed to tell you his real name.

Davo' is after Stan Blake. The foreman knows he'll usually find Stan here and the foreman knows about Stan's problem. It's a problem for Davo' as well because he likes Stan and sympathizes with his plight. But the foreman is caught between his like for Stan Blake and his duty to management, which means if Stan keeps on coming to work pissed he'll have to report it and Stan will get the bullet.

The foremen in the mills are usually recruited from the men on the mill floors, ex laborers and operators of machinery. Jimmy can see they're caught between loyalty to men they used to work with and loyalty to management, who expect them to come down hard on the men when needed. It's a twilight zone many of the foremen find themselves lost in, former work mates refusing to have anything to do with them, members of management refusing to socialize with what they see as an upstart worm wriggled straight out of the dross of the mill.

But Davo' manages better than most. Jimmy can see he looks a lot like Paul Newman and goes about giving everyone that sparkling, blue-eyed grin and the men cannot help but like him. As well as this Davo' carries about with him an enormous pewter teapot. He seems to drink cups of tea all the time, usually with the men as he goes from site to site on the floor of the Skelp Mill doing his job. This pewter tea pot prop makes him look faintly ridiculous. It's as if he doesn't take his job seriously even though he does.

Seeming to not quite take his job seriously appeals to the men whether they know it or not, thinks Jimmy. This larrikinism identifies Davo' as one of them. The men of B crew feel that Davo' is just pretending to be a foreman, it's all an act, he's pulling the leg of management on behalf of the rest of the men on the floor.

"Come on, Stan. Wakey, wakey. That's it, on yer feet. There's work to be done but before that I'll make yer a nice cup of tea to get rid of some of that beer yer've downed," says Davo'.

Jimmy the Kid watches Davo' help Stan Blake up the stairs of the crib room. It's not the first time he's seen this foreman help the man back onto the mill floor, sober him up, and coach him back to the twist chute to do some work.

But Jimmy knows that in the back of Davo's mind is the thought of what might happen if he finally reports Stan Blake to management.

If Stan gets the sack the men will just as likely go out on strike even though Stan Blake deserves to be sacked. And Davo' will find himself ostracized by the men on the mill floor, who like him, and management, who loathe strikes and the loss of steel production that goes with them.

Jimmy the Kid struggles up the stairs of the crib room carrying a box filled with the vegetables. The chooks are still in his fridge at home but he's arranged for one of the men, who's actually taken the day off, to meet him at the side gate at an appointed time and hand over the plucked and trussed birds.

Jimmy is short of breath and his legs ache from the sores that are forming more regularly on his legs these days. And it's getting harder to heal those sores. Jimmy's been told by his doctor he's got diabetes but that doesn't stop him meeting the others after work at the Staggering Hunter and drinking six or seven schooners every night — or morning if they've been working dog watch. He knows he shouldn't but he just can't bring himself not to drink with the others after work and, besides, he hasn't anyone to go home to. Hasn't seen either of his ex-wives in years and his children live far away.

Waddling across the mill floor, wheezing like a steam train, Jimmy has to stop, put down the box. Greg Burrows comes to his rescue picking up the box and asking Jimmy where he wants it taken. Greg Burrows is at the mill for a short time because he's a uni student. The works employ several hundred at the end of the academic year. It's a PR exercise and the money comes in handy during the year for the students. Many of them, like Greg Burrows, will labor for as long as possible before going back to the antiseptic and hallowed halls of Newcastle University.

Jimmy grins as he follows the young man. He remembers the first week Greg spent at the mill assigned to Jimmy, who was supposed to look after him. The first thing Jimmy had to do was to convince Greg not to call him Mr. Kid. When the other men on B crew heard him call Jimmy that there was no end to the ribbing Jimmy received, on the mill floor, in the showers, in the crib room, every fucking where.

But Jimmy still remembers the fear in the young man's eyes that first week, the way he sat next to Jimmy in the crib room and did not eat, confused, intimidated by the other men and their foul language, the aggressive manner they even managed to bring to a game of five hundred. Cursing, slamming down fists on a table if they lost a hand.

It took Jimmy a long time to get Greg Burrows involved in the life of the mill, if you could call such an existence a life, ponders Jimmy. Greg

Burrows was like the new kid at school, on the outside just ready to be bullied by the others if he didn't hurry up and fit in. And his quietness, his shyness made him a marked man unless Jimmy did something fast.

There was only one thing to be done so Jimmy took Greg home after work and taught him to play five hundred, an almost instant passport into the world of the mill and the crib room. True, Greg got his fair share of abuse as he messed up more than a few games, but he caught on quickly and soon was one of the best players on B crew and therefore in demand. It's difficult, Jimmy thinks, to underestimate the importance cards play in the lives of the men.

And as he became more accepted, as the men began to forget he was a uni student and not one of them, the more Greg Burrows opened his mouth and gave as good as he got.

"Burrows, yer fuckin' dreadful at hot tying and fuckin' dreadful at cards," one fitter declared to cover up the fact that he had messed up with his card partner, Greg Burrows.

"Tim, yer wouldn't know the difference between a good hand and yer arsehole," returned the quiet Greg much to the delight of the others.

In fact it became a game of sorts among the others to get Greg Burrows to shoot off his mouth and give one of the others a tongue-in-cheek dressing down. It amused the permanent members of B crew to see the quiet young man come down to their level and wallow there.

"When are you going to stop drinking?" says Greg Burrows to Jimmy as he places the box of vegetables on the floor near the metal box.

"What?" says Jimmy feigning ignorance, surprise.

"You know what I mean, Jimmy. Look at that sore on your left leg, it's getting bigger," says Greg.

"Look, there's nothing the matter with my legs. Why are yer lookin' at them all of a sudden? Do yer fancy me?" says Jimmy.

"Have it your own way, Jimmy. You know what I mean though," says Greg and walks off.

"Fuckin' smart arse uni student," mutters Jimmy. "Look after 'em and they think they can run yer fuckin' life for yer."

Jimmy the Kid heads for the side gate where he knows the Birdman will be waiting. The Birdman works at the mill performing a number of jobs. He never seems to have one particular job but floats from site to site, doing whatever the foreman for that shift tells him. So he's like a migratory bird, flying here and there so the men call him the Birdman.

But there's more to it than that. The Birdman has a number of other jobs outside the Skelp Mill, jobs he seems to wander in and out of.

Some of the men see him collecting empty glasses at the Staggering Hunter, others see him panel beating in his backyard, others see him driving a taxi.

It's his job as a taxi driver that has come in useful for Jimmy. As the fat man reaches the side gate, he sees the Birdman waiting there with the cab and the boot already open. Inside are the twelve chooks placed in gray, plastic milk crates the Birdman has stolen from the local milkman over the years.

Next to the chooks are two big metal eskies full of crushed ice, from the servo' down the road, and bottles of Gala Spumante. The bubbly is for the washing down of the baked chooks and vegetables if Jimmy manages to get the job done.

"Thanks, Birdman," says Jimmy. "What do I owe yer?"

The Birdman waves his hand, gives Jimmy back the key to his flat. Grimaces as if to say he is insulted by the question. He rarely speaks so he doesn't say anything now, but takes hold of two crates of raw chooks and starts carting them toward the mill. Jimmy manages one crate and leaves the others and the two eskies of sweet, tooth-rot bubbly to the Birdman.

The Birdman completes the job quickly. There's no fat on the man and that's because he spends his life working. He sends money back to Greece to his parents and relations.

Once in a while the Birdman disappears. He goes back to one of the Greek islands to visit his parents and aunts and uncles. There he is greeted as a hero, a saint of sorts. Then he returns to the works and Mayfield East where his circle of labor continues a lifetime of toil, but the man refuses to yield. He is driven by something most of the men on B crew cannot understand. The men see the Birdman as hungry for work and therefore to be despised to a degree.

Some of the crew, when they pass the Birdman on the mill floor, mimic money by rubbing their thumb and index finger together in his face. This usually happens when the Birdman is doing a "doubler," a sixteen- hour shift. The men mimic money with their hands and say to him: "Doubla', plenty money."

The Birdman labors at many jobs, does long hours at the Skelp Mill in the hope that one day there will be enough money to bring his parents to Mayfield East to spend the remains of their lives.

Jimmy the Kid places the chooks in the metal box with the vegetables and slams shut the big metal door. News has been spreading among the mill about what he is up to and there's almost a buzz of excitement, of expectation among the men. Jimmy stands in front of the big box and wills the heat of the reheating furnace to do its job. The theory is the outer skin of the furnace is so hot it should heat the metal box and bake the chooks and vegetables.

He hears the voice of Les, the crane driver, as he swears blue murder trying to stack the steel billets neatly so they won't topple over. The electric crane picks up four or five of the steel bars and Les must place them on the skids. The skids are a series of big steel arms that shuffle back and forth sorting the steel billets into size and length, into some sort of pattern before they're pushed into the reheating furnace.

Normally Les would do this standing on his head but he's as cranky as buggery with fatigue like the other men, and with anger comes mistakes, a loss of confidence in his ability to do a job he's been doing for years. Jimmy watches the small man leaning out of the cabin of the crane, straining to find the best resting place on the skids for the load of steel bars his crane is carrying.

Les lives in Cooks Hill, far away from the industrial suburbs of Mayfield and Tighes Hill where most of the other men of B crew live. Les is a mystery. He's a bachelor, a man who doesn't socialize with the rest of the men. One or two of the others on B crew have seen him sitting in a café in Cooks Hill drinking coffee as they drive by. But that's it. You won't see Les in attendance at one of the get-togethers the Skelp Mill Social Club puts on usually at one of the local pubs or clubs.

So Les is treated with a certain amount of suspicion. A man who doesn't mix, who keeps to himself, will never have an easy life in the mill, Jimmy thinks as he watches the crane driver finally deposit the load of steel bars on the skids.

•

Later, finally, Jimmy thinks it's time and he opens the door of the box and the smell of roasted chook and vegetables is overpowering. Jimmy's mouth waters. He slams shut the door and goes around to the front of the furnace where Michael Green operates the furnace door. The furnace door is where the almost molten bars come out of the reheating furnace to be fed through the rollers.

Jimmy gives Michael the nod and Michael allows a hot metal bar to come from the furnace mouth, then he shuts the furnace door and reverses the rollers so the bar does not go straight through the rollers but remains stationary, cooling very quickly. When the bar has cooled to a sombre gray with only patches of hot orange here and there,

Michael puts the rollers back into forward and feeds the "cold" bar into the first roller and runs.

The steel wraps itself in a question mark around the roller but there's no siren to signal a cobble. Someone's managed to disconnect it. No one from management comes to the window of the office block to check why production has stopped. The crane doesn't move toward the trouble spot to drag out the steel. In fact the rollers stop; every piece of machinery comes to a halt.

The men gather on the mill floor and Jimmy the Kid appears pushing a foreign order steel trolley on which are twelve smoking roast chooks and piles of baked potatoes and pumpkin. He goes among the throng handing out cardboard plates piled high with food. Behind him comes Marco Stavros handing out glasses of Gala Spumante.

Jimmy the Kid is called Jimmy the Kid because his name is James Kid. But there's more to it than that. He looks like a kid. He looks like Billy Bunter with his fat knees but without a school uniform. But he's not just a kid, he's a child — a child with the innocence of a child, a child with the compassion of a child, a child with the luminosity of a child shining from the flabby folds of his face.

The men stand together and they toast Christmas day with the Gala Spumante. They toast their families at home. They toast each other.

They toast the blessed and sacred silence.

QUARRY GIRL

Inspired by a painting of the same title by American contemporary artist Leslie Anderson.

EMILY STANDS UP TO HER THIN BONY ANKLES IN THE icy water of the quarry. She tries to see down beneath the green and blue sheen, searching for something in the deep black chasm of water. But she cannot find anything — not the ripple of a fish nor the stirring of a leaf fallen from one of the trees that crowd closely like a gang of men to the edge of the quarry, nor the brief breath of slight wind wounding the water. The pool is a blind eye.

She feels the water grasping her ankles, fastening like hard metal chains, holding her in place as though the quarry will never let her go, never let her turn around, walk away back through the larches and pines to the humidicrib warmth of her parents' house, the place where her mother is roasting meat and vegetables for tea and Emily's father just home from work is sitting, still ready to bounce his only daughter on his knee.

Emily feels the slippery plate of rock beneath her feet and suddenly she feels as though she is about to topple, fall down into the water. She imagines a cold claw grabbing hold of the straps of her purple swimming costume, dragging her into the deeper water, pulling her below the surface against her will, not allowing her a choice.

Instinctively Emily clinches her toes like an ancient primate trying to keep a foothold on the slimy limb of a tree in some primeval forest, but she feels her small toes, blind white worms, slide, slip. Her tiny scream rents the air, a closed dome of northern chilliness, then all is silence. She has not fallen, she stands still, waiting.

Emily looks down, sees the rock upon which she is standing, a blood-colored shelf of stone, the same color as her long thick thatch of hair that brushes and bristles like electricity against her pale, sensitive skin. She looks at the moles scattered like thrown sand, the blemishes ghostly like the ends of the fingers of another person buried in her flesh struggling to get out.

She imagines some of the boys from school hiding in the trees at the edge of the quarry pool, the spiteful boys who grab her when she's walking along a school corridor alone and grind their already hammer-hard hands against her new breasts, pinch her nipples until she squeals and runs from their cruelty, tries to escape their resentment of her blooming body that is alien to them, confuses them. She flees from their taunting gravel voices, stinging stones about her grandmother.

The boys have sneaked through the yellow and red and green flames of the forest leaves, crawling on their hands and knees, Emily thinks. She turns her head away from the pool and peers into the candle blaze of leaf light imagining the boys' black eyes glittering like shiny cold mica in their puffy and pimpled adolescent faces. The thought that they may emerge from the trees and form a circle around her makes her stumble again. She limps a few more steps into deeper water, the rock shelf is covered with slimy slippery weed. She struggles to stay standing; she struggles to keep her imagination in check.

Emily knows what she must do. The boys and girls at school have spitefully revealed the story of Emily's grandmother, telling the granddaughter of her grandmother pursued by three men, taking the young mother against her will, raping her, leaving her alone and cold among the winter forest of trees. Emily's friends, some of them grandchildren of the men who raped Emily's grandmother, have told her the story bit by bit like installments from a soap opera, the tellers drawing out the truth, teasing and tormenting Emily, finally telling her with a gloating glee spread across their grinning faces how Emily's grandmother, in her shame and despair, cast herself into the quarry where she drowned.

The quarry was made by generations of men from the small settlement, made by the men who abused Emily's grandmother and men who knew the story, listened to it over and over as they sat eating, taking a break from the hard work of cutting, chiseling stone, tearing, blasting out blind dumb earth, leaving it in blind dumb heaps, nothing changed, no strange and magical transformation made by a lapidarist, polishing the stone, revealing hidden strata to be marveled at, to be understood as more than raw bits of rock.

Emily steps further into the pool, looks down at the bulge of her puppy fat stomach, blushes, screws up her courage, suddenly lunges into the water that grabs, grips her like hands. The cold tears the breath from her lungs as though a bully has punched her in the belly. She struggles to stay afloat, desperately treading water, her white legs a maze of movement beneath the water, making small surges of ripples that run outward in circles, lapping the edge of the quarry like light but persistent knocks on a door.

She stills herself. Takes a breath. Dives. Pulling herself down into the dark depths. Willing herself toward the bottom, the place she has told herself for months now she must reach. The breath in her body pounds like a hammer. She holds it in, scared to let the essence of her life trickle out in a slim stream of bubbles. Emily is close to panicking as she feels the water become a cold tomb of stone, but something stops the fear.

She feels her new body, her almost woman's body lengthen, become lithe and strong, and she pulls apart the water, kicks her legs hard, touches the bottom of the quarry, relief and jubilation coursing through her. Emily bunches herself into a ball, rights herself ready to push off the bottom, looking forward to breaking the quarry pool surface. But she stops, the breath inside of her lungs intact, still. She stands upright on the bottom of the pool because she can, and then, slowly, almost languidly, she sets herself free from the bottom and slides through a vein of light reaching down from the sky above into the stone strata of water.

Emily breaks the surface and her cry of joy is a migratory bird returning home. She strides from the pool, her strong thighs parting the icy water, her feet sure on the slippery shelf of submerged rock. She looks down and her stomach is gone; it is flat as though she has been sandpapered from head to toe. Emily finds her towel and wraps it around her waist, walks out of the quarry into the trees, seeking the track to take her home. But there are two boys from school there, in front of her, barring her way.

But they falter in their menace, she can see. Her red hair, wet, is the color of bright blood pulsing. It shocks the boys, they take a step back away from the girl they terrorize in the dim cold school corridors, the woman who now blazes as brightly as the leaves on the trees surrounding the quarry.

Emily squares her body to them, steps one step closer. They take one step back, lower their eyes, look at the ground. She takes another step. They cower like animals beaten, their faces half-hidden by long greasy hair. Emily feels her body harden, the muscle cord and hump, her bright turquoise eyes flash like lamps. She raises an arm, ready to strike them, punish and pummel them, but one whimpers, the other falls to his knees.

She lowers her arm, bends slightly from the waist and touches each boy lightly on the head with the tips of her fingers, then brushes past them, leaving them behind, the young woman heading for home.

Emily opens the door and marches into the house. Her mother pauses from peeling vegetables, raises one eyebrow and eyes her daughter with interest.

"Come on, Emmy, come and sit on Daddy's knee and I'll bounce you up and down," says her father, sitting in his chair near the fire, his face split with his perpetual boyish grin.

"No thanks, Dad. Not now, not anymore," says Emily.

THE RESTAURANT DE LA SIRÈNE AT ASNIÈRES

Inspired by a painting of the same title by Vincent van Gogh.

THE BRICK AND SHINGLE OF THE BUILDING HOUSING
the restaurant is silver. At a distance the building looks like the balding
head of an old man with scrubby patches of sparse hair fading to gray.
So off-putting is the building that when male pedestrians come around
the corner into the town square, they are often rendered immobile by
that balding pate of gray brick and masonry.

You can see them if you sit at a table outside the front of the restaurant
or if you sit at a table at the window inside; they stop and stare. And
you can see the looks of incredulity ingrained into their faces as if the
lines of worry and consternation had been carved there with a hammer
and chisel by some sardonic sculptor.

Their hands go up to their heads, venture around the back where
they pat the bald spots they know are there because most of them,
each morning, mirrors in hand, stand in front of their big bathroom
mirrors screwed to the walls and ponder their naked scalps. They look
away from the mirror, most of them, and try to ignore the clearings of
shocking pink flesh they see in the undergrowth of gray hair.

Some of them try to make a joke of it. They tell their children that
when the wide-eyed siblings inquire about the bald heads of their
fathers, that it's where the moths have been eating the hair during the
night. There was nothing the men could do about it because they were
sleeping so soundly when the moths escaped from the wardrobes in
the bedrooms and feasted upon the banquets of hair. They would have

woken and swatted the moths away and so saved their hair, but they were so exhausted from working hard every day to feed their families and pay the bills, they felt nothing when the softly dusted wings of the moths fluttered upon their skulls.

To come around the corner into the main square of the town and see a building that reminds them of their early morning rituals of masochism and their children's increasingly acute questioning on the matter as they get older is upsetting to say the least. The men, middle-aged, old, and some quite young, squint into the distance searching for something to relieve the colors of age that assault their senses and their pride.

There is a yellow railing of wood that runs along the front of the restaurant; it stands out like a ribbon of golden hope against the silver and gray. For many of the non-plussed men, the golden color is the color their hair used to be, that blonde color that once upon a time harvested every ray of sunlight and dazzled the eyes of women passing them by. In the good old days, women stopped in the middle of the street and turned back to admire the tall, young men with the corn-colored masses of thick hair.

It is needless to say that these thoughts of past golden glories eventually depress the men because such ponderings sharply highlight thoughts of their present naked pates. Many of the men get so upset they turn away from the building and decide to eat somewhere else. It is just too confronting to sit in a restaurant that reminds them of their mortality.

And that is another thing — the Restaurant de la Sirène at Asnières is crumbling. You can see it clearly when you stand up close. The bricks are split with age, and the boards are warped with weather like the damaged spine of an old man. The building is a decaying, moldy monument to the men who look upon it.

Some of the men toss their heads, dismiss the matter because they are still young. They laugh at the older men stranded in the town's square with the look of horror on their faces. But even when the younger men seat themselves in the restaurant with their cups of coffee set before them on the tables, they still twitch and itch as if someone has dropped a fleck of bone down the back of their collar.

The sharp shard of imaginary but real bone nicks and cuts, irritates, and they usually only drink one cup of coffee and leave as quickly as possible. They never turn around, these younger men, but bustle off to offices and factories where the tedium of pens and paper and desks and hammers and tongs and bellows and pieces of hot metal obliterate their fears.

All the men — the ones stranded in the square, the ones who venture briefly into the restaurant — drag themselves home in the evening to wives who cuddle and caress them. Women who are soft, caring, affectionate but cannot understand the sudden rage of their husbands when the women accidentally stroke the thinning spot at the back of their heads or touch the slackening muscles of the arms of their once better halves. And the rage drives the men to take their wives to bed where the husbands, determined to defy time, make love for hours until some of the wives beg for mercy. But only some.

It is only in the mid-afternoon that some men will venture across the cobblestone desert of the town square to the restaurant, and that is because the sun, low in the sky, manages to illuminate the sidewall of the building. The color of gold is strong, the bricks and boards shine like a motherlode of the precious metal. Hurrying across the square before the sun sets and the gold is lost, the men sit at tables at the side of the building. They nestle closely into the hot bricks and boards, feel the heat in their bones like a bath of warm water freeing up their joints and limbs.

Feeling almost young again, freed of their ailments of impending old age, the men manage to smile, some even laugh, greet each other across the tables like naughty school boys staying away from school and merry in their complicity.

But as the sun sinks in the sky, as the shadows creep and deepen to purple, then black, the men stop laughing, they become grim, their grins are lost. They see the tide of darkness and the attendant cold coming across the square, and they all know they have to leave. To stay, to eat and drink any more is unthinkable. Fleeing like rats from a sinking ship, the men scurry away from the Restaurant de la Sirène.

All of this puzzles and upsets the owner of the restaurant, Jacques Mort. The poor man has tried everything to attract a male clientele to his establishment, but to no avail it would seem. Free coffee and glasses of wine at certain hours of the day are just not enough to entice men into his restaurant. Well, not for long — sometimes one or two, unable to resist free wine, come along. But their drinking could hardly be called quaffing, let alone appreciation, so quickly do they guzzle down the wine and run back across the square.

Even the name of the establishment — the restaurant of sirens or mermaids — isn't titillating enough to persuade men to spend time there. No thoughts of seductive beautiful women waiting for them at the tables inside the building enter the heads of the men when they are frozen with fear upon looking upon their brick-and-mortar mortality.

But there are two women who come to the Restaurant de la Sirène every day. They spend most of their day there, sitting at their respective tables, waiting for the men to come to notice them. It has been a long vigil for the two women, something like waiting in the darkness for a light to come to show the men the way to their doors.

One of the women is a painter and teacher. She sits there, dressed in her long dress woven out of many colors of wool. She looks as though a rainbow has come out of the sky and wrapped itself around her body. She is a flare of colors that burns brightly in the dimness of the restaurant. This woman sits in the window looking out onto the town square, a candle of colors burning brightly to attract some of the men who are rendered immobile by their fear of age and death.

The painter sits there, looking at the small knots of men on the other side of the glass. She knows she should venture out onto the cobblestones to confront the men with her body swathed in many colors, but she knows she cannot do this. The men must be able to see her themselves without any interference from her. They must perceive her presence sitting at the center of the square of glass.

She knows what she will do if one of them finally spies her; she will take him out of the square away from the building of age and death. To her studio she will lead him where she will dress him in paint-bespattered rags, hand him a paint brush, teach him how to hold it correctly, hand him a palette of paints of every color, and command him to begin to paint.

The woman knows she will stand just behind the man, ignoring his balding head, concentrating on what he is making on the blank white canvas, perhaps placing a restraining hand upon his shoulder should he become too rash and threaten to ruin the painting. But most of the time, she knows, she will be the softest of breaths at his back.

The other woman who comes to the restaurant is a prostitute. She comes to ply her trade amongst the men who come to the restaurant. She is dressed in a long black gown and her eyes are as black and as blank as the coal the wives of the men throw onto the fire on winter evenings to keep their husbands and children warm.

This woman knows that if one of the men sees her, she will take him from the Restaurant de la Sirène to the small flat she rents at the back of the town post office. There she will take his money and his clothes, and when it is all over, she will not even recognize his face should he come back to the restaurant to seek her out.

Sitting in the restaurant, the two women, aware of each other but not acknowledging each other's presence, wait patiently for the male customers to come. They wait for the men who sometimes venture there and sometimes catch the briefest of glimpses of one of the two women. You can see the shock register in their faces, whether it is the painter and teacher or the prostitute.

But most of the men stand in the square, the seconds, the minutes rise like the shallows of a sea tide lapping at their feet.

THE ROOM

Natasha bows her head, tucks it into her throat, and hopes nothing will disturb her. She has rolled over on her left side facing the wall of the room. It has been a long night and early morning, and all she wants is some peace. She's so tired she hasn't taken off all of her clothes. She lies there clad in black stockings and a long soft flannel blouse pulled up revealing her round fat bum and her legs like smooth tree stumps.

She looks look a piece of sculpture, white and hard and shiny, but that is an illusion because her skin, her flesh is soft and hot to the touch. Once you place a hand on that flesh you allow your fingers to stray across her bum or down her legs — you cannot stop. You must continue; you are compelled to undo her blouse and pull it open, cradle her heavy breasts in your hands, lick and suck her blood plum nipples. You must open her legs and explore the insides. You must kiss her bony knobbly knees and lick the runeled stretch marks on her belly.

And of course there is her mouth, hidden now, but if you rolled her over you would see how full it is, as fleshy as a Dutch tulip in full flower. Then you would have to kiss it and slip your tongue into it, find the inside of her mouth, her tongue as slippery as a pink moray eel that will, you can be sure, entwine itself around your tongue until you think it might tear your tongue out by your roots leaving you speechless forever.

That way you will never be able to tell anyone else about her. You will not be able to open your mouth and spill out the words, revealing where Natasha lives, what she does, what she looks like, what she feels like, all of her — her bum and her legs and her mouth and her vagina.

Now, as she is slipping into slumber she hears the sounds as short and as sharp as rose thorns pressed, jammed, rammed into her flesh, leaving red wounds that open, split wider like mouths full of decayed and pitted teeth, mouths with the stench of bad breath withering, wrinkling her body.

Natasha tries to keep her eyes shut, she cradles her arms around her head over her ears, trying to block out the sounds, but the sounds are sharp knives, scalpels that cut through her arms, paring away the flesh so the sounds bury into her ears like parasites burrowing into her, feasting upon her bones and blood and tissue.

Natasha opens her eyes and looks at the wallpaper. Its pattern is so old and faded she cannot tell what the figures are. They are blurred to a mess of anonymous color, and the rolls of wallpaper are beginning to peel from the wall, long rolls descending slowly from the ceiling like big sticky bales of hay that might continue peeling one night when she is asleep and roll over her, bundling her into the roll so she wakes a prisoner in a sticky roll, her thrashing arms and legs sticking out of the ends of the roll.

Natasha closes her eyes again, but she knows what she will see and that compels her to open her eyes. She cannot help it; it is something that happens every late night or early morning when she gets home and gets into bed. The horror of it is something she can depend on, something stable in her precarious life.

She sees the first small, crawling humps beneath the wallpaper, the silverfish that swarm under the paper, a mass of movement like a mucky, muddy, smelly Seine spring tide — the silverfish. They explode out of the tears in the wallpaper, and Natasha watches in horror as they maraud across the floor, disappearing into the cracks of the wooden floor boards just before they reach her bed.

But it is not over, she knows. The wallpaper humps into bigger lumps like hidden growths, tumors of cancer, and then they begin to move, slowly at first, almost tentative, but speeding up, hundreds of them, crawling down the wall beneath the paper, stopping just before they come into the morning light, antennae twitching about like small sharp swords, and then bolder. The cockroaches muscle their way into the day, great, big, brown, shiny, armored creatures cascading to the floor.

They march like a ragged army toward Natasha, but not all of them disappear into the cracks of the floorboards like the silverfish. Some of the cockroaches climb up onto Natasha's bed, and she screams, swatting at the cockroaches with her open soft palms. She brushes them away and they hobble off like sulky school boys brought to heel for their errant behavior.

But it is not over and she knows she will hear the sound louder than the other vermin, and she does — the scuttle of cruel, sharp claws in all of the four walls of her small room.

Moist pink snouts poke out of spaces between the wallpaper and from holes in the floor; all of the four walls of the room are infested. Natasha sees the coarse whiskers twitching and the noses smelling her. The rats pause as one for a second, then begin to march from their hiding places. They swarm over the floor, grunting and squeaking, their long shaggy-haired bodies scraping against the wood, their long fleshy tails whipping about like the whip of an overseer driving slaves.

The rodents advance on Natasha, and she pushes herself up from the bed on one elbow and waits for the confrontation that comes every late night or early morning. The rats reach her bed, and all of them stand up on their hind legs, place their front clawed paws on the bed, leaving prints of mud and blood, and poke their heads over the edge of the bed, their black, beady rapacious eyes rake Natasha's flesh, their heads spasm from side to side, and then they begin to hiss and spit at her, slug slimy rat saliva that speckles Natasha's body and scant clothes death gray.

But she spits back, hawking hard pellets of yellow and green mucus she brings up from her tubercular lungs. She keeps on spitting at the rats until one staggers back a step and goes back down on all fours. The others follow suit, one more and then two more and then the others fall back on all fours. They keep on hissing. Natasha keeps on spitting at them until they are driven back into the walls behind the wallpaper and below the floor boards.

It is not over. It will only be over when the syphilitic bridegroom death comes and carries her away.

CAUGHT

Bᴏʙ Tᴀʏʟᴏʀ ᴘᴜʟʟᴇᴅ ᴜᴘ ɪɴ ғʀᴏɴᴛ ᴏғ ʜɪs ʜᴏᴜsᴇ ɪɴ Mayfield East, the street that led directly to the front gate of the works. The house he bought with Denise when they married, two months after Bob started at the works, twenty years ago. He sat in the car and he could see the fish he'd speared, not long ago, packed in plastic on the front seat. The final flare of the gills and the blood working its way in fans under the thick plastic.

Bob took hold of the fish, got out of the car, slammed the door behind him, and went to the back of the house where he found the board he used to clean the fish. Took his knife to cut away the head; an unusual thing for him to do with Bob usually leaving the head on so his wife and kids could see just how big the fish were he'd speared and brought home for them to eat.

The man averted his eyes as the knife crunched through the backbone and took the head of the groper from its body. Bob threw the head into the bin and angrily slammed the lid. Back to the fish, he scraped the saw-teeth of the knife back along the flanks of the fish. The scales a bright blizzard of silver and red that grayed his face and hair so that he seemed to have aged in a small passing of time. A storm of scales, reminding him of the difficulty he'd had spearing the fish, the difficulty he'd had getting back home, took him away — for the time being from his house, his anger, his disgust with himself and the works — to the sea.

Bob Taylor peered into the blizzard of small silverfish, a storm of scaled bodies catching the light from the sun that shocked the eyes of the skin diver. Bob stopped swimming, held his breath a bit longer, and waited for the school of fish to pass him by. The small fry a scarf of silver movement that whipped and stilled about him. Bob Taylor almost out of air and about to lose the big fish he'd sighted just before the school of small fish obscured his view.

He calmed himself. Told himself there was plenty of air left in his lungs, told himself he'd held on longer than this to spear a decent fish. Told himself to continue the pursuit and not panic. Told himself he'd pull the black rubber right back and load the shaft and aim it carefully at the fish he'd selected. Bob would not be turned away from the hunt and the fillets of fish that would steam on the dinner plates of his family later.

He saw a rent in the veil of silver scale, and Bob Taylor swam through the opening into the green and blue with the javelins of light that pierced the surf swell falling about the body of the skin diver. Bob kicked hard with his legs and used his flippers to slide quickly through the water after the big fish — the big silver drummer he was sure he'd spotted at the corner of a rock ledge.

Bob caught sight of the big fish again, the small mouth and head sticking out from the brown arch of rock that spanned deeply below the platform. The skin diver jackknifed his body, clutching his spear gun while diving down. He could see and feel the shadows of the rock fishermen standing high on the rock platform above him slide over his skin.

The fish off and running — a long tubular length of large scale and muscle. Colors of bronze and blue-gray that had Bob Taylor indecisive because he thought the big fish was a drummer, but he wasn't sure any more. Not once did he see the blue and the reddish line markings that didn't belong to a silver drummer.

But Bob Taylor, almost out of breath,was tempted to shoot to the surface to fill his lungs. The panic losing him his judgment, his determination. The skin diver raised the spear gun, not bothering to think, to look closer to see whether the fish was a drummer. A quick aim and the shaft released, the barb shocking into the side of the fish. It struggled among the lengths of brown and golden seaweed and kelp growing broadloom carpet thick from the floor of the ocean. The fish struggled among the gaff-shaped swirls of its own blood.

The length of the spear shaft whipped back and scraped the ribs of Bob Taylor: blunt steel wounding the flesh taut on the tent peg rib cage of the diver. Hooks of blood came from the body of Bob Taylor and mixed with the scarlet escaping from the almost spent body of the fish.

Bob Taylor, took hold of the shaft, acutely aware of the sear of salt water in the wound in the side of his chest. The diver shot upward, and the sunlight in the water felt like knives in his eyes. Bob Taylor broke the surface, taking in the fresh sea air, holding up the shaft, seeing the body of the groper.

"Nice one mate. Spearing illegally now. Gropers aren't allowed yer stupid bastard," from one of the fishermen standing on the rock platform above the head of Bob Taylor, above the funeral wreaths of red blooming in the water.

Bob drove away from the sea and soon he could see the gray monoliths of steel mills growing out of the line of trees. The humps of black and gray like the backbones of dinosaurs rising out of the flatlands of mud and swampland. He could taste the smell of steel making and associated industry already; a bloom of stench that flowered as far as Merewether and the coastline when the wind was blowing the wrong way. And Bob Taylor could hear the thump of metal in rollers and the shock of gas exploding in the flux of steel being born as he snaked over the Tighes Hill rail bridge.

The sight and smell and sound of the steelworks taking hold of him and the clean salty smell of the big groper in the bag next to him, lost. The sound of steel being made like a hypnosis that had him miss the turn off the main road to his home. So he had to go the long way around, and as he drove he thought about the first time he'd seen the steelworks, in the first light of day, laying like a trick on the landscape. Transforming the mills so they seemed like rolls of money, coins tipped and rolled over the flatlands.

He came north from out of the cold of Melbourne and shot off the main highway that led onto the tropics of Queensland and the smoky Glass House Mountains and the Barrier Reef a line of coral colored red and blue and green and too many other colors for Bob Taylor to remember. Heading for the university on the Queensland Coast where he had a place waiting to study marine biology.

Twenty years ago now — the time when he'd stopped in Newcastle for a couple of days with friends intending to surf the beaches and then head north to study. But stayed when he took a job at the steelworks because management was begging for operators and laborers. Bob Taylor taking the job and telling himself he'd quit at the end of the month and arrive at the Queensland uni with an extra couple of hundred dollars to help keep him in the first year of study.

He'd been seduced, he knew, by the big money to be earned working in the hot and dirty and dangerous conditions of the steelworks. The marine biology left behind him; Bob Taylor not bothering to write to the department to tell them he'd not be coming to study marine biology so caught up was he with work and three shifts about and the money that poured into his bank account.

Bob Taylor sat at the table and watched his wife and children eating the fillets of groper.

"This is beautiful, Dad," from his daughter.

"Yes, this fish is the best-tasting fish you've speared," said Denise. "But are you sure you won't have any?"

Bob Taylor shook his head. Looked away from his family shoveling the illegal sweet meat of the groper into their mouths. Bob Taylor felt his hand go to his rib cage. Felt the blood soaking his shirt. Held up his hand and looked at the salt and spice of his life turned black.

THE RELEASE

DULCIE FELT IT. STANDING AT THE SINK, PEELING THE potatoes for tea. She felt it. A groan and shudder that fissured into her chest. Took the breath from her body, turned the blood backward in her like a tide receding, leaving a hard flat mirror of sand reflecting torn clouds, black crows creaking like rags of grief. Instinctively. She straightened herself. Locked her limbs into place to stop herself falling, arched her spine like a lynx, her back muscles like wire rope against the final nerve-hair shudders. Beneath her feet. Raised her mica eyes, coal black, as if the unconsciousness flowed in a seam in her.

Dulcie knew the tremors. She'd felt them before when the pit took her two uncles in one collapse. Jack and Fred, buried away in the earth, tombed up away from the smell of the surf spray scarfing up in funnels of light and water above Burwood Beach, buried away from the eucalypts towering in spurs of growth over the rocky scape of Glenrock Lagoon and Murdering Gully.

All gone now, her uncles, her last relations. Scots who'd sailed the rush of the roaring forties, salt-skittled around the Horn, heading for the new land and the new pits that were black and oily and consuming like the pits of Devonside. Away from Devonside, with its tenements, gray and slated and slick with drizzle, a swallowing into half-light and smoky fires after the hours beneath the earth.

The uncles had spoiled Dulcie. What with no families of their own, a dull journey into the darkness of middle age. Except for Dulcie, a shining child who welcomed them back from the pits of Merewether, took them into the cottage with the fire wheeling out rings that splashed light across their blackened bodies. A fire Dulcie constructed from childhood, long after her parents had died, long before Henry Abbott swaggered into her life with his careless boyishness.

Not that Dulcie's luminous figure was enough to take Jack and Fred from the darkling. They would break out of the cottage. Like clumsy thieves. Head for town and the pubs. Roll back in like schooners in high seas off Nobby's Breakwater. Stagger up the unlit scar of earth that was Union Street. With their mates from the pits. Mates below the earth, mates who made the choice. Turned their backs on the fire of family affection.

They took their careless, drunken staggering down into the earth — once too often, full of port and brown muscat — the story went from the foreman. Jack and Fred wondering into out-of-bounds areas. Gas there for three weeks. They lit their pipes. And Dulcie heard it. Then. Below her feet, below the iron cauldron swinging like a metronome, full of mutton and veges; the night's tea, not eaten.

•

Dulcie looked out into the wild sea of buffalo grass that was her back yard. Green fire in the noon, just turning to a pale tide of evening. A sea swell of grass growing untamed from the black soil. Below it, the hit-and-miss mines of coal. Lacerations lashed out beneath the conglomerate by men with picks and wooden props and a few proposals of prayer.

Merewether and Glenrock and Murdering Gully — a warren of tunnels and shafts, a dice-roll of miner's cottages across a thin skin of earth termited out. Below. A nest of blind albinos subsiding their own houses. Waiting for their deaths beneath a ton of rock, a flare of gas skinning them alive to soft jelly and jarred bone, waiting for the walls and roofs of their cottages to disappear into the "rat" holes they'd gouged out.

Dulcie looked out into the grass. They'd be coming for her soon. Coming with the news. She knew. Just as they'd come, caps in hand, heads bowed, with the news of Jack and Fred. The messengers, not looking her in the eye. Speaking the news of Fred and Jack back into the earth. As if they wanted the memory, the crushed and torn flesh, the bloodied muscat mouths, the smashed bone to be buried away from them. With the uncles, with the half-rotten wooden props and the yellow birds in cages caroling until gas burned the pearl notes, dropped them to the floor of the barred cages.

Dulcie remembered Jack and Fred the day before the collapse, the day before their deaths. How they'd returned with the cage and the dead bird. They ignored. Went out to town, to the pub, left the bird for Dulcie to bury. Careless. Fred and Jack. Not a bit of notice taken of the gas that had claimed the canary.

●

Dulcie watched her children, Susanna and Michael. They hadn't heard it. Felt it. Still playing in the sea of grass. Pulling the long whip strands of green around them. Taking away the sun in caves of grass. Up the back yard. Dulcie would watch them disappear into the green tide. And it was as though they'd been taken from her. By water.

It was the only time she really left the kitchen, the laundry, her places allotted by Henry. His insistence upon her labor after his boyish grin formed into a shapeless gash as though someone had pushed a fist into it. After the courting, the marriage, the death of the uncles, Dulcie's life began in darkness, before dawn, chopping the logs to kindling. Dulcie's life finished in night with the washing up, the scrubbing of Susanna and Michael in the metal tub, brushing their hair, tucking them away in beds. Dulcie, in between the walls of darkness, the cleaning and cooking, the clothes turning over in the copper, Henry's coal-stained clothes she rubbed with pumice stone to try to take away the black dust that stayed.

Dulcie would rush from the tubs, full of piles of soapy, steaming garments. Not see Susanna and Michael. Wade into the buffalo grass like a woman walking into the ocean. It rose around her ankles. Reached her waist in wind-whipped waves. She'd plant her feet. Squarely. Down into the soil. Bend into the grass. Moved by a sea of wind, stiffening out of Glenrock, rifling out and down the flat sandy plain of he Glebe.

Dulcie would coil her body as though she were in a shore-dump surf. Defying the breakers that rose without warning, from froth and under current to six feet of green claw in front of her breasts.

Dulcie would reach into the green. Search for her children. Find Susanna. Reaching out for her mother as if it were all a joke. Susanna's lopsided grin that made it alright. Susanna thought. Would always think. Casual. Like her father. Slouching off back through the grass jungle. Heading for the ice chest, a cool drink, while her mother searched for Michael.

Michael, hard to find, to haul out of the green currents and undertows. As if he'd been taken by the surf off Burwood Beach. Michael's cry, like a bird, slanting off across water, to somewhere else. A carrion cry of a crow, black and creaking and feeding, like the fiber and grain of timber torn slowly asunder. And she'd see his mouth first. Coming out of the grass, a wide gaping maw of demand, like a young bird demanding to be fed, and he'd latch his fingers, like claws, spiky, prickly, into the flesh of her neck, her breasts. Slobber spit and mucus. Pull tighter. Drain the oxygen from her lungs. Wouldn't let go for hours. Sometimes. Dulcie would feel him, his tongue, lapping the sweat that rivered down her neck and pooled in the hollow above the ridge of her collar bone. Michael, taking the salt from her body. The goodness.

Dulcie watched them now. Their blind play. She peeled the carrots. Threw the shanks of lamb into the pot. Waited for the coming of the news. Of Henry. Her husband. Put it out of her mind, just as she'd put away Fred and Jack after the funerals.

She remembered the funeral, and Henry, sobbing. As the coffins were lowered into the red earth, hacked out in winter. Henry, shuddering, spasming his grief, his anguish. Unable to hold it back. To stand upright, with an arm around Dulcie. Henry under the great wet wheels of water hammering down from the sky. Hunched over as though he were still underground with Jack and Fred, still mining coal. With his mates. But, at the graveside, Henry was some dismembered life form, a soft jellyfish mass. Blind, in the wet mud of the graveyard.

Dulcie. Stood. An obelisk of non-porous stone, the water sliding off her hide, plastered with the sodden cotton of her dress. Dulcie, impervious to the bitter cold that bit her nipples to a sore hardness. As though she were pregnant. Suckling some invisible flesh, her nipples sore from bony gums draining her.

Dulcie rammed a piece of dead black wood, willed the fire into being below the pot. Added a generous dose of salt. An essence that Henry hated. The drying out, the cauterizing pinch of the gullet as the lamb and vegetable soup went down.

To Dulcie, a sweet pain — salt into the wounds of her mouth. She remembered the salt-laden liquid the night her uncles died. Liquid that stung her tender mouth like a metal bit in a pit pony's mouth. Salt-cured her throat until her voice was a whisper. Tearing silent her howls of anguish and grief. But her voice came back, no longer the long fluted note. But a coarse worm of a whine that pulled up her children. Short. And her husband, who missed her milk-and-water mewl of submission. Gone, as though a hard callous of skin had grown out from the trunk of veins and arteries that formed her throat. Grown out in spurs and roots and branches of hard flesh, a beef jerky hide that bound her up — her bones and blood and gristle — into a straight tower, that stood. Apart.

Apart from the hands and demands of her husband. Henry stayed away from her after that. After the funerals. Months would pass and the need for her flesh would be too much. But he'd stop, in the moonlight of the bedroom. See her. Turning. In the mirror, see her arms, the heavy flesh, matronly, and the heavy brass bangles clamped like yellow rings of magic into her biceps. He'd see the flesh squeezed in thick ripples from the rings of metal. And Dulcie, squeezing them tighter, into the skin, a pain she took with her every day to remind her of Jack and Fred, to jab her eyes into a flare of attention. Not to be careless with Susanna and Michael, her family. All that was left.

To be careful, not like Henry with his clumsy coal miner's hands raking her soft flanks the way he clawed out the coal from the gut of the earth; Henry in the black of the bedroom, rank with dried sweat. Unable to wait. A black, mindless unconsciousness, jack-knifing into her the way he pick-axed out a ton of coal a day. And his curiously lukewarm sperm slithering into her like a sheltering snake. And his withdrawal. And his back to her. Her, lying. Spread eagled. Outraged. By his carelessness. His stupidity.

No more, since the cave-in took Dulcie's uncles, and grief took Henry. Henry banished. As though Dulcie had turned him back down into the earth, where he belonged.

•

Dulcie watched the night come down. And heard it — the cry of the front gate, opened.

She watched the two men come out of the darkness. Slowly. Struggling. Trying to be born into the final light, to form their flesh for her eyes. They stood there. Waited, while she came to the back door, their eyes, a rock shelf wedge of black beneath their hats. And their ridiculous stove-pipe trousers, too short, showing their thin ankles, as though the bone might snap, as though they'd fall, unable to hold themselves up.

Dulcie watched them. Not a word from her to make it easier, to help them say the words. Words like fish hooks, barbed into the flesh of their throats. Their hands fidgeting final flakes of light. Hands like kites without tails — no direction, no purpose. And she started to hear their words, strange rumbling sounds like the distant boom of surf at Burwood Beach during a king tide.

The owner stood in front of Dulcie, the owner of the pit, the coal company — tall, waxen, in the kitchen of the miner's cottage. Dulcie watched him move about in his black suit, too big for him. Great baggy sags of fine cloth hanging from his arms and back and stomach like the slack skin and muscle of an old man. He seemed to move about in the bolts of cloth, like a thin man finding openings and pockets he didn't know about.

Dulcie could see the long ferret's throat and the Adam's apple working up and down as if to hold back an unpalatable obstruction. Working up and down like the floats Henry had used on his line when he fished off Burwood Beach, bobbing up and down, below the surface, hard to tell if there was a fish or a dark undercurrent, hidden, runneling under the rock platform shelf, below the frothy mess of the surf.

Dulcie half-expected the owner to melt from the heat of the open-hearth fire. His waxy fingers and face to pool away from the chalky bone, the wax to run between the boards of the floor until there were only the organs grinding in the bird-shell skeleton.

The words were coming out. The condolences. The hopes. Commiserations. For Dulcie. About Henry. Dulcie watched them come in the tide turn to twilight. Melodious syllables and consonants rolling out of his mouth like ocean waves rising, covering the rotting corpses of shags and cormorants and gulls, sand-encrusted, opaque-eyed, on the beach. Watery words in long soft lines, trying to take away the deathly mute sorrow. A sea change that only salted the wounds.

"Very sorry, Mrs. Abbott. Your good husband, Henry, one of our best workers. Still hope, only two days now. A strong man, Henry. May be still alive. Have gangs of men working 'round the clock."

Dulcie only heard the black spaces between the jerkings of words, black openings she could see into, see down into the earth where Henry lay. Beyond words.

She turned her back on the pit owner and stirred her soup, turned her back on his false hope, his wax-works hands of meaningless gesture. Flickering automations, like the pit machinery, pulling men out of the earth, turning them back down into darkness. Every day.

She turned back. She could see the smooth half-moons of his fingernails, manicured, dancing like silver blades. Cutting up the air. Slivering into the soft night velvet, the way the black rock and props cut into the eleven men and boys. Drowned in the earth.

Dulcie knew the owner, knew his wife. The woman, sitting on the balcony removed, one floor up, above the street, sitting, waiting, wrapped in her fox stoles. Dulcie would see them as she walked past, the dead animals and the heads, resting on the plump shoulders of the powdered and puffed-up woman. Fox heads with black bead eyes and mouths ajar, the teeth, sharp, yellow, as if they might snap shut into the flesh of the waiting woman.

Two of the last foxes, hunted down in Glenrock, a bloody bantu of blacks and miners ordered out by the owner. Ordered into a line, given drums and fifes and clubs and orders to drive the foxes from the brush. Foxes for his wife, but, tricksters, substitutes for her husbanding's presence. Dulcie knew the woman's cold resentment, saw it in her eyes, in the twitching pits behind the powder, the same black glass marble eyes sewn into the heads of the foxes draped about her form.

The woman, waiting for her owner-husband, knowing, as Dulcie knew, as all the Glebe knew, where he was. Away from her, away from their children, in the city. In Hunter Street, down the West End, in the brothel he half-owned.

Dulcie knew the man left for Sydney, regularly, on the clippers. The miners of the Glebe knew the coal they chopped out left Newcastle with him to go to Sydney, to countries across the ocean. The rich core of Newcastle taken off, elsewhere. And the pit owner soon to move, the rumor went, sell up his house and move to Sydney. An absentee owner, away from the town, waiting by Sydney Harbor for the profits to sail through the heads.

He was still speaking. The words washed about Dulcie's ankles, a rising tide. Dulcie took him by the arm and led him down the dark gun barrel of the miner's cottage, took him to the door with words still spilling out of him. She led him out, put him out through the front gate. Went back and found the iron-bristled broom.

Swept the house from top to bottom, as if to sweep out the owner's litter of speech, sweep out his waxy half-light and the fermenting vegetable smell of the wet wool of his suit. She could taste his smell and she flung open the windows, the doors. And the sea breeze came in from the beach, spiriting through the house. Like a dose of vinegar and salt scrubbing clean the boards of the coal dust Henry and Fred and Jack had brought home with them over the years.

And she sang. That strange flat chant, that incantation that came from her belly, funneled up into her chest, her throat and came like the grind of sea and sand and rock pebbles on Burwood Beach at high tide. Susanna and Michael stopped their play, came from the sea of grass of the back yard. Came and stood near their mother, near the gravel and rust notes. Notes that bound around the two children in circles of magic, of protection.

●

Dulcie stood at the pit head, on Myer's Farm, not far from her cottage. She watched the troop of rescuers lowered into the earth. Grim-faced, dirty, plain scared, from shift about, digging in the blackness below the earth, below the cold night.

Night fluxed by starlight, coming in silver waves over the ocean. But taken away from the men who carted out the flesh and bone of the earth, who carted out the flesh and bone of their dead mates.

A fall of roof in a cross-cut district, the day for the change of cavil, the quarterly draw for fresh places. The miners had been engaged in removing their tools from their old bords to their new places. They'd reached their bords when a great fall of rock took down men and boys. Sheared limbs from some, taken to the surface, rivering blood back down behind them into the mine. White husks in the new daylight, laid out in rows, waiting for the doctor, waiting for the stretchers, waiting for the undertaker.

The rescue crews were propping every square inch, holding up the roof, still working; currents and knots of rock twisting beneath the earth's skin. And Henry down there had made the wrong choice, drawn the short straw, purposely, a new bord, a careless choice. Like Fred and Jack. Henry knew its reputation — a dangerous place. He had the choice to go to another bord. Family men did. Not Henry, wanting to be among the other lads. Spiced the shift and his damper with a bit of danger. Mining out the coal with a rumble and shudder of fear in his guts that drove him on. Made him ignore Dulcie's pleas for him to keep himself clear, keep himself safe. To keep his children's mouths filled with food. Not to take notice of his mates, the braggarts at the bar after work with schooners of black and stories of how they'd cheated death. Again. Stories that grew with every drawing of a draught. Until they hailed each other hail and hearty, and heroes. Henry couldn't resist.

Had to be in on that. But not strong enough to repel the cold-fire look from Dulcie that shafted into him when he lurched through the door. He'd go off. Sulk. A blackness of silence. Something Dulcie couldn't stand. Silence that chopped into her like school taylor, chopping into white bait off Burwood. He'd turn his back on her. Her sitting on the bed, watching him, watching the wilting, the crumbling of his spine when he pulled off his shirt. She'd see him in the mirror, the whorl in the glass that twisted his eyes to a spiral, a vortex of pale, leached-out almond, the strange mercury dribble in the mirror that slurried away his mouth and chin.

She'd turn on him, like the tide turning and flushing into Glenrock Lagoon, a high violent tide of water breaking through the sand barrier, raking out the silt and sediment from the silent creeks and stagnant body of the lagoon.

"What do you think you're doing?! Henry Abbott!! Drinking with your mates? Working that bord?! Two men killed there last month! Will you be next?! And who'll feed Susanna and Michael then?! If you're dead, or without an arm!?"

Even his violence was silence, a mute, methodical fury of open palms cutting through the air, smacking, smashing into Dulcie's face, bruising her breasts, making her eyes into muscat grapes. But she'd stand there, a coil of hard flesh, as though she'd been steel-chiseled out of rock; she'd stand and take the blows, until he'd exhausted himself.

Look at her with disbelief. See her feet planted into the floor boards as if she'd grown from the grain of the wood itself. As if she was a prop of tree fiber, exaggerated in the night light, seeming to hold up the roof and walls of the miner's cottage.

And he would run from her. Sulk out into the night. Away from Dulcie, away from his family. Back to the pub.

•

She could see him now. Dulcie, above the earth, could see him, knew the rock plate that covered him, saw his dead white face with the bloody tear across the brow cut through the skull bone into the soft tissue of the brain. Dulcie could see him, felt him, dead.

The fall was extensive, the roof crushed so only four or five yards per shift could be cleared and timbered. Men scrambled out at intervals. Afraid of further collapses, afraid of being entombed, afraid of finding bodies. Bodies that easily could have been them; bodies that followed them out of the earth to their homes, to their sleep, rising pale and bloody in the black sleep of the miners, who woke, shuddering like the pit in collapse, sweating like the pit ponies, pulling skips of coal to the surface.

Miners in a foul and black midnight, sitting at rough-hewn gum slab tables, worn smooth by the arms and hands of men taken from them. And wives at a loss. Unable to help them, comfort them, until the turning tide of day washed light into the darkness.

Men, who feared a tender touch may cave-in their rock-and-wood resolution, split, asunder, their propped up bar-room afternoons with the S.P. bookies and the poker hands and the smoke and the beer.

Rumors flew like scavenging gulls around the Glebe — wild rumors of the thinness of the barrier between the collapse in A pit and B pit. Stories of the ease with which the bodies could be secured. Indulgence — a way out for the owner, the foremen, the men. Hope against hope, the way they staged the pit pony races every second Saturday in the bush, near Glenrock.

Miners and bosses in the eucalypts, with a ring hacked through the trees and some rough mattocking of the clay surface so the horses could run. The miners there with their shillings and zacks, or more, and their plunges on the rumored long shot. The sure thing that would come home, they were told, they wanted to believe. Believe that the horse would take away the rent burden for a couple of weeks, with enough left over for a spree in town. Until their rumor hobbled in at the rear of the field, carrying a fourteen stone jockey employed by the S.P. bookie who covered all bets at all odds.

Years later the rumor of the barrier was dismantled, two and a half chains thick, the barrier between the two pits. The rumor dismantled, just as the pits were dismantled with the coming of the steelworks that took the miners into another unconsciousness, a black, oily humming of shift work, day in, day out, month in, month out, year by year, a metal and mechanical hypnotism, wheels and steel rollers and sprockets and chains and black belts and spiraling hot metal that seduced away the disgust, the distaste of the men. And turned back out through the gates of the works, tired men. With just enough ignition spark to blacken eyes, to stumble, half-asleep, carelessly, into the working arms of machinery that took away limbs, sheared away a livelihood, a family.

The bodies were raised. As if the rescuers were divers in bell helmets with grappling hooks, hauling out the corpses from the sea of black rock. All bodies recovered, except Henry's. Two days more they searched. Without remuneration. Until the owner ordered the rescue shaft cleared.

There was a great deal of water and work would be extremely dangerous, he said. And the company would be commencing to draw coal from a section nearby during the following week. Better the rescue closed down and the men directed back to work the new seam.

Henry, lost in black unconsciousness that left Dulcie in the kitchen, peeling the vegetables for tea, scrubbing the black river loam from Michael and Susanna in the tin tub, tucking them into bed.

Dulcie saw Henry in her dreams. Unchanged Henry, no transformation, the mirror-twisted eyes and oxbow mouth and shifting chin, a reality, now, rotting in a last resting place in blackness.

Dulcie would watch herself move near the ruined roof of the shaft, passing over the body, the shapeless slack blue ink mouth frozen in death, but stopped up, like the shaft, stopped up so no excuses came, no drunken rages. Dulcie saw his shuttered eyes, the pale blue washes clamped over by ashen lids and she saw the smashed limbs already mulched back into the oily coal, rotting back into some obtuse, blind strata of rock.

Dulcie felt herself trapped by Henry's body, held down in the ground. Unable to release herself from Henry. She calmed herself, focused her eyes in the darkness. Further down in the shaft she saw the movement come at her in a pulse of energy. She moved, willed herself further into the earth.

The pit pony. She could hear its heavy breathing. Twelve days imprisoned, but still standing upright, below a crack in the roof from which came a trickle of water. Dripping down onto a foreleg he licked to stay alive.

Dulcie saw the current of energy sinewing under the starved-tight hide; veins and arteries pumping and the pony's red eyes furnacing in the darkness. She saw the electrical storm of defiance, of energy, in the bunched muscle tied tightly to the rodded bone of the frame. She felt the energy like lightning in her body fiber, fluxing into her.

Dulcie watched herself, astral through the roof of the mine, passing up through the conglomerate and the root fiber that might snare hooks into the cotton of her garment, hold her down in the earth. But she passed upward, a smooth length of irresistible energy breaking clear, ghosting back over the night-black suburb of the Glebe. Shaping her conscious self, creating her memory of herself that shed the shell of Henry Abbott, the memory of her uncles.

•

Dulcie held on for a month. The coal company owned the cottage she rented. She left before she was kicked out.

Took Susanna and Michael away from the Glebe, away from the pits and the owner and the vibration of miners just below her feet.

She took her children into the city, into a flat where she worked, self-employed, as a seamstress, twelve hours a day. Poor light and light money, but enough to pay the rent, the bills. Enough to release them.

THE ALYSCAMPS, AVENUE IN ARLES

Inspired by a painting of the same title by Vincent van Gogh.

MONIQUE WAITS BETWEEN THE ROWS OF TREES, THE trunks covered with great coats of shaggy green moss. There are crinkles and bumps in the wood because there is shrapnel buried in the grain. The Prussian troops shelled the town and the surrounding countryside. Hot lumps of metal slammed into the trees, many were destroyed, some were left standing with hearts of steel and iron. The wounds from the Franco-Prussian War are clothed, smoothed by the moss. Sometimes, red sap weeps from the lacerations in the trees.

Toward the crowns of the trees, the color of the leaves changes to canon-flame yellow. But when Monique waits for Jean in the evening, she thinks the trees look like lampposts made of weathered green metal, as though the metal of war has taken away the sap and leaf of nature. She can never be sure what the trees will look like when she comes to wait.

Last week, when she came to meet Jean in the middle of the day, the trees looked for all the world like soldiers standing rigidly to attention. Soldiers dressed in dark green uniforms with headdresses of yellow feathers waving plumes in the faint breeze coming off the river not far way. They looked so much like soldiers, Monique, making sure that no one was watching her, went right up to the trunks and searched for the rifles she was convinced the trees must be carrying. Only after close inspection, did she assure herself there were no rifles with metal bayonets attached.

There is grassland on one side of the walk lined by the trees and ample space between the tree trunks for Monique to escape into the open fields.

The grass is lush, seeded on flesh and bone beneath the soil. But Monique always feels as though she should stay on the path made of orange stone pounded to small pieces by the prisoners in the gaol of the town. She is fearful that if she steps off the path onto the open grassland, she will miss Jean, that he will stride along the walkway, discover she has not come, and leave in a huff, perhaps never to meet her again, a punishment for her not keeping her appointment at the time and place they agreed upon.

Monique knows how difficult Jean can be to get on with, but she thinks she has come to almost adore the man. She knows she is treading on eggshells every time she meets with him. Every time they talk she is on edge because she is scared she will say something to upset him. It is part of his nature, this tetchiness, a nervous habit that makes him take the young woman to task over mere trifles.

Like the other day when Monique came to meet him wearing her black felt hat. Jean had never seen it before, but he stopped dead in his tracks when he saw the woman's curls of hair controlled by the black cap of felt jammed down close to her ears. Monique knew from the expression on his face that the hat displeased him: the petulant down-turning of the corners of the mouth, the left eye twitching, the bristling of the sparse graying hair on his head made a man not used to dealing with the unexpected to the slightest degree.

He sulked for the rest of the meeting. Jean wouldn't look at Monique because he couldn't stand the sight of the black hat. When she got home to her cottage beside the river, she removed the hat, sat on her back step fondling the soft black felt, wondering what it was about the hat that so upset the man she had been meeting regularly for three months now.

As she sat on the sandstone step, watching the river meander onward past her stone cottage, Monique could see the gravestone of her dead husband, already lichen-covered, the lettering starting to fade with the weathering of wind and rain. It seemed such a short time ago when Marcel was still with her, plowing their one field, milking the cows. Then he was gone. One small lump of lead was all that it took, leaving Monique with one son to bring up and little in the way of money coming in.

Almost at the end of her tether, Monique was at the point of selling the farm and moving to Paris, where she might find work as a seamstress in one of the factories of the capital. Loath to leave the farm and the grave of Marcel, Monique held out but despair won the battle of attrition.

She went to see Jean, the town's solicitor, to sell the property. But by the time their meeting was at an end, the man had persuaded her to stay on the farm. He was prepared to pay her an allowance to keep body and soul together. In return, the man asked only that Monique meet him on the walkway three or four times a week. It was a strange proposal, one that bothered Monique, and she only accepted it because it meant staying where she had been born and had lived all of her life.

But Jean had always been the perfect gentleman, difficult to get on with a lot of the time, but the man, in his mid-fifties, kept his hands to himself, had not even requested a peck on the cheek from Monique when he met her. Indeed there was an almost stiff, courtly grace to Jean, something not seen in the shambling gaits of the local farmers.

It entranced the woman, that walk that was almost a dance as if Jean, when he walked toward her on the path, was dancing across the polished floor of some hall full of lords and ladies dressed in formal attire with an orchestra playing. When the widow saw him coming to meet her the first time, she had to suppress her mirth because he looked so comical. But really, her barely controlled laughter was from nervousness of experiencing something so different, so foreign to her. That a man, not a woman, should move through the world in such a way was intimidating to the highest degree.

It took the woman some time to get used to Jean and the way he behaved when they met. There was a ritual the solicitor always went through, an extravagantly elegant removal of his gloves, one by one, gently pulling at each finger until the leather covering came free. Only then would the man bow to Monique, offer his hand, and wish her good day.

It was so comical at first, Monique often dissolved into a lather of guilty giggles. Jean would stand, waiting patiently for the woman to regain control. Then he would continue his ritual by offering her his arm, which she took, and he guided her along the pathway of orange stones.

It was all very different from the attention paid to Monique by one of the veterans of the war, a farm hand who'd belonged to the same regiment as Monique's dead husband. The farm hand, red-faced, shy, would knock on her door, but when she answered the poor man could find few words to tell her how he felt. Rather, the words were replaced with a series of terrible farts that sounded like gattling gun fire because the veteran was so nervous approaching the object of his adoration.

The resemblance of the man's flatulence to rapid gun fire made the situation worse because the veteran of the Franco-Prussian War, badly shell-shocked, was always convinced that the Huns had returned and he was under fire again. As a result, the man farted more and more until Monique gently shut the door out of pity, leaving the poor peasant confused and even more embarrassed.

Monique related the story of the farm hand to Jean, laughing when she told the lawyer of the man's uncontrollable farting. They were walking along the path of broken stones when she recounted the story, Jean stopped dead, removed his arm from the crook of her arm, turned and looked at her in a way she'd only seen once before. That once was one night when the Prussians were thick among the fields and woods of France. Monique looked through a crack in her front door.

She was barely able to stifle her cry of fear because the looks on the faces of the invaders were not human, they were not men but machines, men of steel and oil, driven to kill and maim without thought or feeling. Never had Monique seen such inhuman expressions in the faces of men before. So when Jean looked at her this way, she was fearful for her life. But the lawyer turned on his heel, left her standing there on the path, and she didn't hear from him for almost a month, although the checks supporting Monique and her son continued to arrive regularly.

When Jean finally summoned her, she went demurely, half scared, not knowing what to expect from this strange and intense man. But Jean was all civility and graciousness in his treatment of her. He did not mention the story of the veteran.

The meeting went as most of the others had gone, but there was an increased intensity to Jean's ritual dance, his formal greeting of Monique. As he approached her, the lawyer stepped gracefully from side to side, swayed his head back and forward, held his arms out elegantly as though he was partnering some invisible woman across a ballroom. Monique should have found it ridiculous, she should have laughed, but she couldn't.

There was such a desperate seriousness about the man's actions, she couldn't find any humor in them. Instead, they made her flesh rise in goose bumps. She held out her hand as he came up to her and waited while he ceremoniously removed his gloves. She breathed a sigh of relief when Jean took her hand, shook it, and wished her good day.

That meeting passed without incident. Monique relaxed a little, and she found she felt a sense of reassurance when the older man had his arm placed through the crook of her arm. It was as if she breathed freely for the first time in a long time. It seemed to the young woman that she didn't know just how on edge she had been, and it took this man, leading her along the path, to show her just how ill at ease she had been for such a long time.

The smell of newly mown grass came from the fields. The clean aroma seemed to seep into every cell of her body, relaxing the way she walked with Jean, even though he made sure it was a walk of great formality, treading the path in a way he defined clearly in his head.

It was only when he wished her goodbye, took his guiding arm from hers, and went on his way did Monique remember the smell that came from the river during the war. The French dead floated in bloated battalions down the waterway; the stench was almost beyond endurance. Months after the war came to an end, the farmers and townspeople were still finding pale, leached limbs caught in reeds, caught on fishing lines.

As she waits on the path, Monique sees the trees on the other side of the walkway with a wall of stones running along the flanks of the trunks. She tries to look away, but cannot; the red stains are still visible in the stones locally hewn and cut. The stains are the blood of men and women of the town when the Prussians took them prisoner, lined them up, and executed them. Many of the town's houses and business premises are still empty.

And Monique has been told by some of her friends about Jean's wife, how she was among those shot that evening when her husband was in Paris on business. When the solicitor returned, he was beside himself; Jean holed up in a house in the town square with a dozen other townspeople, and the men, women, and children, armed with guns, proceeded to pick off the Prussians whenever they strolled into the town square.

The complacency of conquerors was soon replaced with alarm and anger when the rebels accounted for more than a dozen soldiers. Prussian soldiers came from everywhere, shooting at the house that was heavily barricaded with wooden shutters and furniture placed against all entrances. The Prussians lost their tempers as more of their number were claimed by the snipers. A barrage of return fire tore the house to shreds, cutting apart shutters and walls, tearing open the ceilings of the small bastion.

But Jean, mad with the death of his wife, continued to fire even after the others with him had been killed. The Prussians were pulling away the last of the barricades when an unexpected counter attack by the French Army forced the invaders to flee with Jean pouring as much lead after them as he could manage.

The story went that Jean collapsed in a fever, the townspeople took him from the house, and two women nursed him for weeks before the man fluttered open his eyes. But even though his body survived, the man's mind was broken by the loss of his wife and the knowledge that he'd become as bad as the invaders, an animal, who'd destroyed so many human lives without the slightest feeling of remorse or horror at the time.

It was almost a year before Jean could find it in himself to resume practicing as a lawyer. It was forever on his conscience that it was the business of the law that took him away from his wife when the Prussians killed her. But the townspeople and farmers encouraged him to go back to his office. They told him they needed him because he was the area's only solicitor.

So the man went back to his modest chambers, but he was never the same after the war. There was an anxiousness about him, a jittery movement that seemed to infect every limb of his body. The people of the town, mindful of his heroics against the invaders, kept a close watch on him. Women cooked his meals, farmers came in from their fields for a friendly chat. They didn't want him doing harm to himself.

Now she can see him coming up the path, his walk is smooth, not awkward the way she's seen it before. The movement is formal. He steps gracefully, waves his arms about, steps up to her and smiles. The shock of that smile leaves Monique breathless. There is light in his eyes, the deadness she always saw in them has been removed. He shakes hands with her, takes her arm, walks her right to the end of the path. And steps off.

A cry of alarm escapes from her. They've never left the path before. They've always turned around when they reached the end and walked back to where they began. But her resistance is slight. She gains courage from the strength of his arm and the smile that grows wider on his face when he turns his head to look at her.

Into the town square they go. It is almost silent, only a small struggle of the noises of commerce can be heard since the war. Monique cannot see anyone, but then a few faces appear at windows. Jean leads her into the middle of the square, releases her arm, turns to face her. He places one hand at her waist, he places one of her hands on his shoulder, and he takes her other hand in his other hand.

Carefully, with great consideration and deliberation, he begins to waltz the woman through the dust of the square. She has not danced before, not in this way. She is tense, but the more they move about the square, the more she relaxes.

As they progress around the circle of buildings, a man steps out from a doorway. He is carrying a violin. Placing it under his chin, he slaps the bow against his leg, plumes of dust are shed. Swiftly the bow comes to the strings, the music begins, the dance continues, more faces come to windows to watch.

BLOOD

GEORGE BULL DIDN'T LIKE THE JOB, BUT IT WAS SLOW.
He hadn't had a fare in two hours. So when the operator gave him
the blood job off the Mayfield Rank he took it. Could have refused it,
but the money got the better of him. He could put up with taking the
plastic bags of blood from the abattoir at Mayfield West to the labs to
be tested. A decent fare if you could put up with liters of blood sloshing
about in the bags on the passenger's seat next to you. Blood taken from
the cattle the abattoir slaughtered. Day in, day out.

George Bull felt like one of those beasts in the slaughter yard. Every
day, seven days a week, George drove the cab. Twelve hour shifts for the
owner; sixty percent to the owner, forty for George. Enough to feed his
wife and kids, enough to pay the rent so long as he didn't stop.

And the day work was murder. Twelve hours in the heat and glare
of light off the metal bodies of cars, off the black tar of road rolling on
forever. Great sheets of heat stewing George, boiling him live like a
lobster in a steel pot.

He had no choice. Only day work, fifty years old, and the glaucoma
in his eyes had put a stop to the night work. The darkness was too
much for him now. Too difficult to see, to find his way through the
black. Ferrying home drunks who gave him a hard time because they'd
had a bad night, because they'd had a shitty life.

A relief, of sorts, to get away from the night work, but no big money
on day work. Mostly owners driving day work. George had to push
hard to scrape a living. Cut throat, he did his little bit of cheating, like
all the other drivers.

Owners who didn't start till eight or nine in the morning and
knocked off at two in the afternoon. Owners who pretended the taxi

game was some sort of gentleman's club where you politely chatted on the rank with other drivers. If they were owners. Not George. He was a shit for brains driver, the bottom of the pecking order. The owners managed him a nod, but none of the elite jumped into his car in the queue to chew the fat.

"And cheatin' bastards some of 'em just like their night drivers!" muttered George.

George had a theory about owners and their drivers: the night work driver had the same character as the owner of the cab. The really greedy cheating owners invariably had really greedy cheating night work drivers.

George wondered, as he drove the blood, about the move he'd made with Denise and the kids. Whether it had been a good idea moving from the Central Coast to Newcastle. After work. Things had been grim on the orchard just outside of Gosford. Ten years he and Denise had toiled out a living from the crops of oranges. Just enough to get by. Until the bank raised the interest on the loan. They were hungry. Denise got notes from school about the state of the kids.

So they left. Stories of plenty of jobs in the steelworks reached the Central Coast. They sold up, paid out the mortgage, loaded a few sticks of furniture into the ute, and like Steinbeck's Oakies, rolled onto the highway on smooth bald rubber tires, heading for the Promised Land.

Newcastle was not the Promised Land. There were no jobs in the steel mills. B.H.P. was pulling out, setting up a mini mill, the rumor went. A mini mill with a few jobs, a mini mill spitting out designer steel for export.

In desperation George went on the cabs, rented a place in Maude Street, right opposite the Commonwealth Steel. A main drag with a thunder of traffic that fractured the foundations of the weatherboard federation, fractured the nerves of Denise, made it difficult for George to sleep between shifts.

Even at night, with only a trickle of traffic, the clang and smash of metal from the Comm. Steel tormented George like a green fly around cattle.

And George and Denise, a long time since they'd come together. No sex, no touching, no tenderness in the circle of work and kids and half-sleep. A deep hungering below the surface.

George breathed deeply. Tasted the sulfur air. Heard the blood swishing next to him. Wondered what was going to happen, what was going to break the cycle, the vicious circle that shackled him every waking and sleeping moment.

The answer came when he was wondering, not concentrating. The answer came in a fully-loaded semi that shuddered into the red and white falcon.

The cab, riddled with rust, fell apart around George. The doors skidded down Maitland Road in a long bellow of metal on tar. The roof landed on the footpath. The wheels continued on, in formation, without a body or axles, toward the city.

And the blood exploded with a sound like a chisel cutting open a padlock. A crimson, sticky flower that drenched George red. He swallowed some of it. It couldn't be helped.

George sat there, in the wreckage, between the axles, gagging. But the thick blood stayed down. Wouldn't come up. Was there to stay inside of George.

•

They scrubbed George down at the hospital. No serious injury. Only shock, and having to put up with the jokes.

"Bloody lucky there, George," the young intern grinned at him.

"Hard to get off," the nurse said as she scrubbed George with a bristled brush. "Still, they say blood's thicker than water."

His family came to see him — Denise and the two kids. Brought him flowers and fruit and chocolates. Chattered about school. Denise talked about her boss, the solicitor, who was giving her a hard time about her typing speed. But the chatter died.

They eyed George. Doubtfully. Denise and the kids didn't say anything. But there was something different about George. Something about the pallor of his skin. As though the blood had seeped under and forged a fire in his flesh. And Denise didn't like the way her husband looked at her. Great big rolling brown bulls' eyes that fixed Denise without gentleness.

And his voice. There was something wrong there too. A coarse bawling tone to it as if the words bolted up out of George's throat like animals clearing an electrified fence.

Denise herded the children off. Used her umbrella like a cattle prod to get them out, away from the hospital, away from George.

George came home. In a cab. Denise didn't go for him. Denise watched from the front window, watched George disagreeing with the owner of the cab. The owner who'd brought him the long way round. She watched as George tore a door from the cab and hurled it across

Maude Street. She watched the frightened owner push the shift into drive and hit the accelerator. But not before George lurched into the cab and took hold of the owner's hair with both hands. The cab took off and George took the owner's scalp. As clean as a Red Indian with a tomahawk. And the scalp blood, a thin line of hot spots that bubbled and hissed on the molten tar of the road.

Denise saw the thick covering of red coarse hair as George undressed. A hide of red growing from his crotch, spreading in a thick fibrous growth up his belly. Reaching out thick red fingers toward his chest and throat.

And then she saw it, the thing between his legs and his inhuman eye on her. She almost fainted, but George took her. Threw her on the bed. Denise on all fours and that unmentionable huge thing. Over and over. He couldn't stop. And his harsh roar coming up out of the pit of his stomach.

Monday, Denise exhausted from climaxing. George was going in to see Henry Saunders, her boss. To explain she wouldn't be in. Denise should have dreaded it. Should have feared losing her job. Instead, vaguely waved the kids off to school. Closed her eyes and slept.

George scrabbled up the stairs of the chambers. His feet made a clip clop sound. People stared. Then the lift and the dreadful gamy smell, the smell of animals in a compound, made the nine-to-fivers gag.

Young, freshly-washed women, and men in three-piece pin-striped suits, lurched out of the lift. Headed for the nearest wash room. Stripped to the waist, scrubbed themselves with small caches of soap as best they could.

George Bull approached the reception desk. Empty, except for a brass bell with a button. George hit it, pushed it through the walnut veneer of the desk. The brass clang was a "sweet, uneasy sound" in the dim portals of eggshell blue.

The receptionist came. Turned up her nose. Got Henry Saunders in a hurry. George tried to explain about Denise and the hard times they'd had. But the words clogged like black pudding in his throat.

"No excuses, Mr. Bull!" said Henry. "Your wife's had many chances. I don't know why I've bothered with her. Why don't you people just go back to where you came from? You're not fit for city life. The country's for you."

The words, a red rag to George. A snorting anger steamed from his dilated nostrils. A strange, waxy, blood-drained expression came to Henry Saunder's face.

George charged, butting the sanctimonious solicitor out of the office, along a corridor and into a wall. Henry Saunders suffered internal injuries. And cuts and bruises later when the State Emergency Service cut him free from the wood and gyprock of the wall.

George left, but not before he fixed his rolling maverick eye on the receptionist. The young woman screamed. Then sat, mesmerized, flushed and strangely wet with a desire she didn't dare attempt to explain to herself.

But it was next door where George really went on the rampage — a branch of the bank that had raised the interest on the loan on the orchard.

George stood out the front shaking his head from side to side as though bothered by flies. His left foot pawed the pavement. And he charged. Right through the plate glass sliding doors. An explosion of glass that branded his hide with nicks of blood. George dismembered every teller booth, tore apart the long waiting counter. Scattered the down-at-heel customers. Stormed into the bank manager's office. Ransacked the files, the records. Found the deeds to mortgages. Torched them. Piled them in a bonfire in the middle of the bank.

Great glorious columns of flames that found the salmon carpet and crimson drapes. Spread as quickly as foreclosure. Until the bank was a furnace, staff and customers outside. Watching the building burn, explode like a tubercular lung. A shell of white-anted out flesh that crashed. Masonry, hot gobbets of brick and molten steel left the taste of vagrancy in every passersby's mouth.

George went back to work. Turned up at his old owner's place. The owner didn't dare refuse him a shift. George took the cab into the cooling twilight of the night shift. His eyes able to see in the congealing black. Clearly. Everything.

He smelled out the fares; smelled the sickly sweet stench of spirits on their breaths before they even saw the beacon of his vacant sign. Saw their drunken black jig-saw constructions in the dark. Pulled up right next to them.

They saw him, his red rolling eye glistening their blackness back at them. They all got in. No one refused. Well behaved. Mesmerized by the eye of George Bull in the black of the rear vision glass.

A final fare for George. One more before he went home to Denise. Denise waiting, lying awake for him.

The four men broke into his cab like thieves. He saw their mouths ajar and their words sliver like snakes.

"Stockton! Driver! No fuckin' worries. Get th' money when you get there. Put y' foot down too! Y' prick!! We wanna get there t'night. Not t'morra!"

Too drunk to notice George's rolling eye, the animal smell. The baiting continued. Until George stopped the cab on the crest of the Stockton Bridge. Orange lights threw bars of black across the cab.

The drunks, untimely ripped from the cab, before they made it home. Drunken protests, then the fear. As George, with Taurean stubbornness, unlatched the fearful fingers clutching the guard rail. Picked up each passenger, hurled them into the cold black air. Thin screams, the white, doughy faces of fear falling, the faint smell of shit, coming back up, on the way down. Four hard lard smacks of bags of bone and gristle and blood bursting on the Hunter River.

•

Six police marksmen shot George Bull dead. George had torn away the barbed wire fence of the Comm. Steel. Torn out of his house. Sick to death of the bell clanging of metal stopping his sleep.

George had torn away a whole corrugated iron panel of the mill, was heading for the operating platform when the bullets came. And the blood. The cement floor of the mill awash with it, more blood than one human body should hold.

George, taken away to the morgue. A postmortem by some curious doctors carved George up into steaks and chops and side cuts.

The media descended like crows after offal. Denise signed contracts, exclusive interviews and articles. Her life of fear with an animal. She took the money and ran, after the funeral.

Bought back the orchard on the Central Coast. Owned it outright with the new double-story brick bungalow she built on it.

In Mayfield, there were men who'd slipped, fallen into the blood of George Bull. Slid and slithered in the thick red on the mill floor of the Comm. Steel.

In Mayfield, the strident calls of shocked wives in orgasm filled the sulfur air. Clip clopping filled the early hours, and the wrenching of steel, the dismembering of the steel mills. The snorting of anger herding toward town.

LEAVING HOME

THE CHOPPER LURCHED IN THE GUT OF THE STORM. HE
held on with both hands to his stomach. Holding himself in order. The
clouds were black, clots of black like matter from an old wound. He
could taste it in the cabin of the helicopter — a creeping mist with
a metallic taste like the edge of the meat clever his wife waved about
when she lost her temper with him or the kids. The pilot reefed at the
controls, fought against the vacuuming spiral of air currents trying to
tear the news helicopter from out of the sky.

Five minutes before, it had all been clear — that azure Australian sky
of his infant years and "God Save the Queen," and the coastline with
its coastal villages in gemstone-cut definition. Villages ringed by gum
forest, squared off by the right angles of streets, a school of arts, the
lakes of red brick bungalows. Towns he'd seen a hundred times from
the air that passed under him with a predictable rhythm chopped into
time by the copter blades. A rhythm as predictable as his life: school,
university, a degree in English literature, a journalist's position on a
small daily, T.V. reporter, then marriage and the kids following on
behind to fill the rooms of the mock Spanish villa he and his wife had
purchased, almost paid off, in the bush of Kuring-Gai.

The storm had screwed around the helicopter in seconds, jolting in
from the ridges and escarpments of the Great Divide. So fast, he and
the pilot hadn't seen it coming. The way he hadn't seen the bush fire
coming that almost took his home only months ago. Only a taste of
smoke, a dice roll of red witches hats snapping two ridges away, but
then, the roller coaster of flame. Screaming down the gully, howling up
the ravine, taking the two houses on either side of his. His wife and two

kids sweating in the cellar, the paint blistered into great welts that came away later like peelings of burnt skin.

The fire unnerved him. He'd started imagining a house of his own, away from the bush, away from his wife and children and their strange distance from him. In his mind he'd dug the trenches for the foundations and single-handedly poured the cement. It was clear in his thoughts, the smell of the sweat as he hauled hundreds of bricks in by hand and mixed more cement, laid the supporting turrets of brick, the walls of the house rising in his mind's eye.

He looked down into the vortex — the spiral of cloud and wind and rain and the sickening white wash of light — a descent into Poe's "Maelstrom." But the fantasy house was the barrel to which he clung and hoped might float him free from the whirlpool. The whirlpool silence of his family who spun themselves around with a chaos of activity — the trivia of computer games, mini golf, *Hey Hey It's Saturday* — that barely involved him — even when he was at home.

He'd flown out of Sydney, north to Newcastle, a human interest story to pack out the thumbnail sketch news service of the early morning current affairs show. Something to go along with the tap dancing poodles, elephants that sang, men who played "Waltzing Matilda" on their teeth with their thumb nails. Something just before the hosts and weatherman fucked about pissing in each other's pockets. He'd hoped it was to be his last story.

He'd accepted a part-time job as a tutor of English literature at a Sydney University, a chance to finish his doctorate on Dickens. Until his wife exploded like the trees exploded into columns of flame in the bush fires. Not enough money to cover the expenses of her bridge night, the Tupperware parties, services on the Volvo. He threw in the chance. Stayed with television and his thirty minute spots, an "Idiot Wind" that blew among the blades of the chopper, blew between the buttons of his coat.

The story, the rate of suicide among males in Newcastle — twice the national average, five times as high as Sydney or any other capital city. Newcastle, just north of his villa, perched on the lip of sandstone. A view from his house into the smoky blue forests of the Great Divide, an opaque blue that swallowed him up when he got home. Spurs of bush rock and gum root he imagined clawing out the foundations of his family home, ripping through the floor boards, cocooning in spirals of wood and rock and leaf around his wife and children, taking them away from him.

He'd lapse back into fantasy. Go to work on the house in his mind. Cutting the wood of the floors and walls to size. Good solid hardwood frame, and the flat expanse of the floor, yellow and golden-grained like the reaping of a wheat harvest. And the walls rising in brick and the tiles of the roof he placed into position himself.

They were going down. He could see the sea, like the shiny green belly of a fly, bloat up toward the helicopter. A heavy sea swell coming up and above it all. Above the shriek of the wind and the jack hammering of hail against the glass was the sea-sound static as if to brush the salt water would incinerate the chopper, blast it into a dying star flame.

He looked sideways at the pilot, seasoned, but shitting razor blades, sweating blood, and his teeth gritted. Worn down horse's teeth with the breath and saliva hissing through the gaps like the sound of the sea hissing closer. The pilot looking for a place to land on the tidal rock platform. Just enough dry rock at the base of the cliff to put down the craft. He gagged as the pilot tilted them almost side on to fit between the rock of the cliff and the wave that lunged up out of the ocean at them. He gripped the arm rests, his hands knuckled ridge tents of taught, stretched skin and bone threatening to tear out of the flesh.

He tried to tighten his fortyish flab, to hold in his insides as the chopper righted itself, tried to stop his intestines from flying out in long snakes like the toy snakes in his daughter's plastic canister that flew out when you opened the lid.

Finally, he felt the dragonfly settle onto rock, but rock slippery with the green weed prized by fishermen who angled the platforms and ledges for elusive blackfish and the occasional drummer. Drummer that would drive back into the black fathoms taking a 1'0 suicide hook, half a reel of line and sometimes the footing of a rock fisherman.

Gingerly, he eased himself from the metal insect body of the helicopter, a blind, vulnerable pupae breaking out of the parent belly. He stumbled, up to his ankles in salt water. He saw his face in the water — haggard, white, and the grid reference of red veins in his cheeks, pinpointing evenings of sweet sherry and beer. Anything to escape the slamming car doors as his wife and kids went out. Almost every evening.

He locked his wobbly knees into place, willed himself to stand upright, felt the sponge clamp of his wet wool socks around his feet and ankles. And the cliffs, sheer rock around him, the same brown as the mock Spanish Villa, blocking out the faint pearl of sun with crypt darkness. He leaned an arm against the chopper, but felt it tilt, tremble, like the pin ball machine he'd bought his son. No games won.

The pilot walked out into the ocean. He could see him up to his waist in water, standing on the submerged edge of a tidal rock gutter, speaking into his mobile phone. As far away from the interference of the cliffs as possible. He watched him coming back to him. Pushing through the water, coming, not as a new thing baptized, but a scared shitless man suddenly old, suddenly near to retirement, his patch of tomatoes up the back yard and the rotting smell of his compost heap with its green tendrils of wild pumpkins easily tameable, easily controlled.

"It's alright mate," said the pilot. "I got through. There's help on the way. Fucked if I know what's going to happen to the chopper."

As if in answer, the sea curled into a sheet of dark green that raked out of the working fluid body, the unpredictable big wave that was always sure to come if you turned your back, if you felt secure knowing that help was on its way. The same way he'd felt when he thought he'd escaped the bush fire with his home still standing. Until his wife slammed the front door after another argument and the gyprocking of three rooms came away in an explosion of thick white plaster dust that settled like an aftermath on everyone and everything.

The chopper was gone like a fresh strip of mullet taken by a big flathead working its way back out to sea. Not a trace left, except for the faint indentations in sand soon washed away by the rising tide.

He huddled with the pilot under the overhang of cliff rock. And waited.

•

The police chopper dropped him on the roof of the TV station. With legs of jelly, he rode the elevator back down to the car park, willed himself behind the wheel, backed out of his spot, coffined by slabs of gray cement.

He crawled home in the city traffic, away from the scrapers and hectares of glass reflecting a thousand suns, orange and dying exhausted into the ocean off Sydney Harbor Heads. A clutter of cars and suburban shadows spilled over his face like acid. In the jam he stopped, took his eyes from the charcoal strip of tar.

Saw back down into laneways and easements, the dark outline of brick bungalows and units and subdivision flats, and villas pretending not to be flats. Saw the tendrils of smoke from chimneys, the pubic curlings of steam, saw the coagulation, the swamp of vapor.

And he thought of the home again to take him away from the swampland stretching away on either side of him.

He imagined the lounge room and the polished boards he fitted himself. He imagined the stain finish, a red mahogany French polished into a lustrous mirror, and he saw himself, clearly, in the grain of wood running without contradiction. He imagined the plaster he rendered into walls and the open fire and the grate he somehow made himself. A blacksmith with forge and bellows and hammer beating the metal to a curved shape to take the logs he would cut by hand. And, with great expectations, he imagined himself as the artisan molding the ornate plaster of the ceiling into configurations of angels and children — not his children, but new children, new souls, clean, with echoes of heaven in their eyes. Flying in every corner of every room.

He made it home. Pushed the car up the steep driveway with leaves and mud fanning out in hairline waves like watery fissures. The driveway, built across a natural water course. A death trap, having claimed two cars of his friends who'd slid sideways off the cement and jammed their Jags in a ravine far below.

He walked in the front door, breathless, ready to tell of his ordeal, a common ground of sympathy with his family. Almost taken by the storm, almost taken by the sea. He opened the door and heard the familiar sounds.

"I don't care, Geremy, we're not going to McDonald's" stated his wife.

"C'mon, Mum," whined Susan, their daughter.

"Yeah, Mum. We haven't done nothin' all holidays!" yelled Geremy.

They stopped. A cursory glance his way.

"I crashed today," he said. He made it sound as though he were trying to win show and tell at school.

"The storm almost got us. Had to put down near the sea. Almost drowned. Waves huge. The helicopter . . . " His voice trailed off, died like the turn of the tide of evening from silver to black.

They turned away.

"We wanna go to McDonalds!" chorused the children of his wife.

"Well, we're not going. And that's final. I've had a bad day," said his wife. "Dora Parkinson didn't turn up for bridge. Had to put up with that stupid Clare Summers for a partner!"

He walked away from them. For the last time.

The house in his mind was almost at the lock up stage. As he climbed the stairs to his bedroom, he began the finishing touches: the deck he built out from the lounge, away from the trees, with a clear view of the coastline. A river of wind washing through the heart of his new home.

And he saw himself adding a loft onto the pitched tile roof, a loft full of the books he hadn't read: Dickens, Shakespeare, Henry Miller, Cormac McCarthy. And racks of records his wife and children forbade him to play. Fifteen years since he'd heard the voice of Dylan creaking into the veins of his soul.

"Tolling for the outcast, burnin' constantly at stake
An' we gazed upon the chimes of freedom flashing."

He heard the chime of the wind above his head. Calling him. He threw his briefcase away on the bed, hauled off his striped shirt and tie. Put on his comfortable shorts, sun-faded to crisps of fabric, his wife always at him to throw them out. Pulled his favorite t-shirt over his head, slipped on his KT26 joggers broken open into banana shapes by age. Pulled away the man hole cover, some tiles, and stood on the roof.

He could see it, his home, floating just an arm's reach away. He jumped, caught hold of the terra cotta tiles he'd laid on the front steps. Heaved himself up and away from his family like a swimmer hauling himself from the baths after twenty hard laps.

He opened the cedar door he'd planed smooth and lacquered. Its red grain mirrored him, every feature clear and highlighted, even in the darkling air. He closed the door behind him.

And disappeared.

THE NARROWS BEACH

Inspired by a painting of the same title by
Australian painter William Dobell.

THE BOY WADED OUT THROUGH THE RUNNELS OF
water. Wind rushed across the lake, dropped dead, leaving the water
flat, unmarked, then springing into life again, making a maze of
markings on the water surface. A cross-hatching of wind stripes so the
boy seemed lost in an expanse of scars. Some ridged hard and white
butting against his body, others vague blemishes beneath the surface
dissolving around the boy's legs.

As he held the hand line, with the hook concealed by a ball of mullet
flesh and gut, blood from the bait spotted the water, the smell bringing
fish close to shore. Carefully the boy pulled back his arm, threw the
spools of line, the hook, the gut, the small sinker spinning across the
sky like web coming from the arse of a spider.

A wind spray of crimson came back like seeds in loams of air
turbulence, spattered the face of the boy, spotted the old cardigan
and gray trousers, stained his clothing with blood. But he had no
time to think about that, wiped his arm across his face, smeared the
blood across the cheekbones straining against the mask of taught
skin.

Quickly he retrieved the coils of line, slowing down when he felt
the slack taken up by the sinker, the weight of the mullet on the end of
the line. He continued pulling the line, keeping the bait on the move,
enticing the fish to strike at the bloody flesh hiding the steel hook.

He felt the pickers, the rubbish worrying the bait, not having a decent
go at the mullet, small jerks that ran like electric shocks up the line into

the hands of the boy. Behind him, in the house, built where the beach narrowed to a point of rock, his mother began to call him home.

The boy tried not to listen, but the woman's cries were like the harsh squabblings of the seagulls when they argued over the head and guts of a fish the boy had caught and cleaned.

Something bigger was at the bait, it was enough to bring the boy's concentration back to the line, ignore his mother, who was on the veranda calling him by the name she had him baptized by. Harder to ignore once she called him by his name rather than "boy" or "you."

"Jimmeeey, Jimmeeey! James Strong!"

But the heavy drag on the line kept the boy concentrating on the mysterious fish, more than interested in a feed of strip mullet and intestine with capillaries of blood and oil leaking into the water. The heavy drag on the end of the line persuaded two loops of line from the boy's delicate shell-curl of fingers. He let the line go.

Wondered what was on the end, had visions of a big leatherjacket with its periscope spike carving through the water. Saw the yellow and brown fans of the fins flick flicking, undulating sinuous movement as the fish pulled down heavily on the bait. The boy could see the mouth open, the teeth snaggle into the flesh, two or three lurching bites before the lot disappeared down the gorge of the fish with the hook taking hold in the gullet.

Ignoring the woman on the veranda, the boy walked a few steps out into the lake placing loops of line back onto his fingers. From the corner of his eye he could see the other house built on the shore of Narrows Beach. Not that you could call it a house — a ramshackle nail-and-tar cobbling together of second-hand boards and rusty tin plonked on pylons the shack's owner had scrounged off the beach when they were washed up in a big blow years ago.

Inside the shack the boy knew his grandfather was sitting, waiting for him to turn up before the boy went back home to his mother. Jimmy wondered, as two more spools of line were taken from him by the big fish, why his grandfather, his mother's father, waited every day for his grandson to come to him with a fish.

Jimmy knew his grandfather loved fish, any sort the boy happened to catch. But it wasn't as if the old man depended on his grandson for food every evening.

A sudden vicious side to side wrenching of the line told Jimmy the fish had struck. He pulled hard but the line went limp. Peering into the few feet of water, as he retrieved the line, the boy could see the hook trailing a few skerricks of ragged flesh and gut. Not far away, in deeper water, the big fish, whatever it was, was digesting a sizable chunk of bait. The last bit of bait the boy had until tomorrow.

The grandson would go empty handed to his grandfather. Although the old man would settle for steak and vegetables that night, it bothered Jimmy. It was important he turn up each evening to offer his grandfather the fish he'd caught for him. A ritual Jimmy and the old man never tired of.

"Oh, what a beauty, Jimmy. And yer say yer want me t' have it?" his grandfather would say every evening to the boy standing there with a pleased grin as wide as the circle of the bay that looped out of the closed cleft of Narrows Beach.

"Oh, I couldn't take such a beautiful fish from yer. Yer take it home to yer mum now," the old man would say.

"No, Grandad, you take it. It's for you," Jimmy would insist.

"Oh, I don't know. But if yer want me t' have then I'll just have t' take it," the old man would say.

He'd hold out both his hands solemnly, Jimmy would place the fish on the creased and cracked palms, his grandfather would hold it up to the last of the daylight, the scales sparkling like treasure found.

So to go empty handed to the old man was a disappointment so keen it hurt as badly as when Jimmy sliced his hand with his fishing knife when he was cleaning his catch one day last year. His mother had called him from the veranda and he'd lost his concentration crouched over a pile of fish on the sand.

As he pulled the line toward him, the scar across the back of his hand glowed whitely in the gloom of evening. The hook was a few feet from him when the whiting darted through the water and grabbed the last bits of bait. Nothing shy about whiting when they strike. The boy pulled in the fish, reached down into the water to his shins, took the whiting from the water. Held him up to the half disc of the sun on the horizon. A small cry of delight from Jimmy when he saw the unusual dark bottle green, the color of moss growing on rock, across the head, flecking the flanks of the fish.

Carefully, folding down the fan of dorsal spines with his hand, the boy placed the fish in the canvas fishing bag. Swung the bag over his shoulder. Left behind the lake to the night, set off down Narrows Beach toward his grandfather's shack.

But that meant passing the house where his mother was still standing on the veranda demanding his return.

"Jimmeeey, you come here now. Put away yer lines and bait and come inside fer tea. And if yer with yer grandfather come home this instant!"

The boy could see her. He stopped, ducked for cover into the thick stand of tea trees. Something he'd done before, hiding from her, but never convinced the wind-wobbling green and yellow shade cast by the crowns of the trees offered enough cover to keep him from the crow eye of his mother.

Holding his breath, he was convinced she could see into the tea trees, could see him crouched down, one hand against the side of the canvas fishing bag, feeling the bucks of the whiting still stroppy after so short a time out of the water.

His fear was because he could see her. If he could see her, then it made sense to him that she should be able to see him. It was like standing in the shallows of the lake fishing and seeing the fish a few feet in front of you. An old fisherman from Wangi Wangi told the boy that if you could see the fish then they could see you, and that made it nigh on bloody impossible to catch the buggers.

But his mother would catch him, he thought. Even if she couldn't see him, she would sense that he was there in the tea trees near where she was standing. He crept through the shaggy-barked trees, holding his breath as he passed so close to the veranda he could see the weathered strips of boards and flashes of the blue dress his mother was wearing.

"I can hear yer, Jimmy and I can see yer. Come out, I know yer in them trees," she demanded.

This had worked many times; the boy's bluff had been called. He'd come from under cover, go to the veranda where his mother smirked her grim satisfaction at him. Took the fish from him, placed it in the ice chest for tea that night. But he'd won a few times, stopped his ears with his hands, kept walking the way he did now.

Bent over like a soldier in no-man's land he was, seeking the comfort of a trench and a cup of tea. Burst from the far end of the copse of tea trees, ran across the sand littered with shell and seaweed. Saw his grandfather standing on his veranda, the big grin splitting open his water chestnut face.

The complicity between the two was a triumph whenever the boy managed to get to his grandfather's shack under fire of his mother's words. Taking the whiting from the bag, Jimmy approached the veranda where his grandfather waited with the words the boy loved to hear, the gestures the boy loved to witness.

At the edge of the copse of tea trees lay an ancient boat with a cabin, the timbers stove in by the elements and by boys with nothing better to do than throw rocks at the old vessel. Broken port windows gaped, the deck boards, long sprung, stuck out like tongues gossiping. Its bow was half buried in the sand, tears of grease and salt wept from the bow boards.

Jimmy could see it when he woke of a morning and looked through his bedroom window; it was usually the first thing he saw. Because he'd rather sit up in bed and look through the window than venture out into the kitchen where his mother would be waiting with breakfast and a lecture on what he should and shouldn't do for that day.

The boy knew the boat belonged to his grandfather; he knew it had been beached on Narrows Beach for years, had lain there for as long as anyone from Wangi Wangi could remember. As he sat up in bed, with the westerly wind whistling off the water, Jimmy would wonder about the boat and why no one would tell him about it.

He'd asked his mother about it, saw her mouth knit into a higgledy piggledy fence paling line of displeasure, saw her thump the saucepan of porridge on the gas ring, the slurp of gray sludge fly through the air slopping on the floorboards. His mother grimly wiping up the mess, then turning on him.

"Don't yer ever mention that boat within my hearing again if yer know what's good for yer! Now eat yer breakfast and get t' school so I don't have to lay eyes on yer," she said.

He went to school with a flea in his ear and never mentioned the boat again to his mother. But that didn't stop him asking about it around Wangi Wangi, inquiring of old men who sat out the front of the pub in the main street. But there was nothing to be told as far as they were concerned, although the boy could not help but notice the peculiar side-long looks they gave each other when he asked them about the boat. And the uncomfortable shifting of their prodigious rumps on the wood of the bench.

•

When Jimmy sat in the kitchen waiting for the porridge to be ready, he glanced at his mother from the corner of his eyes. Didn't dare look at her directly because he knew it would send her off. Something he'd recently discovered — his mother's displeasure at being looked at directly.

An accident that happened when Jimmy cut himself with the knife when he was cleaning the fish and she distracted him with her yell. An anger welled up in him as strongly as the blood welled from the wound across the back of his hand. For the first time, James Strong experienced anger, a white, hot fury at the stupidity of the accident. He didn't mind the blood, the pain. He didn't mind the thick scar that would be there, but he did mind how unnecessary it was, particularly when his mother could see him clearly from the veranda.

His mother had no reason to yell like that other than she'd done it for years to see him jump with fright. A small amusement for her, although to hear her laugh after he'd jumped with fright, you'd have thought it was the pleasure of her life.

But it had been different that day. He'd flung the fish he was cleaning from him, marched up to the veranda, held up his bleeding hand, looked straight at her. The smirk vanished from her mouth, he saw her shift uneasily from foot to foot, saw her look away from his direct look. And then the anger flared.

"Don't yer look at me that way, boy! Get away from the veranda with that hand. It's leavin' blood all over th' place!" she tiraded.

But much to his amazement, as well as his mother's, he stood his ground, thrust his hand over the railing and let the crimson drop all over the bare boards that thirstily drank his blood. His mother backed away, he kept his eye upon her, and she couldn't look at him, let herself into the kitchen from the veranda and yelled at him from behind the cover of the salt-encrusted lace curtains.

"Don't yer look at me that way, James Strong! Keep away and if yer think I'm goin' to spend money on getting' yer an ambulance yer mistaken!"

He left her hiding in the house, walked along the beach knowing she would watch him as he headed for his grandfather's shack. And it was as though the boy's grandfather knew about the cut, sensed the pain. He could not have known from his daughter's yelling because the old man was almost deaf.

He was standing on the veranda of his shack, holding the finest piece of fishing line he could find and a long thin needle. No words were necessary as the boy tramped up the steps holding his good hand under the wounded one, trying to stop the blood falling on the boards.

Quickly the old man went to work washing the wound with sunlight soap and hot water, then dabbing some methylated spirits onto it with a wad of cotton wool, the boy gritting his teeth, holding back the cries of pain. Knowing his grandfather was doing it for his good to kill any infection that might be there from the guts of the fish, the salt, the knife blade, the sand.

A cross-hatching of line stitching so fine, in the hand, the boy could hardly see it. Small beads of blood peeped from the line of the flaps of flesh sewn together. But they soon dried, the — small knobs of blood, the fine line, stopping any more bleeding.

Jimmy didn't go home that night for tea. For the first time in his life he stayed with his grandfather while the old man placed the black iron frying pan on the wood fuel stove. Lumped a knob of butter, a glug olive oil and a squeeze of lemon into the metal, threw in two good-sized bream. That sizzled so the silver skin curled away from the clean white flesh.

James Strong and his grandfather sat on the veranda with the southerly buster bustling up the coast from Sydney, cutting away the heavy heat of the day, wetting the old man and the boy with fine salt spray from Lake Macquarie as they forked the fish into their mouths. Nothing to say to each other while there was flesh to be found on the fish bones.

No words, only a shared smile when the boy's mother started calling him home and the two ignored the sound, kept feeding themselves while the wind howled louder than the woman on the veranda of the house not far away.

•

As the coffin was lowered into the earth of the cemetery in the bush on the western side of Lake Macquarie, he looked at the woman, but he could only see relief in her features. It wasn't what he expected to see. Maybe, he thought, she would find some tears for her own father. But there was no mistaking the brow clean of lines of care, the suspicion of the mouth corners about to turn upward.

Anger furnaced in him and he looked straight at her, her eyes were turned down but he knew the force of his eyes would make her look at him. And she did, glancing up, his eyes hooking her as securely as a big silver hook in the gills of a fish. She couldn't look away from her son and he punished her, made her squirm like an eel wrapping itself tighter in coils of unbreakable fishing line.

James Strong stood on the opposite side to his mother as the diggers began to fill the hole with earth. He kept the line of his look taught; no slack was offered to the woman. And he began to draw her toward him; she could not help it, she had no control. Stumbling in the mound of dug earth she tottered toward the open grave, small dolly steps, closer to the edge. Until the man, standing beside her, a distant relation of Jimmy's grandfather, come from Perth for the funeral, took the woman by the arm, pulled her back from the edge.

Later, in the afternoon, after the funeral, after the relations had come and gone from the house in Narrows Beach, the boy, almost an adult now, went down to the wreck of the boat. Lashing chains and the ropes of pulleys around the hull of the boat, he attached the other ends to the underpinnings of his mother's house.

Bent over double he began to wind the pulleys, grind the winch, the boards of the old boat protesting almost as loudly as his mother when she came onto the veranda and saw what he was doing.

"What in God's name do yer think yer doin'?!" she demanded.

But he ignored her, kept winding the ropes and chains, saw the hull move slightly in the burial of years of onshore wind drifts of sand, heard the hull groan like a man in pain. Kept winding until the hull rose a few inches free of the sand; salt water, grease dripping from the green and gray sludgy bottom of the boat.

"Leave it alone. Don't yer do it!" his mother protested.

Beneath her feet she could feel the pylons, some of wood, some of bricks and mortar, move, quiver under the weight of her father's boat being drawn from the sand of Narrows Beach. She was scared the weight of the vessel would break the pylons that kept her house above the sand and salt water of Lake Macquarie. But she was more scared of whatever had made her son, James Strong, decide to raise the wreck. Afraid of what someone might have told him about the boat and his grandfather still warm in his coffin in the grave not too far away.

Her son left the ropes and chains attached during the night, ready for him to continue the next day. His mother lay in her bed feeling the taught lines of rope and metal underneath her humming like the gut strings of a violin. So when she arose next morning, she was dog tired, too worn out from lack of sleep and fear to berate her son like she usually did every morning.

Over many days, James Strong pulled, pushed, persuaded the old boat out of her sandy grave up the slight slope of beach until she rested only a few feet from the veranda of his mother's house. Placed on trusses of wood, the boat was left to dry in the scorching sun of summer. The boy and his mother could hear the grain drying, the soft whimper of wood as the moisture was taken from it by the heat.

It just about drove the woman mad having the boat of her father sitting there right in front of her house, the hull blocking her view of Lake Macquarie, the sound of its timbers haunting her day and night. And her son drove her to stay inside nearly all of the time now because he spent all of his time working on restoring his grandfather's boat.

Every hour was spent replacing some of the boards of the hull that were beyond repair, the sound of hammering filled the quiet, still air of Narrows Beach, it filled the head of the woman sitting wan faced at the kitchen table.

As he worked, James Strong remembered the words of the distant relation of his grandfather from Perth, the story the old man told him at the wake. How James' mother gave birth to him out of wedlock and almost immediately gave him up to the father to take away. Because she wanted nothing to do with the baby and nothing to do with the shame of being a mother out of wedlock in a close community like Wangi Wangi.

The boy learned how his grandfather went after the man, another fisherman, who sailed toward the opening in Lake Macquarie hoping to reach the sea and take his son from his grandfather, north to Queensland, before the old man found out.

Jimmy's grandfather pursued the father, sailing the boat Jimmy was restoring. It had been a long, slow but vicious struggle when Jimmy's grandfather sighted the boat and boarded her before it reached the open ocean. Badly cut by a rusty blade, the grandfather took the baby in his arms onto his boat and sailed back toward Narrows Beach.

Faint from the loss of blood, the man, old then, struggled to keep from passing into blackness. An alignment of the planets caused a huge king tide to rise, the swell of water in the lake finally taking control from the old man. The vessel taken high into the air by the tide, the old man on his knees on the deck holding the bundle squawking protest. The tide falling as quickly as it rose, dumping the boat into the sand of Narrows Beach where it sat for years.

As he worked on the boat, James could see his grandfather crawling up the beach holding him in the crook of one arm, his grandfather's blood baptizing the tight red and wrinkled ball of his face until the old man reached the cottage and presented the child to his daughter.

•

Under the brightness of daylight, the boy, almost a man, rubs linseed oil into the finished timbers, the boat glows like a fish in a clear fathom of water.

MARIA

*Inspired by a photograph by Eugène Atget
titled* Streetwalker Waiting for a Client.

MARIA SITS ON THE HARD WOODEN STOOL LIKE A penitent. She shifts her ample rump back and forth so the splinters, the hollows, and bumps of the stool rub and make her sore. It is her secret, something she would never tell anyone, let alone her husband, Anthony. She tries to punish herself because she feels guilty. She should be happy or at least halfway content, she thinks, but there is something missing, she feels, when she gets out of bed every morning.

Anthony is always gone, leaving her hours before the dawn to start his toil in one of the fruit and vegetable markets at the foot of the Montmartre butte. There, in freezing darkness, Maria knows, he carts boxes of produce, and when he gets home, his hands are torn and bloodied.

Often she spends an hour or more with a needle ministering to his wounds. She places the tarnished tip of the fine steel in the bright yellow of a candle flame, then prizes out the splinters Anthony picks up from the wooden boxes.

This she enjoys, the closeness as she holds his hand still, bending over it like a palm reader, carefully coaxing out the splinters, feeling his body heat so that by the time she is finished, she is wet and ready for all of him. And, sometimes, he gives some of himself to her.

But it is the loneliness, she knows, that makes her feel discontented; the hours of the day grind by like the cart wheels of the rag-and-bone merchants that pass at the end of the alley. Maria sees them when she sits outside the small, narrow, brick apartment. She would like to go out into the sunlight of the main road and talk to the merchants of secondhand rags and clothes, but she knows this would be taken amiss, taken the wrong way; she would be seen as nothing better than one of the washer women and seamstresses of Paris, women who often resort to part-time prostitution when times are tough, when there are no clothes of rich clients to wash or sew.

So now she sits on the stool, moving her generous weight back and forth, wondering whether she might end up with splinters like her husband. She wonders what it would be like to lie face down on a bed, have someone pull up her black calico skirt, slip down her lace-lined knickers, and gently prize out splinters from the full moon crescents of her bum, gently caressing her flesh.

She blushes, the bright red blood dim in the shadows cast by the buildings of the alley. The brick and wooden tenements beetle over the narrow cobblestone path. Maria is ashamed of thinking such thoughts, and she drives them from her mind by standing, walking up and down the serpentine alley, but not for long because this, she knows, might be taken the wrong way as well.

Just the other day, a middle-aged man stopped at the end of the alley. He'd gotten a glimpse of her sitting in the light and shade and stopped, walked right up to her. He was well-dressed, sporting a collar and tie, wearing a silk jacket and patent leather shoes. Without hesitating, without embarrassment, he'd asked Maria how much.

It took her a few seconds to understand he thought that she was on the game. She jumped up in horror, overturning the wooden stool and rushed back inside, slamming shut the apartment door, hiding on the other side, breathing hard, sweating as heavily as one of the draft horses that plod up and down the main road pulling carts loaded with wares of all kinds, leaving monstrous piles of steaming green shit on the cobblestones.

But, despite herself, she peeked around the edge of the door and saw the man righting her stool. He turned and tipped his hat to her evidently aware of his mistake. He murmured words of apology, and Maria felt sorry because of her reaction. Overcoming her shyness, she'd stepped out before he reached the end of the alley. He turned and looked, waved to her, and she returned his acknowledgment of remorse with the smallest of smiles that opened her full lips, revealing two even rows of perfect pearl-white teeth.

The man hesitated when he saw her smile, not because he thought she wanted him to return and offer her money, but because her smile, her teeth, made him pause. She understood he was showing appreciation for her beauty, something she rarely considers. She's always thought of herself as plain, and Anthony has never commented on her body or her face, never remarked on the sound of her voice. Her voice is her one vanity. She regards it as melodious, even soothing, but her husband seems never to notice, or, if he has, does not consider it worthy of commenting upon.

The woman tells herself again she should be happy with her lot. She has a roof over her head, her husband works hard putting food on the table, there are enough sous for Maria to buy stockings and clothes from the secondhand shop in the next arrondissement. And there is chicory coffee every morning and, sometimes, the luxury of hot rolls and croissants if she is prepared to venture out of the alley darkness and walk the distance to the bakers halfway up the Rue Lepic in Montmartre.

She should be happy and grateful for a man who goes to work six days a week, slaving to keep her, and then takes her up the Montmartre hill on Sunday to worship at the Sacred Heart church. Such a good man, Maria thinks, the way he sits in church, his head bowed, his eyes squeezed shut, trembling and perspiring, in awe of God. Maria sits back down on the stool, peers out into the giant glare of day at the end of the alley.

She thinks about their meeting, how Anthony appeared one morning out the front of her parents' cottage in the French countryside north of Paris. Her mother and father had been murdered by the Prussians during the Franco-Prussian war; their daughter had escaped by hiding in the woods for three days and three nights. After the regiment of Prussians had wreaked their bloody violence and left, Maria ventured from the snow-covered fir forest to the cottage. But she was lost, did not know how to fend for herself until Anthony came along and almost, it seemed to the woman later as an afterthought on his part, took her in hand.

She followed the man, ten years her senior, up hill and down dale, over mountains, across streams and rivers. He told her he was going to Paris and she could come along if she liked. Strange, she thinks now as the strident hungry cries of merchants along the main street reach her, Anthony always seemed lukewarm, almost indifferent to her presence. He had never been driven to keep her by his side. He had never been helpless with desire for her, let alone love her with mindless elemental abandonment.

But she'd had no choice and followed him into the capital, and when he suggested in a flat, indifferent voice that they get married so as not to cause a scandal, she agreed mostly out of habit of agreeing to everything he suggested; after all, by that time she felt only Anthony could guide her to some sort of safety and survival.

Her husband remains a mystery to her; she does not know anything about his past, his parents, or where he came from. He just turned up that day, surveying the smoking ruins of the cottage, his face devoid of emotion, finding a shovel and digging graves for Maria's parents. He said nothing to the young woman, weeping uncontrollably beside the two empty holes in the clay earth. The stranger just kept digging and dumped the bodies into the openings like the sacks of flour that are unloaded by rough and rude laborers from ships berthed at the quaysides built along the banks of the Seine.

Maria sits uneasily on the stool. She tries not to think of her parents, tells herself, as she does many times every day, that times have changed, she cannot go back to live where she came from, she will never see her mother and father again. She gives herself a good talking to, admonishing herself for being sentimental, telling herself she must be more like Anthony who seems to take all setbacks in his stride as if hard times, tragedy, and death don't exist.

The man is impervious to trouble. As long as he can come and go from the alley each day, as long as there are boxes of vegetables and fruit to be shifted, as long as Maria has a hot meal on the table for him when he comes home late at night, then he will put up with the worst privations, the mocking cries of the street urchins that follow him whenever he ventures out from the alley, the poor wages he gets from the market owners, the splinters in flesh, the sometimes sprained ankles and broken fingers.

But it is this automaton-like quality of her husband that worries Maria, and over past days, she has come to link it with her loneliness. Anthony's resolute attitude toward this hand-to-mouth life, his refusal to acknowledge pain, is connected to and contradicts the softness of Maria's feelings as she sits now, wiling away yet another day by herself, her full figure stained with the shadows of light and shade.

The man who offered her money showed more personal consideration to her than Anthony ever has, she knows, now. The man's apology, his appreciation of her beauty before he vanished into the river of humanity coursing along the main road, struck every nerve in Maria, pared the endings until they were raw and tingling for days after the incident. And the man righting her stool, she thinks was like him righting her after she'd fallen over in the alley, and he'd come to her, reached out a hand, and helped her to her feet.

The restlessness is too much for her; it itches and bites and nips at her soul. She gets up from the stool and marches up and down the alley, her long, black, lace-up leather boots squeaking and squealing like the rats at night. Maria often lays awake, listening to them rushing and scuttling along the alley while Anthony, oblivious, slumbers deeply like a man buried beneath six feet of conglomerate rock and clay.

Now she walks to the end of the alley, something she hardly ever does. She peers out of the dark into the explosion of daylight. Gingerly, almost fearing some sort of injury, half convinced that if she goes further a cart will rush by, knocking her head from her shoulders, she pokes her head into the light. It is too bright, her alley eyes are unused to the dazzle and her ears are assaulted by the rush and bustle of commerce.

Her head floats outside of the sea of alley black as though it has in fact been severed from her body. But then the sights, the sounds, and smells of Paris in this arrondissement filter into her body, awaken it, seep down deep like rain water on dry ground.

But she can go no further. Maria is convinced that if she steps out onto the main road she will never see Anthony again. The carts, the milling throngs of people, the horses and merchants will sweep her away through the streets of Paris where she will eventually be cast into the Seine to drown. She pictures herself, her body washed up on one of the mud banks, her naked and dead form, arched and open, gawked at by strangers standing on the embankment. There is an inkling of arousal in the thought, and it makes her wet, a little, makes her take the step into the diamond-cut light.

It is like escaping a dreadful dream. She turns back and looks at the narrow corridor of darkness, and she can barely see the stool and the door that leads into the apartment. The street lays claim to her, she turns her back on the alley, moves her sensuous weight from hip to hip and back, feels her nipples harden, and, for one mad moment, wonders what the men walking and talking up and down the street would think of them if she undid her blouse and showed them those tight pink buds.

Anthony ignores them as if they don't exist. Maria has made roundabout suggestions that she would like him to lick and suck her nipples, but he doesn't catch on, or if he does he cannot seem to be bothered to take up her proposal. Their couplings are like his attitude to a hard life — resigned, predictable, something to be done out of duty because it cannot be escaped.

Carefully, balancing herself on her high heel boots, she totters along the cobblestones like a child freed of its mother for the first time, fearful but thrilled. At first, Maria stares straight ahead, scared to look in any other direction lest someone takes her to task for doing it and demands to know what she is doing out of her alley when she should know her rightful place and stay on her stool tattooed by light and dark.

Worse, she imagines Anthony returning home early from work, for some reason, and discovering her out and about, not sitting out the front of the apartment the way she always does when he arrives. Not that he would say anything, he rarely speaks; his cold looks are enough to cower his wife, keep her in check.

There isn't ever anything malicious in his glance that slides off her as quickly as oil on water. There is no fire of anger blazing in his eyes, but that is worse, she thinks. His agate-cold eyes seem incapable of expressing feelings of any kind. She wonders why he is like that, but it is beyond her, and besides, the big glass windows, showing the wares of shopkeepers, now divert her.

Up and down the pavement, growing in confidence, the woman walks, looking into every shop window, taking in the silk and woolen clothes, the scarves, the displays of precious stones, the array of boots and shoes lined in one shop window, the leather gleaming as shiny as the wet hide of a seal. It is almost too much — this treasure trove of things, all the goods and chattels of the world it seems to Maria, and she almost goes back to the alley.

But she becomes aware that no one pays her any close attention. It is the safety of anonymity that keeps her walking and looking. People pass her without saying anything. Some women nod politely, some men smile with appreciation at her, but no one stops and tries to do her harm with fists or words. Her confidence grows even more, and she crosses the threshold of a scarf shop.

In an instant, the young woman assistant is next to her.

"Would Madam like to try one of our scarves?"

Maria barely suppresses a small squeal. She isn't shocked by the girl's sudden appearance, she is taken aback by the very idea that someone should offer to help her try on scarves. It is almost unthinkable to Maria that she should be treated like a Parisian and made to feel welcome.

"Why, yes, I would like that," she replies.

The woman disappears and returns with a dozen scarves all long and silken or woolen and of all the colors of the rainbow that sometimes arches over the Seine after a spring downpour. The assistant patiently helps Maria try on each scarf. The customer thinks she will lose patience and order her from the shop, but that does not happen. Maria likes all of them, but in the end chooses one long purple silk scarf with embroidery of silver threads running in fine steams through the gossamer weave.

Panicking, Maria realizes she hasn't any money. It is back in the apartment. Fearfully she asks the girl how much.

"To you, Madam, a new customer, only two sous."

"I have the money in my apartment. It is only minutes away. Would you mind holding the scarf for me while I fetch the money?"

"Not at all, Madam, I will place it under the counter until you return."

Maria tries not to sprint from the shop in an unladylike manner. She is in the alley, up the stairs and back out with the money in a mere stitch of time. No matter it is part of the money Anthony gave her to buy food. She returns, the money is handed over, and she waltzes from the shop with the scarf wrapped around her neck. She turns before she walks away, and the shop assistant smiles and waves to her; Maria waves and smiles in return.

She breathes a sigh of relief and continues her adventures along the main street, almost forgetting the time, remembering at the last minute that her husband is due home. She rushes back breathless but manages to throw together a hot meal, and she is there on her stool when he turns into the alley and trudges like a defeated soldier toward her.

Maria ventures further each day. It is difficult to think of Anthony working hard in the markets when there is so much to see outside of the alley. She has hidden the purple scarf in the bottom drawer of the bureau so her husband will not see it. She imagines him livid with rage should he find that she spent some of the housekeeping money on a scarf. But, then again, she thinks, maybe that would be a good thing to see Anthony lose control, to see his cold eyes aflame with passion about something.

She is lost now in the sights and sounds of the street, she sits outside a café and slowly drinks black coffee in a fine porcelain cup. She inspects the strange paintings hung outside the café and lining the walls inside. Smudges and puffs of colors, not clearly delineating the subject the artist was attempting to commit to canvas. But Maria likes the paintings, all of them. They are like looking at something quickly, not seeing it clearly, but still holding, retaining the impression of the glance, understanding the smudging of the experience.

And after, as she walks away from the café, from the corner of her eye she spies a blotch of black, bustling along the pavement on the other side of the road. Maria thinks the woman, if it is a woman, was looking at her, but then the bent figure hobbles down a side street and is gone.

But Maria continues to see her nearly every day. She cannot focus the woman so she cannot tell what she looks like or if she is in fact following her as Maria thinks. The woman is an imp, something strange and unknowable that has escaped from a bottle after someone negligently left the cork out of the top, thinks Maria.

And with the coming of the hunched woman in black has come a change in Anthony — small, almost imperceptible, but it is there, Maria knows. He is uneasy sitting at the table in the apartment, eating his meals. He looks around constantly, usually behind him as if he is expecting someone to be there, as if he feels as though someone is following him, stalking him, but he cannot catch them at it.

For the first time, Maria sees her husband's face change from one similar to the blank stone visages of the gargoyles atop some of the buildings of Paris to one that expresses fear. She tries to tell herself that any emotion on his face is something, but she cannot convince herself, and she sits each night watching him carefully, seeing alarm, anger, and anguish play across his features. She copies him, looking behind where he is sitting, trying to find the person, the thing, that seems to be haunting her husband.

One day he stays at home. He tells Maria he is too tired to go to work, he needs rest and lies down, closes his tormented eyes. Maria knows this is not true. She sees his long, lanky, raw bone form nestled into the feather mattress. It is a body older than her body, but she knows it is capable of tremendous feats of strength and endurance. The man is crippled by something inside of himself, she realizes, something she feels that may have been brought into play by the presence of the black gnome of a woman who dogs Maria's footsteps whenever she leaves the alley to walk the main street of light and life.

Exasperated, Maria goes outside, stands thinking, and then sees the old woman bent over at the end of the alley, the blaze of daylight revealing her sandstone escarpment features clearly. Maria leaps into life, the woman is off, disappearing into the throng of people, but the younger woman is swift, and before the old woman can disappear once more, Maria grabs her by the arm, forces her against the plate glass window of a shop, demanding to know what the old crone wants, why she is following her all of the time.

The hard mica eyes regard Maria with interest. But the woman refuses to speak.

"Come now, Madam, I want you to tell me. I think you have something to do with my Anthony," says Maria, relaxing her grip a little.

The sound of her speaking Anthony's name is a noose around the old woman's neck pulled tightly. Her head jolts backward and up. The expression of resignation on her face tells Maria she is about to speak.

"I . . . I . . . am his grand aunt, Madam Stephanie," the woman whispers as if the fact is a blemish, something to be ashamed of.

"So, Madam Stephanie, if you are related to my husband, why not come and see him, us? You would be welcome, you know."

"No, you do not understand, Madam, I would not be welcome, he would not be pleased to see me at all."

"Well, please explain to me why not."

"Because I am all he has left. I came here just to see him once because he is all I have left. But when I saw him, I wanted to see him more times and you too, because you are married to him so you have become my family as well. Only you and him I have left now."

"But go on, Madam, you puzzle me, you would be most welcomed by him, but you seem to think otherwise."

The woman is a dam finally breached.

"The Prussians during the war killed all of Anthony's family, his mother and father, his brothers, his little sister, and all of his cousins, close and far. The soldiers were like mad locusts, feasting on blood and flesh. Anthony returned from the fields where he had been plowing to find the slaughter laid out before him. But it was some of the soldiers eating the flesh of his little sister that drove him completely mad. I had been hiding in a cellar on the edge of the town and came upon him when he found the bodies. It drove him insane losing everyone except me, but it was his sister, parts of her sliced from her body, cooked on a camp fire, and then eaten that drove the poor boy over the edge. I tried to reason with him, get him to stay with me, but he looked right through me the same way he looks through you at times as if you are not there. He walked away and kept walking. I have traipsed the countryside looking for him and decided to try Paris as a last resort. Only by accident did I see him one day emerge from the alley. I follow him to work, often, but I dare not approach him because my appearance might remind him of his terrible loss, and that might well drive him further into his darkness. I am astonished he has managed to find and keep a job and marry as well."

Maria takes the woman to the café. There they sit and drink black coffee.

"Now I have come to know you a little, I can see that the boy is in good hands. I cannot help him only hinder him if I approach him. I must leave him to you, Maria," Madam Stephanie says.

"But what will happen to you?"

"I still have my home in the country and there is a weekly allowance, a small trust, from my parents. I will not starve or perish from exposure to the elements. Now, Maria, I wish you luck, but I must go. There is a coach and horses leaving within the hour, and if I walk quickly, I will get a seat," the woman says.

She rises, shakes hands with Maria, kisses her on both cheeks, then is gone.

•

Maria sits by the bed and tells him stories about her childhood. Her voice is low and smooth and gravelly. Hour after hour she speaks to him of her childhood, her life with her parents; what it was like to witness the seasons passing, the sowing and harvesting of crops; her father digging a well, the triumph of cold clean water seeping through layers of earth, finding a place at the bottom of the deep cylinder of clay, her father gathering the first of it in a wooden bucket, hauling it up into the daylight, splashing his wife and daughter with handfuls as though baptizing them.

She tells him stories in between her time working in a clothes shop in the main street. Maria comes and goes between the apartment and the shop. She sells clothes effortlessly, and the owner is overcome with admiration for her new assistant, allowing her time away from the shop to dash back home to check on her husband.

The security of the small wage from the dress shop allows Maria to concentrate on Anthony. Now she sits close to him, still telling him stories, and for the first time, she sees his eyes flutter, he turns his head and looks directly at her, smiles. She is astonished after weeks of her husband lying in such a deep torpor, but she does not let it show. Her low and pleasing voice continues.

Unbuttoning her skirt, her blouse, she slips out of her clothes. She sits on the stool in only her knickers, the purple scarf wrapped around her long, white swan's neck. Her nipples are hard. She looks at Anthony looking at them. Maria leans forward, lets him take one in his mouth, feels herself wet like a new mother suckling a baby. She cradles his head with one strong arm holding him close. His hands reach up from the mattress, taking hold of both her breasts.

Maria rubs her hands up and down his back, feeling every knob of backbone, finding the heart beating in his chest, searching for him, finding him in his tears, her tears, their tears that fall.

DARKNESS IN THE FIRE

Dulcie turned her body against the storm barreling in off the ocean. The wind screaming the long plaintive wails of the white cockatoos, skittling across the sand and gorse and scrub of Smelleders Beach. Gravel rain tearing into her face, white flesh fast turning to brown hide under an elemental onslaught. And the sea heaving into muscled hillocks, rolling on top of each other into collapsing arches of black water shot through with lace lines of yellow scum.

Dulcie turned. Faced it. Felt the fury dancing before her, passing into the black of her eyes like a pure stream of fluxed metal the copper works wrought from dull ore not far away. She felt the noise, the yell of wind and surf unwinding, untying the river-twisted sinews inside her. Straightening them into long lines like the swash of surf, hissing like unleashed electricity over the sand.

She felt the wind pull back her hair like an attendant lover tying back the long and ragged locks. Laying bare, sculpting free the face. A structure of bone howling like a fire through the starved skin mask face. And she tasted the salt splitting the corners of her mouth into deep callused gullies.

The wind fire shrouded her dress around her spare frame — a filament of fabric melted into her form. The wind, the storm cold, brutal at her breasts. Breasts no longer full but eroded down by the months she'd scraped body and soul together at Glenrock. Left in widowhood to face the empty gaunt country that bled away in black seams of bush and rock. Like the seams of coal her husband had mined before the gas stink erupted into flame and wooshed in a long crimson vein through the tunnels. Burned Dulcie's husband to an empty smoking cicada shell melted to the wood of a pit prop. His body rattling in the vacuum after the fire had passed.

And she could see the black rags of crows torn in the storm, the mournful cries slanting off over the hill, creaking whispers that would haunt down the plain of the Glebe and perhaps find the ears of miners at tables with their wives and children and the Sunday roast.

Dulcie watched the black wings spread then crumple like bed sheets in the wind: wings carved from earth-core rock, arched, curved in bell-shaped fiber and gristle, blood and feather. They turned their yellow eyes on her, opened the gorge of their throats and twisted her in the mesh of their cries. Crows, the souls of the dead miners burned black by fire; souls risen, but a forlorn flock unable to fit themselves into the channels of the wind, which might take them away to another place. Of silence. Of stillness.

Dulcie turned her back. Struggled through the soft sand of high tide. Along Smelleders Beach, past the flat sleeping eye of Glenrock Lagoon. She toiled up through the moonscape of sand hills. Felt the blades of sand grass sharp and sometimes cutting her soles if she placed a foot at the wrong angle into the grit. A long ghostly journey over the nightmare scape; a stretch of sand that might see her lost. Stumbling for an hour or more before she finally sighted the rock face of the cliff and the black orifice opening of the cave.

A long and lost journey, sometimes, to find the white faces of Susanna and Michael peering out of the earth that was their home. Dulcie would hear their cries, no longer human, but the shrill cries of the gulls swooping down at low tide to peck and squabble over fish or the carcass of one of their own.

Dulcie watched her children — rickety scarecrow creatures, but as fast as foxes, stealing across the sand, their face skin drawn back into hideous perpetual grins and the fire flickers of their tongues between their teeth. Tricksters both of them; Michael with his whining wheedling that lowered Dulcie's guard. Sometimes. And he'd be off, away from her with the rabbit or fish she'd caught. Gorge it all for himself, then come back, turn on the tears, crave forgiveness. Crave the touch of his mother.

Susanna, different. The same. A will-o-the-wisp in and out of her mother's skirts. Untouched. As though Dulcie could never hold her to account when Susanna refused to do her share of the work. Susanna happy to hang upside down from a branch of a gum fifty feet up and draw a crowd of refugees from the tents to look at her. Refugees, once miners and their families. The men out of work in 1894 because of the strikes and the colliery owners digging in their toes.

Dulcie didn't make the cave before her children were upon her, around her heels, her legs, like snapping dogs.

"What've yer got, Mumma? Let us see!"

"Yes, Mumma! We wanna see! Now!! We're hungry!"

"And we're sick of waiting!!"

They leaped up. Dulcie jerked back her head, half expecting them to sink their sharp triangular infant teeth into her throat, slake their thirst, their hunger, with her blood, her salty flesh.

Dulcie gave up the handfuls of pipis she'd harvested from the rock shelves along Smelleders Beach. Howls of frustrated rage. They would have to be cooked, an eternity of waiting for the small salty morsels that would dam back their hunger for a short while.

Dulcie followed their backs, the torn and worn-shredded shirt and knickerbockers and soiled pinafore. She saw the red ulcerations, the runnels of raw red they'd scratched out from the bights of sand flies. Dulcie watched the mouth of the cave take them, like the sea water she'd seen take one of the widowed women who'd been line fishing from the rocks to feed her children.

A flat quiet sea of surface blue and a cobalt sky. Then a heaving, an earthquake of movement at the rock lip and the look of wonder and fear on the woman's face just before the blue closed around her.

And Dulcie saw it all in that split second, that eternity — the woman in the column of water with the summer sun shearing fire through it. A fiery watchtower of working fluid as though the woman was burning, the hair washed out in waves of flame, the cross-shaped figure consumed by currents of fire fluxing through her. And the woman's eyes, she turned on Dulcie, wide white eyes of terror that turned up into blackness of skull bone. Then she was gone.

Taken from the solid footing of the rock shelf. Taken down by an undertow into the dark sea mass. Broken and bloody far below, only a stain of blood flowering in slow coils to the surface. Running in crimson rings. And Dulcie saw it, the poddy mullet, the school taylor, among the wreaths of blood burning on the water. The fish feeding. Dulcie saw them chopping the water, whipping like silver saw blades in the air. Smacking back into the water to feed. To gorge.

Dulcie scrambled over the final sand hill and into the cave. A long narrow elongation the shape of a carving knife, running a couple of yards, then dipping down dramatically under a shaggy mass of gum roots that clawed at Dulcie's hair as she focused in the black. Looking for her children.

She could see them at the end of the cave, the knife point end that closed around them with conglomerate cell wells. She could see their strange insect eyes, like termites, white and goggled and blind and their hands and arms like thin antennae whipping about in pale white fire flashes in the dark. Searching out their food, feeling for their world, so different from the miner's cottage with its bright fire Dulcie had given birth to every day. The rings of fire lighting the frame of the wood, cooking the stews, keeping them warm.

At the beginning of their exile, Susanna and Michael clung to the rock ridge that ran across the entrance of the cave. They'd stayed there all the day like cormorants on pylons. Waiting for their mother to return with food. It took an effort for Dulcie to force them into the cave every night to sleep away from the wind and the rain.

But months went. The elements passed and returned and the children regressed further down into the earth away from the light of day. Dulcie would force them out, take them out into the luminous light running like wires of fire; force them into the surf to wash their grubby hides; force them to walk with her in the gorse and bush where rabbits skittered across their paths.

Now they only came when Dulcie brought food. And it was an effort to make them wait while she cooked it. Even now, in the dark, she could see Michael with two stones, smashing the shell of the pipis, the two of them gobbling the raw sea flesh like the fish gorging the blood of the woman Dulcie had seen swept from the rocks.

Dulcie shivered. She felt the fingers of her husband fish-hooked into her flesh. Michael and Susanna just like him when he'd been drunk or fatigued from the pit, or both. An animal carelessness, a disinterest that had had Henry wolfing down his food, not using his knife and fork, but pushing handfuls of mashed potato and peas and meat into the black cave in his face.

Dulcie was at her wit's end. But she felt the currents of wind and ocean and storm still straightening through her. She planted her feet in the earth and bent forward and with a harsh cry caught hold of both of them. Hauled them, howling protest, to their feet, shook them, rattling them with pain out of their savagery. Dragged them by the hair. Outside.

Didn't let go despite the bodies of Susanna and Michael bucking like fish drawn in on lines from the ocean. Dulcie headed to the bush and the tent settlement built on the shores of Flaggy Creek. Headed for a pair of scissors and a cache of soap.

Dulcie wielded the scissors like shears. Hacked great furrows into the filthy forest of hair on Michael's head. Gave him a good clip around the ear when he yelled. And Susanna shocked mute by Dulcie's tongue that was a long lash of barbed wire taught-stretched between two posts, but cut and uncoiling with ferocity.

"Keep still yer witch!!" she demanded of Susanna. "I'll take t' yer with th' back of me and if yer don't!"

Dulcie took her children from the tent she'd occupied after some of the refugees offered it to her. A place to stay. A place back among the company of other women and children and men. She took her children from the tent after she'd scrubbed them clean in a tin tub in the middle of the tent. Sunlight soap and hot water boiled and carted by the mothers of other children in the tent town.

Dulcie and Michael and Susanna looked at the triangles of canvas, the tents in concentric circles around the eye of their tent. A mandala of human activity — women boiling clothes in an iron cauldron fired by gum wood they'd gathered, men roasting a whole sheep they'd run to ground in the early hours on the Merewether Estate, children clustered on tree stumps learning sums from a teacher with a dirt-ground board and a lump of shale chalk.

Some of the women came to them with apples from the small orchard the men and women had established in the chaos of bush and rock. Careful corridors of green and the golden fruit, a human pattern in the bush.

Dulcie fed her children the golden spheres, a redeemed consciousness that took away the remnant fox grins, the final carrion-gull-call voices soothed. Their childhood, their humanity reclaimed by their mother.

•

Dulcie pulled up. Dropped the apples in the dirt, the golden skin bruised black. When Dulcie came across Joanna Lowe. Joanna Lowe, who went back into the town and slept with as many men as it took to provide her with the pastries she craved. Even though there was enough food to be had in the bush of Glenrock.

A strange arthritic creature, Joanna, full of worms, infested with parasites. Filthy bird nest hair and the way she squatted in front of Dulcie now to pass water just outside her tent. A reminder to Dulcie and the others of their precarious existence. A borderland and the refugees caught between the wild bushland and ocean, and the estate of Edward Christopher Merewether with its tight knot cluster of cottages and farms barricaded behind paling fences to keep the creeping sand hills at bay.

Dulcie stepped around Joanna but the taste of the woman's smell was in her mouth as she made her way back to her tent. And thought about Susanna and Michael and the way they were regressing. Her son and daughter passive and uncaring about anything other than their bellies.

Her son and daughter fighting her tooth and nail when she tried to bathe them or cut their hair. Dulcie unable to enlist the help of the other women in the camp. The refugees walking past Dulcie's tent. Avoiding Susanna and Michael who were no longer children to them.

The two among the camp conjuring up worst than mischief. Two tricksters: sand dropped into food, the apple trees blighted when Michael and Susanna drove copper nails into every trunk, vegetables dug up and scattered. Susanna caught squatting over a cauldron pissing onto clothes boiling clean. Michael caught twice setting fire to a tent.

Dulcie dreamt it. The sheet of flame folding through the trees in silence, in her sleep. She woke and smelled it — the smell an acrid knife edge. She lit the kerosene lamp.

Saw Susanna and Michael were gone, their beds as empty as sin. Dulcie could see along their paths in the night. Could see her children, crouched with a lamp lighting a fire in brush then moving on and lighting another. Their gleeful eyes shining in the dark as the flame hammered up the trunks of gums.

The whole camp was up. Dulcie helped them fold away the tents, lump together their few belongings. They fled with their goods and chattels to a ridge above the fire. That ran in long lines through the bush like ribbons in a child's hair.

And then the change in the wind as it broke away with the coming of day. The refugees watching the tide of fire turn and rise like a swell of water off Smelleders Beach. A front of fire that ran in wave sets falling upon each other until a solid wall of crimson cut back down toward the woman after her children.

The refugees saw the column of flame fly up only feet in front of Dulcie.

Saw the fire take Dulcie from the outcrop of bush rock. Saw the flame engulf her, the woman held up in the burning blackness. Her hair in waves of flame, the red currents running through her cross-like body. Her arms spread out as if to fly but too late as the fire worked and washed like fluid about her body.

THE LOVERS

HE ARCHED OVER HER PREGNANT BELLY. FITTED
himself into the curve like a swimmer diving into a rip, but not
struggling. Swimming out to sea with the cable of movement into deep
blue water. New unchartered fathoms where the sun, lover's fingers,
traced into a blackness far below the swelling skin of water.

Something new for both of them. Her, six months pregnant, and
taking a lover; him, without a child, moving across her body with a
gentle exploration that might part the flow of her tissue to find the
child, swimming within, waiting to be born out of the uterine fluid. A
child that wasn't his that belonged to the woman's husband. But, was his.
As though he'd swum through a watery darkness with his own wife and
her refusal to bear him a child. As though, for years, he'd been "a pair of
ragged claws scuttling across the floors of silent seas." Feeling his way
in the black, a primitive organism, a jellyfish without a backbone to
give him shape to stand him upright, a vague shape of soft vulnerable
flesh pumping, liable to tear himself against hidden rock, a reef of coral
as sharp as the tongue of his wife.

"I won't have your baby! If you don't like it you can leave!"

The blackness of their years together a watery grave, water that filled
their mouths with a bitterness, a hostile stand-off that was a deep sea
trench shafting down just below their clumsy bodies. Bodies swimming
right next to each other, but blind in the night of the ocean, sightless
to each other.

She looked at him, her lover, and the easy way he had of moving
over her heavy form, the skillful way he avoided the baby inside her,
avoiding injury as his hands traveled her flanks, her thighs. The way

157

his mouth found her nipples, barely touching their tenderness. Moving on. She looked at him. Him with his thinning hair and she could see the relief map of red veins in his cheeks from drinking, from blood pressure, from age. A relief map that was like the map of dark veins rivering through her belly and her breasts, an estuary of swollen blood flooding to the delta of her womb and the child to be born. A rich redness of blood, pumping just below the surface of her stretched flesh. New blood he could feel, with his tongue, his fingertips like river loams of water coming up from below the ground. Passing into him, and the movement of the child a tide turning under a full moon. A vortex of movement coming down into the water, taking him out of his unconsciousness away from his wife. Into the light slanting down into the warmer surface water. Warm water that was a bath of touch and taste and smell as he found his lover and her big belly and her eyes that jetted out blue streams at his very touch.

He moved back, a seal sliding through water to her breasts. The nipples ringed with concentric circles of pink like still tidal rock pools with a stone disturbance dropped into them. Him the disturbance as his tongue tip traced every hair follicle bump of the blood plum nipples. And took them, gently, into his mouth, barely sucking. Not to cause her pain. But the pleasure of being wanted. Of watching his delight as he lost himself in her.

Her joy in being lusted after. Different from her husband's indifference, different from her husband's fear of her body growing larger in their marital bed. Starting to take up room, encroaching onto his side with her belly and legs. And his comments.

"I can't fuck you. I just can't. You're disgusting. That way."

And his back in the mornings as he left for work leaving her on the bed. Stranded like some sea creature on a beach at low tide.

•

His lover's mouth found hers; pink anemones closed fast upon each other in a tidal pool of warm water. Their bed. And their tongues like sly reef fish among a sea of swaying weed that stretched along a scar of water.

Her lover was a life force, coursing through her, taking her through the final difficult months of pregnancy and her husband's coldness. Her lover would take away his penis. Still erect. Happy to have found the configurations of her body. Without coming. He'd tell her

"Learn to take. No need to give back when you've already given."

Something new to her, after her husband. She tracked the history of her husband in her mind. Like feeling her way across the growth rings of a tree that had fallen and fossilized to petrified wood deep below swampland. And the coming child not enough to fire the marriage back to life. Only an artisan, a lapidarist could take the shattered rings of petrified wood and cut and polish them to a high luster finish. Even then the grain, dead, unmoving, below the artificial finish.

She picked over the shards of the time with her husband. And his taking, never giving anything back. She remembered his desire for his first child and his behavior at the hospital.

He was unable to witness the birth, refused to be there to comfort her through the wrenching spasms that tied her muscle and sinew into convoluted knots of pain. Her husband came in after, after the blood, after the sweat, after her face chiseled by pain into crevices, after the child had been cleaned of afterbirth and wrapped respectfully in a blanket.

She still saw the look on her husband's face as he went to his son. Ignoring her. The look of gloating triumph as he nursed the bundle that guaranteed his manhood to the world, to himself. And she'd watched through exhausted clear eyes, her husband wading out into the corridor like a man wading away from her into a flat stagnant ox bow lake of water.

Not a word to her. Took his son and she heard the hard cash sounds of his mates.

"He's a beauty, mate!"

"Finally held y' mouth the right way."

"Always knew y' had it in yer!"

The matey sounds came back in, covered her like wreaths of zinc lilies. As though she were on her deathbed.

She remembered her husband's silence, a razor blade that pared her nerves, when she suggested another child. Like going cap in hand to beg from him. Then his outrage.

"Christ, we've got a kid! I've got my son. We can't afford another!"

"I want to try for a daughter," she declared.

"Why?" he'd asked, nonplussed.

It had been a bitter battle. Her demands that they have another child sent her husband into a lethal silence that lasted for weeks, a silence that tore away pieces of herself, her identity as she moved through the dark gas tunnel of quiet attrition.

She'd lose her temper. Scream and shout, and he'd even deny her

her anger with his bland chartered accountant objectivity. Treating her like one of his clients without a head for figures or tax. Someone to be led to the light, patronized, step by step, into seeing the financial impossibility of her natural needs.

She remembered her revulsion and humiliation when she took him by force the night he rolled in drunk from the end-of-the-financial-year office party. Took him swiftly to get it over with. Her on top tearing the sperm from him before his cock died. Became a collapsed mass of soft sea sponge.

And later his surprise in finding her pregnant. Six months since he'd made love to her. Determined not to let her have her way. And his suspicion, his accusation that it wasn't his child. He dragged her to the DNA blood testing and the results sealed his parentage. But he still denied her himself.

He drew away, coiled back like a moray eel into a dark crevice.

He left her with her pregnancy, he left her with his silence like an abortionist's stainless steel instrument at the mouth of her womb.

She looked down and saw her lover between her legs, his head pink and vulnerable like the child that would come soon. The innocence of the child, his innocence. She felt his hands on the inside of her legs and the electric hair wisps of pain coming from him, almost gone, but there like hairline fissures in bone. His pain in not having his own children, but his joy in feeling the new child just above him, a soul about to enter earth to rest upon his shoulders.

She felt him, his breath at her vagina, and his tongue. She felt his breath, his soul, passing into her body. Traveling past the memory of her husband, traveling in the spice and sea current of her blood, traveling into the curled coil of flesh that was her daughter. Waiting to unfold into the air, into their arms.

LANDSCAPE WITH THREE TREES AND A HOUSE

Inspired by a painting of the same title by Vincent van Gogh.

MADAME DIGS IN THE EARTH, LOOSE LIKE SMALL change as she fossicks among the soil looking for the buttons she buried there as a child. Her father told her that buried buttons would grow into three trees of gold with fruits of diamonds. She would be a rich child, and he wouldn't have to work anymore in the fields planting and harvesting.

So Madame, all of four years old, took all the buttons she could find from the house to bury. Indeed, she went through the wardrobes of her mother and father, and with silver scissors, she cut off all the buttons from shirts, suits, dresses, and the odd hat. Madame, as she looks for the buttons, remembers the sounds of horror and anger even after all these years.

The voice of her mother is still clear as if the old woman has not been dead five years and mouldering in her coffin in the church yard at the back of the house where Madame lives with her husband.

"Muriel Gachet, come here this minute! It is you! I know you are the one who has done this!" her mother yelled from the upstairs bedroom.

But Muriel was more interested in getting to the open patch of bare soil at the front of the house to plant the buttons. She wasn't scared of the leather strap her mother would use on her. She was scared she wouldn't have a chance to plant the buttons because her mother would take them from her the way she took the money Muriel found on the road the week before.

Her mother demanded that Muriel show her what she had in her hand, but the child did not understand, at the age of four, why she should show her mother everything. It was only when her mother prized open her fingers one by one that she relinquished the coins, and then only after Muriel had yelled and screamed. Muriel squirmed in the clutches of her mother like one of the eels her father caught out of the river not far from the house.

Madame Muriel sits in the dirt looking for the buttons, but she cannot find them. She wonders about the three trees that grow there, not trees she's ever seen before, strange wild things with leaves like the long hair of a redheaded princess banished into exile. In the morning light, the leaves flux, and many of the villagers draw their shutters because the red light is like a fire.

They scare some of the men and women, these trees that are not native to this region. Many of the men and women have tried, in the darkness of night, to cut down the three trees. But it is as though the trees are protected by rings of magic of some kind because none of the villagers have been able to reach any of the three trunks to take an ax to the wood.

Men and women whisper about traveling from their cottage at night and walking for miles, it seemed to them, to get to the trees but not being able to arrive there. Yet, they all know that it is only a few paces from most of the cottages in the village to the trees in front of Madame Muriel's house.

Madame continues to look for the buttons, but she cannot ignore the rising of the wind that breaks away from the river and bustles up the slope. Soon the wind will get up into the leaves of the three trees shadowing Madame as she looks for the buttons. The red and golden leaves will lose all configurations that define them as leaves, and the trees will look like Roman candles of fire burning bright messages no one can understand.

A weird phosphorescence lights the whole town, but some of the villagers forget it is the light from the trees. They think it is the return of the Prussian soldiers burning, pillaging, and looting their way across the French landscape. They are afraid, and many old men, with long memories and scars of torture, have been seen at these times to tip over wagons in the town square to form a barricade to fight the invaders.

The other villagers do not laugh at the old men. They approach them with consideration, gently taking hold of arthritic hands to lead the old men away to the tavern where they are made to drink deeply of wine until their fear subsides.

The light from the leaves of the three trees is like a fiery branding, and it seems impossible to remove, just like a tattoo of coal dust in the flesh of a miner from the pits on the outskirts of the town. Madame Muriel stops looking for the buttons as the wind howls like a hound among the branches of the trees. This sound and the conflagration that burns just above her head are too much for her. Despite her stubbornness, her will to do what she wants and nothing else, she stumbles from the trees to her house.

Taking refuge inside, she stands at the upstairs bedroom window to look at the trees. Long burning brands of branches twist and unravel until Madame thinks the eels from the river have slithered up the river bank and taken up a new home in the trees.

The branches whip and lash about in the wind, reminding Muriel of the story her mother used to tell her when she was a child: the tale of Medusa who had snakes for hair, the woman who would turn you to stone if you looked into her eyes. Muriel realizes it was not a story so much as a threat from her mother who could not control such a willful daughter.

"If you do not behave yourself, Muriel, I will see to it that Madame Medusa visits you tonight and makes you look into her eyes. You will become a little stone statue, and I will place you in the garden for the birds to sit upon and do poos on," her mother told her.

And it was the only thing that scared Muriel. Nothing else worked. Muriel did as she wished, and her mother's desires were like fish that swam in the river — a flash, then gone. But the story of the Medusa terrified Muriel for years. It was a tale her mother used often, and the child knew when it was coming because her mother would fix her with an eye that was almost as terrible as the eye of the Medusa must have been.

Madame Muriel's father did not help matters between the child and her mother. He doted on the little girl, often coming home at lunch time just to see his precious Muriel. He was laughed at because it was unheard of for a man to go home to see his child and not eat his lunch in the fields with the other farmers and agricultural workers. But Pierre Gachet did not care what some whispered behind his back about him being soft in the head. He lived to see his little Muriel, and his wife was only too acutely aware of it.

As she watches the trees afire with light and wind, Madame remembers how her father would fight with her mother, then leave the house and take his daughter away from the scene of battle to the river. Sitting on the riverbank, he taught her to thread and tie a hook onto a line, push a worm, dug from the fallow piece of land at the front of the house, onto the steel, and then toss the lot into a cable of current clear in the river.

Father and daughter caught mostly eels, which they took home to Madame Gachet who cooked the creatures in salted water and jellied them in tin trays with parsley, dill, and chives. Muriel's father took the eels to his wife as a peace offering, because he knew she loved the soft jellied flesh with the salty taste. As for Muriel, she didn't care if her father made amends with her mother or not, just so long as he was there to take her fishing or tell her tall tales about planting buttons that would grow into golden trees with diamonds.

Muriel knew her father was pulling her leg when he told her such stories, but many times she wanted to believe they were true, especially the story of the buttons. She thought that if he were a rich man with gold and diamonds from the trees, he wouldn't need to plant and harvest wheat and corn and could be with her all the time.

From the bedroom that was once the bedroom of her parents, Madame Muriel watches the storm of wind and fire shuddering in the three trees while crows fly high in the air, crying their mournful cries like black rags of anguish. The house passed to Madame and her husband when her mother died. Not that Muriel's mother would have left it to her one and only child. That was something her mother made clear to her for years.

"The only reason you're getting my house, Muriel, is because your father managed to tie it up for you with the crooked lawyer in the village. If I had my way, you wouldn't have it," her mother told her.

The old woman lived downstairs in a room like a cave burrowed into rock. She was a troll living beneath the stairs, and no one, especially Muriel, could move from the upstairs to the downstairs, or in the other direction, unless the old woman knew about it. She would jump out from her small room and cross-examine whoever was passing. There wasn't anything she didn't know about the house and its occupants.

Muriel would have turned her mother out for the sake of her family's sanity, but there was no choice in the matter. Her father had made sure his wife would have shelter until the end of her days, although he probably would have delivered his daughter from his wife if he could have managed it. It was just that the lawyer advised him that if he was going to leave his house to his daughter and not his wife, he should provide something for the old woman. Otherwise, the matter could end up being dragged interminably through the French court system.

Muriel's children ended up being pale timid creatures thanks to their grandmother who made a point of terrorizing them whenever she could. The old woman turned the little boy and two girls into beings that were the opposite of their strong-willed mother. The old woman relished this revenge of sorts on a recalcitrant daughter who had made her life a misery for years and had stolen the heart and soul of her husband from her.

Now, it is the fury of the old woman that Madame Muriel sees in the trees. It is as though the old woman has burrowed her way from the grave in the churchyard and taken possession of the three trees. Trees of gold with diamonds they are not; they are masts, crosses of fire that burn in the wind and the light of the day. They are the mad eye of Muriel's mother when she looked with such hatred at her daughter. And that is why Muriel has begun to search for the buttons her father told her to plant.

She believes, out of desperation, that if she can find those buttons and sew them back on the clothes they came from, the old woman will leave her in peace. Muriel is at the end of her tether, she has rummaged through all the boxes in the cellar of the house and found all the clothes that belonged to her parents. She is desperate because her children have left their home and will have virtually nothing to do with their mother.

Muriel's son and two daughters are more than uneasy when they come home to visit their mother. They are afraid, and they do not stay more than a few minutes, just long enough for their mother to see her grandchildren. Then they're off like the catfish their grandfather used to catch from the river. Pierre Gachet would put salt on their tails, and the slimy spiked creatures would madly slither across the earth, disappearing into long grass where some unfortunate villager would find them when they stepped on the poisonous spikes.

Muriel looks away from the burning trees. It is too much for her. It is as though the fire is in her veins, in every cell of her body, burning, causing her pain. She looks out across the fields, a hundred acres of good fertile land that stretches from the river up to the house and in every other direction as far as the eye can see. And the doubling of the size of Pierre Gachet's original farm is due to the efforts of Muriel's husband, Marcel.

No matter what the villagers may say about Marcel acquiring the farm and the house by seducing the owner's daughter, Muriel knows, in her heart of hearts, that Marcel has made the farm a growing concern. She squints into the distance and thinks she can see him. But she's not sure; indeed there are times when she's not exactly sure what her husband looks like. It is the time of planting, and Marcel is up well before dawn and returns late at night when he is a blurred wan visage in the lamp light at the dinner table.

Marcel is unaware of his wife's grief at the isolation of her son and daughters from her. He doesn't seem to sense her loss, because he is so bound up with the farm, making it pay every year, planning which fields will be planted and which ones will remain fallow. A man different from my father, thinks Muriel with some bitterness because she misses being spoiled by her father, she misses being made a fuss over, she misses being the one female who matters the most to one man.

The wind dies and Muriel descends the stairs, pauses near the bottom of the staircase because she still expects her mother to spring from the room under the stairs and give her the alligator-skin edge of her tongue. Then she rushes forward like a scared child, out into the light that is dying as the wind subsides. Moving through the quickly gathering gloom, Madame Muriel goes to the three trees.

Down on hands and knees, she tears her nails clawing at the earth. She digs out under the trees and burrows beneath the roots, convinced she will find the buttons. They are seeds in her mind burst open with the roots coming from them, tendrils of hairlike roots attached to the buttons. Or she might find her mother sitting there quietly underneath a mass of roots shaped like a crown, the old woman sardonically, spitefully grinning at her the way she did in life.

"See, I will always be everywhere you go. You cannot escape me even if I am dead," Muriel's mother might say to her daughter.

But Muriel doesn't find her mother. She finds one button, and it is enough to make her dig harder and deeper. Another button is recovered, and the woman continues digging, placing the buttons in the pocket of her smock. In the back of her mind, she wonders how many buttons she buried all those years ago. She cannot remember, so she prays that if she can find some of them and sew them back onto the clothes, it will be enough to placate the restless vengeful spirit of her mother. Her thoughts are as irrational as imagining eels coming from the river, slithering up the trunks of the trees to make the leaves. But Madame is beyond the grace of reason. She is engaged in a struggle of bits and pieces cobbled together to make something powerful enough to free her.

Scrambling back to the house before night falls, Muriel takes the buttons from her pocket and, with trembling hands, begins to sew them back on the clothes that lie on the bed that once belonged to her mother and father. The suits and dresses are laid out. They are musty and dusty with age. Some fall apart in Madame's hands, and she panics, thinking there will not be enough left to hold all the buttons, not enough to lay her mother to rest.

Once the job is done, she carries the clothes outside and places them in the trees. Coats are buttoned up around trunks, shirts are buttoned around branches, dresses are buttoned to crowns of leaves, and some hats adorn the twigs of the three trees. A mutilated scarecrow it looks like, thinks Madame as she walks backward away from the trees. The buttons blink at her like the eyes of the town's cats in alleyways at night. But she sees herself reflected in those small shiny mirrors, and she averts her eyes, sickened by what she has beheld.

In the morning, Madame Muriel awakes, goes to the big bay window of the bedroom and looks out. The trees are gone, and in their place stand a winged horse and a golden sword. The vision is there for a few seconds, and then the horse and the sword disappear. All that is left is the fallow ground with nothing growing from it.

THE LOAN

SUE WILLIAMS BUSTLED OVER THE GREEN LINOLEUM. Looked at the watch pinned to her uniform. Behind. Ward round only half done when it should have been finished. Behind her head, Mrs. Jenkins's buzzer demanded the pan, the pan and a chance to lay about her poisonous tongue.

"Should buy the old bat a broom. Maybe she'd fly back home," sniffed Sue.

She checked Mrs. Brown. Drawers full of shit. Again. Sue stripped her off. Sponged her down. Replaced the soiled sheets. Put back Mrs. Brown like a body in a coffin. The bed looked good to Sue despite what she'd just cleaned off it. She'd been on her feet for ten hours, and more to go.

George Mackeroff was off again. He started at dawn. Just like a rooster George was. As soon as it was light, his mouth broke open and the terrible howling and wailing started. It went on to mid-morning until George exhausted himself. The other old people did their best to cope.

"Georgie's a bit senile now. That's why he does it," said Myra Standish in the room next to George.

"You wouldn't find me carrin' on like that in a month of Sundies," declared Marjorie Marsh. "I come from a respectable family. None of us 'ave ever lost our marbles. And even if we did we wouldn't carry on like that terrible Mr. Mackeroff."

Myra and Marj were always at Sue to get George Mackeroff moved away from them. They drove Sue mad with their demands — a campaign was closer to the mark. They'd spoken to the nursing home's superintendent about the matter. Marj's cousin was a distant relation of the super.

"I've got me ways and means to fix you, young lassie," she told Sue. "I've got friends in places. You'll see. You'll be sorry you've not moved that shocking creature of a man."

Sue moved down the ward. The bustle was all facade. She was out on her feet. "Dead knackered," as Bill, her husband, put it when he got home from the office. Being chief accountant for Bailey Manufacturing was a very demanding job. So Sue was told, every week night, and sometimes on Saturday and Sunday too.

Sue had taken the casual nursing job at the home to pay the extra heavy bills now that the three boys were all in high school. Two days a week snowballed into four shifts. She had to adjust. Fast. She made all the lunches for Bill and the boys and froze them. Teas were likewise. Enough pasta salad to last the week, chocolate slice in long wide slabs that filled the fridge shelves, and pre-cooked steak and veges or chicken wrapped in plastic ready for the microwave.

"Excuse me dear."

The voice broke into Sue's thoughts. Mrs. Forester, eighty and rheumatic and very considerate toward Sue. Sometimes.

"I do hope the eggs won't be runny again this morning." She smiled a worn-down, yellow smile at Sue. Difficult to be short with Mrs. Forester. Eighty and still all charm. Two hands adorned with diamond rings testified to the male admiration she must have commanded.

Marj and Myra hated her on sight. That's when they got close enough — about two feet — to give her the once over.

"Some things never change," thought Sue as she fluffed up Mrs. Forester's pillow and lied through her teeth that the poached eggs would be firm, not runny. Sue remembered Myra and Marj's reaction to Mrs. Forester.

"More paint on 'er than the Mona Lisa!" snorted Myra.

"Strumpet!" declared Marj flatly.

Sue also remembered Bill's office party at about the same time. Dragging herself up to the restaurant after the shift was over. Walking down the posh marble corridor, almost knocking herself out on one of the columns, she was so tired. Then Bill performing. Two beers and he was off. Almost off with his secretary by the looks of it. Blonde and nineteen, sitting on Bill's lap. Giggling and grinding her big healthy bum into Bill's crotch.

Funny thing, though, Sue couldn't be bothered to get angry. That bothered her. Not having the will, the energy, the purpose to flare up and drag the bimbo by the hair off Bill's lap. Sue ended up asleep after two gin and tonics.

She woke in the dark. A small man, the waiter, was gently shaking her. Bill had gone. And all of his employees. The waiter called her a cab. She went straight home and died. Tomorrow was a 5.00 a.m. start and another long shift.

•

Sue moved into the next ward. Slats shuttered out the light; dark bars fell across her face and down her plump hourglass body. Disintegrated shards of light and dark cut her face to ribbons. She pulled open the slats. Gray-faced Mrs. Green smiled in recognition from her bed. She barely made a small ripple of substance under the sheets, just a shallow range of foothills almost eroded flat by her eighty years of existence.

No one visited Mrs. Green. No family. The gossip was that she left her husband and sons forty years ago. Left them in their corrugated shack in the New England district. Left them to plant and harvest the wheat and survive the grueling summers. Left them to chop the wood to fuel the stove and cook three meals a day for a small army of farm laborers.

Sue often wondered what the last straw had been for Mrs. Green, if there had been something, a breaking point at all. She knew Mrs. Green had spent her last forty years in boarding houses. Usually one bedroom flats with the gas on and a small bathroom all in one. Yet the woman showed no emptiness, no yellow fields of wheat haunted behind her hard, mica eyes.

Mrs. Green's eyes followed Sue from bed to bed. Sue always felt them on her. And she would always come back to the woman's bed. Chat a bit longer. Watch as the woman's eyes looked into her. Took Sue's hand, Mrs. Green's old hand with long bone fingers as delicate as carved ivory. Held Sue's hand clasped firmly as if transferring some inevitable and terrible knowledge.

Sue could feel Mrs. Green's eyes on her now as she moved from patient to patient in the ward. It seemed to go on forever; a journey that never varied from shift to shift, from day to day, from week to week. A daze of waking and walking and cleaning and comforting and cooking. Nothing unusual broke in. Not even Mr. Alexander, seventy and predictably lecherous, pinching her fat bum as she bent over him to re-arrange the bed clothes. That was part of the course.

Mr. Alexander was as close as she got to slap and tickle these days. Bill was burdened with numbers and balancing the books. It took all of his time. Not even Sue's black lace body stocking did the trick any more.

They slept far apart now in the bed, a no-man's land of unspoken barbed hostility between them. Trenches dug, some night, for reasons neither of them knew. When they did meet, squeezed in between the working hours, the silence was a dark gas that burnt out their throats, strangled the notes of humanity before they escaped from the locked jaws.

•

The kitchen staff had begun their rounds. Hard metal clanking of trays brought her back. One ward to go. She was looking forward to her holidays — three weeks with holiday pay. A respite and maybe, just maybe, a chance to get things back together with Bill. She just hoped that nothing unforeseen would happen. Like Bill, last Spring, trading in the car on a brand new Falcon.

Sue hadn't minded the new car. It was the fact that he hadn't told her what he was going to do. And then the deceit of pretending it was a surprise gift for her. Some gift. An extra shift a week, on top of what she was working, to make the repayments.

Still, only two days to go. Perhaps they'd go away for a week. She'd have to fight Bill to make him spend the money.

•

Sue yawned behind the wheel. Swung into the drive. Bill was washing the Falcon. She almost crushed him between the bumpers of the two cars, sent the bucket of soapy water flying all over him. She sat there giggling.

Then she stopped. She looked at him. He looked like an eel, a white long whip of flesh without bones, leached of pigmentation, leached of life. He blinked his white eyelashes, the pink, thick groper lips pouted displeasure. She shivered.

Then, his smile, his business smile he used when dealing with staff or customers, came back. She looked at his teeth — two long rows of flathead teeth, small and sharp and ready to see-saw through the toughest of lines.

"Gooday, sweetheart," he chirped.

Something froze in her. She eyed him with suspicion.

"Good news," he said, as if he were declaring a holiday.

"Oh yes, what's that?" she asked.

"The bank's given me the loan."

"What loan?" Her voice was a flat line on an E.C.G. machine registering death.

"Oh, I meant to tell you," he said off handedly. "I've purchased a small block of flats. Three weatherboard flats. Y' know — negative gearing and all that. The bank's loaned me eighty thousand. It'll mean you'll have to work your holidays for a few years. Extra pay on top of your holiday pay."

Sue stood there. She felt Mrs. Green's hand still holding hers. The image of the long, delicate fingers blocked out his face. Mrs. Green's hard chips of mica staring from the old face barred away the straw-colored hair and albino flesh.

●

Sue stared down from the top floor of the boarding house. Behind her, in her one room, veges turned over slowly in one gray pot on the one gas ring.

She sipped her gin and tonic. Self-imposed solitary. The boys saw her. Occasionally. It didn't hurt any more. Two shifts a week at the home were enough to keep her.

She nursed herself now. Two years it had taken, two years of coping with the silence, coping with herself, coping with the regular sleep, coping with the regular meals.

The swimming had helped. She'd surprised herself. Caught the bus into the Ocean Baths every day. The first two months were murder. Forcing herself through the salt water. She was all elbows and still unable to put her face into the water to breathe out.

She built it up, laps with rests between each one, then, gradually, two laps at a time. Then finding she could put her face into the water. Being able to breathe out into the thick, green silence around her. The salt water scoured out her eyes, her ears, cleansed her skin, sandpapered away the fat. Baptized her.

Finally, the rhythm came, a languid almost careless freestyle that took her effortlessly through twenty laps a day. In the great green gloom of the salt water she was alone; no hands reached out to stop her, to drag her down to the rock bottom of the baths.

Now, she sat, still tasting the morning's salt water through the gin. Below her, a magpie swooped down, close to the ground, almost smashing into the squat, cement garden gnome, but then, by instinct, soaring, caroling up, and into the sky above the boarding house.

FROZEN

AGAINST THE CHOPPING BACKGROUND OF SEA AND cloud the figures formed solid masses of gray, solid in form and size but somehow blurred at the edges like figures in a snowstorm that threatened to explode across the canvas, dominating the landscape.

From this distance, he could see them moving in purposeful silence with the occasional hoot of joy cracking through the air like icy hail.

Really, they were of another world, or so it seemed; apart from the summer landscape, the three of them. They played on the shore with concise abandon. Studies of cold flesh, panting on the flat mirror sand, they sucked in the sea air in long drafts and blew it out like winds across a tundra.

They stood in a ring, holding hands — those square fleshy hands like metal-hard ice shards. With their heads flung back, they laughed and laughed, but in silence, for him, from this distance.

They bent forward, all three, in unison, clasping their knee caps, their heavy breasts quivering with laughter, their cleavages cut with deep sharp shadows.

They were still holding hands, completing the circle. The tide hissed in, washing about their feet in cold sheets of froth and shattered strands of seaweed. Drawing back into the dark green body, the waves sucked sand from beneath each instep. The three slowly sank into the beach, still holding hands, still forming that ring of gray dresses.

They sank, but their legs were like the wooden pylons of a wharf, thick and strong and ready to withstand the fiercest waves and the most furious storms. Wind snapped their hair like scarves of sleet under the brims of their hats, but each stood like chess pieces, each one a queen capable of removing any other piece from the game.

From the shadow of the cliff, between the road and beach, a dog appeared, curious but wary. He watched it move forward in jerky spasms, its black matted coat of some use against the blight coming from the three women. Lowering its head, it moved hesitantly toward the small throng. One turned her head and a whistle was chopped away by the wind. Encouraged, the animal trotted to the three.

He watched, the circle only broken when one stooped to pick up a piece of leached driftwood to throw it up the beach for the dog to fetch.

Time and again the beast returned with the wood dripping between his friendly jaws. The three grew tired, held hands and ignored the dog. The animal regarded them with curious and puzzled brown eyes. He saw the dog darting around the ring yapping madly, his red tongue lolling from the side of his mouth. One of the three women would occasionally look over her shoulder, her face splitting into a silent, frozen laugh at the antics of the animal.

Now they were leaving, trudging heavily up the sandhills sparsely covered with dune grass like the head of a balding, middle-aged man. Their legs sank deeply into the sand like legs into snow. They moved certainly toward the road, toward him sitting in the car, waiting their return.

It was twilight, and the haze of salt air swallowed up the dog running in confused lines up and down the deserted beach.

Before they reached him a shroud of cloud flocked in off the ocean, the cloud a dull gray with a zinc-colored lining. It settled above his car. He felt the shadow lower the temperature in the Datsun. His wife and daughters were closer.

He started to shiver. Then it hailed a rush of muddy water frozen to rocks of ice. It didn't stop. It piled up around his car like snow in a savage New York winter. Piled up in a rising Plimsoll line that sank him in Siberia. Until the car was entombed in a slick ice carving of a Datsun 120Y – smooth, grooved indentations in the ice in line with the red runnels of rust that cancered the whole body of the car.

The state emergency rescue service got him out with ice picks and axes. He sat there buried in the car, watching the orange uniformed figures through the windscreen, through the foot of ice, blurred bends of orange movement like figures from a dream that would vanish should he dare to awaken. Vanish and leave him there, lost in the frozen waking reality with his wife and daughters on the other side of a barricade the emergency crew had erected around him. As if he were out of bounds.

He could see the pewter color of the three women, strangely still, composed, without any flurried movement of alarm. Seemingly as still as pack ice floating placidly out of the Arctic, shearing open the hulls of unsuspecting ships.

His wife drove them home. He sat in the back, purple and blue with his eyes popping out like cubes from an ice tray. They wouldn't speak to him. Not after the embarrassment he'd caused them. All those people curiously milling around the frozen Datsun and the shame of having to get in the car with him after the N.R.M.A. man jump-started it with leads. The embarrassment of owning a man who was foolish enough to get himself buried by a hailstorm.

It hadn't been the same since he gave up his job as a solicitor, their disbelief when he took a gardening job with the Council. They'd stopped talking to him when his pay packet thinned to a few notes. No more trips away each year and no more new clothes when they wanted, no more restaurants or computer games. A prison sentence of cell silence.

He remembered his exhaustion. Wore a body bag of fatigue, still. The work of turning the soil and planting was the circuit breaker that took the pain from his muscles and joints.

He remembered his office and the matter he'd been working on. A turning point — a man trapped in cold storage over night, frost-bitten, lost toes and fingers and his nose. He'd come to him to lodge a claim for compensation, but he couldn't remember the legislation. A statute he'd known word for word. No concentration, as though it had been him caught in cold storage, his brain frozen then carved like tissue slices on glass slides under a microscope.

And then the children's court, the final hoarfrost. After fifteen years of practice, forgetting to read all of the brief. His client, seventeen years old, eager to plead guilty, get it over with, get a slap on the wrist and get out.

And he forgot, forgot to read the witness statements with their descriptions of the beating the victim had taken. And the magistrate sending his client to the District Court. His client close enough to eighteen to be dealt with in an adult way.

He remembered the magistrate's face, the hardened flesh drawn across the bone, flesh like crevices in ice and snow ready to take down lost solicitors and clients into a grave of cold. He heard the rumor, later, like a chilly fog, that the beak had terminal cancer and had hardened his stance toward the children who came before him. Not the usual warm fatherly advice, but a freezing, a frost of retribution that rimed itself upon every kid who came before him; a bitter enactment of chilling death that waited to cut and nip and pierce and pinch the flesh of the magistrate. His wife and kids took up where the magistrate left off.

He sat in front of the TV watching *Escapades on Ice*. He sat there eating his frozen TV dinner, smoked cod cured in the snow bound wooden huts of Norway. He tried to taste it but the flakes of fish were still frozen. They stuck to his tongue like flesh to dry ice. There was no smell, the vegetables steamed a sterile sleety plume of vapor, micro waved into being by his wife. Through the muffle of carpet and drapes he could just hear the clank of cutlery coming from the kitchen and the glacial grind of the voices of his wife and daughters. The three of them sitting at the kitchen table with the leg of roast lamb and the gravy and the mint sauce and the crisp baked potatoes and pumpkin.

And he thought he could hear the champing and chomping of their jaws shearing, rending meat and tendon and fat and gristle from bone. And he thought he could hear the cool clink of crystal glasses and the glob globbing of chilled Chardonnay ringing like cold metal bells.

He'd almost finished his fish when it started. He thought it was the ceiling peeling, but it wasn't. A fine white powder of snow fell on him out of the boreal heights of his lounge room. He looked up, too confused to move, and a whirlpool of wind filled his mouth, his throat, with ice shards. He spat. Spat the ice and snow and blood cut out of his tongue and throat and cheeks by the steel hard filings.

The wind moved into a bluster, whipping about his ears like words of scorn from his wife and daughters. The snowstorm convulsed around him, wrapped him around the way his wife used to wrap herself around him in bed, the way his daughters used to cling about his form for affection.

He was being buried. Again. He couldn't move his legs, frozen in a body bag of snow. He felt his heart pumping, knocking against the cold white bars of his ribcage like the engine knock in his old Datsun. And he felt the tide, the fume and foam of snow rising up over him.

State emergency came for a second time that day, but with an undertaker and a doctor to declare the cause of death. They prized him free of the vinyl lounge chair like a frozen fish finger prized from a plastic packet.

"Hypothermia," pronounced the doctor, scratched his head and looked at the ceiling.

The undertaker and his assistant put on their mittens and carried him out. Slid him, frozen, into the hearse like a carcass of meat in an abattoir.

His wife turned to her daughters and said, "C'mon girls. Come and finish tea before it gets cold."

MARKET PORTER

Inspired by a photograph of the same title by Eugène Atget.

PIERRE LEANS ON HIS SHINY BLACK CANE. IT IS HOT IN the middle of Paris near the markets. It is only early, barely seven in the morning, and already he is perspiring, the dirty runnels of thick salt water running down his face. He surreptitiously wipes his puffy cheeks, trying at the same time not to smear the thick pink powder he stole from his wife's bureau back in the tiny apartment in Montmartre. Pierre plastered it carefully over the lines and pits in his face, hoping to hide his age so that he might continue to get work as a porter in the markets.

Besides, he thinks, as he looks at his powder-blotched hand, I've been working here for years, decades. They won't forget me; they'll remember what a good porter, a good worker, I was. Still am, he tells himself, but he feels the cane slip on the cobblestones made slippery by the congealed lard of slaughtered animals hauled across the narrow square to be strung up for sale.

He almost stumbles, just rights himself in time as some of the younger market porters stroll past. They greet him with familiar hellos, chide him good-naturedly, calling him granddad. Pierre despises them and refuses to acknowledge their existence.

He pulls down his big round straw hat almost covering his eyes, blocking out the sight of their muscular arms and big hands, their easy animal gait. The men cannot see the anger in his eyes. They cannot see the hurt as well. In his heart Pierre knows they are not being unkind to him. It is just that he is jealous of their youth and strength, their ability to cart and carry heavy boxes of fruit and vegetables and dead animals about the marketplace without the slightest sign of fatigue.

Once upon a time, before that mad Baron von Haussmann tore down the old heart of Paris so dear to Pierre, the porter could work all day, and at the end of his shift he was always ready to take on more work, and ready, always, to make love to his Eugenie when he finally got home and slipped in under the beetling brow of the Montmartre butt and into his small apartment, perched halfway up the Rue Lepic.

Now he is weary and he hasn't done any work today. He is waiting for some of the produce owners or one of the market overseers to come along and offer him paid toil. Pierre flatters himself that his loss of strength is more than compensated for by his dapper appearance. His cane once belonged to a duke, or so he was assured by the antique shop dealer; his long smock once belonged to a prince, so said the back-street peddler. The smock is draped about Pierre hiding, he hopes, his corpulent body. His exotic hat is an object of envy among the other porters, he tells himself, and his hand-tooled leather boots, polished by Eugenie early every morning, should be enough, he convinces himself, for an overseer or owner to hire him.

And even if he can't manage the work anymore, he is entitled, because of his years of long and loyal service, to get help from one of the younger porters, someone who might serve as an apprentice to him, thinks Pierre, puffing his chest out with importance and pride.

Pierre remembers Monsieur Le Grand, one of the big owners of produce in the markets, years ago. Le Grand brought eggs, vegetables, and fruit by the crateload to the market every day, and he always sought out Pierre, telling all in the marketplace that Pierre was the best market porter he'd seen, that his blood should be bottled, and the other porters, far lesser men, should be made to drink small sips of the thick, vital, bright red substance to make them into the tireless worker Pierre was. But not too much of that blood for each man, Le Grand always warned. He said that too much richness of strength and determination might harm some of the pale shadows of men who slouched about the market, barely able to stand upright, let alone cart a box full of sheep heads across the cobblestones.

Ahh, those were the days thinks Pierre, and he pulls himself upright, balancing his weight between the cane planted in the cleft formed by two cobblestones and his other hand, which holds the ornate cast iron lamp post. He stands slightly forward, hoping to disguise his hand gripping the post. He holds onto the ornate metal head of a snake cast by some mad artist in a garret or a cellar somewhere, he thinks.

That's the trouble, says Pierre out loud. Since Haussmann ruined the city and the Bohemians came to stay, things have gone to rack and ruin. One of the lady shoppers, passing him, gives him a strange look. Pierre realizes it is because he was talking out loud to himself. He pulls himself together, grits shut his teeth, but bites the tip of his tongue so the blood spatters down his fleshy double chins. I must stop talking to myself; people will think I'm mad, he chides.

Only the other day his Eugenie had stopped in the middle of dusting their Montmartre apartment, went over to him where he was sitting with his legs raised so his puffy ankles would go down and said: "Good God, Pierre, you've been talking to yourself for the past half hour, and I don't think it's that glass of wine you're drinking. For goodness sake, man, be quiet. I can't think to do my housework. If you're going to talk to yourself, go into the bedroom and sit in front of the big mirror. At least that way you'll have someone to talk to."

Her mocking words had been close to the vinegar sting of sarcasm, and they'd hurt Pierre. He loved his Eugenie with a passion, even if not much of that passion translated any more into love making. He got out of the chair with difficulty and left, but not before a parting sling shot of hot acid words hurled by his wife caught him.

"And if you're going to use my face powder all of the time, then you should go out on the streets with some of the working girls. At least if you sell your fabulous body to some desperate men, we might be able to pay the landlord the rent on time."

Pierre blushes at the thought of her words. The heat is thick like the molasses that arrives in big stone bottles in the market from Africa, and he feels faint. For a moment he thinks the iron snake he is holding onto has come alive. For a second he is convinced it will bite him, sting him to death. It is a delusion, he tells himself and forces himself to stand still, not to cry out in fear.

It's not the first time he's imagined such things. Last week, on the Sunday, when he was climbing the Rue Lepic to buy bread from the bakery near the summit, he imagined the loaves of bread had turned into sharks, and they were swimming out of the bakery door down the incline toward him. He'd screamed, afraid they would tear him limb from limb, devour his flabby body with their rapacious jaws of iron.

The baker, drawn by Pierre's screams, had come from his shop and looked with only mild interest at the terrified man. Passersby had regarded him with amused curiosity until Pierre got himself under control, went into the bakery, and, gritting his teeth and ignoring the jibes of the baker, purchased some of the man-eating sharks. He took them from the shop, holding the bag at arm's length convinced, still, that if he held the warm loaves close, the escaped beasts of the sea would bite him.

Now he forces himself upright once more. His head swims, the cobblestones of the market rise and fall like a big tide, rushing down the Seine during the spring thaw; shoppers float by him; market vendors seem to expand and contract as if they are made from some strange plasma, as if they are alien forms of life. And they are to Pierre; they no longer know him, no longer care about him.

Suddenly he is brought back, everything stills. The smell, the stink is rank, so strong it brings back images to Pierre's mind, pictures of the occasional live wild animals that used to be sold in the market. He turns and sees the big black and yellow striped Bengali tiger in a wooden cage being manhandled across the market square by four burly market porters. The animal opens its mouth, the stench hits Pierre like death, the men sweat and curse with the heat and the heaviness of the animal. Their fear makes them weak, Pierre can tell, and who could blame them, he thinks. The long tarnished teeth of the animal are only inches from their bodies.

Then the tiger screams and roars, the noise echoing against the building walls of the marketplace, stopping every man, woman, and child in their tracks. Pierre sees the fear etched on every face, and this gives him some solace, some satisfaction he cannot fathom.

The tiger is placed on a stone stand in the middle of the square where he will be sold to the highest bidder, probably a circus owner or a rich man wanting something exotic to roam the park lands of his estate to amuse his lovers and wife. The wooden crate and the animal disappear from Pierre's view. He is dizzy again and reaches for his mustache, which he regards as his one vanity. The magnificent edifice of hair, plastered with wax under his nose, is his good luck charm, his talisman he has stroked and worried about for years.

He touches it, but there is almost nothing there other than a bare line of graying bristles, and then he remembers, almost sobbing with the grief the memory brings to him. Last week, after work, he'd sat in the cool of evening on the front step of his landlord's apartment, waxing his mustache the way he did almost every night. But he'd put too much wax on the hair, saturated it so it hardened into a long line of hair and wax.

He'd fallen asleep, and one of the gang of urchins that marauded up and down the Rue Lepic came along, took hold of the mustache, and, with one strong yank, tore the adornment from under Pierre's nose. The pain was excruciating but not as painful as seeing the ragged boy, running down the hill, holding Pierre's mustache above his head, yelling to his grimy comrades that one of the working girls had just donated her muff to his collection of bric-a-brac.

The prostitutes, who ply their trade up and down the Rue Lepic and along the Boulevard de Clichy, have a reputation for whipping up egg whites and plastering them through their pubic hair. Sexual tastes come in all shapes and forms in Paris.

Soon, the whole street knew of Pierre's loss, and for days, he had to suffer the jibes and jokes from his neighbors about renegade escaped hairy caterpillars and the dangers of loss one might have to bear when munching the vagina of one of the working girls. The girls were inspected by government authorities once a week for syphilis. The butcher on the Rue Lepic suggested that a deputation from the street should accompany the inspectors to see if Pierre's mustache could be discovered and reclaimed.

Pierre has had enough; he can't keep up his pose of strength and sartorial magnificence any longer. He slumps over his cane, eventually stands up straight, and decides to go to the small café at the edge of the marketplace. Here, he thinks, I will revive myself with coffee and a plain roll. No butter is needed to make it slide more easily down his pelican gullet of a throat.

He sits at a small table and fishes into the pocket of his smock for the franc he is sure is there, but it isn't. But that won't matter, he thinks. The café owner has known him for years, they are almost comrades, almost friends. The big, bald, bullet-headed man comes to Pierre, and the porter is taken aback for a second by the look of distrust that creeps like river mud across the man's face.

"A cup of black coffee and a roll without butter if you please, monsieur," says Pierre in his best merry and bluff voice.

The café owner leans on the edge of Pierre's table. The man's hands are enormous, and for a moment, Pierre forgets to be afraid because he is jealous. He would like to have those hands because he would always have work if he had them. But then the fear takes hold of the old porter, and he struggles to meet the cold, hard, iron gray eyes of the owner.

"Show me the color of your money first, Monsieur," he demands in a voice sharper than the blade of the guillotine.

Pierre reaches to rub his throat, but he can't find it among the multiple layers of fat chins that spill down to his grimy white collar.

"W...what do you m...mean, m...monsieur?" he stammers.

He grins at the man. Pierre looks like one of the African monkeys that used to be sold in the market, creatures that always wore a perpetual grimace like a frozen smile as if they were pleading for mercy and compassion from their captors and future owners.

"I mean that your credit has run out. You owe me at least ten francs for rolls and coffee and you cannot have any more until you pay me," says the owner, who turns on his heel, pauses a moment to present the disdain of his back to Pierre, then marches off.

Pierre, blushing bright red, rises, totters away. The markets are a roiling ocean of confusion to him. He searches out his iron pole and takes hold. Hanging his head, he closes his eyes. He does not care any more about keeping up appearances and hoping for work. He takes no notice when the screams of horror and terror rise in the marketplace. His head still hangs in defeat like the head of one of the bullocks, its throat cut from ear to ear, its body hauled up by a chain for the market butcher to carve steaks from to sell to shoppers.

The commotion grows louder so that Pierre cannot ignore it. He raises his head and there, standing next to him, is the Bengali tiger, crouched back on its steel haunches, ready to spring. Its jaws are open, its teeth glow dully. Pierre, for a mad moment, thinks it is smiling at him.

"Go on, piss off you bastard! Go and have a good laugh at my expense with the others," he tells the beast.

The tiger, maybe having grown used to the human reaction of fear to its presence, seems puzzled by this short fat man speaking angrily to it. Its muscles relax a little, it turns its head to one side and regards the porter with glistening eyes in which the jungles of the subcontinent still live dimly.

"Go on, piss off, I said! Go away!" says Pierre.

The tiger does not move. Pierre opens his eyes and sees what he thinks is a throng of market shoppers crouched low, hiding behind boxes and doors, whatever is at hand, looking at him with fear and relief. They look at him that way because once the porter is eaten, they think the tiger will not eat them.

Pierre, seeing the attention of the throng focused on him, loses his temper, stands up straight, and strikes the tiger with his cane. The animal is infuriated and the roar is terrifying, sobering Pierre, wrenching him back to reality. He looks at the big cat and finally realizes it is the tiger he saw carried past before, and he understands that it has somehow escaped.

The tiger screams again, bunches it hard neck muscles, and the porter sees that it is about to spring, and he will be killed. Desperately, he thinks, and an image of his wife and her cat rises in his brain. He sees Eugenie and the way she scratches her cat, Leon, under the chin and between its eyes, and the porter hears the purr of contentment. Pierre knows he has no choice. His life is miserable, but continuing to live a miserable life seems preferable than being eaten alive by a tiger in front of so many people. Such a mess, thinks Pierre. All that blood and my poor white body would be revealed to all and sundry, and they would laugh about it later.

Carefully he reaches forward, leaning on his cane, and carefully he reaches out. The tiger growls a warning, but Pierre manages to scratch between those cold and merciless eyes. He continues scratching a bit harder when the tiger doesn't bite off his hand. Gradually the tiger's eyes close, his body relaxes, his head lowers. Pierre has to bend forward more to reach between the eyes. The pain of stretching down is excruciating, but the porter thinks it could not be worse than being eaten raw.

Fleas from the tiger's fur hop onto Pierre's hand. They bite hard, drawing the man's sugary blood into their bodies. Pierre grits his teeth, stopping the sound of irritation from escaping. He does not want to bring the tiger out of its torpor.

From the corner of his eye, the porter sees the shoppers, some of them standing, some of them moving a bit closer to the porter and his tiger. Clearly they are impressed, Pierre understands. He bends even lower, slips his hand under the thick muff of the tiger's chin and begins to stroke and scratch. The beast begins to purr, but that purr sounds like a growl of anger, but the old porter keeps on. Besides, he is beginning to bask in the growing admiration of the shoppers and market vendors. With satisfaction, Pierre notices the look of awe and respect on the café owner's face.

There is movement behind the crowd. Someone, it seems, has been found to do something about the escaped animal, hopes Pierre. And he is right.

"Keep on stroking him there, monsieur," says the man, dressed all in white, holding a long black whip and wearing long black leather boots.

By luck a traveling circus has set up close to the market, and their lion tamer has been called upon by one of the market overseers to come and save all of his customers.

"Now, when I tell you, monsieur, step away from the tiger. Keep on moving away so I can confront the cat. All will be well once you do that. He will not harm you once I am between him and you," the tamer says.

Pierre continues to scratch; the tiger's eyes are almost closed. Its head almost rests on the cobblestones.

"Now, Monsieur, my brave lad, move away as quick as you can."

Pierre doesn't need to be told twice. He steps away, the tiger does not move, Pierre takes more steps. He is dizzy and he begins to fall backward, but the arms of the admiring crowd catch him, pull him to his feet, then raise him high above their heads. The last thing Pierre sees before he looks up and sees the blue oblivion of the sky above him is the tamer brandishing his whip, holding the mad animal in check, and the young porters, advancing on the tiger with the wooden crate.

Pierre is pleased with the attention, flattered by the praise of the shoppers as they carry him on high toward the café. But the old man is reminded of his father's death. His father was a coal miner in the Loire Valley and died in a mine collapse. Pierre remembers, as he is sat at a table and the café owner plies him with coffee and dozens of buttered rolls, his father's body brought home held high by fellow miners, the corpse left on the kitchen table for Pierre's mother to wash before burial.

But that sobering memory vanishes as he answers the breathless questions of the shoppers. He replies that he was not scared for a moment. He tells them he has been a porter in the markets for years, and there was no way he was going to let a mere tiger upset the daily routine of selling produce. His newfound admirers stuff many francs into the pocket of his smock, and Pierre pretends to be embarrassed, pretends not to want the money, but he makes sure he stuffs the coins and notes further down into the pocket to make way for more.

A market overseer hires a horse and carriage so Pierre goes home in style. The horse steps high and fast, but news of the porter's heroic deed travels faster. When he gets to the Rue Lepic, the crowd is dense out the front of his apartment. Pierre alights, and immediately he is besieged by well-wishers and the curious, wanting him to tell them how he tamed the tiger. Pierre obliges his many devotees many times, and they ply him with drinks and food. They run up and down the steep street in straight lines, fetching delicacies for the porter to consume.

Pierre looks up into the black sky, the stars circle in bright wreaths of fire. He drinks the Green Fairy, many glasses, but he feels unaffected, as though the spirit of the old man is now more than a match for the deadly green spirit.

Finally they let him go, and Eugenie helps him to the couch in the small sitting room. He lies down; his heart is beating hard like the hammering of the steel foundry on the banks of the Seine just south of the city. The walls of the apartment seem to melt, and Pierre sees the man and woman when he turns his head to one side. His mother and father stand on the cusp of a room Pierre did not know was there. They smile at their son; their radiance falls upon his bloated body and sweaty brow. He smiles back.

But suddenly, Eugenie stands in front of him, blocking Pierre's parents from his view. The light of their radiance dims, almost eclipsed by the almost naked and plentiful body of the woman. She wears black stockings and high-laced, black leather boots, the same as the washerwomen and seamstresses of Montmartre wear.

"Now, my darling Pierre, you have tamed a tiger, you have tamed the marketplace, and you have tamed our creditors. I think it is time for you to tame me as you used to do," she says.

The woman thrusts forward her plump pubis. Pierre looks at her with horror. He wonders if he reaches out and scratches her under the chin and between her eyes whether she might go away.

MONTMARTRE PATH WITH SUNFLOWERS

Inspired by a painting of the same title by Vincent van Gogh.

IT IS SPRING IN MONTMARTRE. THE LAST TIME IT sleeted was two weeks ago when Jean Paul was coming back from visiting his mother on the Rue de Clichy. The sleet caught Jean Paul half way up the Rue Lepic, drenching him to the bone. The water ran down his back and the ice was in his hair. Only now, as he sits in the sunlight is he throwing off the influenza and the mongrel dog cough that came with it.

Next to the veranda where he sits with a glass of muscat to warm his blood and bones, the sunflowers nod their heads heavily over him. The shadows of their round featureless faces move back and forth over his form; the rhythm is as unsteady as an old woman rocking in a rocking chair.

Jean Paul sips the muscat and he wonders if it would not be better to have the influenza afresh. Far better to be confined to bed, sweating with a fever than even consider what he might have to do. He squints up into the sky, but it is blue and bare with not a threatening cloud in sight that might dump some ice on him.

Throwing back his head, he downs the glass of muscat in one gulp and ventures out into the day rather than sit on his veranda stewing over his impasse. Out along the cobblestones of the path he goes, and the sodium flare of the sun makes the stones burn golden, the color of the silk spun by the silk worms his daughter keeps in a box beneath her bed.

Flames of light rise up his legs and to another pedestrian he might look as though he is burning, hanging up in the luminous air. As he descends the Rue Lepic, he sees Madame Toulon, bustling out of the bakery with her cane basket full of loaves of bread. The grim determination of the old woman, in her eighties, is almost comical, but Jean Paul cannot laugh at her.

As she begins the upward climb, she sees him and smiles a smile that would charm the whores on the Rue de Clichy, selling their bodies and bargaining their souls if need be. Madame Toulon salutes him. She is an old friend of Jean Paul's mother. The two went to school together in Montmartre when it was still a village of windmills and quarries and market gardens; a time before the Parisian houses crawled their way up the steep ridge, but the old Montmartre has vanished as quickly as the beauty of a young woman's face.

"How is your mother, Jean Paul?" the old woman demands of him.

"Still the same. Not worse, not better. Still in the land of the living."

"Ah, that is good. Where there is life there is hope," declares the woman, as though her words are set in stone, and all Paris would do itself a good turn if it took note of their wisdom.

But Jean Paul, although he does not contradict Madame Toulon, knows this is not true. Where there is life there may well be misery he thinks.

He pauses and watches the vigor of the woman as she ascends the hill with her load of bread. Jean Paul knows she lives alone, and he knows she will spend hours preparing herself a meal of beef and mushrooms with wine and cream, the way she does every day. And he knows the last thing she will do before she bolts the door and settles down for the night, will be to push shut the heavy metal front gate to her house. Something she has always done and doesn't see the necessity to change her habit despite the weight of the gate, and despite Jean Paul having offered to come around every evening and close the gate for her.

At the foot of the street, Jean Paul comes across Madame Vert, a distant cousin of his mother's, a woman in her middle sixties, who has lost her mind completely. Jean Paul addresses her as aunt but the woman, not that old, looks vacantly at him, turns away and continues to walk the cobblestones, stooping every now and then to pick up dog shit she places in the pockets of her apron tied around her waist.

Anger rises in Jean Paul because the woman should not be out by herself. He knows her son, Pierre Vert, a civil servant is not so civil to his mother. In fact she is a burden to him and the son rarely crosses the river to this arrondissement to see how she is faring.

"She does not know me any more, so why come to visit her?" Pierre told Jean Paul the last time they met.

Jean Paul follows the woman, gently places his hand under her elbow and steers her toward the Avenue Rachael where she lives in one room in a boarding house next to the entrance of the cemetery. Bravely ignoring the stench of dog shit, Jean Paul guides her up the stairs, girds his loins, plunges his hand into her apron pocket because that is where she keeps her key and brings it forth bearing only a little dog shit.

Unlocking the door, he takes her across her threshold and sits her down in the lumpy chair she has sat in for forty years or more.

"Monsieur, who are you? Where am I? I do not know this place! Please take me home at once!" she commands.

Jean Paul resists the urge to weep. He unties the apron, takes it from her, goes to the window and throws it out into the cobblestone gutter. Turning back to her, he sees a glimmer of recognition.

"Ah, Jean Paul, your mother will be worried. It has been a splendid lunch and the wine was so good. Please come again and talk to me. I like your talk, you are witty and there is little of that left in Paris today. But that is enough. You must be on your way dear boy before your mother frets for you," she says.

She turns her head for a second, turns back and looks at him and the recognition has vanished. A look of bewilderment clouds her face; she frowns at him, places the end of her thumb in her mouth and gnaws at it with her ground-down teeth.

Jean Paul leaves the woman, locks her in for her own safety and tells himself he will return later with some food. He walks down the slope of Montmartre to his mother's house.

Knocking at the door he waits, hears the uncertain shuffle of feet coming down the dark hallway he knows so well because this is the house where he grew up with his mother and father. There is only his mother left now, his father is long dead and his brother and sister live in the west of France. He has not seen them in more than ten years and both have ceased to write to him or their mother.

The door opens; the wan face of Jean Paul's mother peers out of her darkness. He sees the lipstick smeared across her cheeks, the powder on her neck, the jumper worn inside out, the shoes on the wrong feet. He weeps and it begins to sleet. He stands there. Ice and water cover him. His mother smiles uncertainly at him.

HOPE SPRING ETERNAL

WALLY WILCOX HITCHED UP HIS TROUSERS AND PULLED the plastic belt in another notch. The ten and twenty cent pieces weighed down the K-Mart casuals. His pockets bulged with heavy metal.

"Christ!" he thought, "I'm going' t' need a bloody walkin' frame t' get t' the track with all this shrapnel."

Wally looked at himself in the full length mirror. "Gone t' seed a bit," he thought. He pulled in his beer belly. The seventies body shirt didn't help matters. His distended navel looked like a sink hole.

"Chere's plastic bloody surgeon 'ud have trouble with me," he muttered at his reflection. "Monday morning a new diet and some walking with Midge. Stroll away the kilos and freeze me balls off at 5.00 a.m.!"

Wally slicked over the remaining strands of hair, plastering them to his pallid pate with hair oil. He wiped his oily hands down the sides of his trousers. Pulling back his shoulders, he rolled out of the bedroom like a sailing vessel in high seas. He prayed that his lower back would hold up under the weight of the considerable coinage in his pockets.

Midge was in the kitchen. Her fluorescent lime green tracksuit hit George between the eyes like a slab of molten metal hitting heavy rollers at the nearby steel works. Wally steadied himself against the laminex snack table. Midge's bright green plumage did not color co-ordinate with the ten schooner hangover he would probably nurse to lunchtime. He felt as though the wild white horses, running through water under moonlight, in the woollies print on the wall, had made their way into his head.

"That friggin' Clarry Kelly," thought Wally. Just come up to the rissole for one beer', he had said. No such thing as one beer with Clarry Kelly," whinged Wally to himself.

He slumped onto the vinyl-covered kitchen chair. Midge had disappeared.

"Christ, where've y' gone Midge! You were here a second ago!" yelled Wally. Wally thought of the DT's. Had he imagined Midge standing in the kitchen? How long would it be before rows of elephants, each holding another's tail, floated past his eyes?

His wave of terror receded back into the ocean of his unconscious when he heard Midge's voice coming from far away. He lurched to his feet and swayed toward the faint sound.

"Down here Wally. I'm down here!"

Wally found Midge on the floor. Doing sit-ups of all things. Her chirpy robin's voice grated his hung-over nerves raw. The sight of her compact healthy body jerking up and down rhythmically filled him with disgust and faint self-loathing.

"Come on down and win a prize, Wally," chattered Midge without losing pace or rhythm or breath.

Wally turned away. Sickly he lit his first cigarette and gulped coffee into the wreckage of his middle-aged body. His stomach made a loud churning sound somewhat similar to the garbage disposal at full munch.

Midge's only-slightly-pink face rose from behind the kitchen bench. She eyed her husband, hunched over with a hacking cough, the way a butcher eyes a freshly slaughtered beast.

"Wally I've cooked your breakfast for you."

"I don't want any breakfast," he moaned through a cloud of blue smoke. The scene was reminiscent of the good old days of the steelworks in full production.

Midge reefed open the stove door and tip-toed with a ballet dancer's grace and a surgeon's precision and timing toward Wally. She carried a loaded steaming plate. She stuck the plate right under Wally's nose. The mere smell was enough, but the sight of greasy sausages, rashes of curled bacon dripping fat and poached eggs quivering disdainful yellow eyes at him, sent Wally flying for the outside dunny.

Clarry Kelly arrived half an hour later. Wally, somewhat wan and worn, was ready to go. Midge looked at the two of them

"You certainly wouldn't buy a used car from either of them," she thought. "That's what they look like, used car salesmen in their parrot-colored shirts and cheap trousers." Wally in his platforms, looking like a groupie from an Engelbert Humperdinck concert; Clarry in that faun safari suit and his stupid big smile that made Midge's best cut glass bowls quiver and ring in her china cabinet.

They were going to make a fortune they both assured her. "Hope springs eternal," she thought. Wally told her to book the tickets on the P. and O., and he was only half joking. This from a man who returned from his last race meeting dead drunk and with an irate S.P. bookie in tow. Wally had met the bookie at a pub afterward.

Midge cringed to think about the incident. Two thousand dollars in debt Wally was to the bookie, and his wallet full of moths on crutches.

The bookie threatened dire consequences and a visit from the thugs from the tugs. Midge had heard about the thugs from the tugs. Everyone had. Big boys in blue overalls who coiled the thick ropes at the end of the shift; steered the tugs in the harbor and made a small packet on the side, sorting out welchers for S.P. bookies.

Midge parted with the Kingswood there and then. The bookie reversed the immaculate green machine down the drive. The last thing Midge saw was the bookie's gold incisor tooth grinning back at her the last fiery rays of the setting sun.

She turned to find Wally stretched out on the front lawn snoring so loudly that Mildred Muddle, the neighbor across the road, and one woman neighborhood watch, came out and complained. Midge grabbed the garden house and roused her slumbering spouse with an icy cascade of tap water.

Of course, by this time, the whole neighborhood had come to watch. Wally, ringing wet, drunk and stroppy, bounced on the balls of his feet round the garden challenging anyone to fight, including Mildred Muddle's dog. Mildred's dog, an affable cross of canine midnight matings, licked Wally's face. Wally slipped and Midge found herself in the casualty ward of the nearest hospital until 7.00 a.m. the next day.

•

Wally and Clarry paid the cabbie. Clarry insisted on the driver taking them all the way through the car park to the main entrance itself. Clarry tipped the cabbie fifty cents and left the man open-mouthed and staring at the solitary silver coin in the palm of his hand. Thirty cars or so had arrived since their entrance. There was no way the cabbie was going to get back to the main drag in a hurry.

The two intrepid punters paid the entrance fee. Wally, a good, slightly-lapsed Catholic, dropped a dollar coin in the wooden box of the fat, Salvation Army lady sitting at the entrance. Under his breath he prayed his good deed would bring them luck.

The second race was over and the two scrounged through three bins before they found a discarded race book thrown away by a punter who'd already been taken to the cleaners by the bookies. It saved the two a couple of dollars. Two dollars was useful, especially toward the end of a meeting when you needed a steak and onion sandwich to soak up the endless number of seven ounce beers.

Wally and Clarry headed for the enclosure to watch the parade for race three. Number seventeen looked good to Wally, all skin, and bones sticking out of him everywhere, not an ounce of fat on the big bastard and Malcolm Johnston in the saddle to boot. A big fan of the Malcolm was Wally; Malcolm patron saint jockey of the penniless punter in need of an outsider getting up.

Wally bolted for the ring. He only came with forty bucks and it took a week of whinging and wheedling and being nice to his mother-in-law to get that out of Midge. There wasn't much left by the time he got in and bought his first beer. He headed for the ring with a strong feigning of hope growing in the pit of his stomach. He surveyed the odds. Some had number seventeen Loser's Luck, at tens, others at fourteens, others at twenties.

Wally reckoned the bludgers were bank managers moonlighting as bookies; they were that cautious. He watched them watching each other's odds through their binoculars. It only took one to turn down the price and the rest followed like traders at a stock market crash. Occasionally, one would be hit with a big bet. You'd see the blood drain from his face, then one of his bag men scurrying around the other bookies laying off half the money on the big plunge.

Wally scanned the odds again. They weren't moving. "Wouldn't bet the sun 'ud rise," he muttered to himself. Last minute before they jumped. One bookie raised Loser's Luck five points. Others followed. One, just for a show of bravado, pushed number seventeen up fifteen points to forty to one. Wally jumped, probably faster than Loser's Luck would jump from the gates. Twenty bucks on the nose at forties: eight hundred dollars if Saint Malcolm was in the mood to walk on water.

Wally joined Clarry, just to the right of the finishing post. Clarry was mid-way through his fourth seven already and looked half shot with those red hard-boiled eyes rolling around in the holes in his head. "You friggin' what!" shouted Clarry. A woman dressed in a short black skirt, black nylons and high heels, moved away from him. "I had twenty bucks on the nose at forties," answered Wally with irritating calmness. "Jesus Christ, and the next race's the second coming is it?!" roared Clarry.

"Well, I reckon it's a good thing," stated Wally with a smug finality of all mug punters.

"So's the young Sheila across the road from me," snorted Clarry. "And she'd probably beat this glue factory if she ran barefoot up the straight!"

Wally squinted into the autumn glare. He could see the horses milling about in the distance at the twelve hundred meter mark. He thought he could see the colors of number seventeen: purple and orange and Malcolm bobbing up and down in the saddle like a buoy in the middle of the harbor.

Clarry stood looking at his feet and shaking his head. The two were hemmed in by a crush of punters from the betting ring.

The horses jumped and the cloud of dust made its way around the rails toward them. At the turn, purple and orange was pulled to the outside. Hooves thundered; a physical presence as keen as the excitement of the punters.

"Go you beauty!"

"Come onnn! Come onnnn!"

"Sss! Ssss! Ssss!"

"Give it to the bastard, Malcolm!" shouted Wally.

As if in compliance, Malcolm drew the whip. In the straight he was five wide and still three lengths from the leading horse. He plied the whip without mercy. Wally could hear it smacking into the bony belly of Loser's Luck as Johnston went to town on the big gelding.

Clarry was yelling with Wally. Dust from the metal hooves rolled into the screaming punters. Women, on the verge of hysterical tears, pounded their hapless partners with purses. In his excitement, Clarry grabbed Wally by the throat and almost throttled the goggle-eyed punter. Malcolm wielded the whip like an overseer and the race finished with three horses strung across the track in a dead even line to the naked eye.

A second photo was called for. Wally waited, promising God he would turn up for Mass next Sunday, if He let Loser's Luck get the nod. Loser's Luck did get the nod, by the shortest possible margin; by a bee's dick Clarry later said.

When the result came up, only Wally and Clarry cheered, while the punters tore up their tickets and moved back to the ring to continue the battle with the bookies.

Wally was the only one in line at the bookie. "And thank Christ for that!" the bookie told him as his bag man thumbed out eight hundred dollars in twenties.

Wally and Clarry headed for the members' stand. They paid their money and mounted the hallowed stairs to a seat right in front of the winning post. Clarry disappeared into the bar to get beers, while Wally pondered the form for race four.

Malcolm was on another outsider at twenties in the paper. Wally felt the comfortable bulge in his wallet in his back pocket. Clarry arrived with the beers and treated Wally with awed deference. It had been a long time since he'd seen anyone win like Wally had. Nothing was too much trouble for Clarry, now. He trotted off to get the great man a steak sandwich and hoped that Wally's talent, or arse, or whatever you wanted to call it, was still hotter than the cold hot dogs they served at the public canteen outside the betting ring.

When Wally told Clarry what he'd picked for the next race, Clarry almost choked on a piece of gristle in the middle of his steak sandwich. He kept his mouth shut though: especially when Wally forked out five twenties as a stake for Clarry to while away the afternoon.

Clarry watched with disbelief as Johnston's mount in the fourth, Punter's Pride, scooted home for a short half-head win. Wally wagered one hundred bucks on the nose at thirties. Things were looking up. Wally was starting to see that clear crystal water and the P. and O. Liner churning smoothly through the tropical air toward Fiji and Suva. He could taste the salt air and smell the sun tan lotion. His day dream fluttered out before his eyes like goodbye streamers thrown from the upper deck of the ocean-going vessel.

"Midge 'ud be thrilled t' bits," thought Wally. "Make up for some of me past misdemeanors," he said to himself. He could just see Midge in a black one-piece swimming costume. She still had the merchandise in good shape. "Probably have to keep an eye on her, what with these older women goin' after younger blokes. All the rage. A nip here and a tuck there and there's a tribe of Tarzans after y' missus."

Race five and Clarry watched in growing awe as the master punter picked Pope Malcolm, The Magnificent's mount to win. Another outsider and another win at big odds.

Wally and Clarry had become a minor center of attention at the meeting. Punters followed Wally's every move. The bookies started following him with their binoculars and mentally calculating how much was left to pay on their mortgages. Wally moved through the multitude with the assurance of a messiah confident in his ability to turn water to wine or feed the throng with loaves and fishes. Or, at least, give generous handouts. Clarry had to forestall Wally's generosity. A broke punter casually asked for a loan and Wally immediately obliged with a twenty dollar note.

It was blood to sharks. Down-and-outers arrived with glassy lizard smiles and open palms. Wally dispensed twenty dollar notes like Social Security on pension day.

Clarry bustled Wally away from the growing herd of the hungry. He steered his mate back to the members' stand. Here they were found by two blonds in their late twenties. The two girls arrived in short skirts and high heels. They sported smiles framed by thick shiny-wet red lipstick. Their voices ran like honey over the two baggy-eyed punters. Clarry knew both of them: working girls. He'd seen them working the crowd at the races before. Tasty bits they were too, but a bit spicy, even for two diggers up on their luck for a change. Still, the rolled down tops of black stockings revealing taught white flesh was food for thought.

Wally was thinking. Clarry could see him. His mouth was open and the shorter blonde was dropping salted peanuts into it and pouring more beer after them.

Things were getting out of hand. The girls were on their fifth champagne cocktail each, at seven bucks a go. Their laughs clattered like hard gold dollar coins. Wally looked at the short one and wondered if Medicare covered triple by-pass operations.

Clarry was getting toey. The next race was due. He managed to get the long purple fingernails out of Wally's flesh long enough to get him to read the form guide for race six.

Wally's eyes found number ten with Harry White on it. Clarry looked questioningly at his mate. Malcolm was on number twelve at good odds, but Wally insisted his intuition knew best. They held the girls over with a bottle of Bollinger which cost Wally, Clarry estimated, the best part of a week's wages.

The two swung from side to side like metronomes in the circle. Wally plunged a thousand on number ten. Bookies around the ring withered like caterpillars cut in two. Other punters rushed them laying all money on number ten.

Coming round the turn, number ten, fast and frothy, was in front by five lengths. Wally and Clarry were already declaring him the heir apparent to the great front runner, Scotch and Dry. Then, number twelve, Ye of Little Faith, whipped home by Malcolm, came out of the clouds to win right on the line.

The exodus of ruined punters swarmed like refugees out of the gates. The bookies sported grins as bright as blood-red carnations at a funeral. Wally and Clarry, dazed in sobriety, checked their dwindling funds. Still two grand left. "Maybe a day trip to Sydney on the train, rather than the P. and O." thought Wally.

The blonds had gone. Clarry caught a glimpse of them on either arm of a bookie leaving early.

There was still one race to go.

The two punters downed two more sevens each and attempted to focus on the form guide. It was late afternoon. Shadows congealed through the members' stand like the life blood of punters splashed on hard and stony ground.

The intoxicated twins lurched into the ring. It was now or never decided Wally. His drunken, devil-may-care attitude led him to plunge the two thousand on the nose of number nine, Last Chance. Wally and Clarry were certain that Johnston would ride this home for them.

Unfortunately, Malcolm was riding number eleven, Out of Sight. The two punters, in their alcoholic frenzy to make good, had misread the form guide. Two thousand dollars on the wrong horse was something that Wally would try to blank out from his mind in later years.

The spectacle of Out of Sight spearing down the straight and thundering home with Malcolm riding hands and heels, haunted Wally in many midnight hours.

Number nine came in last. The two stumbled from the track digging deep into windy packets for shrapnel to get a cab back home. The cupboard was bare.

The two men were picked up by the cops as they tried to walk the five kilometers back to Wally's place. Clarry had stretched out on the median strip for a snooze. When woken, he abused the two coppers in no uncertain terms which was unfortunate because the two young constables were going to taxi home the two drunks without any bother. Instead, they locked up the two loud mouths.

Monday morning found Midge at the pawn brokers with Wally's signatured set of Arnold Palmer golf clubs. The broker gave her just enough to bail out her hung-over and shame-faced husband.

As for Clarry Kelly — well Midge wasn't pawning her new washing machine. Clarry Kelly could rot.

THE BOY'S BOOTS

THERE IS A SMALL CAFÉ IN SYDNEY ROAD, BRUNSWICK, barely a hole in the wall with a few tables and chairs and a menu no longer than a page with large, child-like printing on it. Inside the café it is warm. It is filled with customers because the pasta and the sauces that go with it are famous along the umbilical strip of tar with traffic teeming into and out of the city of Melbourne.

On a mantelpiece, above the heads of the diners, sits a pair of boots, they are old boots, the leather is cracked, torn in places. They are small boots that once belonged to a boy, who drowned in the Hunter River near Newcastle in NSW.

The boots sit there and some of the customers, when they look up from their meals think they can see the small remains of river sediment encrusted in the leather. Others fancy they can trace the shapes of the small boy's feet in the leather.

Everyone, who dines in the café knows about the boots because the owner of the café, Mary James, is the owner of the boots and she tells any new customer her story about the boots that belonged to the boy, who was only seven when he drowned. The mother of the drowned boy gave Mary James's great-grandmother the boots and they were eventually handed down to Mary.

But the real interest that arises among the regular customers is why the mother of the drowned boy gave the boots of her dead child to Mary's great-grandmother. The customers can never really decide why the boots were given away.

But whenever a conversation is struck up on the subject of the boots, Mary always comes from the kitchen because she senses that words are being spoken about the mystery. It is something that has bothered her ever since her mother handed her the boy's boots, through the car window just as Mary was about to drive out of Newcastle to settle in Melbourne.

And there is that rich-red-silt smell to the leather of the boots that reminds Mary of the Hunter River when it is in flood. An odor Mary used to smell when she lived near Newcastle. The smell haunts Mary, even when she is in bed, upstairs, trying to sleep after a hard day and long evening in the café below the bed.

Sometimes Mary wakes with fright because the flood-river smell has her convinced that the Hunter River is flooding, rising up through the floorboards of the top story of the tenement in Brunswick. It is then that Mary's husband, sensing her fear, wakes, reaches out in the dark and pats Mary's stomach, plump from child-bearing, strokes it tenderly until he hears the soft snore of his wife begin.

But sometimes the gentle hand of her husband is not enough to soothe Mary, she gets out of bed, walks softly along the corridor, checks on her three children sleeping soundly in their bedrooms. Sometimes she will go into one of the rooms if she cannot see the face of one of her children. She leans over the bed, finds the face, turns her head sideways, close to the face of the child, checking that her son or daughter is still breathing.

The next morning, after such a night, Mary is wan, tottering about the café and kitchen from lack of sleep. She looks as though she has been taken from deep water by a fishing net, she looks as though the loams of water have washed away any sign, any feature that identifies her as Mary James. The customers sense it, word seems to spread along Sydney Road and the café won't do the business that day it usually does most days.

When Mary is ovulating, when the blood is thick between her legs, she cannot rest at all during the night, she constantly checks on her children and the next morning she is a ruin barely able to cook the pastas for her customers. Not that the customers say anything.

The women, sitting at the tables, look with concern at her, they dare not even glance at the boots sitting like small tombstones on the mantelpiece. Female hands reach out, as Mary, carrying full and empty plates, moves among the tables, the hands touch her, gently. No words are spoken. It is a communion of grief.

CHILD MINDING

Susan feels dizzy, but she tells herself she cannot afford to be ill because her daughter-in-law, Joanne will arrive soon with Susan's two grandsons, Michael and Malcolm. Susan child minds the two boys five days a week, and sometimes seven if her son, James goes away for the weekend with his wife.

Susan stands before her bedroom mirror and sees the lines of age etched deeply like furrows in an overworked field made barren by excessive planting and harvesting. She peers myopically at herself, her form blurs as though something is jarring inside of her body. She looks vague as though her identity has been lost or stolen from her.

She feels short of breath, but she wills herself to apply her make-up, plastering the powder thickly over the cracks in her flesh so that Joanne and the boys will not notice. Not that they would care, thinks Susan, the anger suddenly flaring up in her like an explosion on a distant sun, then puzzling her to think she could think, feel that way.

Her two grandsons are her reason for living now that Susan's husband has been dead almost a decade. Michael and Malcolm are the reasons she gets out of bed in the morning, Susan tells herself. And Joanne often points that out to her mother-in-law.

Joanne's parting words as Susan and her two grandsons stand at the door to wave the woman off are inevitably: "You should be grateful, Mum, having the two boys almost every day of the week. Not many women your age have such an opportunity. I dare say you'd be in the cemetery next to your husband by now if minding Michael and Malcolm hadn't given you something to live for."

Susan's son, James, says little, always deferring to the flint-like good sense and dragon temper of his wife. Susan knows he is uneasy at times, often ringing her in the middle of the week to ask after her health. Perhaps, thinks Susan, he feels ill at ease because I put in a full day most days with the boys. But as she wriggles her way into her foundation garments and takes another look at herself in the mirror, she ponders the possibility that perhaps he is checking on his investment, making sure his mother is healthy enough to go on looking after his children for nothing. After all, he is an investment banker. His life is stocks and bonds.

Susan walks unsteadily down the stairs from her bedroom, goes to the door and the car slides like a slug into the driveway right on time. She watches as Joanne and the two boys bundle from the car; they look like Visigoths about to ransack Rome and other cities of culture and quiet learning.

The issue of not being paid for all of her child minding flits through Susan's mind as she watches the woman and her two sons advancing up the drive; the two boys resemble their mother, with the same lizard-like glassy eyes, and, for one moment, Susan expects the three to go down on all fours, to slither toward her tongues flicking out, capturing flies and other insects, crushing them with gluttonous glee between long strong reptilian jaws.

Susan had asked for a little small change to cover the expenses of feeding the boys two meals a day, not to mention the cost of taking them out sometimes for the day. But she hadn't expected the reaction from her daughter-in-law and son.

"Well, Mum, Joanne and I have discussed your request, and we both feel that if you want payment for looking after Malcolm and Michael, then you're not much of a grandmother. So we've decided to make other arrangements for the boys to be minded," said James with a voice as flat as a flat line on an ECG machine

Susan had always been proud, always carried herself with confidence and dignity, but the removal of her two grandsons had been more than she could bear especially when it became clear that Susan and James would not allow her to see the boys at all. It was punishment for asking for a few dollars to cover the expenses with her grandsons to help Susan survive on her old age pension.

After a month of not seeing her grandchildren, Susan rang her son and daughter-in-law, demanding to know why she had been ostracized, but more importantly wanting to know when she was going to see Malcolm and Michael

"Well, if you can't look after the boys without demanding payment then I don't think you deserve to see them at all, and James agrees with me," Joanne told her mother-in-law.

The standoff-off lasted two months and ended with Susan on the phone, begging her son to allow her to see her two grandchildren, telling James she didn't want any money, and she wouldn't ever again ask for it. The boys were returned to her day care, but not before Susan received a dressing down from Joanne, and a warning from her that if such a thing happened again, then Susan would never see her grandchildren.

Now the two boys push past their grandmother and run to the kitchen because they know a plate of sweet biscuits is on the sideboard, waiting for them. Susan, as she watches her silent daughter-in-law turn her back and walk to the car, hears Michael and Malcolm wolfing down the biscuits. Susan watches Joanne drive off; the woman never waves these days, never turns her head. The older woman sees the profile outlined by the late-model Jag's window; the jutting granite jaw, the implacable look of determination and defiance, the hair pulled back severely so the forehead projects like some ancient Inca statue of a god that demanded the blood of human sacrifice.

The older woman clutches her chest, checking that her heart is still there still beating. For a mad moment she is convinced her daughter-in-law strode up the drive brandishing a knife, sinking it deeply into Susan's chest, slicing her open, tearing out her heart and taking it with her to work at the real estate agent's office. Susan, terrified, imagines Joanne opening a filing cabinet drawer, and tossing the bleeding heart in with the files of houses and flats sold, the sales complete and obsolete, the obscene amount of commissions stuffed safely away the agency's bank account.

Before she can go inside to attempt to care for her grandsons, Susan sees Mick Brown, two doors down. He smiles and waves to her, then turns his attention back to his swarm of grandsons and granddaughters. He bends over the little boys and girls, and Susan is reminded of a beast of burden, a creature in harness commanded to toil until it drops.

Mick's wife died from Alzheimer's two months ago after the illness slowly robbed her of mind and body over seven years; the long goodbye. But the woman had been a grandmother to the bitter end, her sons and daughters-in-law bringing their children to be minded even when Maria Brown was in the third and final stage of Alzheimer's, and didn't know where she was who she was let alone any of the names of her grandchildren.

Susan can still see the wasted specter of the woman, hobbling down the street her madcap gaggle of grandchildren running amok, running circles around their grandmother, taunting her, teasing her because they knew the grandmother she once was had gone, and this one was to be made fun of while she still existed.

Susan closes the door wanting to hide from the sight of Mick, but it is the memory of Maria's funeral that causes Susan to place two fingers on the soft underside of her left wrist to check that her pulse is steady, to maybe check if the pulse is still there.

Maria was placed in the earth in the morning, Mick and the supposed loved ones leaving the cemetery after a brief mumble of words from the minister. By the middle of the afternoon of that day Mick had taken over from his wife, attending to a seething knot of grandchildren, minding them late into that evening, the man not allowed time to mourn the loss of his wife. He told Susan later that his sons and daughters-in-law said to him that it was best if he started child minding immediately, better that he begin the day of Maria's funeral because that way he wouldn't have time to grieve; he'd be too busy to notice Maria was gone, they said.

Susan walks into the kitchen now, she looks at her two grandsons; they hold the empty plate up and both of them lick the final sugary crumbs from it. The woman thinks they cannot be her flesh and blood; they seem strange alien creatures to her, like things that have crawled out of the sea from the deepest depths of one of the deepest subterranean canyons.

Malcolm and Michael are not of her world. The old woman clutches her chest again, her heart lurches, and she is convinced that she has died and is looking at the children from the other side. She has left their world, the world of their parents, and she feels relief surge through her.

Then she is falling, the kitchen sideboard, the cupboards and stove and fridge tilt, turn on their sides. She feels the tepid kitchen air rush past her face, and she feels the hard linoleum floor crash into the side of her head. The last thing she hears before the tidal wave of blackness sucks her down are the boys giggling.

She wakes and she is being lifted into the ambulance by two large men. Mick Brown called the blood box. He'd seen the two boys sitting in the drive holding the barrel of biscuits between them, feeding their faces their lips greasy with the lipstick of chocolate. When he asked them about Susan they'd shrugged, said something about their grandmother sleeping on the kitchen floor. Mick had dashed into the house his own tribe of grandchildren left in the driveway where they declared open war upon Malcolm and Michael.

The squabbling squad of warring grandchildren is still hurling names at each other, still pinching and punching as one ambo' places an oxygen mask over Susan's face.

Mick tells Michael and Malcolm that they must get in the ambulance to go with their grandmother to the hospital. They refuse, telling the man to fuck off. Mick grabs them by the scruffs of their neck and hauls them into the ambulance. They spit like feral cats, but the ambo' slams shut the door locks it, breathes a sigh of relief. Mick gathers his tribe of savages and leaves.

At the emergency ward nurses and the rare doctor come and go, fleeting apparitions of care and concern. Susan feels as though her heart has burnt itself out like a star in a far galaxy imploding upon itself, reduced to charred particles lost in black outer space. She feels her soul knocking against her body, searching for a door to escape through. Next to her bed Michael and Malcolm squabble over a coloring in book one of the nurses found to keep them quiet.

Then Joanne is there, a dark clot in the room as though she has emerged from some corner of the ward where she has been consorting and malingering with golden staph viruses. Susan sees the look of anger on her daughter-in-law's face. It smites the old woman and she dies. Her soul peeps out from the top of her head, seeing Joanne and the children; then the soul is off out of the body like an inmate escaping from gaol after years of hard labor and mistreatment.

Susan looks down and sees the shimmering silver umbilical cord still shackling her soul to the shell of her body. Desperately she wriggles, trying to break the cord to free herself. But she is stilled by the appearance of what seems to be a long black tunnel with a blinding white light growing larger at the end.

Out of the light emerge Susan's parents dead these past forty something years; they are radiant, the looks of love on their faces cradle Susan's soul and she is overcome, overwhelmed by their welcoming affection.

"It is time, darling," says her mother.

"Time for what?" asks Susan.

"Time to leave. You have completed what was set for you. You must come with us," says her father, reaching out a hand his glowing finger tip almost touching his daughter.

Susan is filled with happiness. She reaches out to take her father's hand, but then hears her daughter-in-law, speaking spitefully below her.

"Now, this won't do, Mum, pretending you're sick, pretending you're dead. James and I expect better than this. Now stop playing possum, open your eyes and get out of that bed. I'll drive you home and you can look after the boys until I get back this evening. It will be late because of all the work time you've made me lose."

"I can't go with you," Susan says fearfully to her mother and father.

"Your time has come, darling. You are no longer of that world," says her mother.

"I can't go because I have to look after the boys," says Susan.

She feels the silver cord trembling, and, for a second, she thinks Joanne has spied it, taken hold of it and is pulling Susan back down into her body.

"God is waiting to talk to you. He wants to review your past life and He especially wants to talk to you about not making a doormat of yourself the next time He sends you back to earth," says Susan's father.

"No, I can't come with you. I have to return to mind Malcolm and Michael," she says.

"God's wishes come before your former daughter-in-law's wishes and the needs of your former grandchildren," says her mother.

"No they don't," says Susan.

Looks of mild shock and bewilderment pass over the heavenly faces of Susan's parents.

"You don't understand, Mum and Dad. If I leave with you Joanne will come after me when she eventually dies. She'll track me down in heaven and punish me for not returning to look after her kids," says Susan.

"You're talking about defying God," says her father.

"Sod God! Better defying God than defying Joanne," says Susan.

"But you'll have been sent into another body and another life by the time Joanne dies," says her mother.

"In that case Joanne will see to it that when she dies she consults with God. She'll make Him send her back into another body close to me on earth, and she'll see to it that I'm punished. It's no use telling me she won't remember all of this in her new life because she will. Not looking after her children is something she won't forget or forgive no many how many reincarnations," says Susan.

Susan hears Joanne's voice rising up beneath her like a poisonous river tide of scum and debris.

"I'm just about out of patience, Susan. I'm telling you only once more, open your eyes, get up and stop fucking me about."

The giggles of Malcolm and Michael are like handfuls of blue metal flung at Susan's soul, tearing it, lacerating it. Susan rolls over, away from her parents; she takes hold of the silver umbilical cord, and, painfully, she hauls herself back down to her body and squeezes back into it. She can smell the rank decay of her flesh, the mouldering of her bones, but she keeps hold grimly, opens her eyes and gets out of bed.

Despite protests from nurses and one doctor, Joanne discharges her mother-in-law. The younger woman grips Susan's arm and frog marches her down the front stairs of the hospital, reefs open the door of the jag parked in a doctor's only parking spot and pushes Joanne into the back seat.

On the way home, Michael and Malcolm sit on ether side of their grandmother, holding her arms, their small fingers digging deeply into the woman's flesh, bruising it purple like tattoos of ownership. Susan feels like a prisoner being escorted by two miniature thugs. She looks up and sees the dead cold stone eyes of her daughter-in-law, staring at her in the cold glass of the rear vision mirror.

"You just wait till I get you home!" spits Joanne.

THE DOME

LOOKING UP THE OLD MAN COULD SEE THE LACE WORK of the dome shining in the sun. The old man traced the pattern of the iron, the familiar metal leaves, urns and flowers that were still there just as they had been when he looked at the dome for the first time almost seventy years ago. When he was a child, his hand in the soft hand of his mother as the woman and boy traipsed across the parkland, dodged among the wheels of creaking carriages and walked up the incline to the dome.

The dome had always reminded the old man of different things, depending on the time of the day and whether he was with his father or mother, or by himself.

When he came with his mother the dome looked like the round curl of a cat sitting comfortably in a lap. His mother would go right up to the building with the boy by her side and the two of them would stand and look at the sun passing across the porcelain and metal curve of the dome.

Neither would speak because the arcing of the sun in the metal and porcelain tiles fascinated both of them so there seemed no need for words. Not like at home, when his mother was all a dither running here and there, fussing about his father even when the man was still at his office and wouldn't be home for ages.

The boy's mother made her husband her life and spent hours every day washing his clothes and toiling over a slab of metal iron she spat upon. The boy remembered the spit, the breath of her life sizzling and jumping on the iron that had been heated over the open hearth. He remembered the spikes of saliva diminishing in height as the spit evaporated and his mother went to work on shirts, pants and ties while the dinner roasted in the kookaburra oven next to where she was standing.

Sometimes, when his father was away on business in another town, the boy and his mother caught the tram to the dome when it was evening. They would stand and watch the whirl of stars forming in the skin of the half sphere as night fell. A different painting the stars formed from the set line of the sun during the day; the stars cartwheeled, it seemed to the boy like the bright Catherine wheels on cracker night, spitting circles of light to celebrate the birth of the Queen. Sometimes the different formations were like dancers whirling about each other on a dark dance floor. Never bumping into each other, each couple knowing the limits of their orbit in the night-sky mirror of the dome.

But there was always that special moment, for the boy and his mother, the once-a-month moment when the full moon rose reflected in the dark dome and rode among the stars. Sometimes a cheese-yellow moon with a sea green aura as though the ocean, the moon had risen out of, still held onto the orb and would pull it back down to drown again. But it didn't happen and the moon floated in the crescent of the dome.

At such times the boy's mother couldn't contain her excitement. It bubbled over.

"Oh it's lovely," she would say. "It was worth the tram trip just to see it float up among the stars and settle there. It belongs there."

They wouldn't go straight home when the full moon was in the dome. Not like they usually did because the boy's mother saw it as her duty to be on hand to cater to any of the whims of the man she'd married.

But when he was away and the moon was like a queen sitting on a throne, the boy's mother would insist they walk up and down the streets to admire the contents behind the shop windows. Darting like reef fish in and out of side streets they went with the woman illuminated by the excitement she found in her freedom to come and go as she pleased. For a little while.

The old man sat and looked at the dome and he remembered his mother's face when he was a boy. The flesh smoothed by the colors of the things behind the plate glass windows; brass pots, silver vases, red woolen jumpers, gold earrings, black iron frying pans, cream-colored calico swept bands of color across the woman's features until the boy almost didn't know her.

He had to wait until they walked away to the tram stop to go back home before the bright things for sale drained from her face. The tram, far away, rumbled up the hill toward them like a metal troll let loose to reclaim children who'd enjoyed themselves too much for their own good.

It was different when he went to the dome with his father. The dome looked like an English bowler hat sitting squat on a bald head that was hidden from the public. The boy imagined a giant hand coming out of the sky, removing the bowler-hat dome and revealing the hair-bare head of a man. He imagined the brow of the giant head wrinkling with embarrassment and consternation because it had been revealed to the world.

The boy's father would stare at the dome and he would shift from foot to foot uneasily as though he was seeing what his son saw and was embarrassed just like the bald head of the dome was embarrassed. Self-consciously the boy's father would remove his bowler hat and scratch his forehead, then scratch his scalp that was covered with the finest of blond hair. But the boy always thought of his father as being bald because the shocking pink pate of the man showed through the soft, downy cover of hair.

Father and son went to look at the dome because the boy wanted to. His father took off his city-office hat and scratched his head because he was non-plussed as to what his son found so interesting about the dome.

It was only when the boy got older that he realized his father wasn't thinking of the dome as a bald man. Later the boy came to see the irritable twitch at the corners of his father's mouth. He hadn't noticed the mouth-corner tics before because his father always seemed so tall and far away. As tall as the dome the boy sometimes thought and craned back his head to look at his father the way he craned back his head to look at the dome.

It was when the boy grew taller that he could see the face of his father clearly and the ill-temper of the man jumping like a cut black snake across his face. The taller the boy got the closer he came to the irritable face of his father. It became a choice, he knew, now that he was an old man sitting on a park bench and looking at the dome.

It was a choice he had to make when he was still very young. The old man remembered his resistance, his not wanting to think about it, but it became unavoidable when one day, toward evening, the boy came to the dome by himself.

On the way home from the city by himself for the first time, he knew his mother would be waiting anxiously at the front gate of the Victorian bluestone for him. His mother's face had been a wan moon of concern in opposition to the angry twitch of her husband's mouth and mustache. A battle of wills his mother lost and his father won by insisting his son catch the tram by himself.

The boy got off the tram near the park instead of going straight home. Walking across the afternoon-shaded grass, he went right up to the dome and watched the turning of the tide in the porcelain and metal tiles. The low tide of sunlight pushed backward by the river rush of night until the dome was split in two with the sun and daylight on one side and the moon, stars and night on the other.

The boy watched, holding his breath as the dome seemed to quiver in the middle like the earth trembling as an earthquake rode through rock plates buried deep in the earth's crust. Fearing the dome was about to crack open like an early morning soft-boiled egg smacked by a giant silver spoon, the boy backed away. He half-believed he would be drowned by a high tide of egg yolk and white that would spill from the broken dome and wash about him with its sticky viscosity.

But the building settled and the sun surrendered to the night. The moon rode into its place and the boy knew his own mind for the first time.

Riding the tram back home the boy could see the dome in the glass of the tram windows. He got off and the tram rattled away with the moon and stars committed to a hundred panes of glass. All of them vibrating as the tram crunched over the tracks. As though the moon and stars were about to be shaken out of the dome the boy feared, but it didn't happen. The moon and the stars stayed in their galaxies and the boy was breathless with, strengthened by the knowledge.

She was standing there when he came to the gate. He couldn't control his smile as she pushed open the metal to admit him. And when she took him in her arms and he heard the sob of relief in her, he didn't pull away. He kept close to her with her smell of roses and fresh-baked bread. Even when his father strode angrily down the gun barrel hall of the house, the boy still allowed himself to be held by his mother.

Only when his father jammed his fingers between their bodies did the boy let go of his mother and only because he was afraid the prying fingers of his father might hurt her. The boy looked at his father and the anger shifting his office-procedure demeanor into an edifice of cold distaste that approached dislike.

As the boy grew he became aware of his mother's unhappiness but he could never see it, could never put his finger on what it was that caused her to weep once her husband had left for work.

One day, in the first week the boy had left school and started as an apprentice underwriter in an insurance office in the city, he came home early and let himself in with his key. His mother had forgotten he was no longer a school child and he walked into the parlor and found her there standing in front of the full length mirror. With her blouse undone and her heavy breasts moon white in the mirror.

He could not move, breathless with the beauty of the woman's breasts. Then he saw the bruises beneath the skin like lengths of brown kelp beneath the surface of the sea. He moved behind his mother and placed his hands on her shoulders. She turned her head away, the flush of blood rising up her neck as she wept with shame.

The boy, the man, waited at the front door of the house for his father. When the man pushed open the gate, raised his eyes, saw the anger in his son, he knew. The man froze and it was only the pleading of his mother that stopped her son from hitting his father. He punched the bowler from the head of the man and his father stood there with his by-now bald head with the furrows wrinkled into his brow.

No anger curled his mustache-covered lip and his face was blanched white with fear as the bowler rolled down the cobblestone gutter. The man never hit his wife again.

The boy and his mother settled back into the house as though they had always been tenants there but had somehow suddenly found the money to purchase the residence and do and behave as they pleased when they were within its walls, within its garden of ferns and trees.

The father still came and went to work but it was as though he didn't exist for the boy and his mother. And the boy took his mother on the tram to the park and the dome every day.

Looking at the dome through the veil of evening silver light, the old man could still see the woman, his mother long dead, standing at the perimeter of the building, still enraptured by the moon in the dome. And the old man half fancied he could see himself standing next to her, his attention only diverted by the beautiful breasts he knew sat beneath the lace and ruffles of her blouse.

Not that his mother minded. She knew there was nothing in it. She felt flattered, but left it at that. She needed to feel only a small relief when her son finally introduced her to the young girl he worked with in the insurance office. The two women met under the watching eye of the moon in the dome with the son, the boyfriend, on tenterhooks under the bright blaze of the stars dancing in the porcelain and enamel tiles.

But there was no need for the young man to have worried because his mother and his girlfriend got along as though they'd known each other for years. Cynthia even managed to have an effect on the boy's father, who found himself being drawn into the conversation that leaped about the dining table when Cynthia came to tea.

The father, an old man by now, raised his shamed eyes when Cynthia spoke to him. He felt like a man drowning in a sea that spread as wide as the sky above; he felt the silver net of the young woman thrown around his bent back and scrawny limbs. He felt her pulling him out of the black expanse of water where he'd struggled for years to stay afloat.

Cynthia persuaded the father to come with them to the park the next time. And he went with them even though his wife and son could barely find a thimble-full of words for him. The old man sat next to Cynthia as the tram ran down onto the parkland with the dome shining white like a new onion just picked and washed.

Cynthia, under the watchful and curious eyes of the mother and son, helped the father, as curled as a comma with arthritis, from the tram. Holding him up, Cynthia helped the man hobble over the grass to where the dome flashed in the sea of the evening air.

The son and his mother stood back. They did not approach the dome but stood down in the dish of grassland while Cynthia took the old man toward the building.

The father watched the moon ride into the dome and he saw a figure come with it; a mermaid with a bright, silver-scaled tail, long seaweed hair and eyes burning like lanterns in a dark unconsciousness. The mermaid swam among the stars and around the circumference of the moon. And as she swam her tail became legs until she was a woman.

The father stood, transfixed, and his tears fell and stained the dry, cracked leather of the boots he'd worn to work for almost forty years. He turned away when the woman swam out of the dome into the sea of night air.

The next day the son moved out of home and left his mother with his father. The father gave his notice at work that day. He returned home, went to the garden shed and emerged with a spade. Hanging his waistcoat on a tree twig he ignored the pain of his arthritis and began to dig.

It was a long courtship. As long as it took for the old man to dig the garden and plant the roses. As long as it took for the red roses to bloom. The old man, the husband presented his wife with bunches of scarlet blooms day after day for many long months, before the woman relented. She looked up, one morning, between bunches of roses, and placed her soft palm on the cheek of her husband.

The son married Cynthia and they lived in a house on the other side of town from where the son's parents lived. Cynthia worked on in the insurance office but insisted her husband stay home after he showed her some of the etchings he'd completed. Fifty years of sketching and drawing ensued and the name of the boy, the man found its way onto the walls of private residences and the hallways of public buildings.

The old man got up and he wondered how he could continue now that he'd buried Cynthia just two days ago. He looked at the dome and for the first time he wondered what it was like to be inside the building. He entered under the canopy of the dome supported by rows and rows of book shelves. Because the building was a library and held the stories, the memories of thousands who'd put pen to paper.

The old man looked up and saw all of his yesterdays rendered in the vast sphere of his soul; his mother, his father acted out their good and bad marriage, Cynthia strode among their lives and the old man saw her leading him away, as a young man, to begin the life he had to lead apart from his mother and her house.

Leaving the building at night, the old man walked away but he could feel the moon and stars in the dome following him home.

THE DEAD LANDLORD

Inspired by a painting of the same title by
Australian painter William Dobell.

SHE CAN SEE HIS BELLY IN THE GLASS OF THE MIRROR
as she brushes her long flaxen hair. It doesn't move, the mountain of
blubber, and she can't get used to its stillness not after sleeping next to
him for twenty years and seeing his stomach quiver and shake when he
snored. The blubber was like a jelly shaken in a bowl by a child when
her husband's breath exploded from his mouth and the lips farted like
a horse snorting.

She looks again, sees him laid out, dead, on the bed, she stops
brushing her hair, the bristles of the brush are caught in the long yellow
tresses; they stick through the yellow veil like spiny anteater quills. The
landlord's wife cannot move, because she is waiting for his belly to
begin to rise and fall with the breath of his life.

But it doesn't happen, she continues to pull the bristles of the brush
through her hair until they come out the bottom of the mane of corn-
yellow, but she doesn't bring the brush up to the crown of her head to
begin another brush stroke.

Her hand hangs limp next to her side, it is all she can do to hold
onto the brush. Looking in the mirror she moves her body between the
glass and her dead husband's body to block away his image. Replacing
his spent sack of bones, blood and flesh she beholds her form in the
mercury. Like an image coming up from the depths of a dream, still
forming in her eyes, still being born.

But the knot of his pajama pants catches her eye; she has to move to
one side because the bows of the knot command attention. The woman

is compelled to look at her dead husband's belly and she knows why. It is because the stomach was a weapon, not that she could ever tell anyone about it; it was just too preposterous for words to be spent on the matter.

But the woman cannot help but think about that stomach, the way he used to catch her unawares in the narrow parlor, push the flesh of his stomach against her. Pin her to the wall and he'd have his hands up under her nightdress before she could open her mouth to cry out. Not that there was anyone to hear her.

Not that it happened that often, but when it did, it left her wounded, unclean and she'd spend hours in the laundry away from him while he sat upstairs going over his books checking to see who hadn't paid him their rent for the week.

In the laundry she'd boil the copper and pour buckets of steaming water into one of the tubs, sit in it so the scalding water turned her the color the lobsters turned when her husband brought home some from the pub and told her to cook him a late supper.

Immersed in the hot water, she'd scrub herself with a bristled brush and sunlight soap until her soft pink flesh bled. Hours later, she'd open the laundry door, carefully peep around the corner to see if he was there, waiting for her. But once in a long while was usually enough for him and she'd scuttle back to her bedroom ready for the evening. And there, in the bedroom, she'd sit on the bed, look at herself in the mirror, searching for something that might appeal to any man other than her husband, who was always at the pub on the corner by three in the afternoon.

With determination, she places her plump hourglass hips between the glass and his dead body, with an act of will begins to brush her hair with long sweeping motions like the way she arcs her arms through the air and into the skin of the water off St. Kilda beach. Something she's done for years, swimming up and down the length of the beach in the middle of the day, the long laps keeping her big bum, her wharf-pylon legs, her heavy breasts, tight and taut as a the skin of a kettle drum.

Not that it was for him, the landlord; she doesn't know who it was for other than herself. A long meditation of physical effort, her head in the green gloom, trails of silver bubbles coming from her mouth as she breathed out in the salt water, sandpapering from her nostrils the money and garlic smell of him; an escape from the sight of him. The bullying demeanor of his face, the belly, the jutting saber chin with the steak fat marbling of whiskers haunting her awake, asleep.

And as the knots of her hair are undone by the strokes of the brush, she finds a small smile for herself in the mirror. She remembers his outrage, years ago, when he came home from collecting his rents and found her in the kitchen with her hair down. It was the first time she'd released the cascade of yellow, the first time she'd unrolled the severe bun of hair kept in tight place on the top of her head with an uncountable number of bobby pins.

So much steel in her hair it affected the magnets in the radiograms for sale in the shop three doors down. Whenever she forgot, and passed by the shop, instead of on the other side of the road, all of the radiograms began to play. Thirty or more of them set on the one station, playing Mozart concertos until the owner ran back and forth turning off every one.

"What in the name of Christ are yer doin' with yer hair down. Yer look like one of them street Lizzies down in Chapel Street. Put it back up now before I give yer th' back of me and yer tart!" the landlord had said.

She knew better than to argue and soon had her hair back in place, the pins of steel holding its beauty in check, scraping her scalp sometimes so she awoke with trickles of blood dried down her face. And she kept it that way, never let it down again until the lodger came and told her he was dead.

Strange, she thinks as she continues to brush her hair, strange that it was the first thing she did when she went to the room where he counted his rent money. Saw him slumped across the table, the piles of notes and coins scattered everywhere. The first thing she did, even before the lodger and the butcher from next door, carried him out and lumped him onto the bed in their bedroom, was to let down her hair.

When they staggered across the landing with the body, she was raking her fingers through her hair, untangling the knots of years of wearing it up and tightly controlled. Strange, she thinks, as she bends her head to one side, takes hold of a handful of the last few inches of hair, brushes it briskly, how she saw her husband as the butcher and the lodger took him away to the bedroom.

It was like seeing the body in another time and place. As she glances at the body in the mirror, it reminds her of the drowned man taken in a rip in Port Phillip Bay years ago. She stood on the beach, still a girl, when the men carried him from the water. As young as she was she was puzzled by the feeling that the drowned man amounted to nothing for her nor any one else.

And that's the way she sees her husband now. She stops brushing her hair, undoes the buttons down the front of her nightdress, wonders, looking at her small nipples, the size of sixpences, what it would be like to have a man suck them. What it would look like to look down at a man entranced, suckling her like a baby.

She undoes more buttons, looks at her generous stomach still unmarked by the stretch lines of child bearing and she wonders what it would be like to have a man kiss and caress her there.

And between her legs the hair is still yellow, golden as sovereigns. An aunt told her once what her husband did with his tongue there. It is impossible to imagine that, thinks the dead landlord's wife, such pleasure cannot be seen in her mind's eye.

With one swift movement of her fleshy arms she strips the nightie from her, finds her dress, pulls it over her head, drags it down over her body. Looks at the small bumps of her hard nipples in the blue material, runs her hand over her belly, gets up on her high heels she drags out from where they were hidden under the wash stand.

Worn for the first time, the high heels cause the dead landlord's wife to stagger, totter, right herself, look in the mirror. Sees her bum thrust out by the shoes, her breasts pushed forward by the movement the high heels make in her body. Leaving the room, she doesn't look back, doesn't consider the arrangements necessary to be made for the funeral of her husband. Clumping down the steps, the woman holds onto the wooden railing, fearful of falling but determined to make the ground floor and the street outside, waiting for her.

Like a child, standing on the edge of a deep swimming pool, fearful of drowning, the woman stands on the doorstep. Then steps onto the cobblestones. Walks, hears the radios begin to play The Bolero, almost all thirty of them as the owner of the shop, seeing her, rushes about turning on every last one.

LEMON TREE PASSAGE

EDDY SMITH SQUINTED INTO THE BLACK. A LEAD SKY lit by wreaths of lightning. A flash washed out Lemon Tree Passage with a curtain of white fire. Struck into the crosses of the mangroves. In the rain, a tree burned red; smoked black weals into the water. Eddy focused the column of fire. Burning against the wet. Snapping red tongues against the cold. Dry inside from months of drought. Broken by the humid cell of air, off the ocean, dumping fire, dumping rain, dumping thunder that rolled through the cathedral mangroves, across the slate-flat water of Lemon Tree. Rolled into Eddy's shack, the last fisherman's shack left in Lemon Tree.

Eddy felt the noise coming down on him like trumpets blasting awake the dead and dreaming; coming in through the slabs of the shack; provoking Eddy, bruising through his skin. Jangling up the arthritis, worse than the wet did once it got going. Thunder that jarred his bones upright; sent ribbons of pain, like a hundred sciatic nerves, flaring alertness through bone and gristle and blood. Torched Eddy's still and lethargic blood into a King Tide of movement, like Tilligerry Creek in flood, a bulge of water dredging out the silt and mud in the Lemon Tree Estuary. Lemon Tree with its mysterious mud caves beneath mangrove masses of roots that rocked schools of bream and taylor and flathead like babies in blue water cradles.

Eddy, the last one of his kind, like his shack. A crooked construction of sun-cured gum slab, a tilted corrugated iron hat that threatened to slip off, slide into the water that lapped Eddy's back door. Eddy, a crooked construction of gaunt limbs; flesh, salt and wind-cured into brown, beef-jerky hide. Eyes, soft blue lanterns; blue boats burning down to the water line of the estuary as night covered it.

Eddy's shack smack in the middle of an eye of flat green land; the bubbled end of a long thin isthmus that jutted right out into the water of Lemon Tree. Took Eddy away from the shore and the creeping rust of the new brick and tile bungalows not far enough away. Delivered Eddy close to the mangroves. Where he lay, rocked in his hammock by the tidal tows rising and falling; rocked by the wind freshening among the water gums at daybreak; rocked by the sound of bream crunching oyster shells on the razor racks at high tide.

Eddy looked out. Peered into the dim curtain of water. Frozen water. Arrows of icicles stopping his eyes. He could just make out the new brick police station around the point and, in the grave black, the whispered outline of the real estate agent. New, and selling off Lemon Tree in slabs. Not quite what it was. Years ago.

But Lemon Tree was still borderland: mangrove and marsh and magic that came from the deep blue water. Magic that came from the estuary in the bucking silver bodies of bream and whiting and taylor. Magic that shaded Eddy in shadow circles cast on the fisherman by the crowns of the mangrove gums. Magic that came in the unexpected that belonged to outlaws like Eddy.

A crease of light cracked the bed of clouds. Eddy watched the burning tree subside to charred black. He'd removed the glass pane of the one window. Took away the slab of glass, rimed with salt, to see the water and the mangroves clearly. Rain came in in buckets, but it was worth it to Eddy. First to spy out the weather clearing; first out to fish the dreaming depths.

Eddy packed his bait and gear. Pushed off from his jetty in his dinghy, and began to row. He'd scrubbed the hull clean of weed and barnacles the day before. The vessel slid easily like a lover's hands across the skin of the water. It left a long thin scar in the water connecting Eddy's shack with the maw lip of the mangroves. Eddy could almost feel the warmth of his wood burner, back in the shack, pursuing him across the water. Reaching a hot hospitable hand from the hearth into the cold of the masts of gum.

Eddy rowed steadily between the wooden jaws. No longer did the oars dip into mud, as before the rain. Now they slipped into the water and took hold of the blue deep; propelled Eddy easily toward the bream hole.

The sky was still roiling black; great scuds and squids of fleecy pewter that reached down at Eddy like jelly fish tentacles. The same color as the sky the day Eddy buried Anna Maria, his wife. Eddy remembered.

Eddy, lost, dazed, down, out. Comatose, pole-axed by grief, but walking through the funeral, the relatives, the sympathy, the explanations.

"Cancer in such a young woman. Who'd have thought. At her age. No children. Lucky there Eddy. Would have been hard on them."

It was hard on Eddy. Launched himself into his job. Drugged away the pain of loss with work. A hot tier at the steel works, tying red-hot clock springs of recently-rolled metal. Destined for G.M.H. Eddy took all the extra shifts, all the `doublas' he could get. Spent whole weeks sleeping in the crib room. Rocked into semi-unconsciousness by the smash of hot steel bulldozing snub red noses through ancient rolling stock.

Didn't change. Didn't shower. Slept on the wooden benches as the men from A and B crews came and went like ghosts.

The ambulance came and took him away when he collapsed. Fell asleep and slumped over onto a hot coil of steel. Branded him through his greasy overalls; burned and angry, red-blistered spiral above his heart and lungs.

After hospital, he left, started walking away from Newcastle, the works, his home.

Eddy found the spot. A deep mud hole in the heart of the mangroves. Bream country. No doubt. Harry Beachman had shown him the spot. Just before Harry left the fisherman's shack to Eddy. No lease, no contract. Just gave it to Eddy. Ended his exile. Went back north after eight years to his family.

The locals reckoned Harry hadn't been the same since he'd almost drowned in the hole Eddy was fishing. Deep. A mud cave that portaled under the labyrinth of root maze.

Harry was on the way out of Lemon Tree. Driving his beat-up ute. He found Eddy near Tanilba Bay. Walking. He'd been walking for two days. Harry picked him up and took him back to the shack. Few words. Gave him the key.

Harry left. Headed north for home. Where his wife waited. Waited with the empty bedroom of their daughter who'd disappeared eight years ago. Drove Harry mad. Drove him to the highway. Dazed and hitching. Drove him to Lemon Tree.

Eddy kept to himself. Just like Harry had. The locals accepted Eddy and his isolation; his refusal to mix or talk. As though Eddy was really the old Harry still in residence, or a son and heir who'd taken up his due entitlement.

Eddy pulled in a bream. Slipped out the hook. Slid on another blood worm. Cast into the depth black. The isolation suited him. But something picked at his bait. Squire, and bad news. Fish that took all the bait; fish with a spray of deadly spikes that could pierce to a finger bone.

The savage pick picking in the dark reminded him of Bill. Mad as a meat ax was Bill. Lived up the Karuah River in a shack of his own. The only person Eddy really spoke to. Bill and his net and his flagons of port.

Ingenious was Bill. Well, sort of. Rebuilt his shack on a base of empty port flagons. Laid the glass necks into cement and formed a solid square of glass that moaned like a beaten woman under Bill's drunken heels.

Eddy pulled in. The bait was a ragged, bloody mess from the razor teeth of the squire.

Eddy stopped. Felt the tide turning. Saw the whirlpool in the hole twist his boat. He felt the hot spiral scar itching above his heart and lungs. As if it were turning itself. Turning with the tide, the mangroves, the earth turning in the tide of black.

Five more bream and Eddy decided to row up river to Bill's shack.

"Give the wasted bastard some fish. A bit of nourishment instead of that port leaching out the goodness in 'im. Never catches anything with that net. Too pissed most of the time to pull it in."

Eddy pulled himself over the water as black as squid ink winking star constellations in depths where fish snapped at that burning phosphorescence. Eddy looked up, in rhythm, as he rowed. Looked up into the stars that forged a thousand pin points of light in his eyes; looked up into a scimitar of light that might sever his upturned head from his body.

He could hear Bill singing a kilometer away before he made the jetty. Bill drunkenly hollering across the black water. Eddy could hear the shack moving on its slippery glass foundations; squealing in the night. He could hear Bill's rough hob nail boots clattering up and down in the shack. Great angry slaps of echo booming across the water like a canon fired to raise the drowned, the lost.

Eddy tied the dinghy to the jetty. Clambered up the wooden steps, fractured by weather and tide into splayed slivers of wooden tongues. Arguing with Bill, through the night.

"Whose there! Fuck yer!!" yelled Bill.

Angry boots. Door slammed back. Baseball bat at the ready. Port-rimmed wild eyes that saw things in the mangroves if Bill drank long enough and stayed conscious.

Usually visions of his wife rising palely from among the mangroves. Beckoning Bill across the water to her. Three times he'd almost drowned. Launched himself into the estuary. After her. Surfaced, pissed, thrashing out. Churning the water. Just making the jetty. Slumped on the wood. Sobbing. Howling. Like an animal caught in the steel jaws of a trap, but, unlike the animal, unable to chew off the limb, tear himself free.

"It's okay Bill. It's only me," said Eddy.

"Aha. Eddy. Come see. Come see what I've got t' show yer!" jabbered Bill like a hobgoblin storming out of a night dream.

Bill pushed, dragged Eddy around the side of the shack. Eddy allowed the liberty. He felt a bit sorry for Bill since his wife threw him out. Sick of his drunken rages, and her bruised eyes like muscat grapes, ripe and fallen from the vine.

Packed Bill's bags and put them on the pavement. Took out and A.V.O. to keep Bill at bay. Bill at bay, baying like a bloodhound for Susan to take him back. Down on his hands and knees just outside the hundred meter border stipulated in the A.V.O.

Howling like a wolf until the neighbors called the police, who took him away.

The divorce papers served on him drove him from Newcastle to the Tree. Drove him to drink. Even more than when he'd been with Susan.

"Look! Look! Look!" he cried, galloping with glee up and down the jetty.

Eddy looked. And wondered. A convolution of metal pipes, plastic, stops and cocks formed a dragon-shaped still from which bubbled a stench that made Eddy gag. Worse than any marsh gas he'd experienced among the mangroves. An acrid pong that took hold of Eddy's taste buds, bruised them, burned his throat.

"Christ almighty Bill," said Eddy, hand clasped like a surgical mask over his mouth, "what is it?"

Bill proudly walked amidst the foul mist. Petted and prodded the apparatus. Pulled open a metal cap and funneled in a bilious green liquid from an old paint can.

Eddy watched, half-fascinated, half-nauseous, as Bill poured the contents of brimming beakers into the thirsty, metal mouth. Beside the hissing, spitting still, were piles of corrugated iron, sliced and smashed into strips. Bill took a handful. Cut his hands bloody on the rusty teeth. Poured them into the belly of the dragon, hissing, spitting foulness and steam and liquid acid jets that found Bill's skin. Ate it, pitted it with sink holes eating through to the bone.

"It's for her!! Susan!!" yelled Bill. "Alchemy! It turns the iron into gold. Look!!" he commanded.

Pulled out from the arse end, a sticky mess of yellow, Eddy could see the muddy sludge dripping away. Showing the rust and iron underneath. Bill couldn't.

"I'm gonna buy her back! Use the gold t'take her away. Overseas. Buy a big house. T'come back to. She'll come back. Susan will. She will. I'll stop the drink y'know. No more. Like it used t'be."

Eddy pulled hard on the oars. Backed off into the night. Through the sleeve of black he saw Bill dancing; a painted savage howling. Eddy saw the dragon, sulfur and yellow, glowing red eyes; a metal-scaled body that might raise itself from its metal rods.

Turn upon Bill, lash its tail of odds and ends. Tear through Bill's pasty alcoholic's flesh. Eat him whole with it's ugly spiked jaws that ate second-hand corrugated iron.

Eddy rounded the point. Blocked out the smudge of mad fire that burned around the scarecrow Bill. Eddy was shaking. As though the madness had been passed into him. A virus that left him shaking in fever. He shook like a man with the D.T.'s.

Eddy looked over his shoulder. Saw the shack; a strange, ragged, wooden citadel perched on the shallow, cabochon-cut of land, close to the tide line. Through the skeleton frame of wood, the wood burner burned fire across the black water.

•

Eddy could see the turtle in the stand of mangroves. It was wedged between the jaws of two trees. He could see it spiraled around with circles of mangrove; a spiral of trees and narrow water way that would just accommodate the fat-bottomed hull of the dinghy.

Eddy could see, in the final daylight, the creature thrashing to free itself. Resting. Exhausted. Its mud bleared eyes watched Eddy though the bars of wood. Eddy knew the animal. As long as his boat, it had scared Eddy many times.

Many times, lost in dreaming upon the water, eyes half-closed, mind shut down, Eddy had been blasted from his self-imposed stupor by the turtle surfacing right next to the dinghy. Blowing like a whale. Rocking the boat. Once tipping Eddy in icy water. Waking him for the rest of the day.

Eddy put away the oars. The corridor of trees was too narrow to row. He hauled himself by hand, taking hold of branches; dead limbs that cut into the callused flesh of his palms. Pulled through the spiral. Getting closer to the distressed turtle. The high tide rising. Soon to cover the cabochon-shaped shell. Drown the wise and wrinkled old man's head of the turtle. With the strange tower of shell and barnacle built in the middle of the animal's forehead.

Eddy could feel the black eye of the spiral coming to him. Could smell the black mud stench that was the heart of the mangrove spiral. Pulled, willed himself toward it. Hacking with his bare hands through the undergrowth. Left drops of blood from his hands in the water.

He heard, behind him, the suck sucking mouths of toads gobbling his blood from the surface. Scooping it up in their wicked jaws like cream skimmed from a hot pail of milk.

He found the turtle. Lashed the dinghy to a gum. Slid, delicately, carefully, into the opaque water. Felt roots slice his feet. Felt the mud close around his ankles. The black ooze rising like the tide. Water reached his waist. Red-faced, sweating, he broke away branches of undergrowth from around the body of the turtle.

Eddy hauled himself into the fork of a mangrove next to the turtle. Braced his legs against wood and pushed with his shoulders against the shell. Felt the turtle shift slightly between the wooden vice. Eddy pushed, splintered corners of shell. Heard the pain rolling through the soft body inside the armor.

He went back to the dinghy. Took out the small machete he kept for when he pulled in a sizable shark. Waded back to the animal. Eyes plimsoll-marked half way by water. Eddy felt the steady rush of the high tide water at his chest.

Began to hack at one of the trees that held the turtle. Eddy stood in the black mud stink. He felt the toads nibbling at the cuts in his feet and legs. He felt the mud crabs take a strip or two of flesh from his ankles. He prayed that sharks didn't venture into the mangroves.

Eddy hacked and slashed. He could hear the echo coming back at him across the water. Sliding through the spiral of mangroves; bouncing off the distant brick and tile intrusions on the shore. Coming back to nibble his ears the way the toads and crabs nibbled his flesh.

Finally, the tree gave way; a long groan of wood falling and the turtle pushed free by Eddy, floated into the rising tide of the estuary. Its eyes, disappearing, regarded him with indifference as it sank back into the muddy caves of mangroves.

Eddy was exhausted. He clambered onto a lip of mud. Rested a while, then stood to return to the dinghy. Slipped. Flailing his arms in the darkling air, trying to balance himself, but falling. Back ward, onto the fresh wood stakes he'd just cut to free the turtle.

The wood went into his hands, pierced his feet, severed into the vein and artery chord of his neck, gashed bloody his sides. Rivered a tide of blood from his body swirling into the spiral tract of the mangrove. Staining red the dark heart.

Eddy passed into a delirium of half-waking, half-sleeping. As the tide lapped his fingers, his hands, his head, Anna Maria came in the night, among the gums. Not cancer-wasted, but the Anna Maria he had loved. The woman, brunette and plump and heavy-breasted. Arched in the night under the thrust of his body, the salt sweat of their love-making making them slippery like fishes in the water; a fluid coming together, their gasps of mirth and delight above the distant pounding of steel rolled then spun into hot spiral coils at the steelworks.

Above him, her black shining eyes woke him. He watched her ascend into pointed star light. Eddy felt the mud bed below him; felt the tide just slipping to his lower lip. With will he took himself down from the wood.

Screaming pain and blue murder when he wrenched his hands from the stakes; pulled free his feet, strained his chord of neck from the spiky splinters of wood still inside. The wounds would heal later, keeping in slivers of wood. Healed up inside of him. Wood that later became a second fond flesh rubbing next to veins and arteries to remind him.

He slid into the water. Cried out as the salt water cauterized his wounds. Eddy made the dinghy and dumped himself on the wood bottom, then made himself row in the tide-widened passage. His blood slicked the oars and his cries rent through the gums. In the darkness he smelled his way through the mangrove spiral. He could smell the fresher salt water outside the snaking circle; the salt rising in from the heads of Port Stephens. Bringing clean water and fish. Eddy could smell it and he followed his nose, the small craft instinctively finding its way through the loops. Barely bumping against the bows of gums.

Eddy felt the flesh of the raw gashes clawing up with the salt. He imagined the skin and the flesh growing over in thick protective pads; calluses of hide sleeving around his body to stop out the toads and mud crabs.

The salt smell was closer. Through his pain, Eddy could feel the spiral brand above his heart and lungs. He remembered Anna Maria and the itching of the scar receded, calmed as though the red angry weal of raised scar had been washed away.

The mangrove spat him out into clear water. Eddy passed out. In the dark he heard other oars dipping, felt a strong grip on his shoulders. Lifting him from the wood. Down. Back into blackness, away from the pain.

•

Eddy blinked away the blear of salt water tears. Focused the figure through the water. Saw it rise up, over him. Harden to clear outline in the morning.

The head was a broken square and too big for the thin steel rod frame supporting it. The deformity began at the left cheek bone where the jaw and chin twisted alarmingly to the right, resulting in the impression that the man saw everyone and everything from a side-on angle. As though nothing could be perceived squarely but rather inspected perpetually from an odd and alien angle.

"Gooday mate. Thought you were gone. The grove almost got yer. Lucky. Or bloody determined. Or both."

Behind the figure, Eddy could see large windows looking into thick bush. Myna birds fussed and squabbled over red spring blossoms. A cackle of kookaburras chuckled and rolled into a reel of rollicking laughter.

"Be quiet yer stupid buggers!" the man yelled. He hobbled to a bucket beside a hewn-gum table. Dragged it to the window and threw out lumps of gristle and chewed steak. The birds descended snapping up the meat in their hard black metal beaks. Eddy watched them mercilessly hack and flay the dead lumps of meat.

Eddy could hear the hammering of the blade beaks and see the feathered throats gorging.

The dwarf returned to Eddy. Loomed his large head with its liquid eyes over Eddy.

"Y' look okay t'me. Christ, I thought you'd swallowed half the estuary. Even chucked up mud and weed. I was just waitin' for yer t'regurgitate the Titanic."

The man laughed; a bell peal that rolled out into the cathedral gums and was taken up by the kookaburras. A raucous hymn of joyous noise. Eddy laughed. A long time it had been since he'd laughed. The laugh of a man hauled from the dreaming depths of Lemon Tree. A laugh that took him past the haunting of Anna Maria. Out into open waters where his line would find the silver and rainbow bodies of large snapper.

"Yer look good enough for some breakfast. M'name's Alex. C'mon."

The short man lifted Eddy from the bunk. Surprising strength as if it were coiled into his short squat frame waiting for release.

Alex served up steak and sausages and eggs to Eddy. Then went back to his half-finished meal. Eddy watched him chew the sinew of meat then spit the mass into the bucket. Alex lived on the goodness of the juice he could extricate. His twisted neck and throat made it impossible for him to swallow anything other than the softness of eggs and jelly. The pain of hard food clogged in his gullet like a 1'0 suicide hook embedded in the gorge of a bream.

The room was littered with canvasses; oil paintings of Lemon Tree at every stage of tidal rise and fall. Eddy saw the circle of tide running, in canvas frames, through the estuary, from the heads up Tilligerry Creek, the mudflats, brown and black with death in the corpses of pelicans and fish; the jaws of oyster rocks crinkled white and black; the mid-tide lapping up the salt-encrusted pylons of the Lemon Tree Wharf, taking away the bodies, creeping up the boat ramp to cover the rank slime; the full high tide reaching into the mangroves, with prawns and crabs and fish goggling glassy eyes at fishermen in dinghies upon the clear membrane of the water.

Yet, even Eddy's untrained eye could see the paintings missed something; a small indefinable something that made the scenery strain and twist in stiffness. Technically good, but all fish and birds and trees. Only the bare shadow suggestion of humanity.

"Like 'em?" grinned Alex.

"Yeah. Not bad," lied Eddy.

"P'haps I'll teach yer how to run up some of yer own water colors."

"Yeah, yeah. That'd be good," said Eddy.

"C'mon then, I'll row yer back," said Alex.

"Where are we by the way?" asked Eddy.

"Tahlee. Or the back of Tahlee. In the hills."

The two left by a spiral staircase that coiled from the forest floor into the house set on wooden stilts.

Alex pushed off. Rowed only with his strong Popeye arms. Not like Eddy, who'd learned to use his whole body. Eddy hauling his body into the oars with body and soul; large deep strokes. Not the shallow half measures of Alex, despite his strength, despite his potential.

•

Eddy stood on the plateau armed with his brush and board of colors. Alex grinned. The canvas stood on a rough easel in front of Eddy; a blank window of white waiting to be filled with forest and water, and light and dark.

Eddy aimed his eye at the conical hill of green and began. Daubing clumsily at first, but under Alex's technical guidance, managing the colors, confining them, letting them riot with control.

The hill on canvas was not the real bald hill of green, its cedar cut down years ago by timber getters. Eddy's hill was studded with stands of timber and it lost its smoothness. It pointed toward the peak of the canvas.

Weeks passed. Eddy gained control of his colors. Alex interfered less. Let Eddy have his head. Let him bolt the greens and blues and russets onto the canvas. Always the same aspect, from the plateau; the hill no longer a bald old man's pate worn down by suffering. Now transformed by Eddy's brush, moving with a will of its own as Eddy suspended thought. Gave his body up to the movement of gusts of wind rolling down from the Bulahdelah Ranges.

The earth lay below Eddy; an unrolled scroll of mountains and water and bush. But the hill grew from canvas to canvas, towering to the top of each painting; covered with thick bush of eucalypt gums from Eddy's hands. A tower that dominated the sketched in foothills, the puddles of estuary water, the smoke traces of settlement whispered into corridors of green by Eddy's brush.

Eddy took Alex fishing . Taught the painter how to fish. How to tie on a hook and swivel, how to select a sinker, not too heavy, for elusive bream, but heavy enough in a big blow or a strong tidal movement.

Alex, line slick from his own blood, was all thumbs. Pricked and jagged himself with hooks. Lost the bait easily to the ravenous toads and squire. Cost Eddy a fortune in lead when Alex snagged every cast on submerged rocks, bottles, cans. Lumps of seaweed. Alex seemed to seek them out. The snags.

Only after hours of patience, did Eddy see Alex haul in his first fish; a tawny flathead but with rainbow color down the flanks. An indication that the fish had come in from outside. An open ocean fish its gills and scales washed clean by the fresh salt water.

There was no stopping Alex after that. The bream and whiting and taylor came into the boat like silver streaks of intuition and compassion in a dark mind. Alex painted with a controlled fury. The stiffness, the painful straining , went from his paintings. Replaced by a lucid silver light that transformed the squat ugly landscapes into something else; a circle of land and water and sky crowned upon each other.

Alex's high tide washed clean the waterway, bringing, on the swelling blue eye of water, the Sunday fishermen with their wives and children. Eddy saw them in the boats. The loud yellow straw hats to keep off the sun; the mouths fixed in mirth as a mullet bucked into a boat; the pink generous flesh of the arms of the women offering husbands and children thick squares of bread jammed with ham and cheese and pickles; husbands hauling in whiting that whipped forever into he luminous light of Alex's paintings; the boats, laden with families, on the high tide lifted toward the leafy halos of the mangroves.

And Alex now rowed with a vengeance. Putting his back into it; straining every limb, pulling the boat and Eddy and the gear and the bait to spots Alex selected. Spots that never seemed to fail. Alex's intuition settling on schools of fish just below the boat.

•

Eddy was at Tanilba Bay. In the battered burnt orange Datsun 120Y Alex had bought for him. A present from the money from Alex's first exhibition. Sold out, and with enough for Alex's surgery. Long and complicated, but straightening out the man's throat and neck. He swallowed steak and roast dinners with carnivorous gusto. Took in all the goodness, and worked harder and longer on his paintings. Fed the kookaburras slices of raw rump steak.

This was Eddy's second beginning of the journey home to Newcastle. Early that morning, he'd found Merv wandering on the outskirts of Lemon Tree. Merv, wild-eyed and with a will to walk himself into the earth. Bury himself away from the light of day. Eddy took him back to the fisherman's shack. Gave Merv the key. Showed him where the dinghy was tied. Gave him his fishing gear. Showed him how to feed the small metal furnace.

And disappeared out of Lemon Tree. Going back to Newcastle, maybe even to the steelworks. Eddy felt the spiral scar flattened, drained of the tide of dark poisonous blood.

THE GAMBLERS

The driver could see them out the front of the club. Staggering, drunk. He'd taken them there in the cab, hours ago. Picked them up in Waratah from their rented flat. Just below the line of the highway, coal trucks and cars thundering out of Newcastle, just above their bed, just above their heads. Maybe that's why they drank so much; the noise, the fear of a vehicle through the guardrail. All chance.

He pulled up. Her lips were smeared a Mr. Lincoln rose red; roses mulched by time to an almost black blood smudge of decay. Her, tottering on D. Day high heels toward the cab. All rickety and wobbly, the old limbs. Not like when she went to the club to gamble. Crossed elegantly, not a bad set of legs for an old girl. Long and lean, a swimmer's legs without fat. Not now; chimney-rubble legs ready to topple in a high wind.

He could see the sockets where her eyes were supposed to be, black as the night she came out of. Like a dying light, the lisps and sighs of silver of her white jumper. And her mouth opening as black as her black skirt. On the trip there it had been closed. Pink and demure. Now it gulleted open demanding attention.

"Give us a hand, drive. Before I piss meself. Get us home quick honey bun. M' back teeth's under water."

The driver had heard stories about the couple; the grapevine of driver gossip that told about her child. In her forties the woman had still been childless. But determined, against the odds, against the advice of her doctor, the remonstrances of relations, to gamble. Gamble on pregnancy which came home past the post; a daughter, healthy and squawking, opening a pink gummy mouth for the breast.

A real joy to the couple, an unexpected windfall that kept them together. Helped them overlook their differences, their indifferences toward each other. Then the end of the lucky streak with the daughter grown. Married and overseas. Lived in Florence, never wrote, never phoned. Didn't contact her parents, flying by the seat of their shiny pants, heads or tails whether they'd see another spring racing season. Together.

The driver watched the husband, coming, just behind her. Pork pie hat and shiny suit like a refugee from a racetrack, a punter or a bookie turned off the track for corruption. In exile, left only with his wife.

His legs sheathed in the dusty pants, creases ironed in by time, flicked like blades despite his age. A little of the danger left over from the old days; days in back alleys up Newcastle's east end, flipping two up. Heads or tails, a bank of notes or the arse end out of his strides. Heads or tails with her, and others.

They'd both had others, both gambled with other partners. So the driver's father had told him. The driver's father knew them from the old days from the track. He'd seen them there; him with a new woman on his arm, binoculars on the other, trying to search out his horse among the pack coming around the bend, praying for it to break clear; her with a bookie or a professional punter, all over him like a rash, hoping he'd haul in the big win, the big bash. Take her away on a P. & O. to warmer climes.

Until the gambling went on too long. Her with crow's feet at the corners of her eyes, standing out near the entrance of the track, alone. Not even enough left in her purse to catch a cab back home. And him, still on the two-up, but not the familiar lanes and back streets of his youth with a ready fuck to be cadged up against an alley wall.

Age, and only each other; long-priced outsiders that might get to the winning post or the glue factory. And their wicked tongues lashing each other like the snap of an on course bookie's fingers rifling through his winnings.

The driver watched him pursuing her like a blooded gray hound after the hare. Desperate. He saw him claw out his hands. Just a couple of fingers like fishhooks caught her jumper for support, for blind guidance to the back seat of the cab.

"Shit, get yer hands off me, Georgie," came back at the man. An almost voluptuous wiggle unsnaggled the latch of his fingers.

"Sit in th' back yer drunken prick! Useless drunken prick! I'm sittin' in the front with th' drive. He looks up to it."

She fell into the front seat, face in the driver's lap. A low raw rasp of a laugh came up her throat. The driver felt her breath on his balls through his trousers. Was revolted by her, by his own cock stirring. He righted her. Saw in the rear vision mirror her husband, falling in the black glass. A collapsed concertina of brittle limbs on the back seat. His breath creaking like an old-growth forest tree severed, groaning to its death.

"Bitch! Fuckin' bitch!! Slut!!" spat on beads of saliva.

The driver drove. A short fare. Thank God, he thought. He wondered about them, the drink and the gambling. He knew from experience they'd barely scrape together enough shrapnel to pay for the trip. But somehow they always managed. He wondered about them and the trip to the club, earlier.

All lovey dovey, sitting in the back seat. Together. Hands all over each other like a couple of kids who'd just discovered French kissing. And the husband's wad of notes in his wallet, and his grin of optimism as he forked out a ten dollar note and told the driver to keep the change.

The dignified walk of the two as they headed for the bar for the pokies, for the TAB right next door to the club. As if their lives depended on it; a last throw of the dice, a final twenty on the nose of an outsider, a final five dollars worth of five cents poured down the silver gullet of a poker machine. A final stab at each other in the dark.

•

The driver made the flat. Even this late the line of traffic loomed and boomed like a big surf. An unbreakable noise, a threat that never went away.

The driver watched her scrabbling in her purse, the husband looting through his wallet. Together they had enough to make it home. Placed it in the driver's hand with the over-careful flattened palms of drunks.

The driver watched them groping away from him, helping each other up the steep spiral stairs of stone to the flat. Swaying, precariously, toward the ring of headlights in the black. A lottery whether they'd make the front door, and their bed.

THE LITTLE ARLESIENNE

Inspired by a painting of the same title by Vincent van Gogh.

LUCY WALKS DOWN THE DIRT ROAD AND COMES TO THE small harbor of the village. It is still dark with only a hint of daylight on the horizon. She stops, looks behind her and sees the humps of cottages and buildings sleeping like tame overfed dogs. There is a light here and there in some windows but mostly the town is in darkness and Lucy shivers when she looks at it. The temptation to keep walking away from the village is great and she wonders for the hundredth time how she can leave.

Pushing away the thought, she walks the circle of the harbor, heading for the knot of fishing boats that have been out all night netting. She can hear the creak of wood and ropes before she reaches them as though the vessels are talking to her from a distance. Telling her of the miles they have traveled across the blue and green swells of water, along the coast, past towns and cities Lucy has only read about in the books she borrows from the traveling library when it visits the village once a month.

In her left hand Lucy carries a metal pale for the fish. She stops at the usual boat skippered by the same fisherman she always buys the fish from because her father has ordered her to buy from this man and none of the others. Although, as she passes the metal bucket to the fisherman, without a word necessary, Lucy can see the catches of some of the other boats, fish larger, fresher looking than the mackerel and bream the fisherman hands to her in the bucket. And she can hear some of the prices being discussed, cheaper and bigger fish to be had if her father would let her shop and haggle a little. But Lucy's father has purchased his fish from the same fisherman for thirty years and has no intention of changing his supplier.

Behind the fisherman is his son scaling and cleaning the fish and Lucy sees him put his hand into the gut of a large fish and pull a mass of entrails from it. Toss the steaming dark mass over the side of the boat with the water beside the boat boiling with movement. The young man looks up and grins at Lucy, waves a hand covered in blood. But Lucy ignores him, he doesn't need encouraging she knows.

Lucy isn't interested in the fisherman's son and she's told him so a number of times, she's pointed out that she's only fourteen. But that didn't stop the father of the boy coming to the house and speaking to Lucy's father about the matter. Asking Lucy's father, on behalf of his son, for her hand in marriage.

Lucy still remembers the way her father squirmed in his overstuffed seat in the parlor when he sent for her once the fisherman had left with a promise from Lucy's father that he would have a word with her about the matter. Lucy, as she walks away from the boat carrying the fish for the family's breakfast, can still see her father squirming like one of the conger eels the fishermen sometimes catch, long fat creatures that can ruin a net or lines if they negligently twist themselves in knots.

She hears the laughter of father and son pursuing her along the path but she ignores it. Grimacing to herself she thinks how her father, all bluster and blow, tried to gain a promise from her to marry the young man. Lucy didn't deign to reply to her father's demand. She looked at him down her long nose with contempt her mouth a shut purse no one but herself would open.

"Look Lucy fourteen's old enough to marry. More than a few lasses have married a lot younger than that and it did them no harm if that's what yer worried about. Besides the boy's going to be worth more than a few francs once his father passes on. Good money in fishing and worth marrying into. It's a chance too good for yer to miss," said her father when his daughter did not respond to his demand to marry.

Lucy does not wish to marry yet, she knows it is too early, that her body is slight, unformed, incapable of accommodating a grown man. But she does not want to marry someone from the village, she has no desire to spend the rest of her days dwelling in one of the cottages of the village she walks into now the fish flopping and flapping helplessly in the metal bucket.

She mounts the stairs that run up the side of the house where she lives. Jammed between her house and another house, the wooden, rickety stairs serve two families and she comes across Mr. Brun, from the house next door, scrambling down the stairs. They almost collide. Lucy just manages to flatten herself against the wall of her house as Mr. Brun rushes downward. She feels his dark bulk brush against her breasts and she hears his apology.

"Sorry Lucy but Susan's in labor and I have to get the doctor."

He rushes into the darkness and Lucy can hear the moans of Susan coming through the wall as Lucy lets herself into her kitchen with the fish. But an extra wall of wood doesn't take away the sound of the woman in labor and Lucy knows it will continue until Susan Brun delivers another child into the world.

At night, when Lucy lies in her wooden bed upstairs, next to the beds of her two brothers, who snore and snuffle like moles beneath the earth, she hears the sounds of the Brun children next door. The children of Mr. Brun and Susan move around at night, all six of them seem not to sleep but to wonder across the floorboards of the house.

Lucy can hear, between the snoring and snorting of her brothers, the creaking of the wood as the children walk for what seems hours. It is only near daybreak, just before Lucy is due to rise and walk to the harbor to purchase the fish for breakfast, that the children in the house next door stop walking and sleep. At least Lucy assumes they sleep if the sound of walking ceases.

When the Brun family emerges into the day, with the children half-scrubbed and almost dressed for school, Lucy sees the fatigue in every face of every child. The little boys and little girls all have sad and droopy eyes, they all look as though they need to go straight back to bed for some decent sleep. But Susan shoos them down the stairs where there is a cart, half -filled with other children from the village, waiting to take them to the small school in the next valley.

Mr. Brun is the town cobbler with a shop in the main street the windows lined with shelves of boots and shoes most of which have been waiting for years for the owners to return to claim them. A thin noise of hammering and sewing leather comes from the cobbling shop but Mr. Brun always shuts up early in the afternoon and goes home. It is an established pattern that tells Lucy and her mother they need to peel the vegetables for tonight's tea. Mr. Brun ascending the stairs is a signal to Lucy and her mother that Lucy's brothers and father will be in from the fields soon and expecting their food to be hot and steaming on plates in front of them.

Mr. Brun comes home early to make love to his wife who is always there at the top of the stairs dressed in a slightly soiled black, lacy gown.

Sometimes the two cannot get themselves across the threshold and they make an entwined mass of writhing limbs on the small landing until Lucy's mother clears her throat, as she begins on the vegetables, and the man and woman remember themselves and manage to get inside and close the door. Not that closing the door drowns the shrieks of pleasure, the girlish giggles that emanate from the Brun house.

Now, after she has washed away the scales left on the fish and cut off the fins, Lucy crosses her arms over her nipples where Mr. Brun brushed past her. The feeling, the electricity is still there but she doesn't want to like it. Lucy doesn't want to end up with a wooden warren of children who pitter patter through the hours of the night; children who look like some of the grotesque, bug-eyed fish the fishermen sometimes catch when they've been netting in especially deep and dark water.

Lucy, as she places the fish in hot olive oil in the black iron frying pan, remembers the day Mr. Brun and his wife lost one of their children when the little girl, too young for school, went wandering off by herself. She walked along the main road of the town bustling with people but no one was thoughtful enough to stop the little girl.

And Mr. Brun and Susan were making love, in the throes of such passion neither of them had thoughts or time for their youngest child who might be sitting by the bed watching them or might be somewhere else.

She was found eventually, after days of searching, at the bottom of a gorge close to the town; a deep crease in the crust of the earth with a noisy torrent of water thundering ceaselessly. The little girl lay on a bed of moss her face close to the water and only a few bruises and cuts to indicate she'd fallen a great height to her death. But it was the words of her father Lucy remembers.

"Ah well it can't be helped. We've plenty of others to look after Susan and probably another on the way if I know what's what."

Lucy's family enter the kitchen, sit at the table, wait for Lucy to place the plates of fish before them. One by one she puts the plates down, comes back with a dish of cut lemons, puts it in the middle of the table. Not a word comes from her parents or brothers. Her mother is indifferent to her, her father is still angry with her for refusing to marry the fisherman's son and her two brothers think she's a stuck up bitch because she reads the books from the traveling library.

Once they begin to slide the slivers of white fish flesh from the bones, Lucy knows it is time for her to take the chance of some respite away from them. Breakfast will engage them for almost an hour; not just the eating of food but talk of planting and harvesting. This gives Lucy time to walk out of the village before the day begins in earnest.

She walks into the next valley sits on top of the ridge and looks at the thatched roof of the school. The place she loved to go to learn but the place her parents took her from once she became big enough to help her mother around the house.

Lucy yearns not just to go back to school to learn. She craves to be allowed to teach the children who go there. An impossible dream she feels as the school slides in her vision warped by tears. The creak of the first cart taking children to the school stops her crying.

Lucy rises, waits for the driver to pull up. She gets up and sits on a wooden seat opposite four expectant small faces. They all grin at her as she raises her hand, pauses, drops it. The singsong of times tables rings out as the cart descends to the school. There will be time for Lucy to test them on some geography and history, facts gleaned by her from the books she reads when she can.

The cart reaches the school, Lucy smiles at the teacher waiting. The man allows the young girl to conduct such swift lessons; he pities her thwarted desire to teach. Lucy says goodbye to the children and begins the long walk back out of the valley, leaving the school behind, walking back to her house in the village where the day's toil waits for her.

STREET SCENE IN MONTMARTRE

Inspired by a painting of the same title by Vincent van Gogh.

ELEANOR COMES UP THE HILL OF MONTMARTRE. IN her hand she carries a basket full of eggs of all sizes, some white, some speckled with brown marks, some speckled with hen shit, others a golden brown, some a strange light blue as though some alien fowl has coupled with a hen in the dead of night. The young girl traipses the streets, lanes and alleys of Montmartre after the renegade chooks, the hens that will not be tamed by wire and fences, the chooks that find a nest anywhere they can. In chimney tops, in overgrown backyards among weeds and thistles, in the bowls of outhouses and between the tables of some cafés.

Eleanor spends all her waking time, it seems, foraging for the eggs because her mother is ill with consumption and confined to the bed in the one room they rent, for a few sous a week, in the basement of an old disused windmill. The daughter has not seen the inside of a schoolroom for years for there is a living to be made from the eggs.

After she has loaded the basket until it is brimming with eggs, she descends the Rue Lepic where she stands at the corner hawking her wares and people seem only too willing to take them from the basket and place coins in the palm of her grimy hand. Although last week, two well-dressed, young men stole some and pelted Eleanor with them reducing her to tears, quivering where she stood. Until Monsieur Rouge, the blacksmith, stepped from his forge, took the two men by the scruffs of their necks and held their cheeks close to the glowering red-hot horseshoes he was shaping. Then the men found some francs for Eleanor and went on their way with burning cheeks of shame and a flea in their ears from the blacksmith.

But Eleanor was still left to find her way up the hill of Montmartre to the old mill and her mother. She was covered from head to toe with eggs and soon attracted the attention of the street urchins who cruise the alleys of Montmartre like sharks, sniffing for blood or making it with sharp tooth and claw.

Half a dozen young boys surrounded Eleanor poking fun at the mess she was wearing, suggesting to her they might take her home down some black hole and roast her on a spit over a fire until they had scrambled eggs for tea.

"And, Mademoiselle, we will peel the scrambled eggs from your body and leave you as naked as the day you were born," said one.

"Yes, and maybe we will roast you until you are tender and then we will eat you slowly. Starting from between your legs," said another licking his lips in the most lascivious and suggestive manner, reducing the rest to howls of laughter that became catcalls of desire.

Eleanor, thirteen years old, knew what they meant and she began to run, the mob of urchins following her, pinching her tender flesh. Reaching hands up her dress and squeezing the softest parts of her inner thighs, others finding her new breasts and cruelly squeezing her nipples until she sang out in pain. But life on the streets of Montmartre had bred a strength in the girl, the hauling of the heavy basket full of eggs, the climbing of chimneys and fences to glean the wild eggs had formed a hardening of muscle and bone. So when they cornered her again half-way up Rue Lepic, she turned on them and before they could open their mouths to sneer and ridicule, before they could assault her body again, she let fly with a flurry of punches that flattened three of the young human jackals.

Taken aback, for once in their lives, the urchins paused and Eleanor was upon two of them grabbing handfuls of hair, pulling the two boys to her and biting off the ear of one, spitting it on the ground. Then biting the nose of the other until it hung bloody and flapping. And the two boys became what they really were, little boys, crying for their mothers, who were all selling their bodies for a few francs on the Rue de Clichy.

Eleanor was off, running up the Rue Lepic, leaving the boys behind and with them the notion they should think twice before trying to do again to Eleanor what they just done or tried to do. On unsteady legs the young girl made her way along the ridge of Montmartre to the mill and she could hear her mother coughing before she entered the gate and closed it behind her. The stench of shit in the cobblestone gutter outside the gate was overpowering, a taste as much as a smell, a presence in the lives of Eleanor and her mother.

Going to her mother she delivered the sous and francs and the woman stopped coughing, eyed critically the coins in her hand.

"You can do better than this!" she declared to Eleanor.

Eleanor shrank from her, took a step back from the bed because she knew what was coming, the words as dark and as slippery as the turds in the cobblestone gutter outside.

"You know, Eleanor, Madame Saint Michelle is still interested in what she talked to me about just last month. She has a place in her house for a young girl like you. Once the old ones reach thirty it is the end of them. Their looks are gone as well as their teeth and most of them have some disease," said the mother.

"I'm not doing that. We live well enough from the eggs I sell," said the daughter.

"Well, it's only a thought. Easier earning a living lying on you back than climbing a chimney or a fence and falling and breaking a leg," said the mother.

Eleanor walks the Rue de Clichy with her basket of eggs. It is almost time for the morning break for the working girls and they are her best customers. Not that the whores buy her eggs to eat or to feed their customers daintily cooked omelets.

Eleanor must go to them and she does, knocking at the door and gaining admittance from the madam, Madame Saint Michelle.

"Ah, ma cherie, you have come with the eggs but when are you going to join us and work with us?" she asks.

And she grins a mouthful of teeth capped with gold coins melted and shaped by the blacksmith and rammed onto her rotting teeth. A way of avoiding taxes, keeping your wealth in your mouth so no tax inspector could possibly know.

Eleanor ignores her, takes her basket through the bead curtain to where the girls are lounging on sofas and settees. They are always glad to see her and they dig into purses and purchase as many eggs from the young girl as possible.

Already some are cracking the eggs, separating the whites from the yolks and pouring sugar into the whites then whisking them with spoons or forks. White stiff peaks come into being and Eleanor ignores the usual jokes about the stiff peaks being stiffer than most of their customers. The girls take their combs and dip them into the lathered egg whites then comb it through their hair. The stiff egg whites enable the girls to style their hair into the shapes they desire and their hair will not move no matter what a customer may demand, no matter how vigorous he might become.

But it is the other use that puts Eleanor on edge and makes her take up her basket in readiness to leave. But there is a fascination in the act, she knows, and she pauses just long enough to witness the first of the girls hitching up their skirts, dipping their combs into the stiff egg whites and combing it through their pubic hair. Forming birds' nests for the customers, indigestible meringues for those clients who wish to attempt to eat them.

Suddenly it is all too much for the young girl and she flees the brothel with the witch cackle of Madame Saint Michelle following her, but Eleanor knows she cannot escape that laugh because she must return the next day. The money is too good from the girls. It keeps Eleanor and her mother in food and pays the rent.

Eleanor pauses on the heights of Montmartre. She eyes the crooked paling and brush fence that encloses one side of the windmill and runs along the cobblestone gutter. Eleanor makes a decision and climbs onto the highest crossbeam of the fence. Unsteadily she stands and says to herself that if she can walk the fence to the end without falling then she will not work in the brothel of Madame Saint Michelle. If she falls then she will acquiesce to the wishes of her mother and the madam.

Carefully, she places one foot forward.

GARY

MY COUSIN, GARY, AND HIS FAMILY PRETTY WELL disappeared out of my life when I was ten after we left for Merewether. Before the move, my family lived in a flat above a mixed grocery business in Mayfield West. Gary's father, my uncle, Ken, owned the mixed business and the flat. My mother worked in the shop while my father worked as a tire salesman. The idea was to get enough money together to shift out of the flat to Merewether where my father had lived as a child.

I spent many afternoons with Gary, mostly down the backyard of the premises catching spiders. He was the best spider catcher I'd seen, not that I'd seen many. But he knew how to corner them in a tree or on the ground, and he knew how to jam an empty honey bottle over them, but most importantly he knew how to pick up the bottle, tipping the spider down the slippery cylinder, giving Gary time to screw on the lid.

To a kid like me it was paramount to get that lid on before the spider escaped and bit my cousin or worse, me. Gary was older than me so I looked up to him, and he took me on other mysterious adventures like drying a mango seed on the roof of the shed, planting it later for it to grow. True, we both buggered it up digging up the seed after a month because curiosity got the better of us and we wanted to see whether the hard large kernel had started to germinate. It had a two inch green sprout on it, but, needless to say it died because of our impatience even after covering it up with soil again.

Then there was the subterranean cubby house, essentially a hole in the ground we both made by stealing a tea cup each from the kitchen and scooping out the rich black Mayfield West soil, covering up the aperture each afternoon with an old wooden door. We were convinced that no one, especially adults like my parents and my uncle Ken would notice.

Excavation came to a halt one afternoon when the hole caved in half burying Gary and me. My mother and Ken came running in answer to our screams, pulling us out before we suffocated on black soil. We got a good talking to; Gary got a clip around the ear from his father and told not to be so bloody stupid again. My uncle got a spade from the shed and finished filling in the hole; months of our hard work were lost in a minute or so.

Then there was the attempt to fly by launching ourselves from the roof of the shed. Actually it was just both of us jumping, but flapping our arms like buggery. Luckily for us the lawn below the shed roof was not lawn but a long, thick mass of green grass that cushioned our less graceful landings. However, that didn't always happen, and our desire to leave the earth came to an end when Gary jumped one afternoon, a bit further than usual and broke his wrist on a patch of bare ground just beyond the island of thick grass.

Needless to say we both got another lecture; Gary got another clip around the ear and told not to be so bloody silly again. His wrist was in plaster for some weeks, but that didn't stop our attempt to break the record for the most number of jumps on a pogo stick. Pogo sticks back then were primitive affairs, a bare metal rod with a stiff spring and side pedals molded into the main steel stem that just allowed two footholds.

It was always a challenge because of the degree of difficulty caused by the slope of rough cement that ran from the back steps of the shop down to the shed; the cement was where we always jumped.

At 260 jumps, two short of our record, I fell, landing on my side and breaking my wrist. Off I went to the Mater casualty where my wrist and arm were swathed in sticky white plaster. We looked like twins, Gary and me, both with broken wrists, but it kept us out of trouble. We became brief celebrities in the small Mayfield West shopping strip, every kid wanting to sign his or her name on the two plaster casts.

Evening bath times became complex affairs because I didn't want to get water on the cast because if I did it meant the signatures washing off. My mother patiently washed around the cast being careful not to drop water on it, rubbing around the white attachment until she lost her temper and jammed the wet washer into my ears, screwing it into the canals to take away the dirt and wax and to have the satisfaction of hearing me yell.

Finally the casts came off and we were free to send the once upon a time thick red hair of Ken even thinner and even grayer, and etch the lines of care and worry on my mother's face even deeper. Our next escapade was the great and infamous 1963 billy cart ride down the precipitous Tourle Street hill.

It took us some time to build the cart. We went from door to door, scrounging a wooden box and two prams. We removed the wheels from the prams with difficulty and Gary managed to attach them to two wooden axles he'd made from scrap timber, having spent weeks using a file to wear away the wooden ends so they fitted into the small openings at the centers of the wheels.

On top of the structure we nailed a wooden box that had been used to pack bananas in; the odor of ripe bananas was strong, almost overpowering, but we managed to disguise it by nicking all the pillows from my mother's lounge upstairs in the flat. We nailed the pillows onto the floor of the box and spent many hours, sitting in comfort, playacting out the reality of the big ride, which would be the following Monday, the first official day of the school holidays. We were saving our first run to celebrate six weeks away from the Mayfield West Infants and Primary school.

We sat at the top of the hill on the big day, the vague roar of rush hour traffic far below us. Then we were off, Gary pushing the billy cart, running beside it then jumping in next to me as it gathered speed. And gather speed it did, reaching ear bleeding velocity, bulleting down Tourle Street.

Half way down, we both searched for the brakes and realized we'd forgotten about them. Jamming the bare soles of our feet into the tar didn't seem to do much other than strip the skin from our feet. It was difficult to tell whether we were yelling in pain or in sheer terror.

Across the main drag of Maitland Road we sped right into the middle of the rush hour traffic. The road slopes slightly upward in a westerly direction; not a steep incline, but, that day, for the truckie with a load of skelp steel it was the same as a mountain. He had to slam on his brakes and bring the rig and thousands of tons of steel to a halt. The billy cart slid by his front wheels, and he stuck his head out the window and delivered a stream of invective I only came to understand and appreciate years later when I worked at the BHP during the uni holidays.

Motorists hit their brakes and Gary and I were glad the makers had remembered to fit the cars with means of stopping. Across four lanes we went, the blue burnt clouds of jammed on anchors smothering us, not to mention the continuing stream of blue language coming thick and fast from many car windows. Vehicles turned side on; some rammed into the backs of others, and our billy cart came to rest, hammering into the gutter directly adjacent to the shop door of my uncle's mixed business.

Gary and I were catapulted through the air, tumbling three times each before coming to rest on the linoleum of the shop floor, looking up to see the faces of my mother and my aunt Joyce, Ken's wife, peering quizzically at us from behind the shop counter.

No bones were broken, but our backsides were red and raw for some days. Gary was confined to his house, and forbidden to come near the shop and forbidden to come near me. I got the same orders from my mother regarding Gary. Vague noises were made about sending me away to boarding school, but my parents couldn't afford to do that if they wanted to save enough to get out of Mayfield West, jammed close to the steel works, and build their contemporary brick and tile house on a spur of rock overlooking the city and the sea.

However, when my mother saw all of her silk-covered cushions, smelling of black and bad bananas, nailed to the billy cart box, she was determined to make me pay for new ones. I had twenty pounds saved in my school Commonwealth bank account. Mum took ten pounds from the account, and purchased herself replacement cushions. Not only was I forbidden to sit on the new cushions, I was not allowed to go within ten meters of the lounge on which they rested, bright, soft, new and colorful.

Time was getting short, childhood was passing. Gary went to high school, and he wasn't a good scholar. His father told him that he would be leaving to take up a trade as soon as he was old enough to legally leave. I was still in primary school, and the gap between Gary and me was widening.

But we still had time for one more escapade, namely stealing the cards out of blocks of chocolate in the shop. A confectionery company published color cards of cars old and new, and drawings of what cars might look like in the future. You had to send away for the album which was a thick book with blank squares on which the relevant cards were to be placed. It was almost impossible to eat that many chocolates in order to get all the cards to completely fill the book. Besides, the chance of getting the same cards over and over again was high.

But two kids, one of whom lived above a mixed business that sold mountains of chocolates, stood a chance of getting the whole collection. Gary and me slid the chocolate bars out of their outer wrappers, carefully unfolded the inner tissue paper wrappers and slipped out the cards then wrapped the chocolates back up and put them back in their places behind the glass fronted counter.

It took many months of late night chocolate card nicking, using a torch to see whether the new card we'd just unwrapped was one we didn't already have, but we got the whole collection.

We thought we were home and hosed, and we basked in the glory of all the kids in Mayfield West coming around to look at the complete collection of car cards. Greek, Italian, Irish, English and Yugoslav kids came to look; they were the offspring of the migrants shipped to Australia to be used as industrial fodder in the steel mills.

But then the customers, who'd purchased chocolates, mainly with a view to getting the cards, started coming back to the shop to complain. At first it was a just one or two, and my mother and aunt and uncle thought nothing of it, dismissing it as the fault of the chocolate factory that had missed putting cards in one or two bars of chocolate. But the one or two complainers turned into dozens of irate cardless customers.

It didn't take much for my mother and aunt and uncle to work out who'd taken the cards. My mother delivered her usual ultimatum to me: "If you tell the truth I'll only smack you once, but if you lie I'll hit you twice."

Confessing and only getting smacked once meant dobbing in Gary as well so I didn't say anything. Eventually, after many smacks, I did tell and Gary got a number of clips around the ear and told he was a menace by his father. The sooner he left school and got a trade the better said my uncle Ken. What he really meant was the sooner Gary got a trade the better because it would mean separating him for me.

There were only a few months before Gary left school. That time I remember as him protecting me against some of the less savory features of the adult world, namely Stan Smith a nineteen year old kid cum adult, who rode a push bike at night, and smoked a cigarette perpetually jammed in one corner of his mouth.

I got in his way one evening by accident, so he had to brake his pushie hard. He swung his leg over the bar, got off and grabbed me by my jumper, calling me a little prick with ears. Gary grabbed him from behind and wrestled me out of his grip. My cousin yelled to me to get back in the shop and I did, scuttling inside, peering through the Venetians in the front window, watching Garry do his best to forestall

Stan Smith. But the bigger man gave my cousin a belting, a bloodied nose and bruised ribs.

Gary made up some story and got another clip around the ear and told once more what a useless individual he was. He'd saved me, but he swore me to secrecy because it seemed as though he knew already, somehow, the shallowness of the grown up world, as if he knew that if he explained how he got his cuts and bruises no one, especially his father, would believe him. It was as though my cousin sensed that he had been branded for life with the epithet, a waste of space, and nothing he could do would change that perception of him. There was a strange and sad resignation about my cousin just before he left school.

He landed a job as a trainee butcher because his father knew a butcher, someone who'd borrowed money from Ken and so owed him a favor.

Gary disappeared from my life and soon after we moved away from Mayfield West, leaving behind the pall of industrial smog, hanging over the suburb for the clean sea side suburb of Merewether populated by white Anglo-Saxon professional men and women with kids, who thought their shit didn't stink.

I did manage to get together once more with Gary just before he started as an apprentice butcher. My father picked him up in Mayfield West in the ute my father used to deliver tires to service stations. I was in the front with my cousin, and my father drove us around Newcastle as a treat; we sat in the front as he took orders from service stations or dropped off tires. But we weren't supposed to be with my father.

It was when we were going up Hunter Street that my father spotted his boss, the manager of the tire company, driving the opposite way.

"Quick, get down on the floor you two!" he commanded.

Gary went down, huddling close to the floor, but I didn't. Instead, I knelt up on the seat and said: "But why, dad? Why do we have to get down on the floor?"

My head bobbed up and down above the dashboard as I looked around, wanting, demanding an answer.

GLADYS MONTGOMERY

Gladys Montgomery was not a favorite among the cab drivers. She went to the Workers' Club every day from the Mayfield Rank. A good fare except Gladys faithfully shitted herself before the driver made the King Street entrance of the Club.

Then there was the trip up the steep stairs. Gladys suffered a stroke years ago. Her walk was a shuffle. Her twisted mouth demanded assistance from the driver up the stairs, a mouth with a poisonous, lashing tongue.

"C'mon y' useless young bastard! Turn that meter off! Give me a hand!"

The driver spent the next fifteen minutes helping Gladys up, step by step; an ascent more difficult and dangerous than scaling Everest. The driver, one hand under Gladys's sweaty arm pit, the other clasped like a surgical mask over his face to keep out the smell of bloomers sagging with shit.

And the trip home was only for Christian cabbies in need of some form of penance, cabbies who were absolutely hungry for a dollar or those new drivers who hadn't savored Gladys after ten gin and tonics.

Taking Gladys home was even worse than ferrying home drunken Knights supporters after their team had won, or worse still, when the team had lost. Gladys's command of language lacerated the night air and turned many cabbies purple and pink with disbelief and embarrassment.

"Christ this isn't they way y' stupid young prick! Jesus y' useless! Look at yer! Bet y' couldn't shag f' five minutes without blowin' yer bolt! Not like my Henry. Banged me all night in the old days."

Every cabby, on the trip home, had his ego shredded by Gladys's lethal comparisons of the driver to her Henry.

And Gladys never failed to complain about the fare. Every driver was accused of cheating her, of taking her the long way, of deliberately stopping at red lights so the meter could tick over. Every time Gladys claimed she didn't have to pay the extra dollar for the phone hire charge. Every time she claimed she hadn't rung, she'd been waiting on the rank.

"And for bloody thirty minutes too! You useless bastards should get yer acts t'gether. An old crippled woman waitin' f' forty minutes! And now yer want t' rob her! A pensioner! If my Henry was alive he'd fix yer!"

Drivers would punch back through the computer memory and flash up "Gladys Montgomery, King Street entrance of the Workers' going to Mayfield" on the green screen. The irrefutable evidence bought another tirade of abuse.

"Christ, y' can't take notice of that crap! It's a machine yer stupid young bastard! What, you'd believe a friggin' machine rather than me?!"

•

Merv Smith pulled onto the Mayfield Rank before he saw Gladys. A truck obscured his view. Otherwise he would have hit the accelerator and headed for town empty rather than pick up Gladys. Now he had no choice. She'd already taken his number once and reported him to the Co-op when he took other passengers waiting on the rank. Even if they had been waiting in line before Gladys arrived. Merv had left her steaming and stamping with anger up and down on the one spot.

"Oh Christ, it's you is it!" Gladys greeted Merv. Merv sighed. Held open the door for Gladys. Helped her hobble down the gutter. Took hold of her legs and swung her onto the seat properly.

"Shit! Be careful! I'm not a sack of wheat y' stupid bastard! I'll be ringin' the Co-op about you again, car 207."

Merv resisted the temptation to slam shut the door on Gladys's arthritic curl of fingers. He bent over her instead and clicked her in.

"Don't lean on me!" she commanded. "You've been eatin' garlic. Thought you looked a bit woggish!"

Merv gritted his teeth and began to fold down Gladys's walker.

"Not that way!" she spat out of the window. "Fold the wheels first and the rest collapses yer stupid bastard!"

Merv packed away the adult-proof contraption in the boot. Angry, he slammed the boot shut and dented two walker wheel impressions into the red metal of the cab boot.

"Shit!" he muttered. "I'll have t' pay for that!"

Merv swung in beside Gladys, but there was no smell of pissy drawers, only clean linen and sunlight soap. Something was different. There was a hint of powder and rouge and lipstick.

"What're lookin' at?!" snapped Gladys.

"Umm, nothing, nothing. The Workers'?" Merv asked.

"No, not the bloody Workers'! I'll tell yer where! Don't tell me where t' go yer stupid young bastard! Just start drivin'! Go on! Straight ahead! I'll direct yer!"

Merv grafted the cab onto the flesh of traffic crawling down Maitland Road. It was going to be a long trip.

"Turn left here!" shrieked Gladys. Merv hit the brakes. A coal truck behind almost concertinaed the cab into the car in front. Merv hiked up Victoria Street.

"The Industrial Highway's the way I want t' go. Sandgate Cemetery and don't take all day!" harangued Gladys.

Merv made the Cemetery. Swung the Falcon onto the access road that led to the section Gladys wanted. The car crunched over the wasteland, the yellow weeds engulfing every slab of marble or granite. Only the grimy stone angels rose, here and there, above the forest of waste.

Ragged, blackened creatures, the angels; wing feathers missing, fingers lost, cheeks chipped away by weather and the constant barreling thud of coal trucks not fifty meters away.

The far section of the graveyard was fenced with barbed wire, and beyond, twenty meters from where Merv stopped, was Shortland Garbage Dump.

Papers clung to the wire like lost souls caught between hell and heaven; the breath of decay and death came from the dump with the squalling gulls. Scavengers of the dump, hurtling through the air, snapping red beaks at each other like greedy relations at the reading of a will.

Gladys was the only visitor. Henry Montgomery's grave was a gem-cut square of well-tended lawn in the middle of a jungle of dross and indifference.

Merv, perplexed, watched Gladys haul herself from the cab. He saw the tears of pain in her eyes as she wrenched herself straight and struggled, upright, unassisted, to the resting place of her husband.

Gladys went down on her hands and knees and opened the old fashioned carpet bag she had nursed on her lap. She pulled out secateurs, garden clippers, an ash pan and brush, a plastic bottle filled with water, and a bottle of detergent.

On all fours, the woman crawled the square boundary of the grave. Clipped the grass evenly, pulled away weeds. Then on her knees, brushed away dirt and cobwebs from the angel. Scrubbed its wings white, wings spread in full flight as if the angel might take the slab of stone, Henry and Gladys with it into the pale blue air of the new morning.

Gladys, on all fours with great long rivers of varicose veins that fired her with pain, fired her into action. She poured water and detergent onto the stone and scrubbed every square inch into a white froth. Washed away half the suds with the water remaining in the bottle but not all.

"Oh no!" she wept. "I'm short. There's not enough water to finish it."

Merv watched her on her hands and knees, encircled by a halo of white froth that exploded the pinks and greens and blues of the new light. He opened the car bonnet and took off the radiator cap.

There was a hose in the boot. He siphoned the radiator to half empty. Collected the water in Gladys's plastic bottle and presented it to her.

Gladys took the water and finished the job. With will, she raised herself, straight, upon the rock. Commanded her pain-twisted limbs to take her back to the cab.

They left it, the grave, like a white marble jewel in a black undergrowth of forgotten lives.

Merv drove slowly; found the nearest garage and filled the radiator. Somewhat out of the way to the Workers', but Gladys said nothing.

Merv pulled up in front of the King Street entrance. No words. She paid the fare. No complaints. She waved away Merv's offered arm. Pulled herself upright. Scaled the gutter and headed for the hill of stairs.

Clean. No shitty drawers. An upright resurrection from crooked bones and twisted gristle; a faultless figure as straight as a river gum for one day of the year.

MY UNCLE

My uncle, Ken Musson, worked at the Wire Rope Works in Newcastle for almost sixty years. Back then it was a job for life; once a bloke got hold of a position in one of the industries, he didn't let go of it. The memories of the Great Depression and the suffering it brought were still raw, and Newcastle had suffered a small depression in the 1920s when the BHP was closed for updating. Bad times and unemployment had become a way of life among many Novocastrians.

Possibly, as a result, my uncle was a careful and conservative man. His world was narrowly defined by shift work, home, meals and sleep, broken only once a year by holidays. When his son left his job at one of the power stations at Lake Macquarie, my uncle nearly had a pink fit, seeing his son's leaving of a secure job for other employment as reckless and irresponsible.

Ken's conservative nature affected all of his family. The three sons and one daughter were kept under strict control and, inevitably, some of the children in adulthood couldn't wait to be free of their father and free of Newcastle.

My aunt, Joyce, Ken's wife, wasn't allowed to spend more than she was allocated every week out of the take home pay, despite the fact that they were well off, everything paid for. When my uncle died, his wife lashed out, going on holidays around Australia, spending money on her children, doing up the family home in Mayfield. The immediate family of sister-in-laws and brother-in-laws were horrified, dismissing my aunt as irresponsible, but the truth was they were similar to Ken, conservative, worried about surviving, not inclined to splash money about when they'd lived through the hard times my uncle had.

Ken lived in a short street, and when he retired he became a custodian of sorts for all the families that lived there. He spent his remaining years going from house to house, looking after the elderly and infirm, making sure they had meals to eat, making sure their bills were paid by walking up to the post office himself and paying them, making sure he had time to sit down and chat with the men and women he'd known all of his life.

He invited Jill and me for tea when we first married. My family was made up of a wife and two stepdaughters, but that didn't seem to bother Ken like it did some of my other relations. My uncle seemed genuinely happy that I'd found someone to love and marry. It didn't bother him that Jill and I had made the decision not to have any more children; two daughters were enough, and my wife was too old to bear babies safely.

This attitude was in contrast to my father's attitude; my father never got over Jill and I not having our own children, and I suspect he always considered my two stepdaughters as inconsequential, of no importance because they weren't blood relations. None of this had a part in my uncle's outlook; the supposed narrow man seemed open-minded to me when I compared his attitude to my family with that of my father's, which demanded that he have grandchildren as if by royal command and entitlement.

Ken died of a benign brain tumor; it was so deeply embedded in his brain it couldn't be surgically removed. His eldest son gave the funeral eulogy and during it Darrel made the point that his father had always had an inferiority complex that had prevented him from reaching his full potential in life.

It may have been a short journey from the Wire Rope Works to his house in Mayfield, but I thought my uncle, in his small way, created a life full of caring and compassion, an existence of understanding that many, including his family, didn't see in him.

THE BOY'S GRANDMOTHER

SMELLS OF RUMP STEAK AND POTATOES WOUND through the cool air of the miner's cottage. The boy watched his grandmother frying the thick slab of rump in dripping. She bent over the gas jets of the Kookaburra stove, shoveling the steak back and forth across the slippery, silver pan. On the back gas ring, the potatoes turned over in the gray, metal saucepan.

It was winter, late afternoon, and the blue gas jets threw lines of light against the boards of the cottage. The boy's grandmother was slightly bent. Her halo of white hair shone in the half darkness. The boy could see her nose, pronounced and determined in the cold. Her hands were squares of knotted veins with the skin soft and smooth. He could see her hands moving in the dying light as though they possessed a life of their own apart from the eighty year old body. He remembered the tight grip on the ax as she chopped wood for the fire: fire to stop out the cold that insinuated itself among the skeleton bones of the cottage.

She glanced up and he could see his own soft brown eyes looking back at him. Her face was weathered pink, soft at the flesh-on-bone edges, with the last light of the sun that ran like blood through the lace curtained kitchen window.

A fat pat of butter sat on a plain white plate. They would cut great chunks of it and wedge them into the potatoes then salt and pepper them. Their plates stood, one on top of the other, waiting for the steak and vegetables.

His grandmother was working in the darkness now. She was all black shadow and Indian ink lines except for the crown of white hair that seemed to throw wreaths of light across the surface of the old miner's table.

The boy looked at the table: hewn from local gum his grandmother had told him. Barely planed at all, but the surface was smooth; as smooth as the beach rocks he and his grandmother found on Burwood Beach at low tide.

The table was smoothed from the hands and elbows of miners from the pits: his grandmother's uncles and brothers who had sailed from Scotland to New South Wales to ply their skills beneath the conglomerate earth of Newcastle. They were all gone now; disappeared back into the earth, back into the coal caverns away from the smell of surf spray and eucalypt gums.

His grandmother was the only one left now. The boy watched as her hands tipped the steak from the fry pan, then drained the potatoes. In the last glow from the window, he could see her hands as they switched final flakes of light across the kitchen.

They sat at the table and ate in a communion of silence. The miner's cottage wound him around, cupped him with its shelter. Methodically they chewed the steak and swallowed the brown juice of blood and dripping: the potatoes swam in the rich yellow butter. The boy, from the corner of his eye, could see his grandmother, a darker form against the black shadow of the cauldron that hung from a hook above the hearth of the chimney.

She made her soups in winter in the great black iron pot; stirred the meat and vegetables above the fire that now glowed red in the congealing shadows.

She had lit it hours ago, but she'd let the flames die back to the faintest orange glow. The heat had seeped quickly between the boards of the cottage; escaped from between the decaying flesh of the boards into the icy air outside.

Sitting hunched over his plate, the boy could see the blackness outside like the thick black velvet of one of his grandmother's old ballroom gowns she used to wear when she was young. She would show him the racks of her clothes hanging in the oaken wardrobe. Garments and jewelry from a Victorian age, each gown, each frock, every wrap hole-riddled by moths and coated with thick layers of dust.

The stars in the sea air outside were globes of ice. They fired and fluxed a light that flowed toward him, coming in hard thick shafts that broke into him and his grandmother. He looked sideways and saw her. She was all silver, the color of snail tracks, glistening in the blackness; prisms of light laced and cut her with deep black fissures of age.

He watched her jaw working in the thick lacquer of the light. It was the only movement: the rest of her was frozen and her eyes were gone. There were only black chasms, not the warm brown that usually gave back the light of the day.

The boy shivered. He moved to the fire and took hold of the iron poker. He rammed it into a dead black lump of wood: rammed hard, forcing and willing the sparks to come. They did, slowly in silent spurts. He added kindling, building the mound slowly. He bent forward into the grate and blew life into the dying embers until they flared and caught the careful construction of wood. The fire fought against the darkness moving out in widening wheels of flame.

The whole room was lit now and his grandmother turned back to the fire, turned away from the sterile star light; away from the thin fingernail slice of cold moon that hung above the house in the blackness.

The boy sat on the veranda in the hard crystalline light of the winter morning. He felt the heat in his bones as he sipped his black tea from the metal and enamel tin cup. It burnt his mouth, but he swallowed the heavily sugared, pungent, black liquid. He still shook in the cold. The sun had only just begun to creep into the darkness of the veranda.

He could hear his grandmother at the back of the house. She was singing over the copper, boiling his clothes then rinsing them in the tubs, cast out of cement and small beach pebbles. He sipped some more tea and heard her faint melody coming down the dark gun-barrel passageway. Then the notes faded. He knew she was walking up the back yard with his washing in the cane basket.

The back yard was half an acre of buffalo grass that was only half-tameable. His father had been able to cut the grass half way back to the paling fence, but the rest was beyond mowing. It grew, a thick green sea of grass that he often lost himself in: dense green caves that folded over him taking away the light of day.

His grandmother would wade into it like a woman walking into the ocean. He knew how the grass rose around her ankles, then eddied around her legs, rising quickly to her waist before she found the clothes line. He had watched her many times, the grass wind-swirled into knots and undertows around her brittle form.

He had cried out to her to come back to the house because he feared the ocean of green would snatch away her footing and take her down into the bed of black river loam laid down centuries ago by the lethargic twist of a river.

The boy was warm now. He could smell the wood of the veranda under the heat of the winter sun; dry, weather-leached wood fractured into splayed slivers of gray tongues. The veranda and the railing were fractured asunder with age: the skin of paint had long cracked and peeled and slipped through the cracks in the boards.

The boy heard his grandmother coming back to him. Her quick, shallow breathing came down the black barrel. She sat beside him and squinted into the hard light.

The house was a refuge for him. It took him away from his parents and the endless routine of school and swimming training. He did nothing when he was with his grandmother. They barely spoke. The ritual of cups of tea, reading the paper and meal times, slowed the spinning top. At home, his days were a child's top, painted with bright, colored pictures but whirling at a sickening speed until the outlines of the pictures merged in a mess of anonymous color.

Now, below the veranda, a green honey eater moved among the early crimson blooms of a bottle brush. He watched it, still in the air, feeding, quietly, then moving, to the next flower, and again, suspended, still. Without effort.

The boy's grandmother was completely different from anyone he knew. He wondered about her life. She had spent forty years in the miner's cottage. Some of it had been spent raising the boy's father after her husband died. She hardly passed the threshold of the gate.

Neighbors would murmur a polite hello, or nod their heads to her when she sat on the veranda; but she was always by herself. She rose early in the morning, at 5.00 a.m., cut herself a thick slice of bread, buttered it and ate it with her black tea.

The day unfolded with each chore allotted its own time and space and particular day. It was only when the boy visited that she altered the cycle of her life. Even then the cottage was an island drawn around with magical circles keeping suburbia at bay.

•

Late August, and the boy stood at the lip of the rectangular hole cut into the raw earth. He watched his grandmother's coffin lowered into the gaping, red maw.

It was raining; raining great icy fans and sheets of dirty water, the wind whipped across the sea of stones of the cemetery.

He leaned forward and saw the water rising up the sides of the grave. It was pouring, filling up the grave with wet and the coffin was coming with it; she was coming toward him, coming with the murky brown tide that rose toward him.

Later, he walked with his parents toward the car. It was his last day of primary school. Next year, he would be sent away to boarding school, out west, away from the coast; away from the smell of salt air and the smell of eucalypt gums, running down to the water's edge; away from the miner's cottage that was already sold to a developer, who was to erect six brick town houses on the green tide of grass.

THE FISHING TRIP

"OH SHIT!" YELLED WALLY. THE BARB OF THE RUSTY one-o short shank suicide hook had embedded itself into the flesh of his thumb. Blood trickled into the old cane tackle basket.

"Bloody hell," said Wally. "Lucky I had that tetanus shot last month." He sucked his thumb like a petulant school boy.

Midge eyed him with only mild surprise. She wondered how her husband and Clarry Kelly, his mate, were going to make it to the water. Wally couldn't even rig a handline without doing damage to himself.

"Yes, Wally, it's lucky you did have that tetanus shot," Midge sighed. She remembered the incident without fondness. Wally had arrived home one wintry Saturday night, full of schooners and the misguided determination that he was going to chop wood and make a fire to keep his missus cozy. It didn't matter that Midge was happy with the Vulcan fan heater; she was going to get an open fire.

Wally squatted in front of the old brick fireplace, rocking back and forth like a cane toad, with constipation. The fireplace hadn't been used in years.

Wally crawled into the grate. Peering up the chimney, trying to see the light of the full moon, he was shocked by a tonne of soot which descended without warning.

Midge found him spread-eagled in the lounge room with a thousand lines of exploded soot covering her best Westminster. Wally looked as though he was auditioning for the black and white minstrels.

Midge tried to stop him, but Wally, after seven schooners, was beyond the grace of reason. He lurched into the back yard and headed for the garden shed. Midge went after him but her pleading fell on deaf ears.

Wally emerged from the shed with his newly-purchased woodman's ax and made his way to the pile of ironbark at the end of the yard. One chop was all it took. One chop and one miss, except the shiny silver blade found Wally's ankle. Blood and bad language flowed like champagne at a wedding. Midge dashed back to the house and returned with a tourniquet which she expertly applied.

She drove Wally to the hospital. In casualty, he moaned and assured the other stoic patients that he was going to die. Midge moved down two seats and pretended she wasn't with him.

Two hours later, a nurse, of matronly proportions and disposition, lumbered up to Wally and told him it was his turn.

"About time!" he whinged. "I could've gone on the pension I've waited so long. I'll probably contract gangrene and have to have me foot taken off."

The nurse had been working for ten hours straight. She was in no mood to be crossed. Taking Wally by the ear, she marched him off, amidst a chorus of laughter from the other patients, for a tetanus and stitches.

"Probably got anchors tattooed on 'er biceps," Wally pouted in the car on the way home.

Midge looked at her husband: 10.00 a.m. and he still wasn't ready to go. She'd done her bit: made the cheese and ham sandwiches, a thermos of coffee and a carrot cake cut into slices and packed in her best Tupperware container.

Wally was still having trouble with the blood knots; probably because the blood from this thumb made the line so slippery. As well, there was his vanity. He refused to wear his reading glasses when he was rigging the lines. He'd already tied two lines to the handle of the cane tackle basket, and another to a button on his cardigan.

"Midge, did y' take that bait out of the freezer?" yelled Wally.

"Yes, Wally, the prawns are thawed and ready to go. What about you?"

"Just about ready. Plenty of time. Clarry's not here yet."

Midge looked at the plastic packets of prawns sitting in a puddle on the laminex bench top. Wally always used prawns now. He'd given away using blood worms after the last incident with Clarry Kelly.

The two had organized a trip up the Karuah River from Lemon Tree Passage. They scoured every bait shop in the region until they found blood worms. Wally said that it was like winning the lottery.

"The bream will go bananas when they get a whiff of these on the end of me hook," he said.

Wally had mixed the worms in sand, and for safety's sake, frozen them in a Street's plastic ice-cream container. All was set until Wally and Clarry arrived home from the R.S.L.

Midge was out, at aerobics, so Clarry who had always had illusions of grandeur in regards to his culinary prowess, took over the kitchen.

"Sit back ,Wally. I'll cook the tea. Some nice spaghetti bol."

Wally was in no condition to argue. He lay back in the Jason Recliner Rocker and watched the Knights being flogged by Canberra — again.

Clarry arrived with two steaming plates of spaghetti bolognaise covered with Parmesan cheese. The two wolfed down the continental delight and settled back into the glassy-eyed stupor of drunks trying desperately to stay awake.

It was only next day when Wally went to the freezer to get the worms and found a tray of minced beef and nothing else, that he realized what Clarry had done.

Wally canceled the trip. Green with nausea, he spent the day on the dunny, clutching his stomach. Midge's remarks hadn't helped.

"They say worms are full of protein, Wally. Think of all the get up and go you'll have, Wally."

"Shut up Midge."

"Wally, you'll probably end up like Mildred Muddle's dog when he scrapes his bum down the middle of the road."

"Shut up Midge! You're not funny!"

"Wally, do you think it'd help if I went to the chemist and got some Combantrin."

"Midge!"

Clarry Kelly had finally arrived. Between the two of them, Wally and Clarry had more gear than the local angling shop, except most of it was rusty.

"I can feel it now, Wally. A basket full of big bream and a couple of flathead," said Clarry.

"Not likely," muttered Midge under her breath.

The last time they actually got in the water they caught nothing. True they arrived home with two big flathead, but as Midge pointed out, there were bits of newspaper all over the two fish. The fish mongers was only around the corner she had reminded the two red-faced liars.

Her suspicions were confirmed next day, when she and Wally bumped into Georgios, the fish monger.

"You liked dose fish I sell you, eh, Mr. Wally?"

Wally kept walking, looking up in the air and whistling.

Wally, Clarry and Midge squeezed into the front seat of the Ute. Midge gagged. Clarry had been eating garlic again.

"Christ Clarry!" said Wally, "do y' bath yourself in that bloody stuff!"

"It's good for colds and clearing sinuses," said Clarry defensively.

"It'd clear anything I'd say, including everyone from the shopping center down the road," stated Wally flatly.

•

It was a beautiful day; "Almost good enough to be alive," asserted Clarry. It was a relief for Clarry to get away from his wife, Isabella, for a little while, at least. Isabella had social pretensions that did not sit well with Clarry's job as a government bus driver.

Wally called Isabella "Marie Antoinette, but not to her face.

"Hey Clarry," said Wally, "You should've bought Marie Antoinette along. You could've got her to feed the bream carrot cake."

Clarry was not amused. He'd only gotten to bed at 2.00 a.m. Isabella had him up all hours cleaning the silverware — for the fifth time — in preparation for a garden party she was giving for the local Liberal M.P.

A real house buff was Isabella: buff the silver, buff the china, buff the furniture, buff the bloody Pekinese that always sat in Clarry's favorite chair and left long strands of saliva-slick hair all over it.

They arrived at Lemon Tree. "Bloody typical," said Wally. "The boat ramp's chockers. Bloody holiday fishermen. Should leave it to the professionals." Midge eyed him with growing wonder.

Wally backed the Ute down the green-weed slippery ramp and prayed that the hand brake would hold just one more time. It did, for a time. It was just as the old wooden row boat had been unwinched that the hand brake slipped. Like the launching of the Queen Mary, the Ute majestically slid backward into the green briny. Wally, Clarry and Midge watched in open-mouthed befuddlement as the high water mark rose half way up the cabin.

Luckily, a passing tow truck driver had seen the whole event. Before Wally could blink or think, the driver had backed down the ramp, hitched up the Ute and dragged it out and into the car park.

The tow truck driver grinned amiably and presented Wally with a written bill for one hundred and twenty dollars. Wally and Midge were still lost for words. Clarry wasn't.

"Oh well, Wally, it was overdue for a wash anyway."

In a daze, Wally handed over the money in twenties, and Midge waved goodbye to the perm at the hairdressers as the twin chrome exhausts of the truck disappeared, gurgling richly, over the crest of the hill.

Wally pulled open the door of the Ute. A cascade of salt water bowled him over the asphalt of the car park.

"Christ! Why didn't I just stay in bed?!" he yelled.

"I don't know, Wally. Why didn't you?" said Midge.

"Oh shit! The boat!" yelled Wally.

Midge and Clarry turned to see the row boat disappearing around the tip of the island, opposite the boat ramp. Fortunately, the Water Police were passing. They towed back the rebel dinghy and warned Wally they'd slap a fine on him if he didn't control his vessel in a proper and correct manner in future.

Midge rowed. Wally's thumb was still sore and resembled a giant white salami of bandage. Clarry was still recovering from a double hernia operation after Isabella insisted he move the ornamental fountain in their front yard himself.

"C'mon Midge! Put y' back into it. We wonna fish today, not tomorrow," whinged Wally.

Midge glared back at Wally and pulled on the oars.

She rowed the two convalescents around the point and into the mangroves. She threw out the anchor after securing the other end to the boat. Wally and Clarry managed to bait their hooks by themselves. They fished between the mangroves and the oyster racks.

Midge sat puffing at the back of the boat after the strenuous rowing.

"Be quiet Midge," said Wally. "You'll scare the fish away."

Midge resisted the temptation to scream at the top of her lungs.

Clarry was in a mess. The tangle ballooned into strange inexplicable knots.

"Christ," said Wally, "you've got more knots there than a boy scout's jamboree."

Midge cut away the bunch of grapes and re-rigged Clarry's line for him.

"Life's too short to let him do it himself," she thought.

"Oooh, gee, Wally, I've got something heavy on here," said Clarry.

"Pull it in slowly," said Wally. "It might be a crab."

Clarry hauled the thick line as slowly as his excitement would allow him. Sure enough, it was a crab, but Clarry made the mistake of hauling it straight into the boat.

One enormous and considerably cranky mud crab ran amuck, snapping its claws at available fingers and toes.

"Jesus Christ, Clarry, you stupid bastard! What'd y' do that for? Quick, put a knife through it before it chews off something of value."

Clarry hunched over the nipper-waving menace. He held the fishing knife at the ready. Just then, however, a wave from a passing speed boat hit the wooden dinghy. Clarry and Wally ended up entangled in each other at the front of the boat.

Midge leaped for the knife, and with a savage skill that disturbed Wally when he thought about it later, plunged the blade through the crab's body. Expertly she lifted a sizable morsel of crab flesh into the plastic container filled with salt water.

Things calmed down, for a while. The two were fishing peacefully when the turtle struck. Six foot long, with a barnacle atop its wrinkled and furrowed head, it rose beside the boat wheezing and spouting water and air like a whale. Wally and Clarry jumped several feet into the air. It wasn't the first time this had happened. The turtle had scared them many times over the years.

"Christ," said Wally, "that bastard's scared another six months out of me."

Even Midge had blanched due to the unexpected intrusion.

"And it's so bloody ugly," said Wally.

Clarry was unperturbed. He eyed the turtle's deeply creased visage.

"I suppose it's what you get used to," said Clarry. "Looks like Isabella after a big night on the sweet sherry."

The two would-be anglers settled down to some serious fishing while Midge arranged the sandwiches and poured the coffee.

"Two sugars in your coffee, Wally."

"Be quiet Midge. I'm concentrating."

Midge wished she had bicarbonate of soda, not sugar in the small Tupperware container.

"Christ almighty this bastard's pulled like a freight train" yelled Wally. He pulled in a sizable squire.

"Mmm, a bit small," muttered Wally.

"You'll have to use the hammer on that one, Wally," said Clarry.

"Why do you have to hit it with a hammer?" asked Midge innocently.

"To put a bump on its head so it looks like a snapper," said Wally.

Clarry and Wally doubled up with laughter. Midge wondered what Clarry and Wally would look like with bumps on their heads.

Clarry got a bight next and brought in a good sized bream.

"You beauty!" chortled Clarry.

"That's made the whole trip worthwhile," sang Wally.

Midge wondered at the logic of fishing philosophy, especially with the Ute still half full of water back in the car park.

Wally followed with a larger bream. All of a sudden a life-time dream became a reality for the two: they were among them, and in no uncertain terms.

Every time the line hit the water, a bream hit the bait.

"Christ," said Wally, "I'll have to bait me hook behind me back in case the hungry bastards try t' jump into the boat."

This was heaven for Clarry and Wally. Years, decades even, without a bite, or just another bag of rock cod — and now this. The haul continued: fat, silver bream with gray spines and yellow fins made their way into the boat. Midge watched with growing alarm as the catch spilled out of the boat.

Neither Wally nor Clarry cared. They'd waited years for this.

"My old man was right!" yelled Wally in triumph, between unhooking another bream and baiting his hook.

"What's that?" asked Clarry with uncontainable glee.

"If they're on, y' can catch 'em with a broomstick with a piece of string on the end," replied Wally.

"Broomstick and string!" exclaimed Clarry. "Christ Wally, if y' sent 'em a written invitation they'd come."

The catch continued and the boat settled lower into the water. Midge's feet were covered with silver-scaled bodies that occasionally flopped or somersaulted into the air.

Black turrets of cloud grew from behind the hills rolling north toward Taree. A hot humid glove of air descended, but it was only when the tide had turned, and was on the run-out, that the fish stopped biting.

Clarry and Wally were beside themselves. Finally they had cracked the big catch: enough bream to fill their freezers six time over and plenty to give away to friends and neighbors. Still, Wally found grounds to complain.

"Christ, I suppose we'll be here till next week cleanin' the bastards," he whinged.

Wally could hardly wait to get home to start bragging. He could see it now: Mildred Muddle's shocked face as he presented her with two, two kilo bream, scaled, gutted, but with the heads left on. Wally rarely got a chance to boast of his fishing ability.

Clarry Kelly was day dreaming too as Midge pulled on the oars. He could see his missus, Isabella, for once struck dumb: none of the usual hot tongue and cold shoulder when he turned up with enough high quality fish to feed the M.P. and the rest of the hangers-on, Isabella had invited to her do.

The boat ramp was in sight. In his excitement, Wally misjudged when he should leave the boat.

"I'll just step out and haul it up the ramp," he said.

Gracefully, he stepped into three meters of water. He disappeared leaving behind a trail of bubbles.

"Christ almighty!" he thundered when he reached the surface. He grabbed the side of the boat and tried to pull himself back on board.

"Don't, Wally, you'll capsize us!" pleaded Midge.

Wally wasn't listening. Over the years he'd seen the occasional shark around Lemon Tree and up the river. He pulled and the boat went over.

Bodies of bream filled the water. Clarry and Wally desperately grabbed at them trying to save their catch. They only succeeded in spiking themselves on the sharp spines.

To make matters worse, a passing school of dolphins, swimming for the heads, decided to help Wally and Clarry clean up the fish. It only took five minutes of gluttonous gorging and the dolphins left full of fish.

On the way home, in the rusting Ute, Wally swore he'd never watch another re-run of Flipper again.

ABOUT THE AUTHOR

GREG BOGAERTS was born in Newcastle, Australia. In addition to being a writer, he has been a schoolteacher, a solicitor, a laborer with BHP (an Australian-based multinational mining company), and a taxi driver. His stories have been published in journals, newspapers, and anthologies in Australia and the United States. His first collection of short stories, *Walking Paris Streets with Eugène Atget: Inspired Stories About the Ragpicker, Lampshade Vendor, and Other Characters and Places of Old France* (Shanti Arts, 2013) was inspired by photographs by Eugène Atget. His second collection, *Beyond Sunflowers and Starry Nights*, was inspired by paintings of Vincent van Gogh (Shanti Arts, 2018). He has had one novel published — *Black Diamonds and Dust* (The Vulgar Press, 2005) — and three novellas. Bogaerts attended the University of Newcastle where he obtained a bachelor of arts degree, a diploma of education, and a master of educational studies degree. He obtained a bachelor of legal studies degree from Macquarie University. Bogaerts is married to Jill and currently lives in Buttaba, Australia.

www.ingramcontent.com/pod-product-compliance
Lightning Source LLC
Chambersburg PA
CBHW061518020726
47502CB00006B/2128